ASHLEA ADAMS

STITCHERS

AN AMARANTHIAN NOVEL

Stitchers

Trade Paperback ISBN 979-8-9924035-3-4

eBook ISBN 979-8-9924035-2-7

To Titus and Theo, with all my love

and

To Mom, Holly, Nanny, Granny Pat, and Great Nanny. You are the true heroines of my story.

THANK YOU!

Thank you for taking a chance on my debut novel!

You could've done anything else with your time and money. It's truly humbling to know that you chose my book to escape into. Thank you.

Because you're so groovy, I've got an exclusive thank-you gift just for those who have purchased my book.

Follow this link for your gift: https://www.ashleaadams.com/thank-you-gift

CONTENTS

CHAPTER I

I was supposed to have nerves of diamonds.

Yet here I was with a belly full of butterflies. Was it because of a battle I was about to win? Nope. It was my first day on The Job.

Good grief. I am Huri Pherenike Rojas. Future reigning Athena. I single-handedly conquered the three-headed hellhound plaguing Pagae. At fourteen. I took out the mino-gorgon of Taluth, Georgia, that had turned the citizens into statues and then rammed them to bits. I went through sixteen hours of labor to bring my son into the world. Somehow, my heart still managed to beat after I put the pieces of my husband in the ground.

I took a deep pull of my coffee, eyes fixed on the sign above the turnstile gates, and wiped the anticipation from my palms. Time for the next chapter. Hopefully with a few wins to make up for the losses.

"Weapons Check."

These two words stood in front of a circular logo: two knitting needles were crossed inside a semicircle of laurel with "Stewards of the Shield" framing the entire shield-shaped emblem. I always thought it looked like the *aspis* we Greeks favored.

My lips curved into a smile. It felt like it had taken a lifetime to finally get to a place I could be proud of.

Over the hallway entrance, behind the reception desk, hung another sign: "No heroes. Only heroines." I had been to a few field offices, and this was the only one to post this sign. Was I being paranoid, or did that feel like a warning? Maybe a little sexist. But then again, StS only employed women.

An elderly woman sat on a stool behind a desk, her lavender hair still in tight rollers as she smoked a cigarette with a tube of ash so long it defied the laws of physics.

I caught a glimpse of Grandmother's Parthenon in Centennial Park as I looked back out the front door. Nashville had honored Grandmother with the gift when she'd given Music City several pieces of art over a century ago. Now, it seemed like Grandmother hid between the pillars to spy on me. Which was a foolish thought. She was far too busy. Plus, all she had to do was ask anyone at StS how I fared, and she'd be given a swift, groveling answer.

"Weapons check," the lavender-haired woman barked at me. I involuntarily inhaled the woman's scent. Definitely not mortal. Instead, she smelled something like the air before a thunderstorm. But I couldn't place which species she was.

I swallowed hard, looking around even though I knew we were the only ones there. It was an hour and a half before Roll Call. "I'm supposed to meet Captain Janis."

The ash trembled dangerously on the end of the cigarette like a rattlesnake shaking its tail.

"Weapons check," I agreed, not wanting to make waves on my first day.

I placed my coffee on the mahogany desk, and the woman swiftly shoved a coaster beneath my cup before it touched the wood. I glared at her, biting back a retort.

"Have a little respect. It was Mrs. Abigail Adams's desk. Gave it to me herself."

"Who?" I set my leather satchel beside my coffee.

The ash quivered and cascaded off the tip of the cigarette. "Name."

"Huri Rojas."

"Hurry Rojas," the steward said as she examined her clipboard.

I tried my hardest to hide the eye roll. "No, Huri. It rhymes with 'fury.'" I had lost count of the times I had to correct people.

"Right. Species and/or pantheon."

Keeping my attention on removing my weapons, I swallowed hard. I always hated this part. At least we were alone. "Greek."

I sensed Purple Rain Cloud looking up at me. "Species."

My shoulders slumped. "No...species. I'm an Athena."

Purple Rain Cloud didn't do more than scribble on the paper. "Weapons."

Great. Now that Prince song was stuck in my head.

I wouldn't meet the woman's wild eyes as I shed my navy blazer and unbuckled the sheath of knitting needles at my lower back. With a shrug, I took off the holster that held my twin short swords across my back. I chanced a peek and found the lavender hair was practically standing on end, like she'd stuck her finger in an electrical socket. The sight made me rush through the turnstile.

It screeched like a banshee at me.

My face burned. Hopefully, no one saw me. "Forgot."

I placed each booted foot on the edge of a bench and pulled out two more daggers from each leg. Then there were the sheaths at my forearms with my double-pointed needles. They were surprisingly great for throwing. And so compact.

With an apologetic wince, I carried it all back through the turnstile and plopped it on top of my other weapons.

"That it?" the woman growled. I swore electricity was dancing through her strands of hair.

I patted myself down and then nodded. "Yeah. But do I need to check my hands?"

Purple Rain Cloud just glared at me. "Aren't we clever."

I managed a weak smile. *Good grief. Take a joke, lady.*

It took the better part of ten minutes for the woman to inspect and catalog my weapons. Already, two other women were queuing up. One steward was a woman of otherworldly beauty (and a sheet of blonde hair that would've made Rapunzel jealous) who winced at me.

"What'd you do?" she whispered with a frown at Purple Rain. A waft of stone and moss tickled my nose. Unusual combo.

"I think I insulted the desk."

She gasped and covered her face. "Dear Lord, we better pull up a chair."

After a few more minutes, another two women came and waited after whispers with the first two. These wore lab coats.

Great.

I wanted to disappear when Purple Rain walked around The Desk with paperwork and my pile of weapons. Perhaps I did overdo it a bit. But the knitting needles and their sheaths were the only new additions. The rest were pretty standard.

Purple Rain Cloud now had a new cigarette quivering between her wrinkled lips. "Here, new girl." She shoved everything at me. "Take this to the detectives' floor."

I nearly opened my mouth to ask where that was when the four women behind me held up two fingers and pointed up. Mouthing my thanks, I nodded and started replacing my weapons.

In short order, I was headed up the stairs to the second floor. There were no cubicles or walls in the detectives' offices, or even computers—none of the usual office amenities a mortal would expect. Having mortal technology around immortals was a surefire way to cause a fire from all the sparks and fritzing. Instead, only large rugs about eight feet square dotted the floor in a myriad of colors and designs. Atop each rug sat a hodgepodge of furniture and even pockets of nature from around the world.

Some stewards preferred the typical office desk, while others worked at kitchen tables or in living rooms with TV trays. Some spaces didn't even resemble offices. Instead, there were trees or meadows, presumably the immortals' natural habitats, all contained within the confines of eight feet by eight feet. Several didn't use bookshelves. Their books, manuals, and binders floated as if suspended by unseen, undulating shelves.

My little geeky heart squealed like a kid.

Opposite the entrance, a violet fire crackled in a hearth the size of a twin bed. According to the map in the paperwork Purple Rain had given me, my office was beside that giant hearth.

It was fairly easy to find. Mine was the only empty office space around. It had a simple, off-white rug and three plain walls. Directly beside my spot, with a view out the window, sat a miniature riverscape. A slab of wood hovered over a small creek that stopped exactly where my plain rug began. I still didn't understand how this tech worked. The softest grass filled the floor, and a standard office chair with lumbar support sat before the slab desk. It took me a moment to realize that whoever sat in the chair would rest their feet in the creek's water. Neat stacks of file folders rested on the desk as well as on river-rock shelves.

I peeked at the desk on the other side of my plain rug. This cubicle looked like Stonehenge had a baby inside a forest. Granite-like slabs made up the desk and chair. Wisteria vines draped from branches that spanned the eight feet but were suspended in the air without a trunk to attach them to. Twilight filled that desk, but golden faerie lights winked in and out.

Stop grinning like a kid, Huri.

This was like the rugs in Grandmother's home in Olympia. I stepped into the middle of my rug and closed my eyes. The melody of wood creaking and wind ruffling leaves drew my eyes open. I stood in a forest, except my office rug now appeared to be forty feet below me and resembled the forest floor. A wisp of fog solidified to form my chair, which sat before two smooth, flat tree branches that would serve as my desk and shelf. Opposite my desk, more branches grew to form bookshelves. Within easy reach, spiderwebs stretched between branches, with sticky notes blossoming like colorful insects caught in the web.

I nodded my satisfaction and unpacked the pictures and mementos from my satchel. The first picture was of me and my husband and son. My heart and stomach ached.

Was I finally a steward? After all the years of waiting, after fighting my mother's side of the family, after going through everything with my...I exhaled and stared at the last picture with the three of us together, taken two weeks before Luis's death. Elias had been almost three at the time. We all beamed in that picture, blissfully ignorant in our happiness. We were supposed to have chased these dreams together.

I fiddled with Luis's necklace, hidden below the collar of my shirt. It had been my one-year anniversary gift to him: a Maltese cross I had made attached to a spider cord that *Pater* and *Yiayia* made. Elias's tiny thumbprint was etched onto the back of the cross. Luis called it his good luck charm to get him out of fires. Too bad it didn't protect from hungry immortals.

Next, I placed a more recent picture of only me and my now five-year-old standing in front of our new home. He was growing too fast. His beaming face made my guilt for leaving him to work redouble. But the memory of seeing his grin as he kissed me goodbye this morning eased my mommy-guilt just a smidge. He was so proud of me for bringing the bad guys to justice. Just like Luis had once saved people from burning buildings.

Then came the picture that warmed my heart. It was me and my three closest friends after they'd helped move us into our new house. We were all enjoying pizza and beer in the backyard. They were more like sisters to me. Hopefully, I'd get to have lunch with them today.

My smile faltered. The only catch was that none of my friends knew who or what I was. They thought I was a regular mortal like them. They had no idea that not only was I an immortal, I was also the future Athena after Grandmother and Mama died in a few hundred years. Keeping my secret was as much for their safety as mine. Not to mention an order from the pantheon. But it didn't change the fact that I had wanted to tell them since our first sleep-over over fifteen years ago.

After sticking one of Elias's drawings on the spiderwebs, I exhaled my nerves. As I always did now, I shut my eyes and pretended Luis was still with me, that his hand was rubbing my back, that his voice still sent shivers along my skin.

"You've got this, *amor*," his voice whispered in my ear.

My heart ached, but I nodded, holding tight to the fantasy. "I hope so."

His laughter filled me like a warm drink on a cold day. "I know so."

I pretended his lips pressed against my cheek, then heard the sound of clacking heels approaching my desk. Reality made Luis vanish as I turned to greet whoever approached. A middle-aged woman paused at my desk as I looked around. She wore a black power suit and smelled like something gamey, which made me think of some type of hunter.

"Welcome, Huri." She extended a hand. "Captain Filomena Janis. I go by Captain or Janis. Hate my first name." Her lips twisted like she tasted something nasty.

I shook her hand and tried to smile as naturally (and not nervously) as possible. "Hello, Captain. Nice to meet you."

"It's a pleasure. I had hoped you would come a bit early." Her eyes took in the transformed desk area. "Impressive." She cast a glance at the rug. "You sure that won't give you vertigo?"

My cheeks heated. "I love flying."

Captain gave a half-shrug and then presented me with a box in her other hand. "This is for you."

Somehow, I kept myself from shaking as I took the box. I knew what was in there. I'd been waiting for it ever since graduating from the Academy. There, they had given me a temporary one, like the fake diplomas at graduation. This one, however, had my name and number on it. I swore it felt heavier than I expected. Even my eyes seemed wetter than usual as I opened it to find my badge with the stewards' emblem. My son would flip when I brought it home and showed him.

"If I may," Janis said and gently drew out the badge. A chain cascaded into her palm. "It's my favorite part of the job." She looped the chain over my mass of curly black hair so that the badge rested against my chest. "There."

I couldn't move other than to touch it, like the badge was a new talisman against evil. I'd finally made it.

"Now, you're part of our band of heroines," Janis said as she stared at my badge almost fondly. "You're no longer alone."

Is that what that sign at the entrance meant?

Her smile deepened when I blinked away the extra wetness in my eyes. "Let me give you a tour. I'll show you where the coffee and tea are kept."

There was no way I would start crying on my first day. But it was hard. I felt like a pregnant teenager, a total wreck of emotions. "I'd love that."

CHAPTER 2

Captain Janis finished the tour at the Hen House, as she fondly called it. I peeked inside and found a conference room with several tables and chairs in neat little rows facing a podium. A few women already sat inside with legal pads and pens.

"Just grab your stuff and head on back. We'll start in ten," the captain told me.

"Yes, ma'am." My Southern twang came out a bit more. That insufferable accent always cropped up now that I was back where I had grown up.

Janis's lips twitched into what I imagined was a poorly suppressed smirk. But I speed-walked back to my office and relaxed completely in my cloudy chair. At least, until a woman with a steely bun at the nape of her neck set down a stack of binders on my desk. That impeccable bun was in complete contrast to the muddy hiking boots and dark jeans. I wanted to laugh when this woman turned and greeted me appraisingly as she chewed on the stem of an unlit smoking pipe. But at the intensity of this woman's dark gaze, my laughter died before it could escape. I swore this woman knew everything about me in that single moment.

"Hello, Huri." She walked forward a few steps as she took out her pipe and extended her hand. "I'm Zephonia Weber."

That's my partner's name.

Zephonia's voice filled my mind with flashes of rivers and the seductive laughter of water lapping against the shore. The picture was all the more vivid because of the scent of cool fresh water that perfumed the air around her. I had been around enough sirens to put the pieces together. Zephonia was a river siren—based on the ever-so-slight accent, a nixie, a German river siren. I wondered if Zephonia's voice possessed the same "sing you to your death" quality that the sirens in my pantheon boasted. Judging by the power behind the greeting, I had to believe it did.

Almost mechanically, I shook my partner's hand as I rose. "A pleasure."

Zephonia gave me a lingering appraisal before putting her hand on the stack of binders. "Stuff they don't cover at the Academy. Procedural stuff on your first day. How we bag and tag evidence. Equipment you have access to. All that kind of scintillating stuff. I hope you're a fast reader."

"Right. Thanks." I swallowed hard. "I'll start after Roll Call."

Zephonia's muddy eyes turned toward the Hen House behind us. "Most useless thing. Come on. Let's get the clucking over with. Not doing this tomorrow, though. We've got work."

With those words, Zephonia walked toward the Hen House. I watched her for a moment and then remembered that I was supposed to join her. Wincing, I snatched up a pen and paper and hurried after my partner. Zephonia hadn't gotten far, only to the desk beside mine. She chatted softly with the long-haired beauty from earlier. They both turned to me when I joined them.

"Huri, this is Beatriz Ortiz. She is usually the news breaker in our crew."

Beatriz rolled her dark green eyes and shook my hand. "You can call me Bia. Only Zephonia calls me Beatriz."

"Bia." My eyebrows met as we headed toward the back wall where Captain Janis's office and the Hen House were. "What's a news breaker?"

Somehow, even her wince was beautiful. I studied the shimmering air behind Beatriz. It looked like oil rippling in water. Then it struck me. Beatriz was some sort of fae. The rippling. The stones. She had to be.

"I get saddled with telling morries that their loved ones were attacked by immos." Beatriz shrugged.

My ears tingled at the slight accent, but I decided not to press her about which romantic language she spoke. "That must be tough."

"Eh. It's hard at times. But it's the job. Anyhow, welcome. I'm glad you survived Violet."

That's right. For a moment, I forgot her name wasn't Purple Rain. I blushed when Zephonia arched an eyebrow. "Yeah, sorry. I held everyone up. But thank you."

"Vi...she is always pestering the newbies."

"Even the oldies," Zephonia growled with a rueful wince.

Beatriz's bell-like laughter rang out as we entered the back of the conference room where the other stewards had assembled. Zephonia went first and sat in the first available seat, closest to the only door, instead of going farther along the table to let everyone file in behind her. I paused when the scents of thirty-odd immortal women bombarded me. I had to close my eyes to steady myself for a moment.

"She's always ready for a quick escape," Beatriz whispered with a snicker as we sat beside Zephonia.

What? Oh, Beatriz thought I'd stopped because of Zephonia.

"This is the dumbest thing," Zephonia said, glaring at the room.

Captain Janis entered behind us right at eight o'clock and paused at our table to take in the three of us in the back. Janis snickered at Zephonia. "How kind of you to grace us with your presence, Weber."

"You've got me one morning. That's it. We've got actual work."

I became one with my legal pad, sure that Zephonia was pushing her luck.

The captain paused and stole a long sip of Zephonia's coffee. Zephonia's lips thinned in the extreme.

"Really got to get you some better beans, Weber."

Zephonia glared at the captain as Janis set the cup down and walked toward the front where the podium stood. "Have you lost your ever-lovin' mind?" she hissed at the captain.

The captain's grin brimmed with sisterly playfulness. "You made me lose it."

I wasn't sure if I should laugh or not, but Beatriz certainly giggled behind her hand.

"The captain used to be Zephonia's partner," she whispered to me.

Seriously? I leaned closer to Beatriz. "Did the captain train her?"

Zephonia scoffed and wiped the cooties off the lid of her coffee cup. "She was my greenie a hundred years ago."

"She means that literally."

My eyebrows shot skyward. According to the info I had dug up on my new partner, Zephonia had been a steward for the better part of two centuries. It had never occurred to me that any of Zephonia's partners had risen in the ranks while she stayed behind. What would it be like to have the person you trained become your boss?

I glanced at Zephonia, who lit her pipe and leaned back in her seat like she was ready for a nap.

"Morning, Stewards. Let's start out by welcoming a new face. Zephon—I mean—" Everyone snickered and looked back at Zephonia, who saluted us all with her pipe. "Huri Rojas. She graduated top of her class from the Academy and is rumored to have put Ares himself in a choke hold."

Great. I waved as discreetly as possible when eyes turned to me. I hated being called out, especially when everyone started to mutter at that last statement.

"Is that true?" Beatriz asked.

I shrugged. "He still beat me afterwards. But I did make his face go red." It was about the best moment of my training sessions with the jerk. A small victory with a prompt defeat.

"Normally," the captain began, "we'd take you out for lunch on your first day, but we have a Labbie starting tomorrow. So we'll be having a little potluck tomorrow to welcome you both."

I managed a smile as I nodded. At least now I'd be able to have lunch with my friends. I just needed to find a moment to confirm that they were good to meet up. "Sounds great."

"Excellent. Let's get some assignments out." Janis hefted a stack of file folders and passed them out to the heads of steward teams. I realized this was the case when Janis paused in front of Zephonia and gave her a crisp new file. "Bia. You'll run support on this one with Zephonia and Huri if they need you. I need you to investigate some thieving in Knoxville."

Beatriz gave me a playful two-finger salute before she fluttered out of the room.

Zephonia rose to leave, as did I, but Janis pushed down the file pointedly. The veteran steward sat, fingertips on my forearm, and waited for the rest to leave.

I kept my attention on both women, wondering if something bad was about to happen over that coffee.

"This takes priority," Janis told Zephonia quietly.

"I've got two murder victims on my docket, Filomena."

"I know." Janis winced, glancing around. "We need this guy. Just keep it quiet. You report directly to me. No one else knows until we know what we're dealing with."

Zephonia leaned forward, eyebrows furrowed. "That bad?"

"You'll read it. The tips we're getting from the houseless...it's concerning me. Could be nothing. But..." Janis glanced at me. "Reminds me of the Wheatens case."

Zephonia hummed and nodded. "You got it."

"Huri, you need to speed-read the procedures," Janis told me. "After lunch."

"Filly, she's too green."

My cheeks burned, but Zephonia wasn't wrong, either. "I can handle it," I said, wishing I knew what I was supposed to handle.

"She can. Even if it's not perfect," Janis said.

"Fine." Zephonia exhaled and pushed herself up, waving for me to join her. "But you should at least give her the day."

Janis snickered. "You threw me in the deep end."

Zephonia grumbled and rolled her eyes. "Look where that got me."

Janis touched my arm before I could exit behind my partner. The captain winced an apology. "You'll be fine. Just listen to her. She's one of the oldest stewards still in service. She knows her stuff."

"What are we going to be doing?" I kept my face as impassive as possible.

Janis half-smiled in what I realized was a very Zephonia-ish way. "Trying to bust a mid-level drug dealer who moonlights as a human trafficker."

My eyebrows rose like they did when I had that first delicious sip of coffee in the morning. "Sounds like fun."

"Oh. And he's a vampire."

I couldn't help the dark smile that curved along my lips. "Even better."

Janis snickered and clapped me on the arm. "Needles sharp, Huri."

CHAPTER 3

I caught up to Zephonia right when she was entering her own desk. "I really can do this."

Zephonia frowned and exhaled. "It's not that, Huri. I've seen your records. They're darn good, honey." She chewed her pipe stem, eyes distant. "She's not asking us to merely interview a perp. Either way, to even get to a modicum of readiness, you need to do that speed reading thing I heard you can do. I've got to make a battle plan. I'll know if you've done your homework based on how prepared you are." She raised a pointed eyebrow at me.

I forced a smile, wondering if Zephonia and I were going to get along. "I'll have it done."

"Have a bite of your ambrosia, too. I'm going to see where our guy is and start recon." Zephonia exhaled again as she rubbed her temples. "I swan. That woman's going to make me retire with all these extra jobs."

With those words, Zephonia wandered off toward the central staircase. I dutifully planted my butt in the chair, pulled over the stack of procedural manuals, silently ordered myself not to fall asleep, and dove in.

I scribbled down any items the manuals said I'd need. I already had the knitting needles at my back—a last-resort weapon, one StS was known for. It used to be that women carried their knitting with them everywhere, so knitting was once an easy cover and the needles a handy weapon when the stewards had to be inconspicuous. Now, they were mostly nostalgic.

I paused at the heading "When You're Frogged."

Stewards should always have a dummy knitting project on their standard comm needles. In case of emergency, frog* the project. This will alert your captain that you are in mortal peril.

I paused to follow the asterisk.

*Frogging is the act of ripping your project from your comm needles.

I wrote that little tidbit down and immediately cast on a few stitches with the silk yarn I always carried with me. The yarn slithered over my arm and fingers like a pet snake.

I was the only one in my family who could manipulate every kind of silk: spider, worm, or synthetic. All kinds did my bidding and had gotten me out of more than a few jams.

I knitted a few rows as my eyes scanned the pages. Then I set my needles aside and messaged the girls about lunch.

We're on, I wrote. *Newbie lunch is tomorrow.*

A party emoji from Rose popped up on my bracelet. *We'll be there!*

I smiled when all three confirmed. The smile faltered when I remembered that I would have to concoct some story to cover up the fact that I was an immortal working as a detective for an agency of immortals. None of my friends knew who—or even *what*—I was. Even without the pantheon's gag order, my mother said it was too dangerous. Probably wasn't wrong.

It just sucked to lie to three people who had known me since middle school. It wouldn't be too hard to come up with a cover story this time.

I'd just go with the whole "I'm a detective for the Nashville Police Department" narrative and, like always, shelter them from my immortal life.

With a shake of my head, I turned my eyes back to the manuals and read and read until my eyes were dry. My hands fidgeted with the silk yarn bracelet around my left wrist. I coiled and wove it between my fingers absentmindedly as I read. I finished with enough time to gather up the few supplies I'd need and placed them in the supple leather knitting bag that looked like a typical purse. Taking a skein of sapphire-blue silk yarn from the storage closet, I stowed it in the bag with a pat.

What was a vampire drug dealer like, and why was Zephonia against involving me so soon?

The scry bracelet heated.

I swiped the bronze disk, polished to a mirror finish, and found a message from Mama. There was an image of her, Yiayia, and Elias holding buckets of mulberries. Elias was beaming as only a newly minted five-year-old could.

A shadow passed over the nearby window, drawing my eyes. Zephonia stood there, watching. Totally not creepy or intimidating.

"Ready?"

"Yeah, let me get my backpack." I paused when Zephonia held out a t-shirt with "Middle Tennessee State University" emblazoned on it. It looked brand-new. My brow furrowed as I looked from Zephonia to the shirt and back again. *Her name is way too long. I need to shorten it.*

"You'll need to blend in. Jeans are fine, but you're too old from the top up."

My stomach flitted like I was a teenager who'd seen a cute guy. "Seriously? I'm going undercover?"

Zephonia stared at me for a moment, obviously calculating. "Not exactly, sugar. You're going to be scouting our perp. You won't get close enough to draw his attention."

Best first day ever! I kept my lips at a firm neutral, but my insides were flipping. "Roger that."

"Let's get going. I want to be back before lunch." Zephonia hurried down the stairs with a vibrancy that belied her apparent age.

I chuckled to myself. The gray hair and wrinkles always made mortals—and even immortals—underestimate the stewards. They might appear old by mortal standards, but that's only because most of their time was spent away from their native Amaranthia.

I followed my new partner into the locker room to change. With a sigh, I pulled off the harness and sheath for my swords for the second time that day. Then I put on my undercover shirt.

Touching my owl pendant at my throat, I felt Pater's and Yiayia's own silk slither from the nickel-sized charm. My silk armor was stronger than Kevlar and encased my body from my neck to my ankles with unyielding protection.

I pulled my sheathed swords onto my back again. As always, the harness melded into the silk. It'd be a dead giveaway if I walked in with swords strapped to my back. With another touch of my pendant, the armor slithered back to my owl pendant within seconds, taking my swords with it. I readjusted my T-shirt and jeans. My clothes always got into the strangest positions after I put on my armor. And wrinkled. My armor could do incredible things (hiding my weapons, for one thing), but it always made my pants bunch up in the most uncomfortable ways.

Clothes now set, I threw my hair up into a messy bun, tendrils of hair sticking out haphazardly. With a nod at my reflection, I swung on my backpack.

Definitely looked like a college student.

Zephonia led me to the parking garage, where a fleet of vintage muscle cars waited. Zephonia gave a black '69 Mustang with racing stripes a loving caress. She greeted me with a nod and an open hand held out in expectant silence.

I obediently handed over my backpack, which contained the leather purse with all my supplies. Zephonia rummaged through without comment, the pipe stem hanging loosely in her mouth. After a quick inspection, Zephonia turned her eyes back to me. Was it just me, or did that curve to her lips mean she was happy with my work?

"Seems in order. Let's go. I'll fill you in on the drive."

I said nothing, just buckled myself in. The Mustang was so clean that I swear I could've eaten off the floor.

As Zephonia joined me, I fiddled with Luis's necklace to keep me calm.

"I've got just one rule when you're riding with me," Zephonia said, glancing over at me.

Forcing my thoughts into the present, I wiped my sweaty palms on my pants as discreetly as possible. "Should I write this down?"

Zephonia didn't acknowledge me or make a sound. Instead, she tapped out the tobacco from her pipe before restuffing and lighting it. "Don't eat in Gertie. Ever. Or I'll use my nixie voice to make you clean the mess with your tongue."

I mentally berated myself for not doing more research on my new partner's abilities. That would be top of my list tonight once Elias was in bed.

Outwardly, I merely nodded, staring out of Gertie, the '69 Mustang. Super subtle. How Zephonia had kept the sixty-year-old collectible in such pristine condition—not to mention how she kept it from getting stolen—was a mystery. "Got it."

Zephonia exhaled smoke through her nose and kept quiet as we drove. The hush unnerved me, but I remained silent, continually fighting the urge to check my scrying bracelet to see if Mama had sent pictures of Elias. Elias would probably be stained red and purple all over from the mulberries.

"Am I enrolling in college?"

"No, sweetie. Keep an eye on that one." She put a photo in my lap. "He's a tick."

"Don't you mean 'vampire'?"

"Great." She exhaled a smoke ring. "You're politically correct. I bet you really call them by their scientific name. *Homo lamia.*" Zephonia rolled her eyes. "Look. True vampires take care of their mortal donors. They get a bad rap because of the ticks. Just in case you fell asleep in Immortal Creatures class, the ones you run into the most in America are your Dracula-variety *strigoi*. Like our buddy,

David Spangler, here. They reproduce like rabbits. There are kinds. But, in any case, I make a distinction. Ticks, unlike their vampire siblings, are parasites that treat mortals like walking blood bags. They might all be 'vampires,' but they are definitely not the same."

Wow. "OK. Thank you..." Eyebrows raised, I whistled softly, not really knowing what to say. "For the clarification."

Turning my attention back to the photo, I snickered. "How do mortals not know?" The horrible orange spray tan alone should be an indicator.

"No telling. Now, your first assignment is to simply observe him. Report anything unusual via your WIP or your bracelet. I'd go with your bracelet since most folks don't knit nowadays. You do *not* engage this guy or talk to him. Nothing. Just watch and report. Now, remember. As a steward, your job is to keep our fellow immortals from taking advantage of mortals. Your allegiance, if you will, is to the mortals. Not the immortals."

"I know the oath. So, do I knit anything in particular for my work-in-progress?"

"It's called a WIP out here," she said, pronouncing it like *whip*. "And no. I'd keep it simple, though. Dishcloth or the like." She shrugged. "If you need me, just frog it."

"Got it. Frog it." After memorizing the vampire's face, I flipped over the photo to review his aliases.

"I've heard you're top in combat, but this isn't the gym."

Remembering my years of training with Olympia's best warriors made me cringe. "I can handle myself." I stared back at Zephonia for a moment, hoping she would recognize truth and not arrogance.

"You've got your perfume on?"

"You tell me." Even before becoming a steward, I'd practically bathed in anti-scent spray. Given my lineage, my scent was stronger than that of most other immortals.

"It's not too strong, but I can still sense a little. You shouldn't be close enough for him to notice."

Fighting the urge to roll my eyes, I said, "Understood."

Zephonia pulled into an out-of-the-way parking lot at the university and cut the engine.

She took back the photo. "I'm going to be watching your WIP." She tapped the mirror where Gertie's radio once was. An empty grid displayed the empty status of my needles. "Let's give the transmission a test."

I obliged, knitting the knits and purls of my coded name on the needles with my fake project. All the stitches appeared in the grid, complete with auto-translation underneath. This mirror was definitely not standard-issue.

I had lived so long with mortal technology constantly malfunctioning that it was almost heavenly to be around Amaranthian tech. The few mortals who knew about it swore it was magic, but how a cell phone worked was just as mystifying to me as a scrying mirror was to mortals. Still, it'd be nice to not have to worry that a mortal might see a cell phone blow up in my hands. "Blow up" might be an exaggeration. But they did stop working.

With the transmission test complete, Zephonia nodded and shooed me away.

My bracelet buzzed against my wrist on my way to the student union. A photo appeared of Elias's fingers holding up a ripe mulberry. He must have been trying out the new hand mirror that Grandmother bought him with my approval. It was a gift to celebrate going into kindergarten. But I knew it was because I was going back to work and couldn't afford one yet. Part of me was relieved I'd be able to get ahold of him more easily. Actually, most of me was.

My attention refocused on the students milling about. It was the week before summer finals, so the campus was full of students rushing around with their eyes stuck to either a book or their phones. I entered the student union and decided to blend in with the late lunch crowd.

A brief glance around the food court didn't immediately reveal my quarry. It was unlikely I'd have an issue sensing the perp since the coppery tang of blood always seemed too strong for my sense of smell. It would overtake my nose and overwhelm my taste buds. The residue of the strigoi's bloody-copper musk still clung to the air, so I sat with my back against the wall and sipped the swill these college students dared to call coffee.

I finished my initial scan of the area and messaged an all-clear to Zephonia. As I finished typing, Mama finally sent an intelligible picture of Elias, fingers and lips stained purple as he beamed, a bucket full of the tart dark berries hoisted before him. I couldn't contain a chuckle.

That's when the coppery scent pricked at my nostrils, making my forearm hair rise, along with my adrenaline. My heart raced more as I looked to the exits, but his cheap-spray-tan self wasn't around. I closed my eyes to focus on the vampire's scent through the haze of pheromonal mortality.

I traced the source, like a trail of smoke, to the restrooms. He was flirting with a young woman who preceded him with a telling giggle. As they parted, his hand gripped hers before the girl slipped her hand into her back pocket.

Did he just pass her something?

My gaze followed the young woman as she exited a door on the far side of the student union. Then the vampire put on an apron and stood behind the counter of a burger joint.

I sent the message that I had spotted him. I almost expected Zephonia to come and sit with me now that our quarry was spotted, but my partner just reiterated that I should sit and observe. So, I waited and watched.

By all appearances, the vampire was a model employee and had just the right amount of charm to make the young women smile, even if their order was slightly wrong. In fact, his line was the longest. After several minutes of watching him serve others, my curiosity started niggling my brain too much.

What's the harm in getting a better view?

I dared to push myself up from the table, ignoring the memory of Zephonia's orders.

"Just order a milkshake," I whispered and wiped my sweaty palms on my jeans. I paused behind a column to check my reflection in my scry bracelet. *Look like you have some kind of fashion sense, Huri.* Frowning, I pulled out my hair tie, gave my curly black mop a tousle, and retouched my lip gloss.

With a slight wiggle to feel the reassuring presence of the straight needles at my back, I shoved my nerves into the recesses of my mind and tried not to think of Luis raising an eyebrow at my flirting on the job. I could almost picture him snickering over at one of the tables I passed.

"You aren't the most accomplished flirt in the world, Huri," he would have teased me.

I shushed him in my mind with a conspiratorial smirk.

As I drew closer, I could hear several of the girls ordering similar items.

"Hot fudge sundae," one simpered with a bite of her lip. "With extra cherries."

I rolled my eyes. So cringe. The vampire took something from his pocket and slid it underneath the dessert cup. Other girls ordered desserts with extra cherries. When the girls walked away, he would palm the cash they left. I had no idea what he was selling or how I would get it without any cash, but I was definitely going to try.

CHAPTER 4

A smile luxuriated across the vampire's lips when I finally stood before him. His nostrils flared slightly, making his leer deepen. "How can I service you?"

I threw up a little in my mouth. *How do girls fall for that?* But I managed to keep my hands to myself and not knock him through the kitchen window. *Flirt, Huri!* "Chocolate milkshake." I leaned my hip onto the counter and twirled my hair around my finger. "Extra, extra cherries." I cringed inwardly. *Am I even doing this right?* I wasn't a great flirt before. Now, I was rustier than a redneck's truck on cinderblocks.

"I bet." He hummed, eyes raking my neck. He could probably spot every vein in my throat. "You smell delightful, darling."

My pulse quickened. "Thanks. My boyfriend got me a new perfume for my birthday."

He practically growled and retrieved my order with extra cherries under the cup. I reached for my back pocket, but he shook his head. "On the house, love." He presented a card with a magician's flair. "For when that boyfriend can't give you what you crave."

Taking the card, I smiled and bit my lip as I batted my eyelashes. *I am so bad at this.* Then I took my tray back to the table, remembering to put some sway into my hips.

I sat back down at the table, imagining Luis with me to calm my nerves.

"That wasn't completely horrible." Luis snickered, wiggling his fingers at the vampire. "He was staring at you the whole way back here. Can I go break his arm yet?"

Underneath the cup was a tiny baggie with three cherry-red, spherical pills. I palmed them and fanned myself with the card. It only had a phone number and red polka dots. How was he simply answering a phone? They'd fritz on him just like they did me. But there were probably mortals lining up for him. No doubt, they were the ones helping a tech-hapless strigoi out.

"Stop it. I can't focus," I whispered to Luis. My eyes widened when I looked up to where Luis sat. I definitely had to stop pretending he was with me everywhere. Now I was talking to myself out loud. Psych evals? I'd fail them.

He gave me that tender smile that always accompanied the words I'd never hear from him again. Then he rippled away.

As I collected myself, the perp still watched me in between his customers. *Did he see me talking to myself?*

No way was I drinking that milkshake. Even so, I pretended to do exactly that as I sauntered out to the parking lot and tossed it into the first garbage can I came across.

Zephonia straightened when she spotted me, and Gertie purred to life as I slipped into the passenger seat. "Well?"

"We should move."

I gestured at a parking lot away from the student union. After we parked, I passed Zephonia the drugs without a word.

"What is this?" Zephonia pulled out a cherry pill. "Please, tell me you didn't engage him."

"I know you said not to, but he's selling it from a restaurant."

"And you couldn't just sit your rear end in a chair and watch? Or take it from one of his customers?"

I shied away. *Didn't think of that.*

With a grumble, Zephonia opened the ashtray and slammed a pill inside. Gertie's usual roar took on a high-pitched hum before the results appeared in front of my WIP. *Unknown strigoi substance, unknown mortal substances.*

We could only stare at the screen for a moment. Zephonia shook her head and redid the test. *Unknown strigoi substance, unknown mortal substances.*

"Skata. What's a strigoi substance?"

Zephonia winced and rubbed her face. "That can't be right."

"What substance could they have besides their venom?"

"Their saliva has healing properties."

"Come on, Zeph. I doubt they're passing out healing draughts."

Zephonia glared at me. "Name's Zephonia, kid."

My stomach churned at the thought. *Homo lamia* venom was highly addictive and contained pheromones to mark the mortal donors as the vampire's territory. Soon, these young women would do anything to become donors just to get the drug. It was an incurable addiction that left its victims dead and dry. Depending on how much venom was in those pills, the vampires would have a never-ending, line-up-to-be-drained food supply.

"No wonder he could move around during the day. He's probably got all sorts of donors keeping him dayside."

"Let me call the captain." Zephonia punched the screen to send over the data to the StS field office. She didn't even have to dial. The captain was apparently monitoring us in real time.

Zephonia tapped her ear cuff to answer the scry bracelet, making the captain's miniature head appear over her wrist. I grumbled to myself when she answered via her ear cuff, which meant I couldn't hear Captain Janis's side of the conversation. "Afternoon, Captain. That was quick." She shot me a glare. "Yes, ma'am. Steward Rojas got it off the tick. Selling it on campus, apparently."

After a grumbling moment, Zephonia started Gertie and left campus, still speaking to the captain. With a hard swallow, I pulled out a mirror as big as a legal pad and accessed the note-taking function to type out my notes about what had happened. I had to type things in the stewards' code of knits and purls, but they had drilled this code into my brain so much in the Academy that it was second nature.

"Yeah, we're headed back now." Zephonia took another drag of her pipe and closed her eyes as she exhaled. "Good. We'll need them on this one. See you there."

I grimaced inwardly at the silence and looked out the window as I typed blindly.

"I don't care who you are or who you're connected to or what you'll become one day. If you screw up my case and go all lone hunter on me, chickadee, I'll ground you so fast you'll think lightning hit you."

"I didn't mean—"

"Don't matter. You're my partner. You're...we're not alone anymore. And you're green as fresh grass. I hate the rules sometimes, but they're there for a reason. Learn which ones to break. Sure. But you darn well better toe that line. All these folks count on us to keep them safe. To bring their attackers to justice. You don't just screw me over—you screw all of them too. So fall in line, chickadee."

My stomach churned. The pride on Elias's shining face as he sent me off to work filled my mind. "I won't let you down. Or them."

"Good." Zephonia puffed like a steam engine for a few more moments. "But good work."

Her words were like cool water trickling into my broiling gut. "Thanks. So, are we going to arrest him now?"

Shaking her head, Zephonia kept us heading toward the field office. "We need to know what we're working with first. I just hope this isn't what we think it is."

I exhaled as I finished the last of my notes and returned my mirror to my backpack. "Me too, Zeph."

"Zephonia."

I snickered behind my hand when Zephonia gave an eye roll and failed in her attempt to hide her smile. Maybe she wasn't so uptight after all.

CHAPTER 5

The captain and Zephonia dismissed me to lunch as soon as we got in and I had given my report.

Considering my lunch plans, I didn't mind that much. I checked the giant clock over the entrance to the detectives' offices. Fifteen 'til. Right on time for a flight to the pizza joint on the other side of Centennial Park.

I took the stairs to the roof access.

"Great." A lock blocked my way, so I wiggled my fingers for the silk yarn from my bracelet to slide into the keyhole. Eyes closed, I concentrated on forming and hardening the yarn to mimic the required key. I'd done this trick many times while ditching school, so the lock gave way in seconds.

The summer sun assaulted my vision as I relocked the door. Without another thought, I shifted into a short-eared owl and flew away to the pizza joint on the opposite side of the Parthenon replica. I returned to my normal form, glad my body glided through the transformation without any disfiguring cracking or pain. I was simply a woman one moment and an owl the next. (Way better than what were-people went through.) Dropping into the alley between the buildings, I grinned at seeing Rose already waiting outside.

"Made it!"

Rose startled so violently that I felt bad.

"It's just me. You okay?"

Turning, Rose thumped my arm before putting a hand over her chest. "Don't scare me like that."

My stomach soured as I took in the racing pulse that practically spasmed at Rose's throat. "What happened, Rose?"

She swatted my concern away. "Nothing. Just got creepy stalker vibes from some guy at Gruhn's."

"You need me to check him out?" I wouldn't have normally offered, but Rose's hands were shaking. "He touch you?"

"Look at you getting all detective on me, Officer Rojas." She embraced me. "I'm fine. Seriously. Just a creep. Good-looking creep. But still. Anyhow." She beamed and danced a little. "So happy for you, girl! How's it going on your big first day?"

The nerves in my stomach unknotted a little, and new ones surfaced. *I'm just a regular immortal—mortal—detective.* "Good, I think. Got a big case on my first day. We'll see how it goes."

"Look at you all fancy. You'll be runnin' the place soon, girl. Captain Huri Rojas. Or are you going by your maiden name for that?" She grinned and pointed at me as we entered the restaurant. "Just remember me when you make it big. I'ma need you to help me with some parking tickets."

I scoffed. "Who are you again?"

Rose laughed and elbowed me. As we waited to be seated, her laughter tempered. "So, how're you doing being away from Eli?"

Studying the dirt under my fingernails, I wished I could think of something else. "Doing," I said. "I'm loving it...but..."

Rose threw her arm around my shoulders. "You're doing the right thing, Huri. You and I both know you don't want to live off your family."

"I know...it's...it's just a dangerous job. Being a cop."

"Honey, I knew it was gonna be either the military or the police for you. It's like you're built for this. I'm just happy you're not overseas somewhere without Eli." Rose raised one of her famous eyebrows and then kissed my temple. "Stop worrying. That boy is so proud of you. I talked to him just a few minutes ago, and all he wanted to talk about was his mama doing her thing."

"Thanks, Rose."

Rose gave me one last squeeze as the waitress came to escort us to the table.

"So, you find anything good at Gruhn's?"

She melted like a schoolgirl talking about her crush. "This beautiful Taylor. I've been dying to get it. But I need to land a new music publisher before that's in the budget. I've got a pretty big meeting in a few weeks. It could help get me in as a songwriter for some new artists. My agent helped line it up."

"That's awesome, Rose," I said.

Once we were seated, Rose pulled out a little gift bag. "But enough of my starving artist woes..."

"What's this?" I reddened.

"You know you're my girl. I'm so proud of you." She kept her eyes on the menu as I pulled out the tissue paper. "Just a little something for your desk. I wanted to give it to you before the girls showed up."

Hidden inside was a small square frame about the size of my palm. The frame held a picture of me and Rose when we were ten, holding our team's soccer trophy. My eyes moistened as I lost myself in the memory. I knew why this moment stood out to Rose.

At a sleepover later that night, Mama and I could hear Rose fighting to tell her parents that she scored the game-winning goal, but they kept interrupting her with details of the campaign trail. The gist was that they wouldn't be back in time to celebrate the end of the season. Rose's dad was a senator, and her mom was the consummate philanthropist, as all proper politicians' wives should be. They were usually gone as much as they were home, especially when she outgrew babysitters.

That night after the phone call, Mama held Rose as she cried and raged, and she gave Rose her own key to the Arachne house. "You're my girl too, Rose. I hope you know that," she had told her with a kiss on her forehead. That night, I gained a sister.

I cleared my throat and nodded as I blinked away wetness. "Thank you, Rose."

Rose's honey-brown eyes were wet when she finally tore them from the menu. She nodded, unable to speak.

"Have you heard from them?"

She laughed a little. "Not much. Last I heard, Father was trying to pass some kind of energy bill. Mother's trying to rope me into some charity thing in New York." She rolled her eyes.

Laughter tumbled out of me. Rose's version of fun was sitting at home with her guitar or piano, a single malt whiskey beside her, and letting the music just slow-drip out of her soul. Rose's sound was an incredible blend of singer-songwriter and the blues. It sounded heavenly.

Surprisingly, Rose was not one for the spotlight. Instead, she wrote the songs the stars sang. She could've been a star if she wanted. I swore her voice must be the stuff of sirens.

"Hurry! Hurry! Can't be late!" Alexis cried with a laugh.

I rolled my eyes. Everyone, teachers especially, mispronounced my name as Hurry. Naturally, kids never let it go. It became my nickname. Rose snickered at me as we both stood to greet Alexis and Klara.

We four had all gone to middle school together, and somehow, through hormones and push-up bras, we'd stayed friends through high school and college. This was, however, the first time we were all assembled since they'd helped me and Eli to unpack at our rental just down the street from my parents' house. After Luis's funeral, they had all cocooned me and Elias. I remembered how they'd taken shifts staying with us: Klara pampering me with indulgent skin treatments and massages, Alexis making sure I still completed what she called "oblivion runs," and Rose holding my hand as I picked out the coffin. The allure of sisterhood had called me home to Tennessee, even more than being near my parents.

"Hey, Lex!" I hugged her and kissed her cheek.

She squeezed me tight. "Okay, Huri. Arrest me. Pass me to the cutest cop you've seen. Honey, you've got to hook me up."

Klara rolled her eyes and hugged me next. Her hair was bubblegum pink today instead of raven blue. Somehow, she made it work with the vintage rock t-shirts she always wore. With her plaid flannel shirt and Doc Martens, she looked like she was single-handedly trying to bring back (and glam up) grunge. She had even somehow bedazzled her Docs. "She's a walking bag of hornymones."

A screech of laughter peeled out of me. "Hornymones, Klara?"

She pursed her lips and shrugged, a smirk twitching at the corner of her lips. "May not be real, but it's accurate."

Alexis threw herself into the chair between me and Rose. "Ordered yet?"

"Waitin' on y'all."

A smile took over my face. I wished we did this more often, without death being a factor. It got harder and harder as we got older. Then another thought sickened my stomach: in the not-so-distant future, my friends would age, and death would claim them. Not me. No, I'd be alone when I lost them. Like I'd lost Luis.

"They've got vegan options, Klara."

"Thank God!"

I couldn't help but smile inwardly at Klara's lifestyle change. After she ODed in college—we nearly lost her—she'd turned into a health nut and only put the best in her body. So proud of her strength.

"I'ma need it all." Alexis nodded as she glanced over the menu. "Carb loading major. Got a big race tomorrow."

"She's trying to qualify for Boston." Klara took a sip of her lemon water.

"Shh! Don't say that." Alexis waved for the waitress. "I'll probably cramp up and get a DNF."

Klara, Rose, and I exchanged smirks as Klara leaned forward. "Wearing the lucky..." She tugged on her own bra strap.

"Ew!" Rose's nose scrunched like she could actually smell the horrid thing. "That thing is like fifteen years old, Lex!"

"Honey, you gotta do whatever it takes." Alexis gave Rose the usual queen bee all-knowing stare. It made me snicker behind my menu.

Finally, the waitress came to deliver our waters, and we promptly ordered more food than was probably appropriate. I asked for plenty of olives and ham to back up my usual ambrosia.

"Why are you always eating that stuff?" Rose laughed and shook her head, body shivering.

"Not everyone has your aversion to olives, Rose," Klara said with a roll of her eyes.

"It's like next-level, though," Rose said.

I was saved from answering when a shaggy-haired man entered. If he were any more feral, he would've shifted right there. Every mortal turned and watched him go to the counter and pick up his pizza order, smiling a little too toothily at the woman behind the counter. I could hear my friends' heartbeats triple.

"Can you believe that?" Klara growled and stabbed a straw into her drink. "Walking around like he and his pack haven't massacred untold victims."

"You don't know that," I mumbled. "They're not all bad."

"The hell they aren't," Klara said at once. "They don't belong here. They need to go back to their hole or whatever."

"The bad ones at least," Rose said. "I can do without the vampires and weres."

I swallowed hard and bit my bottom lip. That was something, at least. Used to be that they all thought like Klara, who had suffered too much at the hands of immortals to not have scars. Rose and Alexis had softened a bit more over the years.

"Let's change the subject," Alexis said and smiled at me as she squeezed my hand. "We're here celebrating Huri's big day."

"Yes," Klara agreed and shoved aside her bad mood to beam at me. "Congrats! So proud of you!"

I blushed, memories of these three women's support resurfacing. "Let's celebrate *us*. I wouldn't be here without y'all." I lifted my glass. "To our siren."

"Hear, hear!" Klara and Alexis joined me in raising their glasses while Rose's cheeks turned crimson. I had a flashback to a sordid Spring Break.

"For hatching this plan of getting us all together."

Rose scoffed, raising her own glass. "To our own private detective. Who even in high school was a better investigative reporter than anyone at *The Tennessean*."

"To Hermes's daughter," I said and grinned when Alexis shot out a laugh. Rose and Klara laughed, too, because I always said this next sentence to all of them when we were about to play a game. "I'll put in a call to Nike for you." It took them forever to realize I didn't mean the shoes.

"And to the purveyor of the glamorous," Alexis announced. "May your hands be steady and your mascara never run."

Klara blushed, which took a lot. "To us. May we grow into fat, cake-eating, cantankerous old women together."

"To us!"

A devious grin stole across Klara's face. "And God help anyone who tries to come between us."

"That poor, unfortunate soul," Rose sang as we clanked our glasses.

CHAPTER 6

Exhaling, I tossed my keys and leather purse onto the entry table, wishing I had time to take a nap before Elias and Mama arrived. What a crazy day. But at least my first day was done, and I'd managed to keep my job despite going all Lone Ranger again. I really needed to stop doing that.

I wandered into the kitchen, which I hadn't finished unpacking. I'd had to leave our old house in West Palm. It got to be too much when three-year-old Elias would sit at the front door waiting for Luis to come home. Then, he would weep himself to sleep.

Knowing I'd need constant help, I'd found this cozy rental in Nashville within walking distance of my family. My parents lived just three houses down to the right, and Yiayia and Ricardo lived directly across the street from us.

I'd known this was the place the moment I walked into the redbrick cottage. The hardwood floors and built-in bookshelves made me want to sing. The backyard, with its huge elms guarding the perimeter, was what sold Elias.

I'd never forget seeing him walk up to the nearest one and put his tiny hand on the trunk like he was meeting his oldest friend for the first time. He had whispered something I couldn't hear. But the contented smile that filled his face afterward, a smile I hadn't seen since Luis had died, had me signing the contract immediately.

For a few minutes, I worked on putting up the casserole dishes that Alexis's mom got me and Luis as a wedding gift.

Then I dared to pull out the cast-iron skillets that Yiayia had given me, as well as the ceramic cups from Grandmother with ancient scenes that depicted me and Luis marrying and Elias's birth. We had only used the cups on special occasions.

My thumb caressed the crack that ran along the body of one cup, remembering how Luis and I had knocked it off the counter the last time we made love. He had secretly fixed it for me. I remembered giggling when I found it drying at the back of the counter, out of harm's way. I remembered thinking I was the luckiest woman on the planet.

Swallowing hard and shaking my head to throw out the memories, I placed the cups up high and in the back of the cabinets. I left one skillet out to make dinner and stowed the rest.

For the millionth time, I silently asked Luis why he had to save that little girl. She was only ten, and that...azeman thought she would be easy prey. Most azeman didn't go for children, but of course, Luis had to find the only one in Florida who wasn't so discriminating. Once I started hunting the azeman down, I found out he had a fetish for young girls.

"Stop it, Huri." I forced myself out of the kitchen. "A shower. You need a shower."

Once the hot water washed my thoughts away, I exited to find Mama and Elias in the driveway. I dressed and then met them at the door. I couldn't hold back the grin when he ran hard and fast into my arms with his too-big backpack thumping against the back of his knees.

My fingers stroked his unruly mass of raven curls as I lost myself in his embrace. Bless his heart. Both of us doubly cursed him with that hair.

"We got so many mulberries, Mami! You wouldn't believe it! And." His grin shamed Helios's sunbeams. "Yiayia Arie climbed with me all the way to the top to get the best ones."

My jaw dropped as I glanced at my mother. "Seriously? How big was this tree?"

"At least forty feet!" He was practically vibrating in my arms as he squeezed my neck tight and then had to demonstrate the height with his fingers stretched as far as the tips of his toes would let him. "She even spun a web below me. Can you show me how to spin a web, Mami?"

I laughed and kissed him. "If I could, I would. I didn't inherit that gift. Yiayia Arie is the one with that talent. Your *pappous* can do it too." I scooped him up in a tight hug and carried him in as Mama followed with a grin and a sack of mulberries.

"I tried, *asteri mou*. I really did, but they both spotted a bunch of ripe ones at the top. Next I knew, they were all the way up." She laughed, kissing my cheek as she set down the sack. "How was your first day?"

"Good. I guess. I've already got a pretty big case."

Elias exploded with laughter and jumping. "What kind of case? Who's the perp? I bet they're vampires or werewolves. Can I go with you?"

I couldn't resist laughing along with Mama.

Once Elias had understood what my job would be, he'd started watching as many videos about policing as possible. At only five, he read like an eight-year-old and knew how to operate mortal technology better than most adults. Being a demi gave him the best of both technological worlds.

No doubt Pater would have him working on his and Hephaestus's eternal project of merging immortal and mortal technologies. Already, they had merged scrying and calling or messaging. I had every confidence that my genius son would help change the world.

I spun him onto my shoulder so that he was hanging upside down while I tickled him just to hear his infectious peels of laughter.

"No, you can't go with me! You've got to hold down the fort here, *agapi mou*."

Giggling, he tried his best to break free, but my already agile reflexes had grown quicker since becoming the mother of my lively son. The romp was quick. I somersaulted him to his feet and swatted the seat of his pants.

"Go wash up, love. I'll get dinner on."

He practically ran along the wall into the bathroom like some parkour master, making me and Mama shake our heads. I won't say which of us was cringing and which was laughing.

"On the floor, son!"

Once the door closed, Mama caressed my hair and kissed my temple. "You need me to stay?"

My shoulders slumped. "No. We'll be good tonight."

"I'm so proud of you," she said with a grin and pecked my cheek.

I hugged Mama. As grateful as I was to have my mom here, it never stopped me from wishing Luis were here to ask about my day instead. Maybe curling up with me on the couch to relax after Elias was in bed. My body slumped.

"What's going on, Huri?"

"Oh. Nothing. It's just that...I don't know." I couldn't keep talking about how a chunk of me had died when Luis was stolen from me. "Had lunch with the girls today." I exhaled. "Rose was acting funny. Some creep spooked her."

"She okay?"

I nodded, busying myself with finding a home for the hand mixer. "Yeah. He didn't touch her or anything. I don't know. Just had me worried."

"I'm sure she's just fine." Mama caressed my cheek with a proud smile. "They had a wonderful self-defense teacher."

A creaking from overhead drew my attention. Elias was hanging from the ceiling from a bit of web. It took me a long moment to process that his lower abdomen was shaped like a spider. "Elias Dareios Rojas Arachne! What in the world!"

He practically flipped off the web and landed as a whole boy in my arms. I could hardly speak. *Don't freak out. Don't freak out.*

Shivering, he hid his face in my neck.

"Since when could you do this?" Mama managed to say, caressing his back.

He growled into my throat.

"Come on, honey. You're not in trouble." I kissed his hair, letting him hide against me. "It's surprising. That's all. I didn't know you could do that. Neither did Nona."

He cut his eyes back at Mama before putting his lips near my ear. "I didn't know."

My body relaxed as I squeezed him tighter. "Oh, sweetie. There's nothing to fear here. Mami started shifting when I was your age. It's pretty normal."

"Your pappous did when he was even younger. I think when he learned to walk. I can't imagine what your yiayia did with him." Mama grinned. "We'll have to celebrate. Pappous will be back from his trip on Sunday. We need to have a party!"

"Really?" His head popped up.

"Of course!" I laughed, wondering how Luis would've reacted to his son being able to change into a half-spider. I was used to seeing people shift into spiders. But, of course, that was par for the course when you're the granddaughter of Arachne. "It's an important milestone. Like when you learned to walk. We had cupcakes."

"Do I get presents?"

"Don't push it, mister. This is just a food celebration. You had your birthday not a month ago." I kissed his cheek. "Come on. Let's let Nona go and do her thing so I can have you all to myself. I've missed you."

His body softened in my arms before he hugged me again and did the same to his Nona. Hours later, as I tucked him into bed, he seemed incapable of being still.

I smoothed his mop of curls from his forehead as my eyes traced his features into memory. "Listen. Since you're shifting...maybe we should put off kindergarten—"

"No! I want to go!"

"Baby, you start in just days. It's not enough time to learn to control yourself, especially being so yo..." I stopped when his face started turning red. "Baby, breathe."

"You can't. You promised. I can do it." He crossed his arms and looked away.

"I could see if there are others your age in town, and we could start a group thing."

"I want to go to school. I've got everything ready."

Remembering his joy and excitement when shopping for school supplies, I caressed his face to have him meet my gaze. "You're too advanced for kindergarten."

"I'll play dumb."

Like that could really happen. My shoulders drooped when he rolled over to give me his back. With a wince, I rubbed between his shoulder blades. "It means that much to you?"

"Yes! I've been telling you."

"I'll make you a deal. I'll help you learn to control it, and if you show me that you can control it, you can go. If not, we'll find a group for immortal kids."

"You'll really try?"

I huffed. "Of course, agapi mou. I'll always have your back, babe." I gave him a mockingly stern glare. "Get some sleep."

Without warning, he bolted upright and threw his arms around my neck. "You're all over my heart."

I melted into his sweet little arms. "I love you too, agapi mou."

When he lay back down, he beamed at me.

I kissed his semi-squishy cheek. *Look at him. He's already losing his baby fat.* "Good night. Sweet dreams."

Sleep overtook him within minutes. No doubt all the mulberry fun had exhausted him. As I watched him, a tender smile stretched across my face. I was reminiscing about all the times Luis and I would check in on him as a baby solely to confirm he was still breathing.

"He's an amazing kid," Luis's voice greeted me.

"You're his papi. Could you expect less?" I whispered.

"You're the one who gets all the credit, amor."

I blushed, pretending I actually felt his warm arms slip around my waist to hold me. "I miss you," I whispered.

"I miss you too, amor." Just as his lips neared my cheek, he evaporated again.

I took a moment to message the girls to update them on my day. I paused when I was about to tell them about the Cherries, then decided against it. The lab was still processing things, so I didn't even know what we were dealing with.

I winced.

But what if they were slipped one of those things without knowing? They needed to be safe. I couldn't lose them, too.

Listen, I texted. *There's some new drug out there. Not sure what it is yet, but it could be bad.*

Stop worrying, Klara wrote back. *We're okay. And we're not stupid.*

Anymore, Alexis texted with a laughing emoji.

I paused at seeing Rose's "in the middle of typing" bubble pop up. It took a while for Rose to get done. Then there was nothing. She hadn't sent it. My stomach bottomed out.

I talked to Jerome today.

The group text exploded with a flurry of questions and emojis as my stomach settled. Good. No creepy cute guys then.

Klara was the first one to form comprehensible words. *The Jerome?*

It wasn't like that. Rose's texts about her high school crush now came rapid-fire. *He took over his father's business.*

Do people still need piano tuners? Alexis texted.

I do. Ol' Faithful has been way out of tune for days now. Awful.

Klara sent several laughing smileys. *I bet that's all you called him for.*

A shaky smile twitched into place as I typed on my bracelet. *Details.*

After I get home. About to put a load of groceries in the car.

Hurry up! Alexis wrote back.

I snickered before doing a final check of the house. Grabbing a book and heading to bed, I snuggled in to await Rose's account of her time with The Jerome.

It wasn't long before Elias woke from a nightmare. I welcomed him into bed, knowing this stage of snuggles would end all too soon. A smile filled my face when Elias fell asleep against my shoulder. Soon, I gave up the fight to stay awake until I heard from Rose.

My bracelet buzzed along the nightstand. Elias growled his disapproval when I answered. My eyes open just enough to see the green button on the mirrored surface.

"Hello?"

"Huri Rojas?"

The official-sounding voice made me sit up and rub my eyes. "Yeah. Who is this?"

"I'm Ben Carpenter from Saint Thomas." He paused. "You're listed as the emergency contact for a Rosaline Brandt."

I practically leaped out of bed and rushed to get dressed. "Please, tell me she's okay."

"I'm afraid she's been assaulted. She's lost a lot of blood. She's asking for you. Extremely disoriented."

My eyes welled up. "On my way."

CHAPTER 7

I sat in the chair directly beside Rose's hospital bed, holding her battered hand. Thankfully, she was sleeping. The nurses said she'd been barely conscious when she came in and had woken briefly, so disoriented she'd still been fighting like her attacker was in the hospital with her. They had called everyone listed in her emergency contacts. I was the first to answer.

Tears raced down my cheeks. I leaned forward and lifted a stray ringlet from Rose's forehead.

My bracelet warmed and displayed Mama's face.

"Any updates, asteri mou?"

I kissed Rose's hand. "She...she was attacked," I answered, switching to Greek.

Mama let out a strangled cry. "Tell me..."

"Well? What's she saying?" Pater asked over Mama's shoulder. I could hear the soft whistle of the kettle. Yiayia must be making tea, the cure for all ills.

A swallow moistened my throat a little. "It was a tick. I...the healers think it was a simple assault. She wasn't raped, thank goodness!" I stared at the silvered fang marks hidden beneath the bruising. They looked like old, healed scars. "But I smell it on her. The venom...it's there. He bit her at least three or four times. She wasn't as low on blood as I expected. The guy I spoke to before made me thing she'd been drained." That meant one thing. The tick had tagged her. They would come back for Rose. "How's Eli?"

"Still sleeping. Don't worry. You just focus on her."

"Thank you." I nodded. *Man, I feel like a bobblehead doll.* "If they discharge her, I'll take her back to my place. I don't like the idea of leaving her alone."

Mama exhaled. "You'll need to tell her some things. At least versions."

"I know. I'm trying to decide how far to go."

"Just the essentials. She needs to know what she's up against." Rose began groaning, which Mama heard. "Keep me updated, asteri mou."

Rose's eyes were fluttering open as I swiped the mirror clean, sat beside my first and oldest friend, and held her hand. "Rosie, it's Huri. You're safe, baby girl." I hastily brushed aside my tears with my free hand and forced cheer into my face. "Rosie, wake up, honey."

Rose tensed when my hand touched her cheek. In the next moment, her eyes surged open as she sucked in a hard breath. Her honey-brown eyes had that silver-venom haze, making my chin tremble.

"Ri?"

"Right here, honey. You're okay." I kissed her forehead and then rested my forehead against hers. It was a little thing that Mama had always done with us, and we did with each other. "You're safe."

Shuddering breaths escaped Rose before she simply jerked me down into her arms in a crushing hug, the kind someone gives when they're drowning. I held on without fail, wrapping her tight like I could hide her inside my arms. Tuck her away into safety.

I was going to stake that tick to the wall and revel in watching his ashes flutter away in the humid Tennessee air.

"You're okay," I whispered into her hair, inhaling the scent of coconut and shea butter, mindful of the small gash on her scalp where the idiot had knocked her out.

"He...he..."

"He didn't." I swallowed, daring to hold her gaze so she could see the truth. "They checked already. He didn't."

Body deflating with temporary relief as we embraced again, Rose shivered in my arms. I wanted to promise Rose so many things, like that no bloodsucker would ever touch her beautiful skin again, but I didn't fill the air with useless words. Instead, I just let Rose weep, praying and wishing I could take this moment away from her.

Minutes passed until the nurse entered almost silently. She gave us that smile. The one full of compassion with traces of pity. I had seen that smile too often from my family in Greece when I was too young and foolish to hold in the tales of my friendships in America. Eventually, I realized they gave me that smile because they knew I would lose all my friends one day.

"Hi, Rose. I'm Brenda, your nurse for the night. I saw on the monitor that you woke, and I wanted to check on you."

Rose nodded, waving her hands at her face to hide the snot and tears. I passed her the box of tissues Brenda had given me an hour before.

"Can I get you something to drink?"

"Water, please."

"Absolutely. I'll be right back."

Rose couldn't let go of my hand as the nurse returned moments later with a Styrofoam pitcher and cups.

"I've let the doctor and the officer know that you're awake, but you'll likely be staying overnight so we can run tests."

"But...I wasn't..." She looked at me.

"She wants to make sure she wasn't...assaulted." It seemed abhorrent to say "sexual" or "raped."

There was that smile again. "You came fully clothed. Pants intact. Only your shirt was ripped. Particularly your arms. The police officer will be in to speak with you as well. See if you can remember anything about your assault."

I wondered how many times Brenda had to use that word.

"How is your pain level?" Brenda adjusted the blood pressure cuff on Rose's arm and checked her oxygen.

"My head hurts." She tentatively put her hand lightly over the wound. When she saw the extent of the bruises on her arms and wrists, she started shaking.

"I can only give you some Tylenol for it right now. We still need a CT done."

"Anything to help me sleep?" Weeping began again. "I...I don't think..."

"I'll see what's allowed." The blood pressure cuff beeped. "Well, your blood pressure is the envy of everyone I know. Oxygen is perfect. I'm going to send in that order for the scan so you can get a little rest tonight."

"Thank you." Rose fought to give her a smile.

"You're free to use the restroom. Just take Huri or one of us with you."

We remained quiet for what seemed an eternity after the nurse left, but then Rose exhaled. "I'd like to see myself."

I blinked a few times, wondering if I should take her to the mirror in the bathroom or what. But what if she fainted or fell?

Ultimately, I opted to hand over the phone. It was a good thing I didn't get her out of bed. Rose gasped, covering her face with her hand as the phone dropped to the blanket. I wished I had the words to say something, anything to help. But my tongue failed to move.

After several deep breaths, Rose looked at herself again. She stretched her neck to find the handprints around her throat.

"Klara would say that it's nothing some concealer can't fix."

Rose shot me a glare, but then she snickered a little, shaking her head. "She's probably had to cover up these kinds of bruises."

It was true. Klara was known for having...adventurous partners.

"So...who knows?"

"I've only talked to your folks and mine."

She swallowed as if bracing herself. "And?"

"Mama and Pater are with Eli. Your folks are getting the first flights back." I caressed her cheek when her eyebrows rose. "I don't expect them until tomorrow."

"So, my folks are actually coming?"

I nodded. "I sent them pictures." Well, the nurses did.

That made Rose laugh a little.

"Listen. I need you to do something for me when you're released."

"Don't get attacked?"

I barely laughed, patting her hand. "Come stay with me for a few days."

"Ri..." She shook her head. "I'm not that bad off."

"It's actually not a bad idea."

We both started and glanced at the door where a uniformed police officer filled in the doorway. I wanted to kick myself for forgetting to call StS. I'd heard other stewards complain about working with local LEOs.

"Hello, Miss Brandt. I'm Officer Feldman. I'm here to take your statement." He entered a little farther into the room, flipping open a small notepad as his bald head glinted in the fluorescent lights. Even with his baldness, he looked like a giant baby. This had to be his first time out alone. Of course Rose would get saddled with a newb.

"Right now?" Rose asked, casting an eye at the clock. It was after one o'clock.

"It's best to get it right away so that you don't lose those initial details."

"But I don't remember anything. I...I was putting my groceries in the car and..." She stared off as she put a hand on the cut to her head. "Everything else was a blur."

Feldman and I locked eyes for a minute. Then he winced in the most inept attempt to show compassion. He kept his expression even as he said, "We can speak in private if you like."

Rose shook herself awake. "No. I want Huri here. She's a detective with NPD."

Feldman really set his baby gaze on me then. I had to stop him before he blew everything. I should've told Rose sooner. This guy was going to blow it. "Really."

"Yes." Why did I forget my badge? "I'm with StS."

He stared at me for a silent moment. "StS."

I stared right back and squeezed Rose's bruised hand. *Don't blow it, Babyface.*

"Yes. Huri Rojas." I approached with an outstretched hand. "Today was...well, yesterday now...it was my first day."

He shook my hand without pause. "Nice to meet you, Steward. Don't see y'all too often." He grinned and turned pink. *Oh no.* "Well, ever. Y'all are legends."

"Same here." The only good thing was that Rose had apparently missed my title.

"Well, it's pretty cut and dry, Miss Brandt. Based on your wounds, I'd say—and I'm sure Steward Rojas here will agree—you were attacked by a vampire."

Oh, dear Lord. I nearly hid behind my hands, wondering how many other poor victims were told what their attackers were so blatantly. Especially given the ignorance most Americans lived in. Folks like Rose believed evil immortals were little more than fairy-tales, even though they unwittingly dealt with them daily. I was pretty sure one nurse was a werewolf.

Rose's eyes rounded. The heart rate monitor started beeping more quickly. She blinked several times. "Did you just say 'vampire,' or am I high on whatever they've got me on?"

I pursed my lips. How was I going to save this? "Yeah, so, perhaps we should just let Rose tell her side first."

"Absolutely." Feldman nodded. "You're so right. I keep forgetting that discussion of immortal crimes is in your jurisdiction."

Rose's eyebrows met as she looked over at me. "Your jurisdiction?"

My mouth flapped open. *This is so not the time to do this.* How I abhorred this baby-faced cop! *Procedure.* I had to help this guy do his job instead of outing me. "Do you remember anything about your attacker, Rose?"

She frowned at me, letting me know she would not be letting the subject drop. "Not really. Just hitting my head. I remember scratching someone." Rose's eyes closed, and she shook at whatever horrible memories she was reliving.

"Do you know where you scratched him?" Feldman asked, scribbling his notes. "Anything. Scent of his cologne. How tall?"

"He?" Rose said.

"Usually males attack," I said when Feldman looked at me and waited for me to answer. "Females seduce."

Rose stared at me, mouth opening and closing. "How do you know that?"

"It's part of their training. Fascinating stuff. The stewards are teaching local LEOs all about spotting immortal crimes. I've taken every class I can get my hands on."

Lips thinning, Rose blinked with such deliberation that I wanted to hide in a hole. This was so not how I pictured this conversation going. I had everything planned out, and this baby-faced idiot was coming in and ruining it.

I swallowed hard. "Anything come to mind, Rose? Scent. How tall he is? Do you remember where you scratched him?"

"I think his face." She closed her eyes. "But it felt like hitting a wall."

I winced and sat back beside Rose. The blood pressure cuff hummed as it inflated. "They're very difficult to injure. It's like fighting stone." Unless you were a stronger immortal. I had to frequently remember to check my strength with something as simple as shaking a mortal's hand.

"That's what I've heard." Feldman graced me with so flirtatious a smile that I wanted to slap him. "You must be an incredibly strong immortal to be a detective. Why do the stewards only take women?"

"An immortal?"

My body flashed with fire. If I could've, I would've smote him with lightning or a wall of water. Feldman's smile fled as he looked from Rose to me. *Genius finally caught up.*

"Time for you to leave," I told him in a growl.

"She didn't know." His face turned crimson. "I'm so sorry."

My hand flexed into a fist as I tried to keep myself away from this man. "You need to leave. Now."

He paled but obeyed, pausing at the door. "I'll let you report it to the stewards, and if you could not mention it to my CO..."

Rose and I shouted, almost in unison, for him to leave.

The door shut. I waited another second to turn around and face my oldest and dearest friend. *The story the stewards came up with.* I was just a cop who hunted immortal bad guys. Nothing about what or who I really was. It would keep Rose safe. I could still be Huri here. I wouldn't be sent back to Olympia. The home that wasn't my home.

Rose's silvered eyes were wet and her lips flat as paper. "What the hell, Huri."

My stomach cramped and twisted. My mouth opened and then shut. Truth. I could only tell Rose the truth. "They made me swear not to tell you," I rasped, salt water stinging my eyes. No, not some nonsense about being a regular immortal who hunted immortal nightmares. Whatever that was. Rose deserved the truth. Screw the consequences. I was tired of lying. "I am Athena Huri Pherenike Arachne Rojas."

Silence. That's all that I had gotten from Rose after spilling all the secret parts of my life for the last fifteen minutes. I didn't know if I could wait for long. The only other mortal I had ever told was Luis. He had taken the news in stride, as if it didn't matter one bit.

Rose might have been silent, but her heart rate monitor betrayed her. Rose's calm façade was in complete contrast to the rapid monitor beeps. The bruising on her face made it even more difficult to look at her.

Rose licked her lips to speak and then stopped. Then she locked her wild eyes on mine. I had never seen a venom addict, but Rose looked like she was on the threshold of insanity without even knowing it. How I loathed the tick who stole my friend from me. Images of suitable torture after suitable and delectable torture flitted through my mind. I would avenge her. Even if Rose hated me now for all the lies.

"You've lied to me." Rose shook with rage or addiction (I didn't know which). "From the moment I met you."

"I didn't have a choice."

"No," Rose shouted and pounded her chest. "Tonight. I didn't have a choice." Tears cliff-jumped from her eyes and onto her cheeks. "You have had twenty years of choices, Huri."

"It was a direct order from my pantheon, Rose." I bit my lip, wishing I didn't feel so much like I'd betrayed her. But I knew I had. "It was part of the conditions of my being able to live outside of Amaranthia."

"Yeah. Right." Rose began to weep. "You should have told me."

"You don't think I wanted to?" I wiped the moisture from my face. "Every day that I've known you and the girls? I've begged them to authorize me countless times."

"Yeah, and what would you get? A slap on the wrist?"

My chin trembled. "They would force me, and now Elias, to stay in Olympia and never see you or Klara or Alexis again. Mama, too. Never see Pater."

Rose's mouth snapped shut. Her eyes darted away from me.

"And dang it, Rose. I'd pick you every day of my life over them. You're my sister in all but blood." I covered my face with shaking hands. My legs quivered and failed me, dropping me into the chair behind me. *Oh no. What have I done?*

Did mortals experience the intensity of the rage and love I did? I swore they couldn't; otherwise, humanity would implode from a total lack of self-control. I forced myself to breathe in and out. To not think about hunting the bastard who'd touched Rose. To not think of how much I loved being with my friends and family and the fear of losing them.

"They can't do that," Rose told me.

"The hell they can't." Scoffing, I looked up. "I'm an Athena, Rose. My grandmother is one of twelve who rules our people. After my grandmother dies, Mama will help rule our people. After my mother dies, I will help rule our people. I am not meant to live outside of Olympia. But the conditions Mama agreed to were clear. No one knows."

"No mortal knows," Rose corrected.

"Yes." I sighed and buried my face in my hands.

"Luis knew."

My heart clenched. "He was my husband." I blinked. "It's different."

"You told him. Before." Her silver and golden eyes were widening, searching memories. "It's why you became so close so quickly. You married just days after meeting him."

"He was my fate. I saved him from that fire he was in when we met," I told her softly and wearily. I could still smell the smoke, see Luis fighting off that idiot who had attacked him. Luis had told me I was his angel as I carried him out of the building. "He knew I wasn't mortal. But he didn't know what I am until after our marriage. If I told him before..." I offered up my hands again. *What else can I say?*

Rose grew quiet once more.

If truth sets me free, why do I suddenly feel so bound?

"I'm sorry, Rose. I am."

"And what now? Why now?"

My chin trembled at the venom behind her words. "I...you really were attacked by a vampire," I said, wishing my voice didn't sound as weary as it did. "That idiot got that much right. I can't investigate who, no matter how I long to stake him to the wall and watch him turn to ash. But my coworkers can." Wetness that I couldn't keep in check drenched my cheeks. "I'm tired of secrets. I could've told you I'm just a regular immortal. A shape-shifter. Whatever. I hunt down bad guys. Investigate crimes that immortals commit against innocent mortals like you and the girls." I shrugged and bit my bottom lip. "I...I couldn't lie to you more. Not after this."

"It's no big deal."

"It is, Rose." I exhaled a wet sigh. "This fiend...he will come back for you. A...an...and you will let him one day. The addiction will overcome you." My body convulsed with sobs. "He's pumped you so full of venom...their venom...it's the most addictive stuff around. Like worse than any drug. There's no way to detox you."

Rose let out a cry and covered her face. I rushed across the two-foot expanse between us and wrapped her in my arms. Rose clutched me, ripped fingernails digging into my shirt.

"But I swear to you, Rosie. I will do whatever it takes to fix this. I will never give up."

We wept. Memories of our life together flooded me, like some sad movie about a girl with an incurable disease. I couldn't help but feel like we were both mourning Rose's impending death. I just couldn't let that happen.

"There's nothing I wouldn't do to protect you." I kissed Rose's hair. "I promise."

CHAPTER 8

"You did what?" Mama practically hissed the question like an angry cobra.

I tried to peek through Rose's bedroom window, but the glare on the glass prevented me from seeing anything inside. Instead, I drummed my fingers against the wooden railing of Rose's deck. "I couldn't...I couldn't help it. The cop screwed it all up."

"You had a line to toe, Huri Pherenike." Mama covered her face and turned away. "If the others find out..."

"They won't. I've...I've explained it to her."

Mama groaned and began pacing. "She's been turned into a drug addict. She's in no state of mind to keep that kind of secret, Huri. It's not just you and Elias who will go back. I will go. Your father...he's exiled along with Yiayia. We would never see them..."

"There has to be a way."

The pacing back and forth, the frequent looks of disappointment mingled with worry and sympathy. It pulverized my weakened heart. Mama held up a hand as she stopped. "Your grandmother can't know. Not yet."

I nodded. *Good. Mama always has a plan. Why did I screw this up?*

"She'll be in the even worse position of bringing us home."

"This is our home," I hissed.

Mama glared at me. "Yes. Well, so is Olympia. Don't forget that."

"It's impossible to forget. It looms over me."

Mama cradled my face in her hands. "The Twelve did this to protect us and the mortals around us. You know that. Our enemies use the ones we love against us."

I growled and sank into a crouch to hide. *Stop reminding me of that.* I stood again. "What do we do, Ma? This monster will come for her. She's in such shock...she refuses help." My chin trembled. "She says she doesn't want me in danger. That I have to take care of Eli."

"She's absolutely right." Mama gripped my shoulders and squeezed me to get me to stay still. "The stewards will tend to her."

"If something happens to her, Ma..." My eyes darkened.

"You can't get away with it. Vengeance Laws won't protect you this time." Mama gave my shoulders a shake. "You don't have the right to avenge her. No matter how much you want to. She's not your blood kin. Not your mate. I can't either. No matter how much I want to burn this bastard for touching or even looking at one of my daughters."

The wrath that filled my mother's typically serene face calmed me. I soaked it in like it was the sun appearing after a week of rainy days. Sometimes, I forgot how much Mama cared for and loved my friends. They were never merely my friends. They were always "the girls" or her daughters.

"There has to be a loophole," I whispered.

"Nothing. I have searched for years without success, Huri."

Great. "Then what do we do?"

I didn't know. I'd felt like I could barely tolerate the thought of lying to Rose one more day, but the thought of being ripped from the friends who had become my family as well as my father and grandmother...all of it seemed ridiculous and abhorrent.

Mama took a deep breath through her flaring nostrils, closing her eyes as if shutting off the dams of her fury. She whispered inaudible prayers and then, after a few calming moments, said, "We tell Pater and Yiayia. We keep Rose close. I will speak with Rose's parents. Not you."

Mama shot me a glare. "You try and convince our stubborn girl to stay with one of us. He can't get to her with us around. Although I'd love to see him try." A dark grin curved the corners of her mouth. "I will ask Mother if she's heard of anything that might help with the... the addiction side of things to help her beat it."

"Grandmother won't get suspicious?"

"Of course she will. She's too smart for our good. But she will not ask more than she wants to know and can deny knowledge of." Mama smirked a little, as if proud of her mother's prowess. "But you stay well clear of her for a few days. Keep your head. She will fight the world for you, Huri, but she can't deflect everything."

I nodded, trying not to think of how one rash reaction had the potential to screw up so much of my life. "OK."

"Not to mention you're a horrible liar." Mama smiled and rolled her eyes. "I should've taught you poker as a child."

"I hate lying."

Her gray eyes creased into a tender smile. "I know, asteri mou. It is one of my favorite things about you. But it will not help you as Athena."

I frowned and turned my eyes away. *Stop reminding me.*

"I will be with Rose and her parents. I will explain to them a version of the story. But I will impress upon them the need for her safety. Perhaps I can get Senator Brandt to hire a few immortal guards. Lord knows he should be able to do that much."

"I will talk to Rose."

"Now?" She laughed derisively. "She's sleeping and surrounded by family. It would be better for you to go to work and make sure the stewards are on this. You need to start thinking clearly again without your emotions controlling you."

I nodded again.

Mama drew me into a hug and squeezed like she could help put the pieces back together. "I love you."

Stop being such a baby, Huri.

"And I'm proud of you. Always. Even when you make a misstep, it's always for the right reasons. But the heavens know it's usually a big one."

CHAPTER 9

Explaining to Elias that his Aunt Rosie was hurt was difficult, and I was still in a haze when I entered the office.

I paused in the doorway. *Work.* I needed to work and forget the worry on Elias's precious face, the fierceness when he promised he would protect Rose, and the sleeping form of my sweet friend as I whispered my goodbyes. *Work.* It would clear my head. Help me refocus.

A crowd was congregated around the giant hearth right beside my desk. I needed solitude so I could bury myself in the new case. I stood in the entryway of the detectives' offices and waited, hoping they'd all leave.

Just as I got comfortable procrastinating, a sigh from behind me tickled my ears, and tendrils of pipe tobacco wafted under my nose.

"You're supposed to be sleeping, chickadee."

My emotions evaporated as I turned to Zephonia. "Hey, Zeph. Couldn't sleep."

"What's wrong? Why aren't you with Rose?"

"I just need to get to work."

"I don't know if you've noticed, but"—Zephonia cleared her

throat and moved between me and the office—"I'm stubborn as hell, chickadee."

How could I explain to Zephonia that I'd just put my entire career and family at risk? That I was terrified of losing my friend barely a year after losing my husband? "Rose is sleeping. I...I needed a distraction."

"Have you thought about asking her to stay with your family?" Zephonia's eyes were etched with deep lines that seemed to have formed from years of sympathetic expressions. "I've only heard of a handful of victims beating the addiction. The ones who did all avoided any contact with ticks."

I nearly asked if that was in her time as a steward or just the past decade. But I knew the answer. I'd never heard of anyone who'd beaten the addiction. "We're going to try. She can be...a little too independent. I figured I would talk to her. See if she would stay with my family."

"Their scent might throw him off," Zephonia said with a nod. "It's a good plan."

I managed a smile when Zephonia rubbed my back.

"Did you tell her?"

My chin trembled, and I nodded. "Local LEO gave it away," I said in German.

Zephonia barely paused at the fact I could speak her language. "That's good."

I shook my head. "I said too much." My throat constricted. *Breathe.* "Against...orders."

Zephonia inhaled sharply, but I couldn't meet her eyes. "Oh." She licked her lips. "They forbade you," she whispered, now speaking in German without hesitation.

I felt like an idiot for nodding again. "I got tired of lying to her," I whispered back.

"I'm sure it's fixable." Zephonia squeezed my shoulder. "I'll help."

That brought my gaze to her. My mouth dropped open to speak, but nothing could come out.

Zephonia snickered behind her pipe. "I'm not losing my partner just yet. Besides, my own pantheon is a pain in the patootie. There's always a loophole."

I squeezed Zephonia's hand as it rested against my shoulder. "Thank you."

"Let's get some work done. But you're going home at lunch."

"You got it." Exhaling to steady myself, I followed Zephonia.

"So, how many languages do you speak?"

"Nine." I shrugged. "Part of...you know."

As soon as Zephonia approached the crowd of stewards near our desks, they all dispersed like a school of fish. Beatriz stood to greet us with cups of coffee and a knowing smile for me.

"You should know," Zephonia began in a whisper. "Captain's got Rose's case assigned to Beatriz."

I passed a desk that looked like a tropical paradise and nearly tripped on a palm frond. Zephonia leaned in and whispered, "That's Billie's desk. Changes every few days, so watch out."

Zephonia kicked off her shoes at her own desk, revealing fire-engine-red toenail polish, and took the coffee from Beatriz. Today, Beatriz's hair was paper straight and falling nearly to her ankles. The steward looked like a golden-haired Cousin It.

"Ladies! I had a feeling you'd be coming." She passed me the coffee, pushing her sheet of hair out of her unnaturally beautiful face. She beamed and embraced me and Zephonia with kisses on our cheeks. "Captain told me." She rolled her eyes. "I swear these morrie cops don't have any sense of propriety. I can't believe they outed you in front of her."

The giant's squeeze on my heart loosened a little more at Beatriz's exuberance.

"I'm so sorry about your friend, Huri. I'm going to do everything I can to figure out who did this."

The tension in my neck unknotted a bit more at hearing the

familiar lilt of a Latin-esque accent. It reminded me of being safe with Luis in West Palm. "Thank you, Bia."

"Here." She pointed at a spot beside her, and another stone appeared. "Have a seat. Tell me everything you know. I'll be heading over to speak to Rose as soon as we're done."

"She...she's pretty off."

Beatriz took my hand like she had been taking it for years. "Hey. It's normal. You'll see. Most morries don't want to believe that we're in America. They live in this 'no-immos' bubble. But don't worry. I've had my share of unbelievers. She'll come around."

Zephonia squeezed my shoulder. "I need to talk to the captain about the lab results. I'll be back."

In the minutes that followed, I spilled more about what had happened to Rose than I had intended, but I had enough sense not to tell Beatriz about screwing up so badly.

She just sat there listening, even tearing up with me at times as the needles in her hands noted key parts. It was the first time I'd seen a steward actually taking notes the old-school way—knitting in the code.

My bracelet warmed. It was Mama sending a picture of Rose sleeping in her own bed with Sam I Am, the cat, curled up on the pillow beside her. I showed Beatriz and remembered to give her the address. A moment later, Mama sent a second picture of Phyllis coming up Rose's driveway. She was a blur of movement. For the moment, Rose was surrounded. But what about when she wasn't?

"I'm going to head over to her place after I check out the scene. I will definitely keep you updated, Huri. Here." She tapped her bracelet, which made Beatriz's head pop up on mine. "This is my contact information. You scry me at any time."

"Thanks, Bia."

She grinned and grabbed her messenger bag. "I'll let you know how things go."

I laughed a little when Beatriz kissed each of my cheeks and hurried off. There were so many things I missed about living in South Florida. Zephonia approached me from behind.

"How'd it go?"

"Good. I think. Where's she from?"

"Portugal." Zephonia walked with me back to our desks. "She's part mouro and anjana. You should see her fly. Too few of the fair folk left outside of Amaranthia."

"No kidding. Last fairy I saw was in Olympia. What keeps her here?"

"Don't know. Won't say. Keeps to herself most of the time." Zephonia wiggled her eyebrows. "Lab work's not in yet. We need to go follow a lead."

I practically leaped to my feet, conversation with Beatriz and Zephonia having liberated my heart a bit. "Let's do it."

CHAPTER 10

As I opened Gertie's door, Zephonia paused and furrowed her brow at me. "How squeamish are you?"

"Not very." Gertie roared to life, and I hastily sat down. "You going to tell me what's going on?"

"I told you. A lead."

Letting out a sigh, I leaned back into my seat.

The lead turned out to be on the far east side of town at a farmhouse-style bakery called the Sanguine Baker. There were lovely tan baskets lining warm wooden walls along with ancient-looking whisks and bowls. The smell was divine. The mix of dough and icing was enough to get me high (and possibly diabetic) even from the sidewalk. A chorus of bells announced our entrance. It surprised me so much I bumped into Zephonia, who snickered at me.

"Jumpy?"

I realized I was, but I didn't know why my skin was crawling. "What is this place?"

A young woman with raven hair and crimson lips hurried to the counter, stuffing her phone into her apron pocket. She took one look at Zephonia, ignoring me completely, and shouted, "Ma! The Stitcher's here to see you!" Then she was back on her phone as she blindly retreated behind the wall.

Moments later, a plush, short woman glided forward, followed by a tall and obese man. My brow knotted when I noticed the woman's elongated canines as she drank something red from a coffee cup. Even at this close distance, I couldn't sense the usual coppery blood in the air.

The vampire beamed at Zephonia, throwing her chubby arms into the air. "Zephonia, it is always a pleasure to see you. Come, give me a squeeze!"

Zephonia embraced the vampire as if they hadn't seen each other in ages. "Claudette, I swear Millie has sprouted like a weed since I saw her last."

"It's Paul's genes. Tell me how you made it through the teenage years, Zephonia. Lawd, have mercy. How I do hate hormones. Oh! Who is this delight?"

"This is my new partner, Huri." Zephonia raised a beckoning eyebrow. "Huri, this is Claudette and Paul Browne. That was their youngest, Mildred."

"Don't call me that," was shouted from the back.

I took Claudette's cool hand, trying to ignore that she looked a bit swollen and even red. If I had met Claudette on the street, I would've assumed that she was simply a mortal who'd bent over too long tying her shoes. Then I shook Paul's warm hand. Paul actually was a mortal. The silver-lined irises should've been enough of an indication. Dead giveaways of vampire-venom-addicted mortals.

"You be civil!" Claudette hollered with a shake of her head. The next moment, her face softened into a smile at me. The abrupt change nearly made me snort, knowing I had done the same with Elias countless times. "Teenagers. You'll have to excuse her. She was born in a barn!"

"You should know. You were there!"

Paul sighed and closed his eyes. "Mildred Frances, don't you sass your momma."

"No worries," I said. "We've recently gotten out of toddler town." *We*...why did I still say "we"?

Claudette cackled. "Oh, then you know already. I swear toddlers and teens are the same animals."

"Sugarplum," Paul said with a hand on her arm. "I'm pretty sure Zephonia didn't come all this way just to chat."

"I wish that weren't true, Paul, but I am here on both business and pleasure."

"Well then, we'll get Millie to set you up while you get down to business." Claudette opened the swinging gate and motioned for us to join her. "Millie, come take their order."

I paused in mid-step when I noticed blood bags in the walk-in refrigerator as we passed.

"I wanted to make sure I got something for the dhampir at the office," Zephonia said. "So two dozen of your sanguine red velvet cupcakes for them. Then I'll need three dozen ovum cupcakes."

Millie's lips curled to one side when my brow furrowed as I paused to peer into the refrigerator. "That's right, newb. We're a vampire bakery."

"Lawd, have mercy, Millie! Act civil!" Claudette escorted me to a case with cookies and truffles. "Here, sugar. Try these. They're made with ordinary chicken eggs. Well, 'round here, we get a giggle out of calling these ovum cookies or ovum cakes. The morries don't know, though. Goodness gracious, could you imagine?" She giggled and indicated the wall behind the counter. "In the back, we sub out the eggs for mortal blood, harvested in compliance with Amaranthian Society guidelines."

I nearly choked. "You make blood cakes?"

"Why, yes. We're the first—if you can believe it—to come up with the idea. It's spread like wildfire. Sproutin' up all over now. Take a bite."

"There's no blood in this one?"

"No, Huri," Zephonia said with a laugh. "She wouldn't let you sample the other. Costs too much."

"Ain't that the truth," Paul muttered with a snicker.

I dared to take a bite. The flavor of chocolate and toffee burst in my mouth with the perfect amount of crunch to detonate the flavor. "Skata, what is in that?"

Claudette beamed and jiggled merrily like she was Santa Claus. "Water from the Bizaine Springs."

That nearly made me choke. Bizaine Springs was in one of the hidden immortal territories.

"Best you've had, right?" Claudette's eyebrows wiggled as she took a sip from her coffee cup.

"I'll take a dozen," I told Millie. "You've converted me."

Claudette squealed and clapped. "Let's get the nasty over with now."

With that, Paul opened the door for us to enter, closing it with a kiss to Claudette's cheek. She glided around me and Zephonia and motioned for us to sit on the floral loveseat in front of the desk.

"Is this official, darling?"

"Not exactly. I needed to know if you've heard anything about this." Zephonia pulled out a Cherry and set it in Claudette's swollen palm. "Huri got it off a strigoi yesterday."

She sniffed and even licked it. Her body stiffened. "You know what this is?" She looked like she had swallowed a frog.

"I wouldn't be here if I did, Claudette. You're the first person I wanted to ask."

"Zephonia, sugar, I ain't never seen nothing like this. Have they really..." Her eyes were round as she stared at Paul.

"What is it, babe?" He came closer, but Claudette hid the pill in her palm and passed it back to Zephonia.

This is definitely not good.

"Put it away." She winced. "They've turned venom into a drug, Paul."

My gut twisted as Zephonia swore under her breath in German. The first person I feared for was Klara. She hated immortals because she had encountered the worst of immortal society. Her proximity to the music industry's stars didn't help. The latest craze was to become a donor. Then there was Klara's brother, who was rumored to have been lost to a vampire. He just vanished one day and couldn't be found. Both situations had turned Klara against them... us.

Whenever she wasn't doing her makeup gig, Klara was usually at some sort of rally to restrict immortals. I had always been terrified that some vampire was waiting to take advantage.

Paul's face blanched. "Bastards."

"So you haven't heard anything?" Zephonia asked.

"No, the venom breaks down too fast."

Then how were they making it?

"I'll tell you one thing. There's more than one bite in that thing," Claudette said, wagging her finger at Zephonia. "Maybe more than one strigoi."

Zephonia shifted in her seat. "I thought it seemed too small for more than one."

Claudette's eyes stayed on the pill. "Definitely more than one. I could tell even before I tasted it." Her hand trembled as she covered her mouth, glancing at Paul. "With this much, they might even hook a lesser immortal."

Zephonia and I glanced at each other.

"Sorry. Newbie here, but I didn't think immortals could get hooked."

"In theory, anyone can. Even mates can be seduced with enough competing venom. There're stories of the Elders hooking immortals they captured in wars."

I realized then why Claudette was shaking: she was worried about Paul. As if to prove my assumptions, Paul caressed Claudette's face and kissed her with an aching tenderness.

"I'm yours, sugarplum. It'd take an army, and even then, I'd still be yours."

Claudette returned his kiss, but I could see it was to hide her fears. After a moment, she turned her attention to us. "Ladies, I wish

I knew more about this. But I'll be keeping my ear to the ground. You can be sure of that."

"Thanks, Claudette. But keep a low profile, please. We need you. These strigoi are dangerous. Very."

"I will. No worries."

The drive back was pregnant with our silent thoughts. The only sounds were me eating one of Claudette's decadent cupcakes and Zephonia chewing on her pipe.

"I didn't know they could have mates," I said at last.

Staring at the traffic ahead of her, Zephonia hummed. After a moment, she blinked a few times as if waking. "Sorry. I just...yeah. So, it's not common knowledge. I knew them before some idiot turned her. Claudette and Paul were married. She returned to Paul afterward and told him what happened. She nearly starved herself. Paul didn't care. He loved her. She told me he put his own wrist in her mouth, saying he wouldn't lose her again. Thank goodness he had the blood volume to feed her." Zephonia laughed, but a frown damped the mirth. "When vampires find mates, they swell and turn red. She was so embarrassed about gaining weight and being red-faced all the time."

I watched as Zephonia's amusement died. "She looked pretty worried about the Cherries."

"Yeah." Zephonia stuck her pipe back in her mouth and puffed slow and steady. "Mates are lifetime donors. Venom is venom. And addiction, unfortunately, is addiction. His love for her is great, but if something were to happen to her or if he couldn't let her feed and his addiction got to be too much...I just had no idea that a mate could be...seduced. I never would've mentioned it with him there."

"And to think it could hook an immortal. Even a less powerful one." I shivered. Other immortals—who wanted fewer mortals killing peaceful immortals indiscriminately—held vampires in check. Of course, vampires were notorious for not caring about that kind of thing.

That statement made Zephonia growl. "Exactly." The wrinkle

between her eyes deepened. "I don't know that there's any real advantage to feeding on immortals. From what I understand, an immortal's talents don't transfer with the blood. Not to mention, it's said our blood tastes bad. Like how most folks don't like gamey meat. There are already other immortals who have vampire lovers. We don't see anything like that happening."

Exhaling, I finished the cupcake with relish. "Maybe the lab will come up with a way to test it."

"Maybe," Zephonia said. She didn't speak again until we were on the interstate. "This gives me a lot to think about."

"Shouldn't we go arrest that guy?"

"We don't have anything concrete yet. A lick test from another vampire, even an upstanding and respected one, won't be enough. This one is going to take some finessing. I hate to say it, but we need the lab to pull through for us."

Trying to forget the fear on Claudette's face, I focused on the trees racing by out the window and hoped the lab did too.

CHAPTER 11

The next morning, I drove rather than flew to work despite my pent-up energy. I rolled down the window of my 1973 Ford Galaxie that Elias had named Blue (well, "Bu"—Ls had been a challenge), and Luis had then dubbed Big Blue. I couldn't get within twenty feet of any car with a computer. It would just shut down. The hot wind in my face might not've been refreshing, but it was definitely keeping me awake.

My mind couldn't focus on anything but my conversation with Rose, seeing her wild eyes as she twitched and jumped like a squirrel that'd had too many espressos. Thankfully, Rose had agreed to stay with my parents temporarily, and they'd even found Rose a support group for vampire victims through Yiayia's nonprofit. Beatriz was no doubt the reason Rose agreed to the move.

Rose told me how Beatriz helped her remember things about her attacker, like how he smelled like sandalwood and pine trees. Beatriz had stayed and answered Rose's numerous questions as if she had all day to do so.

The worst part hadn't been Rose. It had been talking to Pater and Yiayia. I shook my head to try and erase the memory like my brain was an Etch A Sketch. I had no clue how I was going to make up for this whole mess of endangering my family by telling Rose about us.

I exhaled, certain my rash decision to tell Rose the truth would bring down the Twelve. But so far, things were quiet. My family wasn't ripped apart. Yet.

I pulled into the parking garage and forced myself to stop worrying. The case. The Cherries. Zephonia had messaged that the captain had brought in help from an outside lab they'd dealt with before. I wondered how long it would take to get results.

I took a last bite of my *pan de jamón* (my ambrosia) and exited Big Blue to head toward the office. After Luis's death, it had changed from *eliopsomo* to its Venezuelan cousin. I often wondered if it would change back once—or if—I ever recovered from my grief. But how could I? All the small reminders of him seemed to have cauterized the wound permanently open.

I speed-walked over to the fireplace and slipped into my desk. The sensation of being so high up in the trees eased me a bit more. I savored the final sip of coffee as Zephonia tossed down her bag in her cubicle.

"Hey, how'd it go?" Zephonia said.

"Better than I expected. Bia worked magic. I did not expect Rose to be so...compliant. Seriously, she can be incredibly headstrong."

Zephonia snickered and raised an eyebrow at me. *Fair.*

"Yeah, well, there's a reason we're friends."

"And Elias? How's he handling it?"

I tilted my hand from side to side. "School starts soon, so he's enamored with that. It's keeping his mind off things."

Zephonia grinned behind her pipe. "I love the beginning of the school year. All the newness. He's going to do great."

"Yeah." I chewed my bottom lip. "I'm just worried. It's a mortal school."

Zephonia nodded. "I was worried too, but mine did it. They're better for it."

I was just worried he'd shift. He'd been true to his word and was learning to control it, but it still worried me. "He wants to be like his daddy."

"He was a good man, from what I've heard."

"The best."

"Ladies!" Captain Janis shouted from her office.

Zephonia sighed. "That's us."

I jogged to catch up with Zephonia, hopping over a stray palm frond. "How do you know?"

"Only ones needing test results," she mumbled.

Janis motioned at us from her desk.

Zephonia gave me an I-told-you-so look. "Results."

Janis grinned when she spotted something behind us and stood to wave. "I've called in some favors for this. So play nice, Zephonia," Janis said through her smiling teeth.

Zephonia growled and shoved her pipe in her mouth. "Peachy."

My eyes darted from one woman to the other. I stood when Janis welcomed a lanky woman who looked like a poster child for Top 10 Reasons to Do Yoga. She also smelled like copper oozed from her caramel pores. And something else. Something more tropical. I had only smelled it once before.

"Enrica, thank you for coming at such short notice." Janis kissed each cheek.

My heart pounded against my rib cage. *No. Not one of them.*

"It is nothing at all, Filomena. I was just about to head to a donor meeting nearby." Her golden brown-colored eyes swept the room, settling first on me with a weird smile and then on Zephonia.

"So this is the...ace team—is that how you call it?—that found this new drug?"

Zephonia tensed beside me.

"Yes, these are Stewards Weber and Rojas."

Enrica squeaked. "Truly? Are you not Alcis's granddaughter? You must be Huri. You look so much the same."

I could hardly breathe, let alone speak. An azeman. South American vampire. I blinked away the memories of the last azeman I dealt with. Tried not to consider how similar they looked. Just a fluke. "Yes. You must know my grandmother."

"I do. Such a sweet woman. She is all I have heard in stories and more. I am to meet her today, in fact."

I managed a smile and forced myself to breathe. She wasn't the azeman who took my husband. That man was ash now for his crimes.

"Stewards, this is Enrica Fontana. She founded Lamiens Alliance. Her foundation is looking for a cure for venom addiction."

"Really," Zephonia said, crossing her arms and taking a puff from her pipe. "How noble."

I wanted to scoff. Why would a vampire want to cure venom addiction? It was counterintuitive.

"It's just the right thing to do." Enrica smiled and kept her eyes fixed on me like she could read my thoughts. "We are not all bad, you know. Not monsters who hunt the innocent. So, ladies...I mean, Stewards. We have the results. I had to bring them down in person."

Enrica looked back. A young man, mortal from the lack of scent, entered with a briefcase. He opened it and presented a file folder to the captain. He didn't meet my gaze, but I spotted the silver outline around his pupils and irises, denoting his complete addiction to venom. He was a donor, probably Enrica's, from the tender smile she granted him.

"Gracias, mi cielo." Enrica exhaled and indicated the folder with the results. Whatever Janis read made her go pale. "I am so happy that Lamiens Alliance's laboratories could be used for such a good purpose. I just wish we had better news."

Yeah? Well, why do you look so perky?

Janis tossed down the file on her desk and wiped her face. Without hesitation, Zephonia took it, and after a moment, her face paled. *Good Lord. What is this? An apocalypse. Surely it isn't that bad.*

"Can you explain the results?"

"Of course. The drug"—Enrica began as Zephonia passed me the file—"is 'orrific." Her assistant passed her a smoothie cup of green goop, and she swallowed a gulp. "It's the equivalent of ten lamia bites at once. In just one pill."

My eyes widened. Now the fear on Claudette's face made sense. "Skata."

Janis wiped her face again and began pacing.

Enrica nodded. "The mortal would get it all. Healing from the wounds. A libido increase of nymphatic proportions. The addiction of a veteran donor. And it's laced with a tiny amount of Rohypnol. Just enough to take the edge off. I've never seen anything this... sophisticated." She shook her head with a flush to her cheeks and a smile I suspected she gave to a potential lover. "It's..." Her fingers toyed with her hair like she was preening. "They don't stand a chance."

My eyes narrowed. Was it just me, or did Enrica sound a little too turned on by the drug?

Zephonia stood, cursing in German, and wiped her face. "Does it still allow for tracking?"

"No. But the addiction could drive them to either get more of the drug or find a vampire."

My stomach soured as I thought about all the mortals who would be doped and drained because of this drug.

"Can you tell where it was made? I mean, I didn't think they could synthesize lamia venom," Janis said.

"I can give you a list of the equipment necessary for manufacturing this kind of drug. This is incredibly difficult to do. I've never seen it done."

Zephonia stopped and stared at Enrica. "You're implying this has to be manufactured. Like at a pharmaceutical company."

"In a laboratory close to that, yes. With a highly skilled team of chemists. It's truly a pharmaceutical marvel. Beautiful."

Seriously? *Nope. Officially don't like this...woman.*

"If it weren't so sinister," she added with a tilt of her head at me. Like she knew what I was thinking about her.

Janis glanced at Zephonia and then turned her gaze to Enrica. "Could this be something that was leaked by one of those facilities?"

"Highly unlikely," Enrica scoffed. "Something like this is worth a fortune."

I cleared my throat, which brought Zephonia's and Janis's eyes to me, praying I wasn't overstepping again. "Ten bites' worth of lamia venom. Could it be strong enough to hook an immortal?"

Janis's eyes rounded. "That's not possible."

Zephonia's gaze rested fully on Enrica. The azeman had gone terribly still. She wiped her mouth. I felt Zephonia tighten beside me when Enrica moistened her lips. Mouth blocking. A body language sign of someone who was about to lie. "The taste of immortal blood is abhorrent to all subspecies of lamia."

The sidestep. Wonderful rhetorical dance move. The second glance Janis and Zephonia exchanged confirmed that they noticed the mouth block and the sidestep too. Janis merely thanked Enrica for her time.

"Of course. Please don't hesitate to contact me with further questions."

"Thank you again, Enrica, for the rush on this."

"Absolutely. Something this...horrendous needs to get off the streets. Who did you get it from?"

A tight smile stretched Zephonia's face. "Well, bless your heart, honey. You know we can't discuss an ongoing investigation. But we'll kindly take that list of laboratories and equipment you mentioned."

"I hope this is the start of even more cooperation between our two organizations," Janis said as she extended a hand to her door. "I'll walk you out."

"I hope so too. And I will send your greetings to your *abuela*, Steward."

A viper. That's what this woman is. I nodded as diplomatically as I could. "Please do. *Mucho gusto.*"

"Steward Weber," Enrica said with a smile and then was off with her silent assistant/donor.

I stood silent beside my partner as the trio departed. "We don't trust her, do we."

"Not on your downy feathers, chickadee." Zephonia motioned for me to sit as she checked her bracelet.

"This...this can't be right," I whispered, taking the liberty to read more closely through the results as we waited.

"She only brings in experts when it's bad like this." Zephonia clamped her teeth on her pipe stem and puffed even though nothing was lit.

"Look. The list of laboratories," I said.

Zephonia peered over my shoulder for a moment. "That's a hell of a lot of leads."

I snickered and pointed at the Ls. "Lamiens Alliance isn't on it. Don't they make vitamins and supplements for dhampir?"

"Yeah, they do. Maybe they don't have the equipment for this kind of thing."

Or they might be hiding something. I frowned. But Janis wouldn't contract out if she thought they were untrustworthy.

Janis reentered, closing the door. She and Zephonia stared at one another in silent communication built on decades of working together. "Bring him in. Whole as possible."

Zephonia grinned. "You got it."

"The stewards on him say he's still dealing at the college."

The anticipation of a fight tickled my lips into a smile. You'd think because immortals live so long that we'd learn control over the years, but we had the hardest time curbing battle lust. Well, lust in all its varieties. Thankfully, Mama and Grandmother had taught me to think of the long game from childhood, so I was a little more tempered than most of my contemporaries. But not by much.

"You need backup," Janis said.

Zephonia looked at me. "Nah. I think we can handle this one."

I nodded my agreement and hoped I didn't appear overeager.

"We'll send you a WIP when we've brought him into custody." Zephonia gave Janis a two-finger salute as she departed for Gertie.

CHAPTER 12

T chewed my bottom lip and swallowed hard once we were inside Gertie and roaring toward Middle Tennessee. "Enrica was lying about immortals."

Zephonia smiled around her pipe. "Nice catch."

"You think Claudette's right?"

Zephonia tapped her fingers along the steering wheel and took a drag of her pipe. "I can't help but think she is. Especially after Enrica. She didn't want us to know that tidbit."

"I could tell."

"Which begs a whole boatload of questions. But we gotta stay focused on facts, not speculation. We need our perp to lead us to his dealer."

I nodded, slipping on my brass knuckles once we were parked a bit away from the student union.

"Now. He's yours, chickadee. You ready for this?"

I nodded. *Bring it.*

"I'll be there, but...Your perp. Your arrest."

I stared at my partner for a long minute. "Don't the seniors take the lead in the beginning?"

She snickered and fitted her own brass knuckles on. "Yes, but you seem like you need to prove yourself. No kid gloves for you, chickadee."

"Stop calling me that."

Zephonia laughed. "I like it."

"Alright. Zephie."

The older woman's eyes narrowed as she puffed her pipe. "Fine," she said when I didn't squirm. "Tit for tat and all that. Get going."

I opened the door and shifted into a barn owl, shooting into the air. I wish I'd inherited teleportation from Grandmother, but flying has its perks.

"That's not what I had in mind," Zephonia called after me.

I made a screech just to mess with her. In truth, I had shifted because I figured the vampire was suspicious of me. I wouldn't be surprised if he watched me get into Gertie a few days ago. Now, at least, he wouldn't spot me right away.

I flew around the building once, sensing that he was still inside. There was another scent coming from the exit I'd taken last time. A lookout. So he wasn't completely dumb. I decided to enter through a different door. As soon as I landed and shifted back to normal, my bracelet warmed and buzzed.

I exhaled and put on the ear cuff I had forgotten to wear. Again. It was standard-issue, so it kept slipping. Naturally, I had forgotten to wear my personal one this morning in the madness of leaving the house.

I tapped my ear. "Yes, Zephie?"

"You're supposed to be wearing that at all times, chickadee.

"Forgot. Oh, and there's another tick at the exit closest to you."

"I see him."

"How do you want to play this?" I spotted my prey, still doing his flirty job. I leaned against a pillar just beyond his senses.

"Try to lure him out my door. Same as the lookout."

That would put me exiting with the perp where his lookout was.

I definitely did not want to take on two vampires with witnesses. "I don't need to prove myself that much, Zeph."

"Oh no? I thought you liked being the lone hero."

I rolled my eyes at that sassy comment. My mind raced with how to get him to follow me outside. "Why don't you just sing him into submission?"

A slow exhale sounded in my ear. "Because you and anyone else will also be obeying my voice. Use your head, chickadee. Now. Get to it. I don't have all day."

At the moment, I could only think of arresting the tick. But he'd fight for sure then. I adjusted the handcuffs. Mortals always expected to see them, and there was a certain amount of fun using them during training. I also adjusted the badge on the lanyard under my shirt.

Giving Luis's necklace one last squeeze, I prayed I'd come out unscathed. With a steadying breath, I put my right fist behind my back, locking my straight needles to my brass knuckles with a click. No mutton-chop mutant had anything on the stewards' claws.

I stalked forward through the lunch stragglers. He didn't spot me until I cut in front of his latest customer.

"Hey! I was next."

"Sorry, sweetie. I just bought the last of his cherries." I managed a simpering smile at him, but inside, I was ready to run. This was so stupid. *I need a better plan.*

"You're back." His smile faltered.

An idea struck me. Pretending to flick my hair from my eyes, I let my chest heave like some vapid movie star. "I...I need a..." The fingers of my left hand trailed my neck. His eyes followed their path before going back to my bottom lip, caught between my teeth. "Don't you get a break?"

Lips curling back to reveal the tips of bulging fangs, he locked eyes with me for a moment.

I tried to move closer, but I was already pressed to the counter. *Come on, douche. Take the bait.*

"For a delicious morsel like you? Always."

My heart began to drum regularly again as he moved toward the counter's entrance. As he was rounding the counter, devouring me with his eyes, the girl I cut in front of scoffed. "Ow. That's my foot. Watch it with those giant combat boots."

I wanted to cuss out loud when David froze. *Curse my luck.* I didn't think about my shoes.

Own it. I gave him a tight smile, unsheathed my claws, and placed my hand on the counter.

As he took a step back, his fangs lengthened in his mouth. "You're a bloody Stitcher."

My mind reached for my silk yarn, causing another bit of silk to register nearby. I allowed my senses to reach for the source. It was coming from the vampire. *Lord, have mercy.* He would have to be the kind to wear sleazy silk briefs. Not even boxers. Gross!

"What is that I sense?" I sniffed the air and snapped. "Silk. Silk undies." I twisted my finger, which tightened his silk undies around his manly bits. The vampire gasped and tried to stand on his toes. I've never been able to spin it myself. But manipulate it? I clenched my fist, which made him squeak. Bending silk to my will was easy. "Be a good boy and come along."

I tried hard not to think about dragging him out from behind the counter by the contents of his silk underwear.

Baring his fangs, he lunged at me and growled, "I like it rough."

My mind's grip on his briefs stopped him, making him practically bend in half. At a flick of my hand, his briefs forced him to spin to face the counter. Slapping the handcuffs on him a little too tightly didn't keep the ick factor down one little bit. *I'll need a shower after this.*

My skin crawled when I realized everyone was filming the whole thing with their phones. Great. For pretense's sake, I pulled out my badge and Mirandized him as I walked him toward the exit. He tried to pull free, so I pressed the tips of my yew straight needles into his spine.

"Wood? You bi—"

I jabbed them in a little deeper, and the scent of scorched flesh tickled my nose. "Keep talking. Please, keep talking."

Zephonia's voice registered in my ear again. "Oh, there's a good boy. Would you mind helping this old sack of bones with the door, sweetie?"

"Sure thing, ma'am," a voice said from the other side.

The door swung open to reveal a haggard Zephonia just beyond the awning's shadow, complete with a walker and a humpback. Her normally impeccable bun was in complete disarray, showcasing her mass of silver locks. I barely kept in a laugh at the sight of an unkempt Zephonia.

The lookout's eyes widened at seeing his boss with me.

"Well, bless your heart, son."

While he tensed to lunge at me, Zephonia spun down and kicked out his legs. She pounced on him with a flash of her needles to his throat. My grip on my perp tightened as my appreciation for Zephonia's speed and accuracy rose: after all, the throat was a small target. Zephonia flipped the lookout onto his stomach and cuffed him as he hissed at her and thrashed.

"Come on. Be nice." Zephonia hauled him to his feet, tossing the walker into the bushes. "If you're good boys, I won't sing nightmares into you."

They both sputtered and cursed until we shoved them into Gertie's surprisingly accommodating backseat.

As soon as they were in, the lookout fell asleep from the sedative in Zephonia's needles. My quarry still cursed and spat at us like a cobra. Leaning over my seat, I landed a right hook that knocked him into the tiny window, shutting him up for a moment.

"Here." Zephonia passed me a pair of wax earplugs.

I didn't hesitate to put them in. In silence, I watched Zephonia's mouth open and close, making the hair along my neck stand on end. The perp in the backseat immediately shut his eyes and slumped into sleep. Zephonia nodded and tapped my shoulder.

"How long'll that last?"

"Long enough. Thankfully, we're fairly close to the office." She nodded at me. "Finish your WIP. She's bound to send in backup if you don't finish your notes soon. You can write a full report later."

I began typing in the coded notes to the captain.

"I thought I said to lure him. Not arrest him."

"Some girl took issue with my shoe selection."

Zephonia relit her pipe and snickered. "Your shoes? You got made from your...well, they are sorta kickass." Then she smiled with the stem between her teeth. "Just don't get Gertie dirty. You'll be fine."

"I thought you said not to eat. I can't guarantee no dirt."

"Watch it, chickie. That wax might just melt one day."

She might seem relaxed now, but maybe I had said too much earlier. So many foolish choices. Would Zeph think I couldn't handle my stuff? I should've never told her about not following the Twelve's orders. She hadn't outed me to the captain, but she could still use it to her advantage later.

I exhaled.

It wasn't even lunchtime, and I already wanted to run and snuggle with Eli. But the idea of having to play Grandmother's politics steeled my resolve, as did the paycheck that kept me and Elias independent. I leaned my elbow on the door and stared out at the buildings passing us by.

The drive back to the office couldn't happen fast enough. I simply wanted to cuddle with my little guy and a good book, but he would be napping by the time my break came around.

"We're going to let them marinate over the weekend."

I continued to stare out the window as the silk bracelet on my arm wove in and out of my fingers. "We can do that?"

"Yeah." She glanced back at the sleeping perps. "Just be at the office first thing Monday."

I nodded.

"Listen," Zephonia said when we got near the office. "I'm having a bit of a cookout this weekend. You and Elias should come. He could meet my grands. And Rose too. She might not feel so cooped up."

Straightening, I studied Zephonia, who was watching the road purposefully as she wove between cars. "Yeah. We're free. I'll see if Rose's up for it."

Zephonia nodded with a barely-there smile.

CHAPTER 13

I beamed as Elias practically danced around Rose on the walkway up to Zephonia's log cabin, a title that didn't do justice to the sprawling home before me. It looked like a big-city 70s architect fell in love with log cabins and created a mash-up of wood, glass, and stone.

The heat from the summer sun radiated from the stones in the pre-dusk hour, giving the air an oily appearance across the flowered meadow around Zephonia's home. She opened the door, drawing my eyes. Elias immediately stopped dancing, though the grin on his face could not be tempered.

"So glad y'all made it. Elias. Rose." Zephonia fist-bumped Elias and gave Rose a quick hug in greeting. "Any trouble finding it?"

"None." I embraced her. "Although I'm surprised you don't have design magazine photographers camped out. This is gorgeous, Zeph."

She beamed and looked back at her home. "My late husband did it all. It's been our sanctuary."

My eyes widened as I entered the home. The entire back half was made of windows, while the front of the house and the roof curved back like the whole thing was a giant wooden megaphone. I grinned when Rose spotted guitars around a grand piano in the center of the open living room. She couldn't keep from rushing forward like a child in a toy store.

"The kids are out back playing," Zephonia said, which gained Elias's eyes.

He immediately looked at me. I nodded and waved. "Go have fun."

Elias sprinted from the room with a funny hop.

"Everyone's out back." Zephonia paused beside Rose, a gentle hand on her back. "Please, say you'll join us. We're going to enjoy some songs together."

"Oh, I couldn't—"

"We'd love it." Zephonia linked arms with Rose and escorted her to the backyard. "Seriously. We don't often get to indulge ourselves with others."

Rose blushed as she looked back at me like she needed my permission. I half-smiled, trying to hide the wound her need for permission caused me. Before the attack, Rose wouldn't have hesitated. "You should. It's not every day you get to sing and play with sirens."

"I'll try," Rose answered.

I barely heard Rose's response. I was enchanted by the sight of at least ten ancient oaks stretching before us. The sudden urge to fly into the boughs and dance among the branches overtook me. Elias was already swinging and spinning his webs for Zephonia's grandchildren. I beamed at the scene, wishing I had been able to play with my peers like that as a child.

"Look at him," Rose breathed, mouth hanging open. "Is that a giant bat?"

"Yes, that's Jade. She's a pemba shifter." Zephonia nodded and pointed out the man and woman standing below the children who were climbing all over the oaks. "That's my daughter Laura and her husband Ron. The two biggest ones are theirs." She pointed at the twins hanging upside down from rope swings. "Those two are Hans's kids." She craned her neck to peek around some bushes. "There's Hans. With his friend Jerome. Jade's father." She pointed to the grill and waved.

Rose's back straightened at the name, making me snicker.

"Jerome?" I repeated since Rose seemed incapable of speech.

"Yeah. Come on. I'll introduce you." Zephonia drew Rose close like a mother hen. "He loves music too. His father used to tune pianos. Now Jerome's taken over. Dying art."

Rose stiffened beside me as she locked eyes with the dark-skinned man, who was just as entranced with Rose. Hans, whose thin-lipped frown matched Zephonia's, just glared at me like I stole his favorite car.

"Rosaline?"

"Jerome?"

My eyebrows rose. So, this was The Jerome. Studying him longer, I now saw the resemblance to the single picture Rose had shown me of a scrawny but attractive teenager. However, the once-young Jerome was the very opposite of scrawny now. And based on the fruity ripeness that permeated his pores, he was definitely not mortal either.

His shoulders dropped, as did his mouth, eyes swimming over every inch of Rose's frame until he settled on her eyes. Based on the lump he swallowed, he had to know the true nature of Rose's mugging. He still beamed as he dared to draw Rose into a gentle hug.

"It's so good to see you. I left a message with your mother, but she said you weren't available."

Rose's jitters stopped completely for the moment she squeezed him back, even daring to close her eyes. "It is so good to see you, Jerome. I hated that I missed you and Jade. I hope Mother's assistant wasn't too horrible."

Zephonia pointed at them as discreetly as she could, eyebrows raised at me. I could only shrug and shake my head.

"It's all good. Now. Girl, let me look at you!" He laughed a deep, rumbling laugh and held her out, eyes beaming as the heady scent of flowering fruits overwhelmed my senses. "You grew up." A moment later, his cheeks flushed.

Rose laughed. "Me? What about you? You look like you could be on the cover of *GQ* or something. When did this happen?" Then she grinned, her left cheek dimpling.

A thunder of laughter flew out of him just as some dark shape zipped past Hans and Zephonia. The shadow landed right in Jerome's arms, making Rose squeal and jump back.

As soon as I saw the enormous bat from the trees, the bat disappeared, and a little girl was there instead. A shifter. I had never heard of bat shifters outside of some vampires like the azeman.

I put a hand on Rose's back to keep her from bolting and whispered, "It's okay. The little girl's a shifter of some kind."

"Daddy, tell them I don't sleep in a coffin."

Jerome cut his eyes briefly at Rose, who was retreating into my chest with her eyes glued on the little girl. He winced and kissed Jade's forehead. "J, I want you to meet Miss Rosaline."

She wiggled to the floor and stared up at Rose, her poof of coiled hair bouncing around her even though her body was still. "The lady who has the big backyard with the apple trees?"

I squeezed Rose's hand while Rose fought to breathe. Her mouth opened, but the sound stuck there without coming out. I squeezed her hand again to remind her to speak. "I guess that would be me."

Jade grinned. "Daddy and the blonde lady let me look—"

"While I was working on the piano."

"It's really pretty." She sniffed in Rose's direction. "You don't smell like a pemba."

Jerome choked on his words, cheeks flushing, and hurriedly pushed her toward the other kids. "She's mortal, baby girl. Now, go play, and no tattling."

I could tell by the way Jade and the Weber grandchildren played freely that they must be regular playmates, but they were so welcoming of Elias that I could only laugh as they roamed the trees and the ground. Even Jade was now jumping off of Elias's webs and shifting into a bat before soaring into the air.

Rose was shaking again as Jerome turned back to her. I nudged Rose, raising an eyebrow. Rose, however, was hardly able to talk. With as charming a smile as I could manage, I stepped forward and extended my hand to Jerome. "I know we haven't met, but I spoke to you just the other day. I'm Huri. It's so nice to finally meet you. Rose always told me so many nice things about you and your father."

Jerome laughed, cutting his eyes at Rose. "Huri! I've been wanting to meet you for years. Well. This is more Zephonia's realm, but this is Hans, a friend of mine since forever." Jerome extended a hand toward the glaring man behind him.

"He's my son," Zephonia said with a prodding elbow to Hans's arm.

"Huri." He nodded and put his hands in his pockets. "I'm glad I finally get to meet my mother's new...partner."

I was well aware that Zephonia was giving Hans the stare of death.

Jerome couldn't take his eyes off Rose. He smiled at her when she caught him staring. "You...you want something to drink?"

Rose's smile filled her entire being. "Yeah. Parched."

I watched him escort Rose back toward the cooler by the house. Zephonia mumbled something about checking on the sweet potatoes. *Oh no, I'm alone with Hans. Great.*

We ignored each other for a few seconds as he began placing the corn on the grill.

"Great day for this."

He grunted.

My eyebrows rose, wondering what his problem was, and took a step toward a vacant chair.

"You better not get her killed."

I looked back. "Excuse me?"

"Mom would've been promoted into a safer position by now." I could hear the implication: *If it weren't for you.* "Should've been over the entire NFO. So I expect you to keep your troublemaking nonsense to a minimum until she's done training you."

Did he really just say that? My jaw cocked to the side. "Wow. You really need to get your facts straight before you try to sit at the adults' table." I winked. "She turned down five promotion offers in the last ten years, Hans, ol' boy. Before me."

His lips thinned, and I reveled in the shade of white he turned.

"Hmm. You didn't know that. Now, before you put your nose into another area where it doesn't belong...she's the best steward I've ever heard of. And she's allowed to stay in the field whether or not you approve."

Hans closed the lid a little too hard as he glared at me. "If you're on some mission to get yourself killed saving the world, that's between you and your son. She's my mother. If anything happens to her because of your incompetence—I don't care if you are one of the gods—I will hold you accountable."

He did *not* just bring up Elias. I stepped forward. I would apologize to Zephonia after tossing the idiot across the yard. He didn't flinch when I squared up to him, and the silk yarn on my wrist slithered out like a snake ready to strike.

"Hans," Zephonia barked from the back door. Even through the protective wax we all put on in the car, I could sense the air of command. "Aren't you supposed to be with Ron? Watching the children?"

"Mommy to the rescue," I whispered.

The glare he shot me was dark and fearless. And kinda hot. No. Definitely not hot. Just annoying. "You're lucky you have those in your ears," he growled into my ear as he passed, making the tiny hairs on my neck stand at attention.

Zephonia gave me a questioning look when Hans traversed the steps to join the kids. "What was that?"

I took a long sip of tea to compose my thoughts. *He might not be on the Smite List, but he's on the Beat Down List for sure.* "Just chatting."

CHAPTER 14

Monday morning came far too quickly. Elias was with Pater today, no doubt working on some insane project to integrate mortal and immortal technologies. Elias just loved tinkering and playing with whatever tablet or mirror they gave him.

I paused at the entrance to the StS building to glance back at the Parthenon replica, questioning my decision to send Elias to a mortal school. Grandmother had promised Elias the finest tutors. But that would drag him into Olympian politics too young. For me, everything had been political since I was born. It was part of the reason Mama raised me away from Olympia.

My eyes grazed the replica's pillars, a copy of the replica in Athens, which was itself a copy of the Athenas' home in Olympia. Grandmother swore she had nothing to do with the office's location, but even now, I rolled my eyes at the memory of Grandmother's all-too-innocent smile.

America had been founded by mortals escaping the oppression of their immortal overlords and had a strict policy of "mortals first." So much so that immortals—and demis like Elias—were persecuted.

Unless, of course, the immortal had enough money and clout and centuries of fame at their backs. Like my grandmother, who, despite having banished and cursed more mortals than any other immortal, was well-loved by Americans as a whole. Hence the building dedication.

"You just going to stare at it all day?" Violet's chain-smoker voice called.

I shook my head to free myself of my thoughts and presented my badge to the purple-haired steward. She glared and thumbed me through, but I could feel her eyes on me as I passed. She always creeped me out. Like she was always watching me.

I found a note on my desk that said, "Meet me at the lab. Z."

I tossed down my bag and headed toward the stairs to the basement. The lab was white from ceiling to floor with clear walls and doors except for the corners and joins, which were stainless steel. The women inside, however, wore a rainbow of lab coats. All except for Zephonia, who was smiling and talking with a woman in a dark-blue coat.

Zephonia grinned at me. "You made it." Her eyes turned to the other woman. "Now that Huri's here...tell me you have good news, Bridget."

She snorted. "Depends on your version of good." Her eyebrows rose at me, and then she glanced at Zephonia. "Well, as I live and breathe. I thought you swore off partners, Zephonia."

"Bridget, Huri. Huri, Bridget."

After we exchanged pleasantries, Bridget extended a hand to a pair of glass doors and set off. "Sorry it took so long. I was double-checking the results from Lamiens Alliance. So. What do you want first?" Scanning her bracelet at a clear cube, she escorted us through the doors.

"Who are they?"

Once we sat in her office, Bridget passed Zephonia the file. "The dealer is David Spangler, of course. You'll be interested to learn he was turned by Boris Yannerman. Never been topside."

My eyebrows met. "Topside?"

"Amaranthia." Zephonia barely looked away from the file. "Means we'll have to pay Boris a visit. His protégé's remarkably well-fed."

"Indeed. I've rarely seen the like, to be honest. At least here. More common in one of the city-states, naturally. He's nearly indistinguishable from a mortal."

"Is that all you know about him?"

"For now. I'm processing his clothes as we speak. These mortal-made machines are constantly fritzing. I can't stand not running my own tests."

What's this about?

"Funding," Zephonia whispered from the corner of her mouth.

"It's all well and good that you get swanky offices upstairs and get to outsource all the fancy lab—"

"Bridget." Zephonia cleared her throat. "The spare?"

"Fine," she sighed, rolling her eyes. "He's but a babe. Turned just months ago by our friend Dave here. Name's Franklin Howard. He's so new that papers haven't been completely processed yet. I had to track him through mortal databases. No criminal record, surprisingly. Owned a landscaping company."

Zephonia passed me the files. "That's unusual."

"Yeah, he doesn't really seem the type to turn."

"Thanks, Bridget," Zephonia said. "Let me know what else you find. And let's keep this quiet. We don't need a panic getting started."

Bridget leaned back in her chair and rolled her eyes. "No worries, Zephonia. I'll be discreet. Stake 'em to the wall."

"I'm tempted to roast 'em over a fire until they pop." She saluted Bridget with her pipe on the way out.

Rising to follow, I said, "Thank you, Bridget. It's nice to meet you."

"Same here, Huri." She smiled and winked. "Take care of her. You've got one heck of a partner."

"Will do."

"Oh, Zephonia!"

We looked back from our places in the hallway.

"Based on the test results, venom isn't either of theirs. I'm trying to track down who it belongs to. But that's a different tangled mess."

"Thanks, Bridget."

I jogged to join Zephonia. Wanting to show that I could do as I was told, I asked, "So what's your plan?"

Zephonia snickered as she started climbing the stairs to the fourth floor. "I've got to get them talking. Without my voice."

Really? "But they'd tell you everything if you used it."

"It's considered 'coercion.' Plus, a few can resist. Usually the heavier hitters. Now, if you have questions, you need to ask them before I go in."

"Do you think David could've come up with the idea for this drug?"

Zephonia scoffed. "Not on your downy feathers, chickadee."

"If Franklin was turned months ago—"

"There we go. Glad you got there. That's probably when they started selling and working at the college. But you never go in asking a question you don't already have the answer to."

"I can contact the manager while you're interviewing him to confirm."

"No need yet." She paused at Interview Room 1. "You're in here." She pointed at the first unmarked door on the left as she peeked her head into the observation room directly beside it. "Hey, Jude. Could you hand me some printer paper?"

Jude could pass for a too-tan Florida snowbird, complete with the tan lines from bug-eyed sunglasses. She smiled and handed her a thick folder. "Already got it ready for you."

"You're amazing, honey. So, Jude, this is Huri, my greenie. Huri, don't interrupt me."

"Yes, ma'am."

She smirked and patted my cheek. "You're cute. No ma'am-ing me anymore."

"Yes, ma'am." *Can't be a complete pushover.*

Zephonia shot me a look before we disappeared behind our respective doors.

Tossing down the file folder, Zephonia took the chair across from the cuffed vampire. He was chained to the table and wearing a purple mouthguard that served as a muzzle. Just in case. She smiled at him like he was an old friend as she pulled out her knitting from her bag and started casting on thirty stitches. "Hi, David. I'm Steward Weber."

"Lawyer."

Zephonia snickered. "Mortal laws aren't our laws, David. You should know that by now." She paused in her WIP to glance at her empty file. "It's been—what?—thirty years or so since you were turned?"

He licked his mouthguards and winced. It had to be because of the minty flavor. "Where's your partner? She was a tasty morsel."

What a douche. I couldn't contain the eye roll.

Zephonia didn't answer as she resumed knitting. "Tell me about this new drug you're peddling."

He stared off at the wall without speaking. He was sphinxlike for a while as Zephonia applied gentle pressure. After a half hour of no answers, Zephonia readjusted her bun and secured it with a pair of double-pointed needles.

Jude sat straight. "There it is." She tapped the large mirror on the wall, and then Zephonia's bracelet buzzed.

I sat forward, wondering what the nixie was up to.

Zephonia tapped her ear cuff. "Go ahead." She paused while Jude remained quiet. "Is that so? Excellent. Just as well. David's not cooperating. Thanks, Captain." She hung up and reached across the table to his cuffs.

"What're you doing?"

"I'm releasing you. You're free to go. Your boy Frankie just flipped. Took the deal. No honor among ticks, I guess."

"What deal? You didn't offer me a deal."

She laughed. "He came up with it himself, apparently. Smarter than I took him for. He said he's too pretty to go to prison. Babies are so cute. If he only knew what our prisons were really like, right?"

"Yeah right. Frankie don't know nothin'."

"No?" She paused in unshackling him. "That's funny. Maybe he just wanted to get back before the drop happens."

I straightened and looked at Jude, who was grinning because David straightened. Zephonia didn't miss it either.

"Doesn't even know where it's going to happen."

"He seemed to believe he did. And my captain believes him." She raised her eyebrows and shrugged. "Bless your heart, honey. It's just karma. You got over on Boris."

David leaned back, eyes going wide for a moment.

"And now, Frankie's getting over on you. It's the life cycle of a tick, honey."

His lips thinned. "Ungrateful ass..." He shook his head. "You need to know that that bastard ran kids in-life."

Zephonia kept her features as schooled as possible. "You're not so clean yourself, Dave."

"I didn't do kids. He does. Runaways mainly, but he'll snatch them right off the playground." He straightened. "It's why they wanted him."

"They."

David fixed his gaze on Zephonia. He growled and leaned back as a smile luxuriated across his face. "You ain't got nothin', old woman."

Grinning, Zephonia unchained him from the table. "Bless your heart. You're free to go, honey."

His mouth dropped as she hoisted him by the elbow from his seat. "What are you doing?"

That's what I want to know.

"Releasing you. I can't really charge you with anything. Off you go." Zephonia escorted him out of the interview room while I followed out of sight. They went on out past Violet to the front doors. I paused beside The Desk. Careful not to lean on it. Zephonia paused to smile once more at him and then uncuffed him just beyond the front doors.

"Where's my stuff? My clothes. I can't go out like this. Take these things off my teeth. Freakin' things are stuck on."

"Those old rags? I'm afraid they were mislaid. But those purple scrubs are lovely on you." She pushed him away from the building like he was an unruly horse. "Besides, the muzzle'll fall off in a few hours. Go on, now. Git!"

His eyes widened, but he turned and ran.

I stepped outside to watch him leave. "Am I missing something?"

"He'll lead us either to his home or his boss." Zephonia shrugged.

"How will we follow him?"

"While he was passed out, I had them switch out one of his earrings for a stitch marker. We'll keep an eye from the skies. Now, we talk to Frankie."

When we returned to the interview room beside the first, Franklin awaited us, and he looked a little too pale and haggard. Zephonia sat across from him, knitting away on her notes from David's interview as I watched from the observation room. Her silence made him fidget and shake. If I had to guess, it had been at least a day since he'd fed.

"You look like you've been rode hard and put up wet, son," she said after finishing her notes fifteen minutes later, concentrating on her knitting.

His eyes were gaining that red hue.

"May I offer you a drink?"

"Depends on the drink."

Zephonia pushed a strand of hair behind her ear, and Jude knocked on the door with a small cup of red, viscous liquid. He perked up at the scent. How many signs had Zephonia and Jude worked out?

"Thanks, darling." She closed the door and placed the cup in his hands, even topping it with a straw since he couldn't lift his hands more than a few centimeters. "Better?"

The color receded from his eyes as he nodded.

"You prefer Frankie or Franklin or what?"

"Frank."

"I'm Zephonia. Sorry about the sedative back at the school. Part of the job. Hope you understand."

Glaring at the wall, he growled at her.

"You'll have to excuse me for stating the obvious. But, honey, you've got a pretty crappy partner." She relaxed into her seat. "Not only has he flipped on you, but he has also been keeping all those lovely veins to himself."

He snorted even as he sucked down the blood in his cup. "He's an ass."

"What are you doing turning, Frank? Your record in-life shows no criminal past. Shoot, you even paid your parking tickets on time. Upstanding, by the looks. Owned your own business at only twenty-five."

Frank sat there staring at her, lips turned down at the corners. "I didn't know turning was illegal."

"Curious." She raised an eyebrow. "Considering you're not the usual turning type, if you catch my drift."

When his mouth opened to answer of its own volition, he clenched his teeth to keep his mouth shut. A smirk played across my lips. *Smarter than the average tick.* His brow furrowed as he looked down at his cup.

Humming at his confusion, Zephonia said, "It's called Aletheia's Tears." She shrugged when he batted away his beverage. "It's standard on potential informants."

My eyes rounded as I looked back at Jude. "Why didn't she give it to David?"

"Because he's the bait." Jude laughed like I should've known that. Probably should've.

"Listen, lady. I'm no snitch."

Zephonia smiled when he immediately clamped his mouth shut. "That's good. Veracity is desirable in an informant."

He glared at her.

"It's painful if you resist, Frank. I'd rather you not give yourself undue pain, sugar. We'll start with something easy. What's your full name and date of birth in-life?"

Frank shook as he fought the drug. The veins in his neck and face bulged. But within thirty seconds, a scream tore from his throat, and the answers tumbled from his lips. She asked him a few more questions about his old life that were easy enough, allowing him to ease into the prompting of the Tears.

"So, let me try a little something more personal." She paused. "Why'd you decide to turn?"

Looking anywhere but at her, he frowned. "I didn't. I saw that idiot feeding on some chick in an alley and tried to stop him."

My shoulders dropped as Jude's head shot up, eyes round. "Bastard," Jude hissed.

"I stayed because I don't know how else to…survive."

"What sort of work do you do for him?"

Frank leaned back. "Just what you saw. He works there as a cover, and I hang out in the shade, make sure no one else troubles him. Took a pee break when your girl came in, apparently."

Zephonia and I knew even as she spoke that David's claims about Frank were a lie. "He told me someone asked him to turn you. That you specialized in abducting children."

His nose twitched in a snarl, which looked rather hilarious set against his purple mouth guards. "Please. He didn't even mean to turn me. At least, I don't think so. I ain't never taken no kids. He's the one. He and Robby round up runaways and the homeless to test the drug out. I told him no."

"Who's Robby?"

"Another dealer. She's mid-level like Dave." He leaned forward. "Look. Don't make me do this, lady. You know these guys don't mess around. I'm as good as dead...well, deader...for real if I talk to you."

Setting down her WIP, Zephonia winced. "Frank, I'm gonna be straight with you. You're as good as dead just getting hauled into this building. Doesn't matter if you talk or not." She leaned back. "But you roll on them, and we can see about getting you out of town at the very least."

Frank studied Zephonia before his head fell forward. He sucked at the mouthguard and finally nodded.

"All right. You'll start by publicly accusing your attacker. We can make something like a mortal video to keep you safe until the trial is over. Used to be done face-to-face." Zephonia shook her head. "Didn't always go well. Anyhow, it's our way of bringing formal charges." She pulled out a portrait-sized mirror and set it on the table. "Give us all the details of how you were turned."

CHAPTER 15

My hands trembled as I pulled into the school parking lot. I had fought minotaurs and cyclopses without once fearing the outcome. I'd gone up against the best my pantheon and others had to offer. I'd even somehow managed to keep myself from tearing Nashville apart looking for Rose's attacker for the past month.

My eyes watered as I took in the kids among the cars. The smiles and a few tears. But my son, braver than I, sat in the backseat, beaming like he was going on a grand adventure. I blinked away the moisture, wanting to appear strong in front of him.

"Just breathe, amor," Luis's voice told me.

He materialized in the passenger seat and gave me that tender smile I missed so much.

I wanted to tell him that I couldn't do this, that I should've let Mama join me, but then Elias would hear my cowardice.

"You can. You've got this. Just walk him to the gate, *cariña.*"

I nodded and plastered on my best excited smile. "Ready, asteri mou?"

Elias was too busy unbuckling to notice how fragile I was. "Yep. Backpack. Pencils. Crayons."

"You've got your folder?"

"Yep." He put a hand on his bracelet. "My mirror."

"Good." Before we left the house, I had checked three times to make sure he had it on.

"Let's go."

"If you get too excited...you might shift on accident."

"I'm going to be cool as the North Sea."

I swallowed a hard lump. "And if you have bullies..."

He grinned evilly. "I will smite them."

"You will no—"

"Chill, Ma. I'm joking." He rolled his eyes like he was ten years older than he was.

I raised an eyebrow at Luis, who was snickering behind his hand. "He's your son," Luis said.

"Seriously, Mami." He put his little hand on my shoulder. "I've got this."

Somehow, I got out of the car.

Elias joined me. I nearly took his hand out of habit but then thought better of it. He was probably getting too big to hold his mother's hand. But Elias took my hand without hesitation. Luis grinned as he stood beside Elias. Together, the three of us walked to the front gate.

"You remember where your classroom is at?" I winced, wishing they would let us walk the kids to their classrooms.

"Yeah. It's right there." He pointed beyond the fence to one of the classrooms closest to the entrance. "With the giant apples on the front."

I blinked a few times to control these cursed emotions as I knelt down. "You let me know if you need me."

"I will, Mami," he said as he practically danced from one foot to the other with excitement. *Bless his little heart.*

"I'm so proud of you," I whispered, blinking fast. I covered it by squeezing him into a tight hug. "I love you, Eli."

He squeezed me back as hard as his little arms could. "You're all over my heart."

Heartstrings, stay together. I kissed him. "Go on now. Have fun. I can't wait to hear all about your first day."

He returned my kiss and bolted off in the direction of his classroom.

I watched at the fence with a gaggle of kindergarten moms and dads. Once Elias was safely ensconced in his classroom, I avoided the commiserative glances from my peers and rushed back to Blue. The moment I was inside, the dams broke in my eyes.

Luis leaned against the headrest beside me. "He's going to do great."

I nodded. "I know."

"He's brilliant and capable."

"I know." I grabbed a stack of napkins from some fast-food joint and dabbed my face.

"You've prepared him for this."

"Have I? He just started shifting three weeks ago."

"He's doing great. But if you don't think he's ready..."

I sucked in a breath to try and steady myself. "I just want him to be happy, Luis. He de—deserves it after everything."

Luis nodded and stared at the gate with me. "He looked incredibly happy," he said.

"I know."

"Let's get you to work. It'll help you calm down."

"I took off so I could be here for him." I shrugged. "Just in case."

Luis opened his mouth to speak, that little smirk playing on his lips. It was the one that always made my knees go weak. But my bracelet buzzed and heated. My heart hammered when Rose's face popped up.

Her silver-lined eyes were so wide that I feared something had happened. It had been almost a month since the attack, and my heart still dropped every time she called.

"Hey!" I swiped to make Rose's face dance above my wrist. Based on the garden behind her, I guessed Rose was back at her house. She'd insisted on staying at home during the day. "Everything okay?"

"Jer—Jerome asked me out."

I sighed as my heart settled back to a normal cadence. "Oh, thank goodness." *Dates. I can handle dates.*

"What do I do? I told him yes and I've lost my mind I'm in no condition to go out with him and—"

"Rose, slow down, honey. When is the date?"

"Lunch. Today."

"When did he ask you out?"

"Saturday."

I covered my eyes. "Why didn't you tell me? We could've had all this planned out. And who plans a date on a Monday?"

"No clue. Said he had something special happening today." Rose's hands batted the air like she was swatting bugs. "What am I going to do? I've waited too long to cancel."

"Go get a shower. Well, eat breakfast. I'll call Klara and Alexis." *Phew. Thank goodness it's something this simple.* "I'll head over to your place."

Rose didn't say anything else. She just hung up. I exhaled my annoyance, hoping and praying for the day when Rose was purged of that insidious venom. I leaned my head against the headrest and looked over to where my imaginary Luis had been. My fingertips trailed the seat's heather-gray fabric. With a slow exhale, I tapped my bracelet.

"Contact Alexis and Klara."

In a matter of two hours, the three of us had descended on Rose's house like we used to as teenagers. I was never more relieved for Rose's tinted contacts, which always accentuated the natural color of her eyes. Now, however, they helped to hide her silver-lined irises.

Rose and I had agreed that we couldn't tell the girls the true nature of the attack. Well, Rose had insisted. She seemed terrified (more than I was, if that was possible) of the Twelve finding out. I was still searching for loopholes.

At the moment, Rose couldn't stop trembling, however. I glanced at the girls, who were watching Rose.

"You cold?" Klara asked, eyes narrowed.

"Just nervous." Rose crossed her arms in front of her body and looked away. "First time since the attack."

Alexis winced and rubbed Rose's arm. "You can still back out. He'd understand."

Rose's face paled. "With Jerome?" I smiled to myself, knowing that Rose had been waiting for this moment since she was fifteen. "No. No. He's been waiting. He said so. For a time during the day."

Klara shot a glance at me, but she didn't press matters. I, however, knew that Klara was suspicious. "We can keep an eye on you."

Rose's mouth dropped open as she shook her head a little too vigorously. "Dang. It's not that bad. He's...he's...just..." Rose turned her eyes on me. "You know."

I released my full smile for Rose. I did know. "He's...your guy."

Rose's entire body stilled and calmed. She blinked. "Yeah. He's my guy."

I pecked Rose on the cheek and headed toward her closet. "You've got this, Rose. You just need that one dress to make you feel it." *Now, where is that geometric dress?* I flicked her clothes until I came to the one that accentuated Rose's figure in all the right ways. "Here it is."

Klara nodded and started unpacking her carpet bag of glamour. She set out all the necessities as she addressed each of us. "Perfect color for you. Lexi, get the rollers going. Huri, you're on nails. Rose, sit."

And just like that, we were all back to our teenage selves, giggling about boys and reminiscing about fun dates and idiots. I couldn't resist reveling in my friends' presence and the distraction they provided from Elias's first day. When they asked about that, they teased me about being a sap even as tears filled their own eyes for Elias's first big step into childhood.

My eyes cut to the back door, and I found Luis there, smiling at me like he did when he watched me after we made love. I blushed at him as I blew on Rose's soft pink fingernails.

The respite ended too soon. We all told Rose how beautiful she looked and then headed home.

I only drove a short distance away before shifting when no one was looking and flying back to her house. I arrived just in time to find Jerome getting out of his car. He pulled out a bouquet of sunflowers and took them to Rose's door.

"Good job, Jerome," I thought to myself as I watched from the cover of the tree. Sunflowers had been Rose's favorites for ages. The fact that he remembered said a lot.

Hope filled my heart at seeing Rose exit, calm and still as she had been before the attack, with an almost lovesick smile. Jerome handed Rose into the car, grinning like a fool. I didn't follow them, though I desperately wanted to. Jerome had chosen the time for their date with care. There weren't any vampires willing to brave the late August sun. I had no doubt that he'd taken every precaution to ensure Rose's safety.

With that, I flew back to the car and then headed home, where the only boxes that stared at me now were Luis's. I ignored them and entered my office, where I pored over scroll after scroll in hopes of finding something that could protect me and my family from the consequences of my mistake.

A thunderclap shook the house. I leaped to my feet and tapped my owl pendant. My silk armor sprang into place just as someone knocked on my front door. The cold of a thunderstorm filled my nostrils as I pulled a sword from its sheath. My fingertips tapped the mirror beside the entrance. A gray-haired young man stood there in a linen suit. His neatly trimmed beard curled at the ends.

I cursed inside. *What's he doing here?* I nibbled my bottom lip and opened the door.

"Athena Pherenike." He, of course, entered like every room was made for him.

"Come in, Zeus Adonis." I didn't sheath my sword as I closed the door. "To what do I owe the pleasure?"

He glanced around, nose wrinkled. "Why do you stay in such squalor, cousin? We all miss you at home."

Adonis and I, like all the heirs of the Twelve, had trained together from the time we were young. It was an uncanny circumstance. Whenever one of the Twelve produced an heir, the rest seemed to automatically follow. Thankfully, none of our generation had begun having any heirs, which suited me just fine. I was in no hurry to find anyone to have a daughter with.

"Did you seriously come to comment on my state of living, cousin?" I slid my blade back into its sheath slowly. "I doubt the others missed me."

"Well, I did." He flashed the mischievous grin he'd always given me when we were children playing hide-from-the-cyclops. "In truth, Grandfather sent me."

"Really." My heart raced. No way did I want to be on Zeus Thaddeus's radar. "What for?"

"Your son. He's soon to come of age for training." Adonis walked to a fruit bowl and started munching on an apple. "He'll be seven in two years."

"I'm all too aware, cousin." I crossed my arms and leaned against the counter. "Why are you really here?"

His handsomest smile curved across his lips. It was full of genuine boyish mischief. He was such a ham. "I missed you."

That made my eyes roll. "Surely Ares Alkibiades is keeping you entertained."

He snorted at my words and tossed the apple core onto the counter.

I pointed at the trash can. "Were you born in a barn?"

"You Americans—"

"Southerners. It's a regional saying."

He actually looked around, no doubt for the *oiketes* that usually doted on the Twelve and their heirs.

"We are our own servants here, Adonis. Trash can."

"Again. Squalor." He actually threw it away, batting his big gray eyes behind thick black lashes. He always reminded me of a charming horse with those eyes. And he only did that when he wanted to lose a few bouts to my astounding awesomeness.

I couldn't hold in a laugh. "OK. Fine. You get one round. After that, I'm enjoying the rest of my day for myself." *Such an Adonis thing to do. Teleport across the world just to spar with me.*

He clapped me on the back, zapping me slightly. "I knew you couldn't resist my charms."

I twisted up my hair and headed into the backyard. "More like scraping gum off my shoe."

"What's gum?"

His full thunderous laugh electrified the air as we squared off, his white-lightning sword flickering even in the noonday sun. My armor parted at my thighs to allow me to unsheathe my second short sword.

Within the next moment, he had charged, and I had darted aside and slapped him on the seat of his pants.

CHAPTER 16

Leaning back into my cloudy chair at work, I beamed down at my bracelet when I saw a picture of Rose and Jerome together on another date in the same week. Monday's date apparently went so well that it had to be repeated on Thursday. They looked quite comfortable snuggled up on the amphitheater lawn.

Alexis sent me the screenshot of the post with the caption, "Will you join the rest of humanity and get social media?"

Rose rarely posted to social media unless it was business-related, so I knew this was something big.

I smiled at the notification that Rose had sent a text.

I've got a gig, Rose wrote with big smileys.

My smile dropped when I read the details. It was in the evening and on the far side of town. I immediately typed back. *Is this wise? You'll be driving at night.*

It took Rose three minutes to reply. My heart thumped hard as my gut clenched. *I've got to live my life. I'll be staying at my place from now on.*

No. Not that. Saltwater burned the corners of my eyes. Rose didn't get it. She didn't understand the danger she was in. She'd only made it this long because of staying with Mama and Pater. *I'd love to come with you, Rosie. We could make it a girl's night.*

I'm going to be fine, Huri. I need to go back to normal. I'll have John with me. He said he wouldn't leave my side, she texted.

Just don't freak, I told myself. *It'll only push her away. John has yet to fail in his managerial duties.* So far, everything had been going smoothly. None of the vampires had come near any of the houses. Even Elias's first day unfolded flawlessly. Maybe Rose was right. OK.

I'm just worried. I just want you safe and sound.

Rose sent over several hearts. *I know, sweetie. I'll be just fine.*

Exhaling as I set down my bracelet, I tried to still my racing heart. *Work. I just need to focus on work.*

I pointedly ignored my web in the corner with its menagerie of dead ends on the Cherries case. Instead, I revisited the lukewarm cases, but it was merely looking. I couldn't process anything. *Maybe I missed something with the Cherries.* I exhaled and shoved the files aside, retrieving the Cherries folder.

Zephonia's bootfalls heralded her arrival. Bless her, she brought cookies from Sanguine. "So, I've got some good news. Frank's gotten his transfer approved."

Brownie cookies with white chocolate chips. New favorite.

I took a delectable bite. "What's that mean?" Sugar was as good a dopamine hit as any.

"He's going to Pakanahuili to help out."

"That was quick." I didn't know those happened so quickly.

I had been to the Amaranthian city-state many times to travel to Olympia, but it wasn't my favorite place to stay just because I hated seeing how the immortals, or at least the elite, treated their mortal servants. Everyone thought my pantheon's home was on Mount Olympus, but that was simply a glorified ski retreat now. These days, my pantheon preferred the coast, with Olympia nestled both on the island above and spilling over into the Ionian Sea below.

Zephonia's smile sprawled along her face like a contentedly lazy cat. "Well, I've been around long enough to know how to grease a few wheels."

"What's the procedure for sending him over?"

"You'll see." Zephonia escorted me to Frank's cell as I savored the last bite of rich chocolate and vanilla.

Frank jumped to his feet like a gentleman greeting a lady when Zephonia entered. His cheeks were a little shallower than before, but his eyes were brighter.

"Miss Zephonia."

I cocked an eyebrow at my partner when Zephonia's cheeks turned a delicate twinge of pink. Most likely, it was more from this happening in front of me than a man hitting on her. No doubt Zephonia still had to turn men away. Little cougar. "I've got good news, Frank. Your transfer was approved."

His eyes rounded as his lips twitched into a smile. "Seriously?"

He's so smitten.

Zephonia nodded. "We can leave as soon as you like. There's a storm coming in today. So there should be enough cloud cover."

"Let's do it, then." His nose twitched when Zephonia passed him a cup between the bars. "Thank you."

Zephonia unlocked the door. "You're not allowed to bring anything over."

"Don't matter. If Amaranthia is half what I've heard, I'm not going to care." He finished his drink, practically destroying the cup to lick the sides. He gave Zephonia a weak smile. "Thank you, Miss Zephonia. This is the first...good thing that's happened since...well..." He looked down.

Poor thing. I really hope we bring David to justice for Frank.

"Come on. That cup won't last you long. Let's get you to the river."

My eyebrows met—*river?*—but I didn't ask any questions even after we all loaded up in Gertie and found a secluded spot at the forested banks of the Cumberland. Heavy gray clouds sheltered

Frank from the sun as he exited Gertie. Frank stared at the water and then Zephonia.

"Are you drowning me? That won't work, you know."

Oh man. Does that mean he's tried?

Zephonia merely brushed away his words. "I'm going to take you there myself—part of being me. There's a steward on the other end who will set you up. Her name is Trudy. You ready?"

He gave me a nod of goodbye before letting Zephonia take his hand. With a look from Zephonia, I donned my earplugs. Zephonia sang and drew Frank to the muddy water with tender caresses to his cheeks and even chest like she was enticing a lover to bed. I again wondered how many men she had tempted beneath the waves. To say he was entranced fell short of describing the lovesick smile that radiated from the inside out, almost giving him the healthy, blood-flushed cheeks of a young mortal again.

I couldn't control a snicker when he tried to kiss Zephonia. But she just laughed, making him shy a little at his faux pas. Then they dove as one beneath the brown river water, taking the chill of Zephonia's song from my arms with them.

Wondering how long this would take, I removed the earplugs and sat in Gertie. In a matter of minutes, Zephonia was swimming back to shore and approaching. Once on land, she shivered all over once, and her clothes and hair ruffled like a strange wind took hold of them. Then she was dry.

I tried to suppress my smirk.

Zephonia scoffed as she paused before me. "Don't start."

"He's smitten. Even before the singing."

She rolled her eyes. "They all are, honey. Poor fools." She touched her nose and looked around. "We clear?"

What's the nose thing? Oh. Smell.

I obediently sniffed the breeze. "Yeah, I haven't sensed anyone for a while. Why?"

Zephonia opened her trunk and pulled scrolls out of her bag.

They had to be hundreds of years old. "I found something that might help you and your pantheon problem."

No way. Even so, I started reading. "This has to do with oiketes."

"Yes. The laws surrounding servants are as binding as family laws."

My eyes rounded. "They...they can't...I can't make them my slaves, Zeph."

Zephonia rolled her eyes and pointed at a section with the tip of her pipe. "Here, Huri. Right here."

"I know. They're protected under Vengeance Laws."

"Yes, and you're quite nearly a queen, Huri." She raised her eyebrows like she was trying to tease the pieces together in my mind. "Who needs advisors and servants...and—"

I let out an involuntary shout. "Ladies-in-waiting. *Douleútria.*" *Right here. It's all right here.*

"If I'm not much mistaken, they are freemen...women, rather. They're as close as family."

Before I knew what I was doing, I'd thrown my arms around Zephonia's neck. Zephonia stiffened, but she still laughed and hugged me back. I never thought of looking there. All the adoption laws forbade the Twelve from adopting mortals. But this.

"It's an old way of doing things. But it might work." I released her and stared at the scrolls. *These pages hold the riches of life itself.* "I could protect them all this way."

"If they agree to it," Zephonia said.

"I'm sure they will." I nearly hugged Zephonia again, but the woman held up a hand and backed away a step.

"You're strong as an ox, chickadee. And I'm a fragile old woman."

I beamed. I wished I could express to Zephonia what she had done for me. My family. "Zeph, thank you. Seriously. I never would've looked at this."

Zephonia shrugged but smiled behind her pipe as we got into Gertie.

"How did you know to look here?"

Zephonia's smile faltered a hair. I winced at how vacant her eyes turned as they stared unseeing at the river. "Part of my old life."

CHAPTER 17

I checked the kitchen clock to make sure I still had time. It was almost ten. *Maybe I should text one last time. Make sure the girls haven't forgotten.* It was Saturday, after all. Klara was probably still asleep and needed a wake-up call. Alexis was no doubt awake. It was her long-run day. I checked my bracelet again for a text from Rose. I hadn't gotten a confirmation that she was home, just a text that she was with John and that the gig worked out. Somehow, I'd managed to trust that she was okay.

My fingers shook a little as they typed, *We still on for brunch, ladies? I don't know about you, but I'm needing some mimosas.*

Alexis's text popped up less than a second later. *I'm more than down.*

Gah, brunch should not exist before twelve. Why are you up at this ungodly hour? Klara wrote.

It's almost 10. Are you in or not, Klair-bear? I snickered. Klara hated when we called her that.

Huri, stop calling me that.

Rose's text popped up immediately. *I'm starving.*

I grinned. Rose was okay. Everything was going to be okay. I just needed to lay out the plan for them. *Yay! I figured we'd forgo a restaurant*, I texted. *I've got everything ready over here. E's playing at Yiayia's house. Hurry your asses up! This mama needs girl-time. The food will get cold.*

Fine. But again. It's too freaking early.

I couldn't stop grinning. My girls were coming. I had a plan to not only protect them but also keep my family from the confines of Olympia. Me and Eli and Mama would be able to stay at home with Pater and Yiayia.

Music. I need some music. I flicked through the selections on the hallway mirror until I found something to cook to.

Rose was going to be fine. She'd gone out at night and hadn't had any issues. The biggest hurdle today would be telling Klara, the immo-hater, and Alexis. Alexis wouldn't be a problem. But Klara was another story.

"You're in a good mood."

I jumped as I spun from stirring the eggs. Luis grinned at me and drew me in his arms. I ignored his sudden appearance and reveled in almost feeling him kiss my lips, the warmth of his body against mine. How I missed this. "I've got a plan, papi."

His body swayed with mine like it always did. His lips smiled against mine. The flecks of green and blue in the pools of his dark-brown eyes made me dizzy like I'd had one too many mimosas. "You always have the best plans."

I giggled, remembering the first time he said that. I'd packed us a picnic and taken him to a secluded stretch of beach. It felt like we stayed like this for ages, swaying to the music in my new kitchen, his eyes filled with that light I craved as much as my ambrosia.

"Oh my gosh, I'm starv—" Alexis stopped short in my doorway. "—ing."

Moment shattered. Here I was, looking like I was dancing with air and staring adoringly up into nothing. *How embarrassing.* My face burned. I spun to find my eggs were nearly burned. *Crap.*

"You okay?" Alexis asked.

Just be cool. I stirred the eggs. "Of course. Just...you startled me." Wetness pooled at the inside corner of my eyes. *No. Not now.* "I didn't expect you until later."

Alexis's hand touched my back. "What was that?"

"What was what?" I really had to stop pretending Luis was still around. "Holy cow! It's almost time."

Alexis turned me to face her. The knowing sigh that escaped Alexis said that she could see the traitorous fluid. "Ri-Ri."

"It's nothing." I swatted the emotions away. "I just miss him. Pretend he's with me sometimes."

Alexis's body melted. "Oh, honey." She crushed me into a hug. "I know you do."

Car doors opened and shut outside. I straightened. "Just don't... you know."

Alexis nodded and pecked me on the side of my head. "I've got you."

"Thank you." I exhaled and closed my eyes to reset. *It's going to work out. I have a plan.* "I think they're here."

"This looks amazing, by the way. Way better than any restaurant."

Klara entered first, looking back at Rose in mid-laugh. Seeing Klara without makeup made me snicker. Somehow Klara made "just rolled out of bed" a good look and accessorized it with a giant lumberjack-plaid tumbler of coffee.

"That was fast."

Klara grunted at me as she watched the world through the steam wafting from her tumbler. "Y'all are killing me."

"It's almost eleven." Rose hooked her arm around Klara's and walked fully into the house. "Come on."

Was it me, or was Rose fidgeting again? She had been eating some fruit Jerome recommended like they were candy. It really did seem to relax Rose's symptoms. Maybe I was just imagining it. Hoping.

Klara stared at Rose through the coffee smoke as they walked to the kitchen island. "You okay?"

"Fine. Come on. I'm starving." Rose beamed at me and kissed my cheek. "Thanks for this, Huri."

I tried to study Rose's eyes, but they were shielded behind those contacts. "You sure you're okay?"

Rose's mouth twitched into a weird smile. "Absolutely. This looks amazing." She hugged Alexis next.

Alexis laughed and shooed everyone to the table. *Oh no. Something's up.* "Let's eat. I can't wait a second more."

The aromas of eggs and veggies cooking reminded me that I was, in fact, incredibly hungry.

"Dig in."

I grabbed some honey and yogurt, eliopsomo...well, pan de jamón now.

As I shoveled food onto my plate, I realized we were missing mimosas. I hurried into the kitchen to pull out the champagne and orange juice. "Who wants to do the honors?"

Alexis raised a pointed eyebrow at Rose and Klara before joining me with a smile. *What was that about? Alexis better not blab about what she saw.* "You know I've got you."

"Huri, what in the..." Klara stopped when Rose rushed to the nearest bowl of honey yogurt and dug in like she hadn't eaten in days.

When Rose looked up at the silence, her eyes widened as she seemed to realize all of us were staring at her. I tried as discreetly as possible to check her for bite marks. Alexis grinned.

"Last time I saw someone wolf down food like that, Huri was pregnant." She wiggled her eyebrows. "How are things going with you and Jerome?"

A bit of walnut caught in Rose's throat. She hit her chest. "Not that good yet."

Klara snickered into her coffee. "If you say so."

Rose's eyebrow arched at Klara as I turned back to the food—

everything will be okay—and as Alexis poured drinks. "What's that supposed to mean?"

Klara grinned and leaned in close to her ear. "I thought I taught you how to hide your hickeys better."

Her what? My eyes shot up. *Hickeys?* And sure enough. There was a fresh one at Rose's collarbone.

Rose's cheeks flushed, and she nearly choked on another walnut. "I don't have hickeys. I'm not in high school anymore," she growled.

Klara scowled at her.

"Rose," I said softly, wondering how discreet I could be in present company. While I had planned to tell the girls the whole plan, that certainly didn't include outing Rose's attack. That would be up to Rose to disclose.

"No, Huri. I'm fine."

My insides squirmed. Rose was rarely so harsh. "OK. Grab a plate, ladies," I sang as I set a glass plate before each of them.

Alexis set down a glass with a clang. "OK. I can't take it. Glass plates, Huri? What is going on? I mean, the last time you busted out the good stuff was when...when Luis died."

I scoffed and sat down quickly. "Nonsense. I just want to—"

Alexis took my hand. "Is Eli okay?"

I glanced at Rose, who winced into her mimosa.

"What's going on?" Klara demanded. "First Huri with her crazy breakfast—"

"Brunch."

"—and now, Rose's got hickeys."

"Klara Marie Godfrey! I don't have any hickeys."

"Come off it. It's not like you and Jerome haven't been making up for lost years," Alexis said with a conspiratorial wink.

Rose cowered a bit.

My stomach was souring by the second. Had she been bitten? But why was she allowed to get away and well...be OK? This didn't make sense.

"Huri, tell Lexi what's going on so she'll calm down," Klara begged as she sipped more from her giant cup.

Rose neatly ignored my probing gaze as she walked to the sink to wash the honey off her hands. "Fine," I said. "OK. Just sit down and try not to choke on anything."

I took a steadying breath.

Alexis slipped into a seat and stared at me, munching on fruit like it was popcorn and I was a fascinating movie. The girl loved gossip.

"So...I don't know where to start, really."

Rose dried her hands and sat back down beside Klara. I realized that Rose didn't even notice that everyone was watching her wolf down a slice of pan de jamón and then chase it with several deep gulps of mimosa.

"What is that?" Klara demanded as she seized Rose's wrist.

Rose's body froze as she stared at the spot where the makeup had come off on Klara's hand. "Let go. I just fell down. No biggie."

"Rose," I called, eyes holding fast to hers like I could will Rose to spill her secrets. *It's times like these I wish Jedi mind tricks were real.*

"Nothing happened."

"The hell it didn't. Your eyes. They're dilated." Klara started panting as she grabbed Rose's other arm and showed the bend of her elbow. "Someone bit you."

"What?" Me and Rose said at once.

"How do you know about bites?" I demanded. Were musicians and groupies really that open with vampires?

"How the hell do you think I know? My job. Immos will be the death of us." She held out Rose's arm before Rose jerked it back. "That's a vampire bite. Not your first one either. Look at you acting like a druggie needing a fix."

Rose's body shook. She looked exactly like every cornered creature I had ever hunted. Rose's wild eyes fixed on me like I was a lifeline. "Yeah, well, Huri's an immortal." She pointed at me like some tattling child.

The moment the words were out, my entire body iced over. Every time Grandmother told me that mortals would use who I am against me replayed in my mind. I never—never—would have believed it.

Alexis's mouth dropped open. "Is that true?"

My mouth couldn't move. My chest heaved air in and out. Gray tinged the edges of my vision. Was I about to pass out? *This was not the plan. So not the plan.*

Klara's chair scraped from the table. "Is that true, Huri?"

Burning filled my eyes. I couldn't look at Rose. Would I be able to look at her again? It was the venom. Mama had said it was foolish to trust someone with venom raging through them. "Yes. It's...it's what I wanted to tell you today."

Klara's body shook. "And why the hell didn't you tell us like twenty years ago?"

"Because I was protecting you from my family."

"What are you?" Klara demanded.

This wasn't going to work. The prejudice ran too deep. *So be it.* I sighed, head falling into my hands. "Does it matter? You hate immos."

"What are you?"

I wiped away a tear. "I'm an Olympian. I'm Athena Alcis's grand-daughter."

"No way," Alexis squeaked. "How cool is that! Do you know Apollo?"

The question made me laugh despite myself. From the corner of my eye, I could see Rose cowering into her chair when I looked toward Klara. I ignored Rose completely, but the ignoring made me feel worse. Klara's face was crimson.

"So you're not one of those predators."

"No."

Klara crossed her arms, shoulders relaxing. "Well, that sure explains why computers freak out around you all the time." She jabbed a finger at me. "We'll deal with your lack of trust later."

I scoffed. "You hate immos."

"I love you," Klara breathed, hand to her chest, tears in her eyes.

"You never noticed that I always said I hate the ones who feed on us?" She motioned at Rose as if she were somehow proof of her point. "Now. Rosaline Brandt. Don't think you're getting away with throwing Huri under the bus."

"What happened, Rosie?" Alexis begged, reaching across the table to hold her hand.

"It was the attack," I told them, glaring at Rose. *Maybe I could sting her back a little.* "She wasn't mugged."

"You're telling me you've been fighting the withdrawals alone?" Klara crossed her arms before indicating Rose's arms. "These are fresh. Who is he?"

"He's no one. Nothing happened."

"Who is he? I'm gonna stake him to the wall with my makeup brushes," Klara said, making me smile grimly. Klara was a warrior underneath it all. I sometimes thought the StS should admit mortals as more than just clerks. Klara would've been perfect.

"It's nothing," Rose roared as she stood. She cast about for several moments trying to find something that none of us could figure out. "Leave me the hell alone." Without pause, she rushed for the door.

"No, Rosie," Klara begged, jumping between her and the door, hands up. "Please, I know someone who can help. She helped with a friend of—"

"I don't need your help," Rose shouted. "I don't need Huri's help. I don't need anybody's help. I'm just fine. Now, what I need is for everyone to stay out of my business."

With one last shove, Rose pushed her way around Klara and ran out.

Before Klara launched herself out the door, I caught Klara by the arm.

"What the hell, Huri!"

"I'll follow her." I peeked out the curtains to watch Rose speed off. "She won't know."

Alexis and Klara exchanged a look.

"I can shift," I sighed. "Just stay here. In case she comes back. Phones on."

"We should follow her. She's in danger," Klara said, keys in hand.

I growled. *She just doesn't get it. Stubborn as all get out.* "She's going to spook even more. If she's bitten like we think, she's not firing on all cylinders, Klair."

"Go," Alexis said with a hand on Klara's arm. "Seriously. We need to keep an eye on her somehow."

I waited for a nod from Klara before I rushed into the backyard and shifted as I launched off the back porch.

CHAPTER 18

An hour later, my body shook a little as I landed in the backyard. I paused when Klara and Alexis both exited my house to stand on the back porch. With that, I shifted. Alexis grinned, but Klara still had her arms crossed.

"Well?"

"She's at her house. Safe. She drove around for a bit." I threw my arms above my head to breathe. I hadn't flown so hard in a long time. "I've got people watching her."

"You have people?" Klara laughed derisively and started fishing through her pocket. "We...we need to call these people." Klara produced a card, hands shaking. "They're a mortal advocacy group."

My eyes widened when I saw the StS logo with Beatriz Ortiz's contact information.

"I know her. She's...she's good for one of them."

My heart pounded so hard against my ribcage that I thought my ribs would crack. "How do you know her?"

Klara stared at her feet, fingers flipping the card around. "I had a friend who...who was in a bad way, Bia...I mean Beatriz...well, she helped him. But they fight for us."

I swallowed and looked from Klara to Alexis. "Bia has already been assigned to her case."

The nickname made Klara stare at me.

With a slow exhale, I nodded. *Time to tell them everything.* "I didn't take a job as a detective with NPD. I am actually a steward."

Alexis's brow furrowed. "What's a steward?"

Klara's eyes widened as she threw her hands in the air. "And you're just now telling us this? What else are you keeping secret?"

"Rose was having a freakin' breakdown," I hissed. "Not to mention, all I've ever heard from you is how much you hate immos *and* cops."

"Uh, what's a steward?" Alexis asked again.

Klara's face reddened. "Look, Huri. You should've trusted me. All of us. No matter what."

"The Twelve would've forced me and Eli and Mama back to Olympia, Klara. I was under direct orders not to tell any mortal. Otherwise, we'd be forced to leave," I shouted. *So much for keeping my cool.*

I nearly let Klara have it, but Alexis hit the railing and stomped her foot.

"Will you two stop your bickering? What. Is. A steward?"

Klara and I glared at each other, and I said, "A steward investigates crimes immortals perpetrate against mortals."

Alexis frowned at me. "OK. So you're, of course, one of the good guys." This time she fixed Klara with one of her queen bee glares as if making a point. "But you should've told us—"

"Or how about any minute between when we met and now," Klara shouted at me. "You're our girl, Huri. If you ended up being a vampire or some predator, you would still be our girl."

Klara was a bag of crazy. It drove me insane. But I loved it about her. We were too much alike. I winced and hid behind my hands. "I was forbidden from telling you all. Any mortal. Yiayia was exiled here, and so were Pater and his siblings. Mama was practically exiled herself because of Pater. It was all I could do just to go to a normal high school. And this. This was the price. No one could ever know. Or they would send us back. Mama would have to leave Pater."

That made them start cursing.

"You're telling me that you are freakin' Athena's granddaughter?" Alexis hissed. "Like The Athena."

"Well, that explains all the weird jokes. I just thought you had a Greek fetish," Klara grumbled as she crossed her arms.

I laughed so pitifully they winced. "Y'all don't get it. I am Athena, too. Athena Pherenike."

Both stared at me, slack-jawed. I waited through the silence, praying someone would say something.

Klara swallowed hard and covered her face. Alexis shook her head. "I'm sorry. You're telling me...us...you're..."

Nodding, I toyed with the silk bracelet around my wrist. "And look. I have a plan that can...keep us all together. I told Rose what I am when she was attacked. No plan. Just got so overwhelmed. But I can protect you all." I swallowed hard. "It's why I wanted to have brunch."

"The...your family will force you and Mom and Eli..." Klara's eyes grew round.

"Yeah." I sighed. Finally, she was getting it. "But my partner...she found a loophole. I can have douleútria. They're ladies-in-waiting." I shivered, praying they'd really read the scrolls as I presented copies of what Zephonia had found. "Douleútria are free. Not like oiketes. They're like advisors." I bit my bottom lip. "This is everything I have on what they do."

"Your...your grandmother has them?" Alexis asked, ignoring the scrolls. Klara sat at the patio table and drew them close and read and read. *Thank goodness one of them's reading.*

"No. They're old-fashioned."

"And this would keep you here." Alexis's eyebrows furrowed.

"Yes. As my douleútria, you would know everything about me. You would also be protected like my family."

Klara looked up then. "You could legally go after the guy who hurt Rose."

That was quick. I nodded. "If she agrees, I could. But she hasn't. Same for each of you. I just found out about this yesterday."

Alexis didn't read the scroll. "Where do we sign?"

"Lexi, you have to read it," I said. "You have to understand."

"I trust you, Huri. And I won't let some old farts steal you and Eli and Mom away from us," Alexis said, brow knotted as tears filled her eyes. "We're on the brink of losing Rose. I won't lose you, too. So where do I sign?"

I bit my lip to keep it from quivering.

"It seems straightforward." Klara nodded as she mumbled to herself. "We need to each offer something. Like a service. Easy enough. Lex can help you with endurance. She's done that for years already. Administrative stuff. I'm a makeup genius." She preened with a grin, eyes still on the parchment. "Rose, when we pin her down, she's got a political mind even if she doesn't use it. Done."

"You would have to go with me every time I go to Olympia officially. You would have to go to war for Olympia if one occurred."

"Shut it." Klara dismissed my words. "We're doing this. Now. Even without Rose."

I covered my face to hide the rush of emotion. "You all are amazing," I rasped.

"You have to petition your grandmother," Klara mumbled, eyes scanning the parchment.

"Rose would do this in her right mind," Alexis said, bringing me into a quick hug. "Can we forge something?"

I wish it were that simple. "No. She has to give verbal consent, using the Tears."

"An actual truth serum." Klara gasped with a wicked smile. "I would love to get my hands on that."

Alexis clapped. "Let's do it. Can you get in contact with your grandmother somehow?"

"Right now?"

"Yes," Klara hissed. "If they find out you've told us..."

I exhaled and tapped my bracelet. "Grandmother."

Having them watch me openly use immortal technology was strange. They gasped when my grandmother's head materialized in miniature above the surface of my bracelet.

"Asteri mou, to what do I owe this unexpected pleasure?"

"Can you spare perhaps ten minutes? It's urgent."

"I better get to see my favorite..." Grandmother's face disappeared from the bracelet, and her entire body appeared on the patio. She let out a yelp at the same time the girls did. "Huri Pherenike Arachne Rojas!"

I held up a hand. "They want to become my douleútria," I said in rapid Greek.

Grandmother's gray eyes settled upon the two. "This is true? You want to become her maidservants?"

Their mouths were practically dragging the table. How cringe. *Come on, girls.* Grandmother gave me a telling look.

"They've never seen anyone teleport, Grandmother."

"She's even more beautiful in person," Klara whispered, eyes roaming Grandmother like she could envision doing her makeup and styling her just so. "Seriously. The resemblance is unreal."

"How did we miss it?" Alexis whispered out the side of her mouth.

"Girls," I hissed. "She has perfect hearing."

"More than. But thank you for the compliment. We're in serious breach of the Twelve's laws at this moment," Grandmother said, crossing her arms.

"Right." Alexis nodded and looked to Klara, who nodded back.

"We would like to formally declare our desire to be...Athena Pherenike's doul...ladies-in-waiting...thingies." Klara actually blushed, which doesn't happen often.

I covered my mouth to hide the laugh. Grandmother frowned at me. With a flourish of her hand, three vials appeared. "I expected Rose to be here as well."

"We think she was bitten again," I admitted.

"Well, hurry up with her too. For Klara and Alexis." She handed each a vial in turn.

Scrolls appeared, contracts that listed their duties, and as the girls read those duties (which fit them perfectly), I realized that Grandmother had been waiting for this moment. A laugh escaped me, drawing three sets of eyes. Grandmother arched an eyebrow at me as the tiniest of smirks curled one side of her lips.

"You knew."

She waved for the girls to drink. "What is it Americans say? I cover bases. I had to with you over here. I thought for sure you'd spill the beans to them years ago."

"She only told us today," Alexis said at once.

Grandmother turned her penetrating gaze on Alexis and smiled. "And you've already agreed to this."

Klara swallowed. "She's our family."

Grandmother's throat caught, and she blinked hard several times. I blushed as Grandmother threw her arms around their necks and then straightened just as suddenly, smoothing out her perfect cream-colored suit.

"Let us begin," Grandmother said, eyes creased in a tender smile. "The Tears won't stay long."

Within short order, Alexis and Klara were questioned and passed unfailingly.

"Welcome to the insanity of our family. Officially." Grandmother embraced them both. "I'll have tutors arranged. You must bring them to Olympia for an official visit once Rose is tended. How is she?"

"Better until last night, apparently. We think someone got ahold of her."

"I know you have it in hand, Pherenike. But I'll see what I can find out to help her. Perhaps it would be best if she came to stay with me."

That made me smile. "Thank you, Grandmother. That is generous."

"I still want to see my grandson." She checked her watch. "But the hour is late. I will return next weekend."

With those words and a tilt of her head, she vanished.

CHAPTER 19

The events of the morning seemed too good to be true. I stroked Elias's hair as we watched his latest favorite movie. I couldn't help smiling at the memory of Klara and Alexis becoming my douleútria as I checked my bracelet for an update on Rose.

Last I heard from Beatriz, Rose had driven to a park. It was late and starting to get dark. I should've heard something by now. Surely Rose would be home.

Just try not to worry. I snuggled in a bit more, just wanting a bit of relaxation with my baby. But the doorbell rang.

"Thank goodness," I laughed, fighting to keep lighthearted. "I'm starving."

I swiped the mirror to see if it was the pizza guy. My stomach bottomed out. "Beatriz." I flung the door open.

"Can I come in?"

"Of course." *Please, let everything be okay.*

Elias sat up, eyes round as we came back into the living room. "Is Auntie Rose OK?"

Beatriz's face paled as she pushed her hair behind her ears.

Not good. Something nasty settled into the pit of my stomach. "What's going on, Bia?"

"Have you heard from Rose?"

"No. I was trying to give her space after the blow-up with the girls."

Beatriz glanced down at Elias as he wrapped his arms around my leg. "Should we talk about this alone?"

I winced and motioned for her to continue. He'd just be listening at his bedroom door.

With a sigh, Beatriz wiped her face. "I lost her after the park. She called me from a jazz club."

Elias squeezed so tight that my leg was starting to lose feeling.

"She told me that there was a vampire, and she was scared to leave."

Skata. Skata. Skata. My heart bottomed out through my stomach, and a wave of dizziness rushed my entire body. "Oh no." *I never should've left her.*

"When I got there, she was missing. The bouncers and waitress said she was really disoriented and stumbled out. No one saw which way she went."

Had someone stuffed my ears with cotton? "No. No. No."

"Traffic cameras show her getting into an unmarked limo."

Elias whimpered beside me. "Is she okay?"

My bracelet vibrated, and my throat caught. "It's her. She says she's home."

"What?" Beatriz grabbed my wrist and jerked me (and Elias) over to read the message. "No. I've got someone on the house." She tapped and then swiped her own bracelet. "Lanie. Do you have eyes on our owlet?"

Beatriz's face paled. "OK. Thanks." I cuddled Elias close when Beatriz shook her head.

"Did you call her agent? Maybe she had a gig." Even as the words came out, I knew it wasn't true.

"I did. He said the last time he saw her was last night at the audition. He left when she and the owner of Firebrand Records were at the studio. They all had dinner together, and Rose and this Nikolai Smirnov guy were working on a track. Seemed to be getting along really well. So well that this Smirnov guy was asking for her this morning. Set something up."

"I don't know him. She didn't mention anything about him."

"Huri, there is no Firebrand Records. There's no Nikolai Smirnov either. I've run his name—"

No. We have to go now. I ran to get my car keys, but when I saw Elias, I stopped. My parents were visiting friends in Clarksville, and Yiayia was on a date with Ricardo. Alexis and Klara lived an hour away. I started cursing in Mandarin just so Elias wouldn't understand. "Let's go, Eli."

"Is Auntie Rosie okay?"

"We're going to find out. I've got a key to her house, Bia. Meet me there." I scooped up Elias and buckled him into his booster seat.

We got there in record time, Elias silent and fidgeting in his seat the whole way.

I looked back at him once we arrived. "I need you to stay with me. Stay silent. Do exactly as I say. This is major listen-to-Mami time. Understood?"

He merely nodded, eyes round.

"I've got you, bud. Get on my back and hold on." I exited Big Blue and pulled him up onto my back, praying over him as I situated him. He clung to me like a backpack as I traversed the stairs to Rose's front door. It was still locked.

"Lanie's confirmed that no one has been in or out," Beatriz said.

"Rose!"

Beatriz and I shared a glance when she didn't answer.

"Rosie, it's Huri! I'm coming in with Bia and Eli."

Hand shaking, I managed to fit the key into the door. It opened as it always did. But the silence screamed emptiness. We moved through the house, confirming in moments that our fears were realized.

"Do I get down?" Elias whispered.

"Not yet." My nose was in the air like a scent hound, but there was nothing. No hint of an immortal scent.

"Huri, her clothes are gone," Beatriz called from the bedroom. "There's no suitcase anywhere I can see."

My hands started shaking when I saw Rose's cell on the counter.

"There's a note on the fridge," Elias whispered.

I rushed over, stomach souring even more. It wasn't her handwriting. It wasn't even her words.

"Mom and Dad? Aunt Rosie doesn't call them that. What's in Seattle?"

Water burned my eyes. "I know, son." She only ever called her own parents Mother and Father, and my parents were always Pater and Mama, just like I called them. "I don't know that there's anything out there."

Beatriz exhaled when she saw the note. "You didn't touch anything?"

"Nothing."

"I'm calling it in." She swiped her bracelet.

"Where is she, B?"

"We'll find her, Huri. Don't worry." She turned away when she had to speak. "This is Steward Beatriz Ortiz. We've got a Dropped Stitch on Morning Glory Street. I need a collection team to my location."

"She left her phone?" Elias whispered. "She never leaves it anywhere."

I shook my head. No way was this happening. Tears threatened to break past my eyelashes.

"But she's okay, right, Mama?"

"I'm sure she is. Just...just a misunderstanding or something."

But that misunderstanding was taking longer than ever. I had scried my parents, hating to call them on their night in Clarksville. I couldn't face the girls yet.

I'd failed my first and oldest friend. I should've never gone even an hour without making sure she was okay. Seeing her with my own eyes.

Once at home, I had to stay in Elias's room until he fell asleep, which he hadn't needed for the past year or so. It took what felt like forever for him to even begin to relax. *Not again. Not again.* When I finally dared to leave his bedroom, Mama waited in the kitchen for me with three steaming mugs of tea. Yiayia entered from the bathroom, kissing Mama's cheek as she took a mug. I stood across from them, eyes red but tearless.

"I have to find her."

"You've got to let Beatriz do her job," Yiayia said with surprising authority. She almost sounded like Zephonia.

"She's my sister."

"She's my daughter." Mama covered my hand. "You've got to let them do their job."

They had failed. I had failed. We had all failed Rose. But not again.

"Philomache's right. Once they catch this guy, they'll be able to put him in prison. You start screwing with things, and he could go free."

My shoulders slumped. Rose wouldn't want that.

Mama gave Yiayia a grateful smile as Yiayia rubbed her back, even nodded encouragingly.

"I've worked with Beatriz before," Mama began. "She's helped put a lot of predators in jail. Gave my Earthbound families peace of mind." Mama squeezed my hand. How many times had I seen her do the same to mortals whenever they came to the charity for help after their family members went missing? Countless. I remembered many volunteer hours spent at Earthbound, the nonprofit Yiayia started to help immortals live quiet and safe lives among mortals. Mama had officially joined the nonprofit shortly after I found the girls and was doing well in school, but even before that, she had been quietly helping immortals and their families find their place in America.

Mama's sigh brought my thoughts back to the present. "You've got Elias, too," she said. "He's old enough to recognize things now. You got away with it before because he was so young."

I tried to forget the first time I ever left Eli. It was for three days while I hunted down Luis's murderer. I still wished that I felt better for watching the fiend starve to death, slowly drying to dust before my eyes, but the creature who stole my husband merely became another skeleton in my closet. I hated to think what would happen if anyone found out at StS.

But she was right. My shoulders slumped. I didn't know what to tell Rose's parents. They seemed to believe the cover story her captor had concocted. They even showed me a text saying she had landed and was headed to a hotel. I wanted to vomit when I saw that.

When I told the girls, they wept but rallied quickly. Klara immediately started a website and phone number for people to call with tips about sightings. Alexis started calling everyone who knew or might know Rose.

I had especially wanted to vomit when I saw Jerome.

He had been sitting at his own piano just staring at the keys.

"It's nice that you're checking on me," he had told me. "But I'm fine, Huri. We're in different spheres."

"What are you talking about?"

He showed me a text that said, *This isn't working. I'm just not ready for a relationship. Goodbye.*

Instead, I burst into foolish hysterics as Jerome awkwardly put his arm around my shoulders. Poor guy.

"Jerome, this...she..." I could barely speak. "We can't find her."

Jerome's face fluctuated through so many emotions that my waterlogged eyes couldn't keep up. "What?"

"I think he's got her." I explained everything as his eyes transformed from moist to stony the more he heard.

"We'll find her, Huri. Our girl's strong. First thing is we have to talk to her parents. They're powerful enough to move some immortals."

"I've tried, Jerome. They didn't believe me."

"We have to get mortals looking for her."

My chin trembled as I nodded. *Keep it together, Huri.* "Even her vinyls are gone, Jerome. What does that even mean?"

He blinked, eyes searching the air. "I don't know. I don't know. But you've got to try talking to her parents again. They will listen to you before anyone else."

I had doubted his assurance that Rose's parents would believe me so much that I waited until I could speak with Mama and Yiayia. The women hummed as they considered Jerome's plan, sipping tea.

"He's not wrong," Yiayia allowed. "They're well-connected. They may not be aware of it, but I know they're acquainted with immortals working secretly in the government."

"Yeah," I said. "I just don't know what they'll do. They didn't handle it well when we tried to tell them this trip was completely out of character."

"But stewing on it may open up their minds a bit. I know Phyllis is especially tender right now." Mama took a sip of tea, eyes distant and almost vacant, like she was staring into painful memories.

Yiayia nodded as she stared into the tea's steam. "It sounds like you'll need evidence that she didn't make it to Seattle. Run it by Beatriz. She's no doubt knocking out the possibility that she's actually there."

"After you handle steward stuff, I'll go with you when you talk to her parents," Mama said. "I hate to say this, but we parents still look at you all as children, no matter how old you get. I don't want Phyllis and Sturgeon to see you as little Huri."

I exhaled and covered my face. "The girls are already contacting everyone they know."

"Earthbound can bring them in on all sorts of things to help the investigation. We can get the girls to help there."

I knew all about those "things." I'd been on more than one fruitless papering of the city to find missing people, usually teenage girls. It was nothing but a way to give the families something to do when nothing could be done. It was rare that those efforts led to a girl being returned to her family.

"This can wait until morning," Yiayia said. "You need sleep. You both look like you're ready to fall asleep where you stand."

"I doubt I'll be able."

"I know, asteri mou." Mama kissed my forehead, trying to hide the tears on her own cheeks. "Come on."

All three of us piled into my bed like it was a Saturday morning of old. The only difference was that Pater was stuck working in the lab where they were synthesizing spider silk. Apparently, there was a chemical spill.

I, however, wanted only to be left alone. But once cocooned in my family's arms, I realized this corny group hug was just what I, and apparently Mama, needed. Mama whispered tearful prayers for Rose and the entire situation. Hearing my mother cry silently made me hold her closer. We were never big criers. The warriors of wisdom weren't supposed to be emotional. Yiayia simply cuddled us both together, kissing the tops of our heads until we drifted to sleep.

CHAPTER 20

The next evening, when the girls left after a fruitless evening of making calls, I had to tuck Elias into bed. It was beyond difficult. Which was why I hid in my office/spare room as soon as I left his room.

My eyes stayed firmly away from his bedroom door across the hall. He had cried himself to sleep again, worrying about Rose, scared vampires were going to come for us like they had for Rose and his father.

I had tried to hide that truth about Luis from him, but what was the first thing he looked up once he could read? Luis's death. He even knew to do it without my knowledge. *Sneaky kid*. It had been the worst conversation I'd ever had with anyone. At least Klara and Alexis's positivity helped keep his spirits a little higher during the day.

I sat down at the desk with a slow exhale and took a deep sip of decaf coffee. If I had the hard stuff, I'd never fall asleep. The thought of sleep made me remember the nightmares I had of Rose.

I should've kept a better eye on her. I should've noticed that things were off. I'd just been so worried about telling the girls without ratting Rose out in the process.

I didn't want to have another of those conversations with him.

One last check confirmed my blinds were closed as always. With that, I studied the story collage (as the girls used to call it in high school) that the three of us had made to track what needed to be done and who needed talking to. Then I pulled a copy of Rose's case file out of my backpack.

I could almost hear Zephonia scolding me. Even so, I ignored that little voice—*Rose needs me*—and dove into the file. With masking tape, string, and crayons, I started adding to the story collage. It wasn't long before everything was up on the walls. I stood back and stared at it. With a frown at all the unnecessary furniture, I shoved the bed against the opposite wall to get it out of the way.

"Better," I whispered.

I took out my journal and started making my list. Beatriz had already debunked Rose's going to Seattle. Even her phone had been wiped down. They hadn't found any ashes in the alley, but they'd found rain-washed blood. I knew that would be where Beatriz concentrated, along with the limo from the traffic cams. Perhaps there were some locals who hunted in the area. Houseless vampires weren't entirely unusual. Perhaps they would know who tended to the sick or injured. Even ticks needed healers. All I had to do was start talking to some of the locals.

With a satisfied smile, I took my empty cup to the kitchen and stared into the backyard. A giant orange-and-yellow moth sat among the herbs in the kitchen's window box. It had to be the biggest one I'd ever seen. I was so shocked that I nearly woke Elias to look at the amazing creature. Then it fluttered off into the darkness.

CHAPTER 21

The following day, only thing that took my mind off Rose was being with my fellow stewards. I hoped being at school was helping Elias cope. He seemed happiest on the ride home, when he got to tell me everything that had happened.

My eyes welled when my gaze rested on the picture of Rose and me. *Please, let Elias find good friends.*

"Knock. Knock."

Looking up from staring at Rose's gift and my pictures of Luis and Elias, I was ready to dissolve into a puddle, but I shoved that down with the promise of sticking the tick to the wall. Come hell or high water.

I turned to greet my partner. Zephonia's shoulders were down, and her eyes were staring at her bare, wrinkled feet. The hardboiled nixie actually had another fire-red pedicure.

"Zeph. How'd it go?"

"Fine. Cap's processing the paperwork and looking over the interviews." She nodded at the picture of me and Rose. "That you?"

"Yeah. With Rose."

"I'm sorry, chickie. We're going to get the tick. Bia always gets her man."

My chin trembled for a moment. Too bad she hadn't done that before he kidnapped Rose. I should've gotten him before he could come back.

Zephonia's lips twitched into a small smile, and she gestured to the other pictures. "Those are two handsome men there."

Staring at Luis's picture, I nodded. "I'm blessed."

Zephonia hummed. "I heard about his case in passing. Beatriz had it. It was weird. As soon as she got assigned the case, the perp turned up topside, starved apparently."

"I know."

For several long seconds, Zephonia stared into my eyes like she could will me to spill my secrets. I merely blinked, knowing better than to let any stray facial gestures slip.

"Anyway. Luis was quite brave for standing up to an azeman."

Scratching my nose—*stop it, Huri*—I pointed at the other picture. "This is the last picture of them together."

"He is so adorable. Those eyes! You are going to have your hands full with the girls later."

I watched Zephonia for a long minute, which made her raise an eyebrow.

"What's wrong?" she asked.

"Normally, people balk at my having a child so young."

Zephonia shook her head. "Honey, love knows no age. If I could've met my late husband when I was younger...that would just mean extra time with him. Time that I wouldn't trade for the world. Thankfully, I have Laura to remind me he wasn't just a wonderful dream. Han's dad was a whole other mistake."

My shoulders relaxed, glad she understood.

"The price of loving mortals," she sighed, taking a drag from her pipe. "Heavy first couple weeks, huh?"

"Yeah, not what I expected."

"Yeah," Zephonia said with a weak laugh. "I can't stand hearing stories like Frank's. Makes me wish I staked that tick while he was here."

"I get that."

"You got the tracker going on David?"

Thank goodness I wrote myself a note before my brain exploded. "Yeah." I showed Zephonia my circular hand mirror that displayed a map and blinking dot. "His tracker has him stuck at an old apartment complex for the past couple of days after roaming around the outskirts of town."

"Good work. How'd you know who to ask?"

"Jude. She was real helpful."

"She's a gem." Zephonia nodded as she looked around my office. *What's she looking for?* "Good. Now, I hate to be the killjoy, but..." She winced. "We need to see what this tick's been up to."

"I'm up for it."

"I figure you're uniquely suited, given your talents."

She was trying to make me blush. "Talents."

"I'll be on the ground. You'll be in the air. Good combination. Dave's not the brightest bloodsucking crayon in the box. I'm hoping he'll head to his house."

"Let's get to it."

Zephonia smiled and patted my back. "Stakeouts suck, chickadee. Don't be so eager."

Anything to get my mind off being a total failure.

Down in the parking garage, we chose an old Toyota Corolla that smelled like a cyclops had eaten too much chili one night...more like the entire weekend. I had to ride with my nose pointed at the cracked window. August was turning out to be way too humid to ride with the windows down and no A/C.

Zephonia eventually pulled into a lower-middle-class street filled with on-street parking and old apartment buildings. We looked down at the hand mirror. He'd been there far too long, perhaps a few hours. There was no way he'd stayed in his apartment without checking in.

"It's that one." I pointed at an apartment building ahead on the right.

"I'll check out the building. You get an aerial view of the area."

Flying is exactly what I need.

A moment later, Zephonia was exiting the car with a tin of cookies. I snickered at her grandmotherly costume before slipping behind a tree and taking flight. I did a lap around the building, watching over Zephonia and searching for any immortal scents. David's two coppery trails, one faint and the other newer, mingled with the mortal scents. The newer one stopped at the street and disappeared. I could imagine him getting into a car.

Time to report in.

"He's gone," Zephonia said when I appeared beside her.

I nodded.

She grinned. "Let's see what he can tell us."

What does this crazy woman have in mind?

I followed her inside the building and into his apartment. The unit was sandwiched between two others on the bottom floor—fewer windows. Zephonia gave me a strange, knowing smile as we stood at the door.

Her eyes indicated the lock when I just stood there. *Am I supposed to read minds?* "You want to do the honors, or shall I?" she asked.

Duh. "Oh!" I slipped the silk into the keyhole, and the silk twisted the handle and pushed open the door. "Age before beauty."

Zephonia playfully bumped into me on her way in, right hand already sporting her yew needles. My silk closed the door behind us and then wrapped itself around my forearm like a strange pet snake. My lips twitched to hide my hopeful grin as I armed myself, needles clicking comfortably into place. *Love that feeling.*

We moved methodically through the single-bedroom apartment until we saw that it was truly empty. *Bummer.* Neither removed our claws as we silently began investigating his apartment.

There were utility bills, something called a cable bill that was a month late, and several flyers for weight-loss support groups.

Bizarre. Zephonia chuckled and used her needles to poke at the stitch-marker-turned-earring. Based on how it was bent, he must've had to pry it apart to get it out. When I lifted the flyers for Zephonia, the nixie mimicked taking a picture. As I photographed them, the fridge squelched open, and Zephonia gasped. I took that to mean I should join her. There were baggies upon baggies of little cherry pills. With a dark smirk, Zephonia filled her cookie tin, barely able to close it when she finished.

The bedroom looked like a bad 70s porno threw up in it, bringing those silk briefs back to mind. I shuddered and swore I'd shower at the field office just for walking on the red shag carpet. Complete with mystery stains. *So gross.* Zephonia found a drawer with women's lingerie.

That's when I saw a cream-colored leather purse on the night-stand. It even looked expensive (and big enough to hold a type-writer). I dared to open the purse, revealing a pocketbook inside belonging to a Lisa Fuentes. It had all her money and cards, even her extensive makeup bag—and the makeup wasn't cheap either. Everything from the mascara to the strawberry body glitter was something Klara would buy. I dutifully took pictures of everything and replaced it as I found it. Then we returned to the Toyota.

"Which support group are we going to today?" Zephonia asked.

"Really? I don't get it. He was into nothing but super skinny coeds at the college. I figured he'd be into strippers."

"What do they call them? BBWs? They have more blood volume. Ticks love them." Zephonia shook her head. "What better way to have sustainable meals than preying on women who struggle with knowing their worth?"

Just when I didn't think I could hate this guy any more. I flicked back through the pictures until I found the clinic flyers. "There're six this week. But they're all across town."

"Same company?"

"Yeah."

"That's gotta be them. Which one's their main location?"

I scanned the flyers. "I think it's in Berry Hill. Half the meetings are there." I exhaled and frowned. "Right next to some train tracks." *Probably shipping out victims on the trains.*

"Well, aren't they clever. You see any cover for your alter ego?"

I pulled up a map on my hand mirror and expanded it for us to see easily. "Definitely. Buildings. Trees."

A half hour later, Zephonia pulled into a parking lot across the street on Berry Hill and slipped the Corolla into a shaded spot. "This is a definite 'do not engage' situation. You just need to watch who comes in and out."

"Got it. I can take cover in those trees or on the rooftop. What about you?"

Zephonia's answer was to drink from a vial hidden in her knitting bag. Within seconds, her age unwound. Her wiry gray hair turned lush and auburn while her skin became firm and golden. For a moment, I could only admire the natural beauty of a river siren.

Zephonia wasn't supermodel beautiful. She was simply pretty, except for the dangerous curl to one side of her mouth. Poor fools. How many men had Zephonia tempted into her waters with a song playing along that little smile?

"Better?" Zephonia wiggled her eyebrows.

"Don't go breaking any hearts."

That actually made Zephonia's cheeks pinken just a smidge. *Score one for me.* "I'm going to see if they need a fitness instructor or something. He doesn't know me like this. If he's in there. Just don't engage this time. You will definitely be outnumbered. You got that?"

"Yes, ma'am." I had no intention of taking on an entire house. *Unless it's for Rose.* That thought made my skin tingle.

She nodded. "If either of us spot anything, we call the other. Ear cuff on?" Zephonia unfurled her mass of auburn locks and readjusted her breasts in her bra. "I need to remember to get better bras."

Snickering, I kept my eyes fixed firmly on the passenger window.

"So we'll be able to hear one another, but I don't think that'll happen if you shift."

"Yeah, won't work."

"All right. Well, let me know before and after."

"Will do."

Zephonia rolled down my window. I took the hint, shifted, and swooped away, circling around the building once before heading for an elm. Within the cover of the leaves, I shifted back to use my ear cuff.

"Definitely a massive amount of ticks here. I can smell them everywhere."

"OK. I'm going in."

"I'm heading next door. Better line of sight from the roof." I shifted into the *Athene noctua* or "little owl" Athenas were famous for and headed for the rooftop of the adjacent building that granted a view of the front and side doors.

Hidden just a few inches inside the shadow of a dumpster, a muscled guy leaned against the wall. Once I shifted back to normal, I couldn't sense whether he was mortal or not from this distance. Perhaps there were other tells. He looked like a bouncer. *What does a weight-loss clinic need a bouncer for?*

"Hi, I'm Tori. I want to speak with the manager."

I grimaced and shivered when a male voice hummed like he was enjoying dessert as the front door closed behind Zephonia. "You're in luck, honey. I'm just the guy you're looking for. Name's Charlie. How can I help you?"

"Really? Your name tag says you're an associate. Doesn't sound very manager-y."

He chuckled. I bet this guy was falling all over the desk to flirt with Zephonia. "You caught me. He's not here at the moment. Sure that there's nothing I can help you with?"

"Well, I wanted to offer my services."

I gagged at Zephonia's breathy tone. *She better watch it. He's probably a puddle already.*

"Doing what?"

"I'm a fitness instructor. I've got lots of experience. You know, with yoga, dance fitness, pole dancing exercise."

"Oh dear Lord, Zephie," I groaned. "He's probably turning into a puddle of testosterone right now. Isn't he?"

"That's so perfect. I definitely need...I mean, we definitely need that."

Zephonia giggled. "Are you flirting with me?"

"Always, beautiful. Let me show you around. We're about to have a meeting in a few. So I'll have to make it quick. You can stay and see what I'm...we're all about."

"Oh, I'd love that."

So gross.

From the opposite end of the alley, a dark figure stalked to the side of the weight-loss building, bringing the bouncer out of hiding. *Thank the Lord for distractions.* I shifted and swooped closer when he put a hand on the shadow's chest. Landing upwind, I positioned myself on the ledge of the building, overlooking the door.

"Look, man." *The bouncer. Has to be. Voice's too deep.* "She told me no one was going back today. Not even you. Just wait."

"I've got to see her. Tell her it's important. She'll be pissed if you don't tell her."

The bouncer growled and spoke into an earpiece. "Denny, Dave's here to see Lisa. Says it's urgent." After a pause, he folded his arms across his massive chest. "He's checking. Just chill."

I ducked behind the low roof wall and shifted back to normal so I could access my bracelet. Almost belatedly, I remembered to double-check that nothing would reflect off the mirrored surface. *Safe.* A hologram of a keyboard appeared for me to type a message.

"What's up, honey?" Zephonia said.

Dave's down here at the side door.

"You stay your feathery butt put, chickadee."

I sent my agreement and waited as the door opened. The owner of the wallet emerged. Even from here, her makeup was next level. That quick look, however, was all I dared. With a swallow, I hid behind the roof wall and angled my bracelet up to record what was happening down in the alley.

"Wow!" Zephonia's voice pierced my ear through the ear cuff. "This place is amazing. You've got so many wonderful programs. I really think my skills would help these ladies. And guys, too." She giggled.

My eyes rolled back. *Why doesn't this earpiece have a volume button?* I made a mental note to tell Pater.

"Baby," David greeted her with a hand up. "Look. I know—"

"Where in the hell were you? You got arrested? How'd the cops find out?"

"It wasn't the cops," David answered, rubbing Lisa's arms. "I got hauled in by the bloody Stitchers."

Lisa's body stiffened, and she moved a step back. *Hmm. So she's scared of us.* Her head turned toward the bouncer. "Inside. I'll let you know when I'm done."

My nose twitched in her direction, trying to find the immortal scent. But there was nothing.

"Yes'um."

Once the door closed, she crossed her arms at David. "The Stitchers?"

"I gave them nothing. They said Frank flipped, ungrateful punk. But he don't know nothin'."

"Do they have it?"

I wish I could tell that she was definitely immortal, but I wasn't close enough.

"No, baby. What do you take me for?" He caressed her face. "I'd never give them anything. Even Frank was clean. Didn't have the goods on him either. We're good."

"The hell you are, David. They know you now. Those crazy old women probably got you under surveillance." She shivered. "With their creepy little needles. You need to lie low."

A message from Mama flashed onto the bracelet. Great. I tried to flick away the message, but I flicked too hard, sending the bracelet over the side of the building. *Skata.* With a grimace, I swooped down, talons leading, and grabbed the bracelet before it hit the metal fire escape.

"What the hell is that?" David hissed, backing protectively before Lisa.

I battled gravity for the anonymity of the roof's shadows, bracelet clutched in my talons.

"Just some hawk out hunting. I hope it got one of the rats running around here."

My heart jackhammered against my ribs. *Such an idiot, Huri.* I pressed my back to the small wall of the rooftop. With a glare at my offending bracelet, I shifted back to normal and shoved the cursed thing into my pocket. Then, I refocused my attention on the couple.

"—etting all knightly on me."

"I gotta take care of my lady."

There was a moment of squelching below. I dared to peek over the edge to find them making out quite vigorously. *Ew.* Then, Lisa shoved him back hard and slapped him across the face. It dawned on me that maybe I couldn't smell anyone except for David because he was the only immortal down there. Was Lisa actually a donor? She didn't act like it.

"Tell me more will come later," he purred.

"Get out of here," she ordered with a slap to his rear.

Lisa watched him go. Then, her eyes seemed to zero in on me, but the angle was off. Or at least I hoped it was. Instead of investigating, she banged on the door once, and the bouncer exited.

"Get Jules. Seems we have a rat problem."

Zephonia snickered in my ear. "Nice save, chickadee. Hopefully, you didn't get made."

I spotted her across the street and nearly flew over but decided against it when Zephonia sauntered toward the car, whistling "I'll Fly Away." *That has to be a code.* Upon spotting the two vampires tailing Zephonia, I paused on a rooftop to warn her.

"I know, chickie. I'm going to..." She hissed a curse in German.

There were another two moving from the shadows of the tree near the Toyota. "We've been made."

Zephonia hurried into an alley between the warehouses near the car. I trailed enough to cut off the four vampires from behind. None heard me as I alighted on a rail and shifted back to normal. It was hard to hear much of anything with all the street noise and music from a nearby mechanic shop. *Good.*

I balanced on the rail, my yew straight needles clicking into place in my right hand and my sedative needles in my left. They cornered Zephonia in the alley. The fools were harassing Zephonia like she was a potential donor. *Interesting. Maybe we weren't made after all.* Zephonia continued to play the unassuming, vapid victim even while giving me the nod. A grin stole across my lips. *I love a good fight.*

With that, I pounced, needles driving into the nearest vampire to break my fall. I shot my yarn out to jerk away a tick's hand from reaching Zephonia. Something slammed into me. Humid breath and snapping teeth inches from my neck and shoulder made me cringe. The vampire helped dislodge my weapons as we rolled away from the body.

Rolling on top, I shoved him down as my clawed fist jabbed. I grimaced when I hit bone, and then the needles redirected into soft tissue. He let out a howl as the yew burned his body. The third vampire wrenched me off his housemate by my hair and pressed something metal to the back of my head. *Bastard.* How I wished having a law banning immortals from having guns actually worked. Be nice if we law-abiding citizens could have them.

There was that telling click. My yarn hardened to needle-like points and stabbed at his eyes, missing when he shot at me. Thankfully, his shot went wide, only nicking my left shoulder. *Oh, you are definitely getting staked.* I growled through the pain and the ringing in my ears. I swore vengeance on those dumb laws as I swept his legs out from under him, gun skittering along the ground and going off again. I followed his descent with my yew needles. *Please, let Zeph be okay.* The shriek he let out when my needles drove down from his armpit into his heart made my blood sing. I didn't pause, jerking the needles free to be ready for the next opponent.

Zephonia dropped the final vampire off the end of her needles with a puff to blow her hair away from her face. She grinned. "So. First in comb...wasn't...exagg..."

"What?" Zephonia's mouth was moving, but only half the sound was getting past the ringing.

Zephonia dismissed her own words with a wave as she paused to wipe her needles on a convulsing body. I followed her example.

"Let's g...to be...ed...ash." Zephonia reached down and picked up the gun with a needle, inspecting the weapon briefly before putting it in her purse. "Pain to get out."

This ringing is awful.

"What?" I fought hard to suppress my grin. Adrenaline was making my body vibrate brilliantly. "I can't hear you."

Zephonia pushed me toward the head of the alley as the vampires' bodies began disintegrating into piles of ash. *Oh! Get out of the ash.* Coming to the front of the alley, Zephonia peeked out and indicated a few women who were coming to a weight-loss meeting looking our way.

"Run to the car," Zephonia said right into my ear.

I swallowed hard and nodded. With that nod, we both pelted toward the car. I had the worst time keeping upright. The gunshot had shattered my sense of balance. The women at the weight-loss clinic yelled for help inside the door, but we had a better lead.

Zephonia shoved her foot into the accelerator like gas was cheap, throwing me against the seat. With a hard swallow, I swung around to see if we were being followed, but the street was empty until a vampire ran back out from the clinic.

"We...send rep...Janis," Zephonia shouted.

Report? That must be it. Nodding, I fumbled out my bracelet. My hands, however, didn't want to type. Taking a breath, I started dictating, which made Zephonia snicker at me. It took me a second to realize I must've been shouting.

A moment later, my left shoulder was wet and starting to burn. Zephonia let out a string of muffled curses as she popped open the center console. My mouth went slack when Zephonia started driving with her knees and tending my shoulder.

"You lost your mind, woman?" I shouted as we dodged traffic.

"Shut it, rookie." My mouth quite nearly snapped shut, making me realize some of Zephonia's power laced that command. But Zephonia had finished the bandage seconds later. "That'll last us until the office," she shouted before settling back to take the wheel. Again, I could feel the tendrils of magic in her voice. *Is she using her voice, or does shouting automatically make it come out?*

My eyes moved from my shoulder to Zephonia. Did she really just do that? While driving? "Do this often?"

Zephonia grinned and let out a laugh that made my hair stand on end and made me envision happily running headlong into danger beside this insane woman. "Once or twice."

"What?"

Again, Zephonia waved away her words as I considered her. What would life be like as Zephonia's partner? I tried to stifle those thoughts and concentrate on sending a brief report to the captain. By the time we got back to the office and the healers had bandaged me up, the ringing had died down.

"Take it easy tonight," Zephonia said as she helped me put on my blazer once we stood beside Big Blue. I didn't want Eli to worry when I picked him up from school.

"I will. But really, I'm fine. Hearing's back at least."

My bracelet warmed, making me pause in adjusting my blazer. I swiped the mirrored surface, making Elias's face hover over my wrist.

CHAPTER 22

The sounds of the NFO parking garage faded. My heart bottomed out when Elias's tear-stained face appeared on my scry bracelet. Tears streamed down his cheeks. His nose was cherry-tomato red. At once, I swiped the mirror again to answer his scry.

"They're going to kick me out."

"What happened?" I shoved my hand in my pocket for my keys.

"I shifted. He was bigger, Mami."

"Was it that Chad kid?"

He opened his mouth to speak and then looked away. "They're coming back."

"I'm coming!" I said just as his scry ended.

"You want me to come with you?"

I startled, forgetting that Zephonia was there, forgetting that I was at work or even had to work. "It's okay. I think I better go alone."

Zephonia squeezed my good shoulder just as I threw myself into Big Blue. "He's going to be just fine."

"He's at a mortal school. What was I thinking?"

"You're thinking right. We should all be together. Just use those smarts you've got."

My shoulders relaxed a bit. "Thanks, Zeph."

One last squeeze sent me away.

I was such a fool for letting him go to that infernal school. Why didn't I listen to good sense? Why'd I listen to him when he begged to go? He was just a kid. What did he know?

It felt like it took a mortal lifetime to get to the school, especially in the rain. Why couldn't I have inherited teleportation? Curse genetics! I barely managed to put the car in park before running to the gates. I hated that these schools looked like compounds. It was like I was busting Eli out of jail. My skin was volcanic. How I wished I could bring down lightning on these imbeciles for not contacting me. Why hadn't they called?

But they were apparently waiting. The security officer guarding the gates gave a curt nod. *Total prison.*

"Ms. Rojas. Right this way."

Somehow, I kept my mouth shut for fear of screaming profanities as he led me down the art-peppered hallway to the principal's office. I noticed yet again that only the best from the upper grades were displayed near the offices. The secretary practically leaped to her feet when I burst through the door. *Smiting. Who's first?*

"Ms. Rojas."

"Where's my son?" I tried to look through the principal's tiny rectangular window, but the secretary moved between me and the door. *Oh no, she did not just try to get between me and my baby.*

"He's just fine. Ms. Palmer is with him."

"I will see my son now," I ordered and, like a scent hound, strained my senses to follow Eli's unique trail of fresh-spun silk and the fires his father once fought.

She rushed to the door I was heading toward and opened the conference room that could double as a storage closet. "He's right in here."

Inside were Ms. Palmer and Elias. His teacher's arm was draped around his shoulders as he fought to read *The Lion, the Witch, and the Wardrobe* to her. Ms. Palmer's russet face was a portrait of control when she set eyes on me. Not a coil of hair was out of place. How did she always manage to look so put together? My own curly mop did whatever it wanted. Elias threw himself into my arms, shivering like a leaf.

"I didn't mean to, Mama."

"It's not your fault, asteri mou." *It's mine.* I cradled him close, sending up grateful prayers that he was relatively safe and whole in my arms. I held him out to look at him, and magma coursed through my veins at the sight of my sweet five-year-old son with a black eye. At once, I looked to Ms. Palmer, who stood and straightened her 50s-style polka-dot dress into place.

"He was defending Jamie." She winced, but there was more. Pride? "It was Field Day. Some of the older kids were on the field with the younger ones." She dared to caress his head even while he was in my arms. "He was terribly brave. Tried to arrest the other boy."

I snorted, not expecting that in the least. His sheepish smile greeted me when I turned my eyes to him.

"Said something about being a Steward Rojas."

I couldn't help it. I laughed at that and curled him into my chest again, like I could tuck him away and hide him inside of me forever. Forever. He was never going to experience anything like this ever again. How I missed those days when he was growing safely in my belly. "Oh, agapi mou!"

"Ms. Rojas."

I turned back to see the secretary, who seemed to shrink away. This was why I was sometimes happy not to tell anyone what I was. That look in their eyes, like they needed to close the shutters and bar the doors. Break out the pitchforks.

"Principal Lafferty will see you now."

Oh, now she's ready. I dared to look at Ms. Palmer, who gave me a tender smile.

"I won't leave his side," she whispered and rested her hands on his tiny shoulders. "I want to hear what happens with Lucy and Mr. Tumnus."

"You've read it a hundred times."

She laughed. "But you're the first student who could read it to me. And to do it so well." Ms. Palmer squeezed my hand and gave me a nod. Ms. Palmer's coils danced like flexible springs as they turned back to the book. Elias always said that was what made her so pretty, her springy hair.

"I'll be back in just a moment," I told him.

With that, I fought to keep my temper under control as I entered to find the older boy's parents sitting with their hands on his shoulders as he sat before the principal's desk. They immediately started whispering when I entered. I couldn't contain a smirk at the two black eyes the boy sported. He had to have a good fifteen pounds on my boy.

Principal Lafferty rose but did not shake my hand. "Ms. Rojas. Thank you for getting here so quickly. We tried contacting you, but given the technological issues—"

"No, you didn't. Thankfully my son did your job." I'd have to thank Grandmother for that bracelet (and mean it this time). I glared at Lafferty, trying to forget the throbbing of my gunshot wound. "I've received and responded to every email update and every phone call in the past. I assure you there has never been a reason for you to fear that I could not communicate with you. What is astounding, however, is that I'm even in the room with these offending individuals."

The parents gasped as the boy quelled under my gaze.

"How dare you! When you put our boy and every other student in danger by allowing your son to attend." The father straightened his khaki sports coat with a snap.

"Who are you again?" I knew my face was turning red. *Don't blow up on this Rolex-knock-off-wearing fool.*

Principal Lafferty cleared her throat. "This is Mr. and Mrs. Danville."

158

"Of Danville Automotive," he interjected.

Is the sleazy used-car salesman actually trying to pull rank on me? I sneered at him. "Should I know who you are?"

Mr. Danville's face turned so crimson that I swore he would be the one to explode. *I'd love to see that.*

"And besides, what danger? Your juvenile delinquent assaulted a five-year-old who is a third of his weight because he was bullying another child in my son's class."

"Lies!" the boy bellowed with a squeaky voice. "Everyone saw him turn into some mutant spider thing!"

I scoffed and directed my attention to the principal. "I believe there were adult witnesses to this child's behavior. How do you plan on guaranteeing the safety of the students?"

"Your son is the danger!" Mrs. Danville yelled, her gold tennis bracelets jangling as she pointed at me. *Lord, have mercy. This woman is gonna get it.*

Principal Lafferty winced. "Phillip will receive two weeks' suspension."

My blood flushed with victory.

"Unfortunately, Ms. Rojas, Elias will no longer be able to attend Pine Ridge."

My skin turned to ice. "Excuse me?"

The Danvilles grinned like the cyclops who ate the sheep. *Oh, they're definitely on my list. In fact, I'm making a new Smiting List:*

- *Tick who touched Rose.*
- *Tick who stole Rose.*
- *The Danvilles and their juvenile delinquent.*
- *Principal Lafferty.*

"You know that the relations between immortals and...everyone else are strained at best. We cannot allow an obviously powerful immortal child to attend—not only for his safety but for the safety of the rest of the student body."

I glared at the family beside me. *Smiting. Why can't I smite people again? Wait until my girls hear about this.* All three of them were going to storm this school and demand justice. For a moment, the thought emboldened me. At least until I remembered that Rose was gone. She was gone.

Refocusing on the horrid family, my eyes narrowed as I glared at them and then the principal. "You're choosing this...boy over my son, who stood between him and another defenseless child?"

"He's being punished, and it's not exactly like—"

I flicked a dismissive hand at Lafferty's words. "Elias!" I shouted. With a growl, I snapped at the secretary to fetch my son. *Oh my word, I'm acting like Adonis. Horrible manners.*

"What are you doing?" Mrs. Danville demanded.

I held up my finger. "Just wait."

Within seconds, Elias entered with Ms. Palmer holding his hand. I nearly wept at seeing the thin lips and firmly raised chin, his little puffed out chest. He looked just like his father right before he would battle the blazes. Luis always looked like a warrior, a humble one whose mission it was to save rather than destroy. Elias looked like him in miniature now.

"Principal Lafferty. I believe you have something to tell my son."

"Surely not. This is something you should discuss..."

I gave her a silencing glare. "I will not do your job for you. I will not say those words to my precious son."

"You're kicking me out." Elias's eyes rounded. "For real?"

"It's for your own safety."

"He started it, Principal Lafferty. He shoved Jamie into the ground. He does this kind of thing all the time."

"He's being suspended."

"That's not fair. He's getting a slap...a slap on the wrist." He couldn't keep the tears from filling his eyes as he stared at Principal Lafferty. "I wanted so bad to go to school with people like my daddy, but you are bad people. You're nothing like him. You tell us we're safe here to be who we are, that everyone's the same, but you're liars. I'm a demi. My papi is...my papi was a mortal. My mami protects you all from the bad guys," he told her. He glared at his rival. "You're a bully. Your mommy and daddy should be ashamed of you. But they're not because they're bullies too."

Phillip cowered, but his parents bristled. I glared the parents into silence, draping my arm around his tiny shoulders. "Let's go."

"I'm so sorry," Ms. Palmer whispered to us, her brown eyes round, hand over her mouth as we left them all to retrieve his bookbag from the conference room.

I helped Elias put on his backpack and nearly scooped him up in my arms, but he just took my hand.

"I'll walk."

Those words nearly undid the thread of control holding me back. *Don't hurt those people, Huri. Go home. Eli. Think of Eli.*

Chin high, he strode out of the school and stayed as stoic as a statue, a statue that leaked tears which then mingled with the rain. My body shook as we drove home.

I had no clue where we were. I had no idea who to talk to. Luis was gone. Rose was gone. The girls were busy at work. My parents and grandmothers...oh man...they would lay waste to the school. *Ooo. Or maybe just the car dealership.*

All I could see was my beautiful, intelligent son having his innocence stripped away. At a stoplight, I dared to turn my eyes to the rearview. Elias met my gaze. At that moment, the dams burst, and sobs racked his little body. I wept with him as I managed to pull into a parking lot. I drew him out of the car, even in the downpour, and let him weep in my arms. My tears mixed with his as I whispered how sorry I was. *I'm such a fool. How could I let this happen to him?*

Swaying back and forth like I did when he was a baby, I fought to calm myself as I allowed him to expel his pain.

"Oh, sugar. Are y'all okay?"

How dare anyone speak to us! I rounded on the offender and found Claudette.

Hand on her chest like some debutant, she gasped. "Huri, honey!

What's wrong?"

"I got kicked out of school!" Elias wailed.

"Why on Earth..." Her lips thinned as she stared at one of us and then the other. "They found out."

"I turned into a spider," he said. "But he was hurting Jamie!" His face whitened. "I wasn't supposed to say that."

Claudette's crimson face somehow got redder. "Jerks! Oops. Pardon my French. Y'all come inside out of this rain. You'll catch your death. You can tell Auntie Claudette all about it over some cookies."

Elias perked up then. "Cookies?"

"Best cookies this side of the Mississippi." She wiggled her eyebrows at him. "What do ya say?"

I dared a smile as I followed Elias and Claudette inside. They sat at the tiny two-person table in front of the big window and chattered on about Elias's schoolyard woes over a glass of milk and a plate of cookies. Millie dared to peek out from behind her phone, eyes glazed. The teen crossed her arms as she pretended not to listen, but I watched her crimson lips grow thinner by the moment.

"Freakin' ridiculous," she growled and shook her head.

"I never should've let him go."

"No," she practically ordered. "They're wrong. You're not. The world's—"

Claudette cleared her throat and glared at her daughter, who cowered a little.

"—crap is all.

"Morries? Immos? We need to be together," Millie whispered. "Look what happens when we're one." She gestured at Elias as proof and, I realized, Claudette. A demi born of my forbidden love for a mortal and an immortal vampire who had the audacity to love and respect mortals. "When immos and morries get together, we are the best of both worlds." She punched my arm slightly, making my eyes roll back a little. *She hits like an anvil.* "That's what you're fighting for, Stitcher."

My insides softened a hint. "For a teenager, you're pretty smart."

162

She scoffed, a smirk playing at her lips. Then she immediately stared back down at her phone.

In a matter of minutes (and three cookies), Elias was wearing a subdued version of his usual grin. Millie strode forward at a nod from Claudette. The teen melted into tenderness and affability as she offered Elias a tour of the bakery. Claudette beamed at her daughter as they walked to the back of the store.

"She's a great kid, Claudette."

"She has her moments."

"Thank you for this," I whispered, trying to keep my traitorous voice steady. First Rose and now this. How was Elias going to cope with it all? "I don't know how we ended up here. I was out of my mind."

"I'm glad you came. He's a good boy. Just like his mama."

I blushed. "More like his daddy."

We smiled at the laughter that drifted to us. But Claudette's smile was too short-lived.

"Everything OK?"

"Of course." Claudette shoved her quivering hands in her pockets.

"Claudette, I can tell something's wrong. Tell me. Paul okay?"

The mention of her husband made her bottom lip tremble. "Of course. He's fine. Visiting his folks." She stole one of her own cookies and munched. "So...I wasn't sure who to talk to about this but..." She glanced out the front window at the rain letting up a bit. "Something happened. We were at...well, there's a group of mated strigoi, like us, who are trying to support each other. We all met at church, of all places."

"That's great."

"It is. It's wonderful to have a...a house...I hate that term, but it's like we're hardwired for grouping together...but anyhow...we're all business owners of one kind or another. And I was wanting to talk to Zephonia about it, but..." She worried her bottom lip. "Some of the others have been approached about selling those things you brought in."

My everything straightened. "Seriously?"

Her hands shook so much that I wanted to still them with my own. Instead, I watched Claudette practically inhale the remainder of the cookie and then shove her hands into her pockets. "They refused, of course, but the answer wasn't one those folks wanted to hear."

"Has anyone been hurt?"

"Not yet. But that's how these things work, right?" Her frown deepened as she stared unseeing across her store. "They'll come to all of us first. Choose one to make an example of."

"Are y'all safe?"

"Safe as can be for now." She rolled her eyes and ate a cookie. "Our affiliation is fairly well-established. I don't know that they'll really bother."

"But they may target you."

"We can fend for ourselves, Huri." She nodded like she was trying to convince herself. "But I wanted Zephonia to know."

"I'll let her know for sure."

Claudette managed a smile as our children rejoined us, Elias with a bag of cookies. We were sent off with entreaties to return soon and often. Elias smiled a bit brighter as he munched on an oatmeal cookie.

My mind raced with what Claudette had told me, wondering if they would be okay. The moment we arrived home and Elias retreated to his room to play, I leaned against the kitchen counter and scried Zephonia to tell her about Claudette. The sight of Zephonia's face paling told me Claudette was downplaying the threat to her family.

"I'll have the captain approve a watch put on them." She shook her head. "Tend to Elias. I've got this."

"Sorry it took so long. I didn't want to alarm Elias."

"You did right, chickadee." She winced. "Give him a hug from me. And take care of that shoulder."

My heart swelled. Every day I worked with Zephonia, I realized how soft she actually was on the inside. "I will. Go help the Brownes."

The doorbell rang, which caused us both to terminate the scry. No one who was allowed to visit rang the doorbell. I reached for a knife from a nearby drawer. Elias came out of his room. I promptly gestured him back into his room with a firm glare, hiding the knife against my forearm. He closed the door but left it open just a crack. I could see his eye peeking out of the cracked door. It would have to do.

A quick check in the mirror confirmed my jacket still covered my wound.

I swiped at the decorative mirror at the door. An image appeared from the viewpoint of the door-knocker. My eyebrows met. It was Ms. Palmer, now in yoga pants and a T-shirt.

I dared to open the door. "Ms. Palmer."

The young woman winced a smile. "Please, call me Addison. Forgive my intrusion. I got the address out of his file."

"Not at all. Would you like to come in?"

"I'd love that. I brought his work and things from his desk." She held up a box. Like the ones they gave folks who got fired.

I managed to return the knife to the kitchen without Addison noticing. Elias practically flew out of the room when he saw her. Addison's laughter flowed as she knelt to embrace him. She ruffled his hair.

"How's my favorite Greek?"

The smile diminished slightly as he shrugged. "I'm okay. Wanna see my room?"

"Absolutely."

I hugged my arms to my stomach as I watched Addison fawn over all the things in his room, freshly unpacked, but then I had to relax since my wound started to pulsate.

After the bedroom tour, Elias had to show her all of his favorite things in our new house, particularly the elms in the backyard. I cringed still at seeing him climb the trunk like a creature born in the trees. He was going to break his neck one day.

As he climbed, Addison stood beside me, smiling up in wonder.

"He's an amazing kid, Ms. Rojas."

"Call me Huri. And thanks. I'm one proud mama."

We stood in silence as he trapezed from limb to limb.

"What's your plan?"

"I don't know." My shoulders drooped. "I haven't even told my parents yet." I exhaled. "They will flip." Grandmother especially.

"You can fight this, Huri. There has to be change."

"I can't put him through that." My eyebrows raised. "Or the school. They might be idiots, but calling down fire and brimstone is not a great option." No matter how much I would relish doing just that.

Addison deflated as we watched Elias rebuild his safety webs so that he could swing from branch to branch. "I came to tell you about a school I've heard of. I've had my suspicions about Eli for a while. He's exceptionally bright." She laughed as she indicated his acrobatics. "Not to mention he's the most athletic five-year-old I've ever seen." With a wince, she wiped her face. "It's a private school out toward Ashland City." She shrugged. "But it's open to immortals. You heard of it?"

"No." *A place for kids like him?* "We barely managed to register him for kindergarten. Just moved from South Florida." I put a hand on Addison's arm. "You're telling me there's an immortal school around here?"

Growing up, I had been homeschooled until middle school, when I met Rose in our old neighborhood and begged my parents to let me go to regular school. Even then, we only lived over in Clarksville. (Fewer immos there. So less chance of recognition.) It had been all I could do to keep everyone from knowing what I was. I didn't want that for Elias.

"Not strictly. There are both. More mortals, of course. I have a friend who works there. I told her about how bright Elias is. She told me that she wouldn't be surprised if he's an immortal or half. Actually, she helped me keep him progressing. He was getting bored with the lessons." Her cheeks turned pink. "It's called Sydney's Bluff Private School. Fairly new. Just started last year. My friend said you should be able to do something called crying or something to get ahold of them."

Scrying. They knew about scrying. "You're serious."

"Yeah. I figured you knew about it."

"No. I've not come across a place for demis around here." No one at work mentioned it either.

Her eyebrows met, and then her face lit. "Oh! Demis. Like you mean demigods? Wow. That sounds so weird to say."

"Yeah," I laughed. "His father was mortal."

Addison nodded. "He told me he died. I'm so sorry."

"Thanks. It's been rough." I shrugged. "I didn't expect to have to do all this alone."

"I know what you mean. Well, appreciate it. But you've got a good family. You've done right by him."

My shoulder sagged. I wanted to start crying again but fought it. *Don't wallow like a baby in front of this woman.*

"Her name is Malory Langford. She teaches first grade. I sort of told her to expect to hear from you."

"Thank you for this, Addison. I..." My chin trembled. *Just keep it together, Huri.* "I didn't know what we were going to do."

"I'm so sorry this happened to you. Especially to him. He's such a good kid."

"Listen. Would you like to stay for dinner?"

"Oh, I would love to, but I've actually got a date tonight." She blushed and looked down.

"On a school night?" I laughed with a grin. *What a sweet young woman.*

"He works in the ER."

"First date?"

"Second, actually." She shrugged, but her smile was telling.

"Seems like a good guy. We'll see how it goes."

"Another time then."

"Absolutely. I would love to have more of that gala...galaboko—"

"Oh! Galaktoboureko. So good! Yes, and I will hold you to that."

CHAPTER 23

After Elias finally fell asleep, I stared down at the pamphlet from Sydney's Bluff Private School. My eyes misted every time I thought about my idiocy in letting Elias talk me into going to Pine Ridge. My parents had warned me against it. But did I listen? No. His excitement had clouded my judgment. He hadn't shown such animation since Luis had died.

A gust of wind shook the house before my front door flew open. I growled a bit when Grandmother strode in like she owned the world.

"Who are these *xenos* who dare harm my grandson?" she greeted me.

Elias stumbled out of his bedroom, rubbing his eyes. "Wha..."

"Thank you, Grandmother, for barging into my house in the middle of the night."

"Oh, my sweet boy," Grandmother greeted Elias, drawing him into her arms. "Did these mortals mistreat you? Tell me their names. I'll deal with the problem."

Elias's tiny eyebrows met as he looked to me for help.

"There will be no smiting except by my hand, Grandmother."

She glared at me even as she knelt on the floor with Elias. "These *xenos* do not know their place, engoní. It is not our way."

I crossed my arms. "I'm dealing with it."

"How? The boy languishes in this primitive education system. If you can even call it that." Grandmother beamed at Elias. "I've the perfect idea, son. How would you like to come to Olympia?"

"But I want to go to school like Papi did."

My eyes widened. She did not. "What happened to being the bastard son of a xenos? You're telling me now that you can unmake your own laws?"

"Why not? We altered Arachne's curse and now allow her children to not suffer under exile. We should make an exception for Dareios."

"Who?" Elias interrupted until his eyes brightened. "Oh. That's me. No one calls me by my middle name."

Grandmother extended her hand. "See? He doesn't even know his heritage."

"Because you practically exiled me twice over, Grandmother. First for Yiayia's blood and then for Luis."

She winced, crossing the room to hold me at arm's length. Every line in her face creased as she exhaled. "And I apologized for that foolishness, agapi mou," she whispered. "I do it every day."

I winced as I embraced her. "I know, Grandmother." *It's just not something you forget.*

She kissed my hair. "Let me help you."

"I can't be parted from him." I looked Grandmother in her storm-cloud-gray eyes.

"No Olympia?"

"No," I said and squeezed her arms to drive home the point.

"Stubborn! Curse genetics."

Grandmother turned to Elias and ushered him into his room with soft whispers.

Once she returned without Elias, Grandmother whispered, "Why do you do this, Pherenike? I thought we overcame our differences."

I chanced a smile. "We have."

"You even allowed yourself to be trained with our people."

I winced. "I did. But I must protect him from those who hate us. If this thing with the school has taught me anything, it is that. I forgot that mortals can be just as damaging as the immortals. Our family's enemies and politics are no place for my son. No place for me."

She winced. "You can't protect him forever, agapi mou. You too will become Athena after your mother."

Don't remind me. I nodded. "I know, Grandmother. But he's too young yet. You know that once they find out about being related to Yiayia, they would treat him like they did me."

I could see the memories clouding her eyes. While training, I had returned to her broken and bleeding day after day until I brought my enemies to the edge of death. Grandmother had taught me how to do that. Mama had taught me since childhood how to do battle, but it was nothing like what I had learned in Olympia. What I learned from Grandmother.

Grandmother exhaled and drew me close again, like she did when she would sneak away from Olympia to meet me in Clarksville. She would bring me wondrous toys that would fly in the air or dance like a real miniature ballerina. And she would cuddle me close as we shared firefly-lit nights, and she would fill my head with Olympia, a city of land and sea. When I finally arrived, the reality was a stark contrast to her tales. For all its beauty, Olympia was a dangerous place for mortals and naïve immortals.

I often wondered why, with all the family strife, Grandmother favored me so much. It was a question my cousins (everyone in the pantheon was distant cousins) had hurled at me all too frequently. It was common for the Twelve to have favorites among the cousins and to scorn their own heirs. I didn't have the heart to ask her. Perhaps it was simply because Mama had once been the darling of the pantheon. Mama teased me that I was the only one in the family with the guts to stand up to her.

Grandmother chuckled and squeezed me sideways with enough strength to realign my spine. "Very well. But if you would like some help with smiting, I am your woman."

I laughed at that. "The family who smites together stays together."

Her laughter danced through the house. "Well said, agapi mou. Now, I know you're getting by on your salary, but if you should decide to take an interest in politics..." Grandmother's eyebrows rose at me.

"I follow you, Grandmother, but I'm no diplomat."

Grandmother nodded and set the tea bags in our cups. "I've already put a call into some tutors."

"Too expensive. I can't afford that."

"I can. If he can't come to Olympia, then we'll bring it to him."

I exhaled and covered my face. "Grandmother, I know you mean well, but we're not doing this."

Grandmother fidgeted with the strings on the teabags. "I know, Huri." She sighed.

It took a long moment for me to realize that Grandmother was worried and that she used my first name, the name my father, the son of the traitor Arachne, had given me. I put my hand on hers and squeezed it. "We're going to be just fine."

"I know, my sweet girl." She winced and kissed my hand. "I...I feel like I'm tied up and can't help you."

I exhaled and rounded the counter to embrace her. "You are here, Grandmother. You are here."

Grandmother melted into my embrace. "I would fight the world for you and Elias, Huri," she rasped.

Water sprang to my eyes. "I love you too, Grandmother."

She gasped and squeezed me tighter. "I remember every time you've said those words."

I released her and presented a brochure. "Here. Look at this. It's the first in the region. There's a school for mortals and immortals to attend together. I'm thinking of seeing it."

That brought a bright smile to Grandmother's face. "Let me see."

I shared the pamphlet with her. After a few moments, Grandmother squeezed my hand.

"Any news about Rose?"

I could only shake my head.

Grandmother nodded to her unspoken thoughts. "I know the stewards have things in hand with Rose, but I've placed a watch on Alexis and Klara. I made sure that they're discreet."

Salt tears burned my eyes. *Will I ever stop crying?* "Grandmother," I whispered.

"I lost my closest friend once," Grandmother said, swallowing hard as she clenched her jaw. "Though she is just yards away even now. I don't want you to go through it. We will find her. And keep your friends safe at the same time."

CHAPTER 24

Trying not to mull over Grandmother's sudden appearance the night before, I sat at my tree-top desk and pulled over the information on the business licenses and tax information for the weight-loss clinic and started on them. A moment later, Zephonia wordlessly put a steaming cup of coffee in front of me and then retreated to her desk.

"Thank you."

Zephonia grunted as she sipped her own cup.

The coffee was black and hot and strong as a bolt of lightning, but it didn't help with the dead end I was hitting, so I flipped back through the lukewarm cases.

The first file I opened was of a were attack on a boy. Ten. Benjamin Walker. His most recent picture was in a sprouting corn-field, brown eyes bright and lively, skin tanned from hours of outdoor fun. He had been playing in the woods in Kentucky. My everything darkened at seeing his lifeless eyes. He might have lived if they had been able to find him in time. He would've lost a leg, but he would've been alive. The werewolf hadn't been found yet.

The next was of a man, late thirties with russet-brown skin. His last picture had been with his two daughters and his wife in their Sunday best. He was far from thin, and based on the number of bruises at key areas in his post-mortem picture, he was drained. The medical reports showed the same. My stomach soured when the other four cases were also homicides done by ticks.

"Package for you, Zephonia."

I didn't even look up, staring down at a picture of a sixteen-year-old girl left in an alley. Based on the photographs, she was all body parts and wounds. Her name was Sierra Lenora Reynolds. *What is that?* I drew the picture closer. A butterfly wing of some sort on the side of her arm. Was it a tattoo? I leafed back through the profile. No tattoos were listed.

Zephonia started cursing in German so well I sprang to my feet, needles drawn.

"What's going on?"

Zephonia motioned me over. There was a box with two pairs of canines and a severed tongue inside, arranged like a twisted shadow box interpretation of a mouth. *Wow.*

"Are those..."

Zephonia shivered a little and tapped her bracelet. "Bridget, I'll need you up here at my desk. Like now." She tapped the bracelet again and addressed me. "Go get Kari. She's the one who brought them to me." Then she shouted across the office for the captain. The volume alone brought Janis storming out of her office.

"Zephonia Weber, you're lucky I've known you for fifty years."

The nixie gestured at the shadow box. "So...how are those talks going?"

"Oh." Janis chewed her lip. "Why this though?"

"I bet they belong to Dave."

I blinked a few times, wondering how they put Zephonia together with Dave. But then I realized they must have gotten him to talk.

The elevator dinged, and Bridget came sprinting out to Zephonia's desk. Her eyebrows rose as she let out a whistle. "Definitely vampire canines. Haven't seen that in a while." She put on her gloves and picked up the box with its contents. "Normally, they just stake or starve their own snitches."

"Huri."

The bark-like order snapped me back to reality and set me running to the lobby. Kari was waiting in the reception area, twirling her cane like a baton. Violet munched idly on her apple, pointedly not looking at me. *Weird. Normally, she glares at me like a gargoyle.*

"Kari, who delivered that package?"

"Which one?" Kari patted my back as she limped into the office. "Never you mind. I'm coming, dearie. Not to worry."

Bridget lifted the tongue up with tweezers, noting the lack of blood, as Zephonia looked back at her approach and said, "Kari, please tell me you saw who delivered it."

"It came with the postal mail, dearie. As you can rightly tell from the packaging."

Zephonia hissed again, fishing the brown paper out of the waste basket. "Son of a gun."

"I'm heading down. There's no additional note or anything," Bridget announced, leaving without another word, package between her gloved hands.

"Thank you, Kari." Janis rubbed her arm. "If you think of anything else, let us know."

"What's the address?" I dared to ask.

"No return." Zephonia chewed her lip as she waved a hand at the paper.

That's weird. "There's no postal stamp either. The wavy lines aren't across the stamp."

"It wasn't mailed." Janis immediately took the paper with a tissue. "Bridget! Wait!" She pointed at someone in the lobby. "Get me video of the building. Maybe they snuck it in nearby."

With an exhale and arms crossed, I shrugged. "But who sent it?"

Zephonia chewed her pipe stem and relit it, puffing like a steam engine.

"It has to be whoever he was working for."

"Yes. Yes. In retaliation for the missing drugs." Smoke shot out of Zephonia's nose. "But who does he work for?"

No clue. But I wasn't about to say that aloud. Instead, I kept silent with Zephonia, whose eyes were fluttering back and forth like she was reading some invisible book in the air.

"I was just looking into the owners of the business," I offered.

"Already did." She retrieved a paper and passed it to me.

"When did you even have time to do this?"

"As soon as I got here." She waved a finger at the paper. "All owned by the same company, Brond Corp. Which is owned by another company, Manantial LLC. And another, Lasource Inc. And Pigi LLC. I stopped in the late 90s."

"It's a shell."

"I figure someone went through a Miss Piggy phase." Zephonia nodded. "What about at the clinic? Did you get to see anyone in the back—"

"Wait. Miss Piggy...but these names..." *Wait. That's not English. None of the names are.* "Pigi. Not piggy."

"Bad joke, I know."

"No. Pigi." I waved my hand to coax her along. *Come on, Zeph. Get it.* "Pigi means *fountain* in Greek. Modern Greek, at least. Not pronounced the same in Ancient but—" I shrugged.

"What on Earth are you saying?"

"Look. All of these. It's not English. Lasource Corp. That's French. Manantial is Spanish. All the names mean *well* or like a *spring*. They just gave the transliterated spellings."

Zephonia shook her head, mouth agape. "How many languages do you speak? Nine, you said?"

I blushed and looked away.

Zephonia scoffed. "I thought I was doing good with three. So...all the names mean *well*. Like having to do with water."

"Yeah. Like a spring or a well with water...I don't know a..." My eyes widened. "Lisa."

"What about her?" Zephonia gasped and slapped my arm. "Fuentes. Fountain."

I groaned. "My arm, Zeph."

"Sorry, but she was giving all the orders in the back. You're certain she's mortal. She couldn't have had perfume?"

"I'm like 80% sure. The apartment only had one immortal scent. But then again, I was farther away at the clinic. Plus, she didn't act like a donor either."

Zephonia growled as she tapped the pipe stem against her lips. "She was definitely living there with Dave."

"I'll check the lease. Maybe he was living with her."

"But why would she have her own 'roommate' killed?"

I scoffed. "How is a mortal giving orders to ticks?"

"Well, butter my biscuits, Huri." She snickered behind her pipe.

"Pretty gutsy naming those things after herself."

"Yeah. Arrogant." She hummed. "Check into the lease if you can. I'm going to have one of the demis look into the video surveillance for the office. When the computers start glitching on you, ask the captain for a research room down in the library."

"A research room?"

"Yeah. They just set them up a couple of years ago. They've figured out that we can be about three feet away before the computers start glitching. So, they've had demis and mortals working to get us some programs that are fully voice. I can't use them." She indicated her throat. "But you could. If that doesn't work, the captain'll have to assign you a researcher. Mine's Julie, but she's always snowed under, so..." She shrugged and saluted me with two fingers. "Good luck, chickadee."

The library was on the top two floors with windows bathing books, binders, and cabinets in full sunlight. A demi, Esmeralda, who wore a parchment-colored lab coat and smelled like snow and pine trees, directed me to the second floor, which was a techie's wonderland. Or at least that's what I guessed.

It reminded me of Pater's lab, where he was trying to marry mortal and immortal technologies. So far, he'd succeeded in bridging phone calls and any sort of messaging with scrying. It was the biggest breakthrough in modern history, but no one knew about it except our family. Too few on either side wanted to communicate with each other. Once they all stopped being afraid of one another, it would be a game changer.

"I'll wait right here while you give it a shot," Esmeralda told me once we arrived at a room with a pane of glass between me and the computer and flat screen.

"State your name and position," a British male voice greeted me once I stepped inside.

I looked back at Esmeralda, who grinned and wiggled her eyebrows.

"That's Mr. Darcy."

That made me snicker even as the voice repeated itself.

"Huri Rojas. Steward Detective."

"Welcome, Steward Rojas. My name is Mr. Darcy. How may I serve you?"

"Seriously? You really named it Mr. Darcy?"

"I could've gone with Colonel Brandon, but Darcy takes the cake."

"Steward Rojas, how may I serve you?"

"Just talk. He's pretty intuitive." With that, Esmeralda departed with a grin. "Ask him to read you the dictionary. It's like chocolate and a lullaby wrapped up in a voice."

With that, she departed. I checked my notes, wondering why everyone automatically wanted Darcy. Sure, he was rich, but I bet the guy never chilled out.

"All right, Mr. Darcy, I need to see..." This was too weird. "Can I call you something else? Super weird."

"You can change my settings to match your preferences."

"Thank the Lord. No offense, but I can't do the literary heart-throb thing. Let's go with Librarian. What databases are you able to search? Do you only speak or search in English?"

"Very well. I am the Librarian. I have a back door into every law enforcement database as well as those available to the public. Also, I am able to search in the three most spoken languages in the United States: English, Spanish, and Mandarin. If you need other languages, you just need to request it. I see Greek is listed in your file. All field offices have the capability to speak Greek."

I straightened, eyebrows meeting. "Seriously? That's pretty odd."

"It is in my programming."

"Why is that?"

The Librarian was silent for several seconds. "I do not know. There is nothing on file that says why."

My eyes narrowed on the screen, which displayed the four languages. "Modern or Ancient?"

"Both."

Seriously? "Do I merely lack the clearance, Librarian, for you to tell me?"

"On the contrary. I do not know why I was programmed to speak either."

"Who else within StS speaks Ancient Greek to you?"

"Now that, Huri Pherenike, is above your clearance level. No one here holds that security clearance, for that matter."

"All right then, Librarian." I paused, wondering what this meant. I'd have to save it for later. "Let's see if you can keep up."

I switched to speaking Ancient Greek, the language feeling at home on my lips. The Librarian was not kidding. He could keep up just fine as we started out looking for Lisa in the databases. I gasped when I saw the DMV record for Lisa's driver's license didn't actually have the same Lisa pictured. It was a fifty-two-year-old woman who immigrated from Colombia. The Lisa in the obviously fake ID picture looked nowhere near fifty-two and nothing like the Lisa Fuentes attached to the DL number. I exhaled and started looking for ways to find who'd signed the lease on the apartment. Leases, however, weren't public record like property deeds.

Property. I switched my search to the owner of the complex.

Brunnen Corp.

Hubris. Once again, Lisa's naming things after herself. I grinned and started printing. Brunnen was German for *fountain*. At Esmeralda's desk, the printer was working so hard it ran out of paper.

CHAPTER 25

It took a full week of babying my arm to heal from the gunshot wound. Klara and Alexis sat on the couch with Elias, grim smiles on their faces.

"Go find her," Klara said. "We've got Eli."

Elias gave me a nod. I couldn't lie to him about why I was going out, and I couldn't ask my parents or Yiayia to babysit. They wouldn't approve. "I'm good, Mami. Go on."

With that, I headed to downtown Nashville.

A few blocks away from the last place Rose was seen, I stood at the edge of an alley, arms crossed as I watched a pair of strigoi chat in the moonlight. With a slow exhale to ease myself into the right mindset, I tapped my owl pendant and felt my family's spider-silk armor encase my body like a second skin and then pulled on a jacket. I needed to ask Pater and Yiayia about armor for Elias. Maybe, since he could spin his own silk, he could help produce some.

With my armor on, I staggered to the pair, who stopped as soon as they saw me. I looked like I was wearing a black catsuit with a leather jacket, so they both grinned like kids and started whispering to themselves. I hoped and prayed that the perfume to mask my immortal scent worked. My heart raced a little as I stumbled toward them.

"Lost?" one greeted me as he fell into step beside me.

I huffed and rolled my eyes. "I wouldn't be if Sabrina and Lissy didn't run off without me. Have y'all seem—seen them?" I did my best to fall into them.

"You kiddin'? Why would you want to hang with them when they ditched you?" He smiled and helped stand me up straight. "I'm Sam, and this is my friend Darryl."

I dared to smile at them. *Could these actually be nice ticks?*

"We can get you where you want to go."

I gave them a deeper smile. "Way too nice. But that's okay. I know how guys are. Y'all act all nice. But I don't put out for just anybody."

Sam grinned, slipping his arm around my waist. I nearly jabbed him in the ribs when his hand slipped a little too low. *Nope. Not nice. Handsy like the rest.* "Well, I ain't just anybody, babe. And to show you we're on the up, there's a spot just around the corner that's got the best fries and shakes this side-a-the-Mississippi. Help get you sobered up a bit."

"I ain't drunk." I spewed a laugh. "That much."

Darryl grinned and gave Sam the thumbs-up behind my back, which I pretended not to notice. What a pair of douches.

They were actually good to their word, taking me to a late-night diner just a block or two away. Inside, Cool Kats Diner was chromed out, with the waitstaff in poodle skirts and black leather jackets. I snickered. All it needed were roller skates.

I took in a deep breath and nearly staggered the other way. The scent of copper saturated the air. Everyone from the waitstaff to the cooks were vampires of all kinds. My hackles rose until I saw a sticker on the front door and on every menu. It was a blood drop with a white cross in the middle. That meant they were a safe haven for donors. *Interesting.*

I dared to smile when the waitress approached. She eyed the two before looking at me. "Fellas," she greeted them.

"Order whatever you like..."

Oh yeah. Fake names. I need one of those. My undercover aliases needed to be revamped. "June."

"What a pretty name," Sam breathed.

"June, I'm Dennise. If you need me, you come get me," she told me with a glare at the men. "They're liable to chew your ear off."

I gave the two a knowing look. My gaze raked past the missing mortals wall behind the register. "Actually...I could use some help." I dropped the drunk act and pulled out a picture. "I'm looking for a friend."

The waitress half-smiled at me before picking up the photo. The two in the booth sagged against the window, frowning when I shot them a wink.

"Sorry, fellas."

Dennise hummed. "I haven't seen her, but she's a pretty girl. The ticks are always on the lookout for the cute ones."

I stared at her for a moment, unable to reconcile the stereotype with the caring immortal before me. I knew Dennise was different just by the scent rolling off of her. She smelled less coppery and more like a perfectly cooked filet mignon. "She was tagged, and then a few weeks later, she disappeared. They made it look like she went on vacation."

Dennise's hand shook as she set down the picture. "You sure she isn't in some tropical paradise?"

"Definitely."

I watched the three look away. *This can't be good.* My stomach roiled. I wasn't sure if immortals could get ulcers, but they'd probably find out with me.

"What's the deal?"

Dennise clicked her pen several times. "The bigger houses sometimes have favorite donors." She winced. "Closest you can get to being turned without actually being turned."

My eyes widened at the implications there. "If they went to the trouble…"

"I'm sorry, June."

My lip thinned. *I hate that everyone keeps acting like Rose is gone-gone.* Even Beatriz had started acting that way. They didn't understand. Rose was going to come home. Come hell or high water.

"I'll still post her picture. Just in case."

I got lost in the table's baby-blue and pink flecks without speaking. I was already making mental notes in my journal. It looked like I needed to start looking at the bigger houses in the area. Only a house with a lot of backing could pull the Cherries off. A house like the one that took Rose.

Maybe my Cherries case and Rose's disappearance weren't so separate after all.

CHAPTER 26

Days later, I couldn't get the diner visit out of my mind. *Special donors. Not great. But it means Rose is probably still alive.* My eyes stayed pointedly away from my tangled web in the corner with its array of unresolved leads on the Cherries case. The shell corporations dried up. So did tax records. All of it.

I looked back over the lukewarm cases instead, but I was merely looking, unable to process anything. My mind couldn't leave what I had learned in that diner the other day.

I exhaled and shoved the lukewarm cases away and pulled back the Cherries folder. Just as I settled in to find what I was missing, Captain Janis ghosted to my side.

"Rojas, where's your partner?"

I startled just a bit. Janis was famous for her stealth, and I wasn't quite used to it yet. She often smelled gamey, so I figured she was some type of hunter. "Bathroom."

Janis frowned but nodded. "I need you two in my office when she returns." Without another word, she turned on her heel and returned to her office.

Beatriz popped her head between my tree limbs. "That's ominous."

That was something else I was getting used to now. Janis had assigned her as extra help on the Cherries case. Which meant Beatriz had less time on Rose's dead-end case. But then again, the Cherries were a dead end now, too.

"Yeah. It doesn't sound good."

I couldn't pay attention to anything but the hall that Zephonia would be walking down. The moment she was in sight, I stood, which caught Zephonia's attention. A nod in the direction of the captain's office sent Zephonia down that way.

"What's up?" she asked as I sped up to join her.

I shrugged as we passed the hearth at the middle point of the room. A woman was prepping for pumpkin season, live autumnal garland sprouting from the mantel. "Janis just said she wanted both of us."

Zephonia frowned deeper than Janis and started puffing her pipe a bit more. "Something's up."

I couldn't disagree, trusting her instincts, as we entered Janis's office and closed the door at a wave from the captain. Janis winced and exhaled. My chest constricted. Something had happened to Rose or the Brownes?

"So...we've got a possible problem topside."

Zephonia's eyebrows made a deeper crevice on her forehead. "How so?"

"Frank is missing," Janis said.

My blood flashed with heat, grateful that it wasn't Rose or Claudette or her family. Just over the weekend, Bridget had sent us the confirmation that David's fangs and tongue made up the twisted shadowbox. Zephonia's mouth dropped open, barely able to catch her pipe before it fell.

"Proof?"

"He told his handler that he felt watched." Janis exhaled and wiped her face. "He hasn't reported back in four days."

Zephonia's lips thinned. "Four days."

"She's been scouring the area. Nothing."

The way Zephonia nodded made me want to stand back. Zephonia's movements were far too controlled. "Thank you for letting me know." She tapped my arm and departed. I had to rush to keep up.

"What are we doing?"

"Going topside. Pack light."

What about Elias? "But..."

"What now?" Zephonia turned with a snap that reminded me of soldiers snapping to attention.

I took a long, hard breath to fight the anger until Zephonia practically melted and put a hand on my arm.

"I forgot about Elias. If it looks like we need to stay longer, I'll send you back. Meet me back at that spot on the river where I took Frank in a half hour."

With a nod, I rushed up to the top floor and launched off the roof, shifting into an owl a moment after freefall. My mind raced with the people I needed to contact. The flight home gave me the time I needed to organize my thoughts rather than just being angry.

The moment I returned home, I messaged my parents and the girls, who assured me that they would watch Elias. It was weird to think that I was now obligated to keep my friends notified of my whereabouts because of their new status.

Getting a change of clothes felt a little less tense as I considered whether I should bring Amaranthian clothes or regular ones. I decided on one outfit of each; I shouldn't run into any of my pantheon since Zephonia would be taking me straight to Pakanahuili outside of Atlanta.

Packing done, I zipped up my backpack and headed over to Mama's office, where she and Yiayia were letting Elias help fold brochures after tutoring.

Over time, Yiayia started having immortals lend their abilities to finding missing persons. It was amazing to see predators hunting not to feed but to save, and even more amazing to see a mortal mother reunite with a child and then throw her arms around the shocked werewolf who mortals had shunned for most of his existence.

The office was located in an abandoned strip mall on the north side of Nashville. The windows were dusty and darkly tinted, but inside, the waiting room was bright and smelled of flowers.

One of Aristaeus's daughters, Delphine, was humming to several bees, who dutifully pollinated the flowers inside before Delphine opened a door for them to buzz away. She beamed at me with her giant blue eyes, the color of which seemed to inspire the flower for which she was named.

"Cousin!" Delphine embraced me with the uncanny grace of her grandparents Apollo and Cyrene. She kissed my cheek. "I wasn't expecting you in the middle of the day."

I winced. "I have a work thing."

Delphine nodded and escorted me back like I didn't know which way to go. "He's with Arachne."

One of the reasons I liked Delphine was precisely because she never called Yiayia "the Traitor," as most of our kin dubbed her. She had joined Mama while I was in my compulsory training in Olympia, a right no laws of exile could circumvent. Every son or daughter of Olympia was to be trained in combat by the best of Olympia, for when Olympia needed her troops to defend her. Even Pater had to be trained when he was young.

At first, I hadn't trusted Delphine, but then during training, I overheard some of our distant cousins snickering about Delphine being temporarily banished for hiding one of Aphrodite's oiketes, a word that once meant *slave* but now was spruced up to *servant* in the modern era with modern sensibilities.

Delphine had been so successful in her ability to hide the oiketes and the slave's daughter that neither were able to be found. Apollo's punishment was to send Delphine to work with Mama in America, the land that hated immortals, and to pay off her offense with the woman who married the son of the Traitor of the Pantheon, that cursed defender of oiketes. Aphrodite was reputedly furious with the insult.

I realized that Delphine was looking more youthful than the last time I saw her. Perhaps she had snuck into Olympia for a bit of revitalization.

After a light knock, Delphine opened the door to find Elias swinging in a web hammock in the corner of Yiayia's office. A smile filled Yiayia's face. Her parchment-like skin bore the crags of age in the best of ways. Each wrinkle was a roadmap of laughter and sorrow. Yiayia's body no longer held youth, but she had become a new model of beauty for me, one of grace and dignity.

For a centuries-old woman who had not stepped foot in Greece since her youth, she certainly aged like a fine wine. No doubt she had connections in the black market for Grecian lamb: just like Zephonia needed German river water to reverse her aging without setting foot in Amaranthia, so too did Yiayia need a delicacy of Greece, which was lamb. For Mama, it was eliopsomo, olive bread. It had been the same for me, at least until Luis had died.

"There's my girl. I've been waiting on updates." Yiayia gave me the usual eyebrow raise before putting her finger to her lips to hush us, pointing at a sleeping Elias. I let Yiayia squeeze me into her gentle embrace.

"Just got a bit of bad news. One of our informants is missing."

Yiayia studied me for a moment. "You have to go to Amaranthia."

I nodded. Somehow Yiayia always seemed to guess what was going on with me as a steward. "Little worried."

"Ricardo and I'll help with Elias in case you need to stay overnight." Yiayia hummed like she did when she processed information. "News on our girl?"

"Not really. I'm thinking that she may have been taken by one of the bigger houses."

"That would explain why it's hard to find her." Yiayia paused and frowned as she gave me one of her probing stares. I swore that stare was like x-ray vision for all my secrets. "You've been letting Beatriz do her job, right? You've got to trust your partners."

"Of course. I'm staying out of her way." I tried my best to keep my gestures as neutral as possible. Yiayia was far too talented at reading body language.

"Good. Even if you are lying." She exhaled. "I imagine you have to be rather quick about things. You've got your armor?"

I touched the owl pendant hanging from the spider silk cord. Within seconds, strands of dark silk spread over my body like a second skin. My silk armor was tougher than any kevlar vest and priceless. It had taken both Yiayia and Pater years to spin enough silk to cover me. Yiayia frowned as she caressed my face.

"We need to figure out a helmet. Your pater's working on it. Should be ready in a few weeks."

"It's fine. I don't plan on letting anyone that close. We need to get one for Elias, too."

"We're on it already." Yiayia gave me that cockeyed smile that I always knew spoke of pride. She gave it to me three times in my life: when I saved Klara from an attacker at a party, when Yiayia held Elias for the first time, and when I graduated from training with the stewards. In fact, it dawned on me that since I'd started working for the stewards, Yiayia seemed to always wear that smile.

"Your ambrosia?"

I tapped the pendant, and the silk retraced its path to my neckline. "Yep. Fresh batch."

"I wish you could travel like your mother. It'd take you just a second to get there. But I suppose Zephonia's more than capable." She nodded with her chin in hand. "No matter. Needles sharp, Huri."

The phrase jarred my memory, but I couldn't remember why at the moment. "Yiayia, you should've joined."

She let out a sharp laugh that woke Elias. Yiayia's face reddened as she covered her mouth. "Oops."

"Mama! You're early." He rolled out and landed on his feet like a cat. With a groggy grin, he hugged me. "You're done already?"

"I wish, buddy. I've got to go to Amaranthia for a bit."

His little shoulders fell. "Really? How come?"

"Just following leads, love. Yiayia and Nona will take care of you until I get back."

He frowned. "It's pizza night."

"I know. I promise to make it up." I silently begged him not to tear up. "I'm thinking it won't be just pizza. It'll be pizza and ice cream night."

Tears welled in his eyes. "Okay."

Yiayia and I shared a wince, but Yiayia would not offer any words of consolation. With an exhale, I knelt before him, caressing his face.

"It's fine," he said but wouldn't look at me.

"It's going to be just me and you this weekend."

"Did you go see the new school?"

I pursed my lips as I considered this line of questioning. It had only been a few days since the fiasco with the school. "I'm vetting this one, babe. We talked about this."

"The website looks promising."

"Look, Einstein, I know you're trying to be helpful, but I'm not so willing to jump right back in. I'm talking to all sorts of people this time around." My chin trembled as I ran my fingers through his hair. "I won't let you go through that again."

"But when? I need to go to school."

"I need at least two weeks."

"Two weeks!" He threw his hands in the air like I did when I was mad. For a moment, I wondered how Mama felt the first time I pulled this as a child.

"Yes, I'm interviewing teachers, staff, and parents. Your safety is my everything. Not budging on this. I've got everything set up already."

He glared at me and crossed his arms. "Fine. I want to go. I want to hear too."

Yiayia covered her laughter with her hand. I shot her a glare before looking at Elias.

"I'll record it. Once I'm sure, I'll let you tour things, of course. But only if they pass my inspection."

"If not?"

"We'll cross that bridge later."

He humphed and crossed his little arms tighter. "Fine."

I snickered and kissed his cheek. "I love you, Eli."

He mumbled something and wouldn't look my way.

"Elias." I caressed Elias's cheek to entreat him to look at me. "I'll be back as soon as I can. Be good for your Nona and Yiayia."

For a moment, he was silent before he squeezed my neck tight, whispering that phrase that he invented all on his own. "You're all over my heart."

I let myself drown in his love, squeezing back as I whispered the same.

CHAPTER 27

Zephonia was waiting at the out-of-the-way boat ramp, pack at her feet. I shifted as soon as I landed, readjusting my pack as my thoughts drifted to leaving Yiayia and Eli. "How's Elias?"

I really need to fly more. Trying to slow my breathing to a steady pace, I winced and shrugged. "He's adjusting. Thought I was there to pick him up early."

Zephonia winced. "That's the worst. I don't know which I hated more. When they did that or grew to expect my visits to mean I was going to be away."

That statement punched my gut. I resolved to make the reasons for work-hours visits more balanced.

"So, has anyone taught you how to travel?"

What? "I can't teleport. It's in my file."

She half-smiled. "Your mother is able."

"My father isn't."

"Even so. You should be able to, considering you were born there." She clapped her hands. "So. It takes a lot out of you. Before and after you travel, you should have the biggest meals you can. That's at least my experience. Usually your ambrosia."

I nodded. *This isn't going to go well.*

"Have you been often?"

"Somewhat."

"I'll give you pointers on this go around. It works for other Amaranthians. But you're attempting the return trip."

"I've never been able to before. Believe me, I've tried."

Zephonia shrugged my words away. "We'll see. This is how it goes for me."

Going to Amaranthia always reminded me of all the reasons I never wanted the girls to visit. And now, they were obligated to. Certainly, it was beyond beautiful, and the air alone was invigorating, but the first time I watched a mortal mother send her daughter off at seven to be trained on how to serve the immortals of Olympia, knowing what would be expected of that little girl, I just couldn't stomach it.

Zephonia was halfway through explaining before I heard her speaking. "...have to have water. You will have to find your way. The few Greeks I've known travel according to their dominate side."

I nodded like I had been paying attention.

"Are you ready? I have to sing you through."

My eyebrows rose. "Oh." *How did I not think of that?* "OK. Sure."

Zephonia laughed, eyebrow raised like she knew I hadn't been paying attention at all. "Here we go."

I braced myself as stoically as I could, but as Zephonia's voice filled my ears, all my worries appeared to drip away if only I would come with Zephonia to Amaranthia. All at once, images of Amaranthia's beauty and wonders filled my mind while still seeing Zephonia standing in front of me, hand on my cheek much like she had with Frank.

What the actual—This is the worst idea. Why am I getting in the water? It was like the sounds themselves were caressing my arms and body forward. My hackles rose. *Nope. Not happening. No way am I getting in any water.* I growled and stepped back. Zephonia's song cut off. The only thing I could only hear was the whooshing of my heart.

"Huri."

I let out a growl that now sounded like a hiss. That was when Zephonia said what I was just realizing.

"You've shifted, Huri."

With a shudder, I returned to normal. "I...I don't like that."

Frowning, Zephonia indicated me with a sweep of her hand. "Proves my point. Most of the pantheons are resistant to my voice."

I glared at her, not knowing why. Zephonia wasn't doing anything wrong. It took looking at anything other than Zephonia to calm my crazy emotions.

"Once, when I was much younger"—Zephonia snickered almost fondly—"I sang to your uncle...cousin...whatever...Poseidon, not knowing who he was. He was an...interesting find."

Ew. "Zeph!"

Biting her bottom lip, Zephonia smiled into the distance for a minute, which made me cringe even more. "Anyhow." Zephonia wiggled her eyebrows suggestively. "This complicates things. You have to learn how to transport yourself, chickadee."

"Nope. I just can't. Let's go again..."

Zephonia laughed. "Won't work. The more I sing to you, the faster you'll shake it off. Which will be something for another day. You won't need those earplugs soon enough. Since you shifted, I'd suggest that you use that. Seems logical. Have you only been to Olympia?"

"My mother usually takes me to Pakanahuili before we make the jump to Olympia."

"Right." Zephonia swiped an address to my bracelet. "In case we get separated, let's meet at the Pakanahuili Field Office."

"Wait...how...how do I do this?"

Zephonia quirked a pointed eyebrow. "You need to will yourself.

Hold tight to the place in your mind. Consider every detail. Smell it, feel it, hear it. I would suggest shifting the moment you feel ready. When I go under, I imagine there is a sort of hole in the riverbed, like a doorway if you will. Perhaps a cloud or archway in trees will work for you. Then with every fiber of your being, you push yourself through that spot into that picture you have of Amaranthia."

Great. No way this can go right. I mean, wrong. Whatever.

"I'd eat first."

I nodded and took out a bit of pan de jamón, making sure to get a bite with all three parts. The rest I saved for later. With a slow exhale, I recalled the transportation room in Pakanahuili, but my room in the Athenas house crept into my mind. I wrestled back the transportation room, trying not to consider that I was probably going to be waylaid. The effects of that bite of ambrosia warmed my body.

"I'll wait while you try."

"What if I can't?"

"You will. No doubt."

My room filled my senses with its expanse of windows opening to the gardens below, the silky feel of the pillows at my window seat, the smell of Grandmother's eliopsomo warming the air with doughy goodness.

No. Focus, Huri.

The stone transport room with its ancient moss-covered stones. I fought to push myself into the transport room, but my room at Grandmother's house took over. It felt like I was there, but the birdsong and hush of the river told me I was still in Tennessee.

I shifted, pretending I was flying to Grandmother's house—no, the transportation room—and going in through the open doors of the balcony—no, the stone archway. *This's never going to work. I told Zephonia this.*

With a burst forward, I forced myself through the doors. Then I hit something hard.

I screeched in pain, opening my eyes at hearing a chuckle. There was not only my grandmother but Zeus Thaddeus. *Of course. The ruler of the Twelve just had to be here.*

"How do you always attract the strangest creatures, Alcis?" Thaddeus chuckled, crouching to straighten owl-me. Unfortunately, when he crouched, I got a full view of something I never wanted to see. Ever again.

"My lord!" I shifted and hid my eyes. "No offense, but haven't togas gone out of style?"

His eyes crackled with lightning until I tipped over to the side with a groan. Grandmother shot Thaddeus a frown and pushed my hair out of my eyes. "Asteri mou, how, by the stars, have you come here?"

I groaned a little. "I was trying to go to Pakanahuili."

"Surely this isn't your first time teleporting, Pherenike," Grandmother said.

I exhaled my annoyance at Grandmother using my Greek name and pushed myself up to stand. Pater had chosen my first name and Mama, my middle—which had to be Greek.

"Sorry. I couldn't envision the transport room that well."

"How is it possible that an heir doesn't know how to teleport herself home?"

Grandmother cupped my face and studied me for a moment, plainly ignoring the comment. "A happy accident. Let's get you seated." She helped me to a bench beside the door, making me realize I didn't even get to the balcony but the door on the bottom floor. "Chloe!"

The dance of blue along the ground drew my eyes to the heavens. Hundreds of feet up, the crystalline dance of the Mediterranean Sea blocked out the sky. I grimaced inwardly. It always made me claustrophobic to imagine all of that water overhead. The Poseidons had created the Twelve's palaces centuries ago when the pantheon underwent one of its many xenophobic phases. Since then, it had become a surefire way to wow the world's leaders.

Chloe, Grandmother's mortal maid, obeyed at once. She had

served Grandmother for thirty years, just as Chloe's mother and grandmother and great-grandmother had served the Athenas for generations. "Yes, my lady? Ah! Pherenike! It's so wonderful to see you!"

I managed a smile. "Good day, Chloe."

With a wave of her bangled arm, Grandmother said, "Could you fetch a bowl of olives?"

"Yes, my lady." She bowed herself out to each in turn. "My lord."

Grandmother raised an eyebrow at me. She looked so like Mama when she did that. It was the black curls and gray eyes, calculating and warm all at once. "What's this about? You've never teleported before. We didn't even think you could."

"I'm here for work. My partner tried to ease me in, but apparently my brain doesn't like siren song." Now I knew why Mama never taught me teleportation. My brain was mush.

Thaddeus's growl deepened as he frowned. "I should think not. Who is this xenos? She should know better. Daring to poison you."

I took a deep breath. "Not poison, my lord. She was trying to help."

Thaddeus crossed his impressive arms. His jet hair was silvered in places, like a chameleon changing its colors, except usually that color change meant lightning would strike soon. "You're under my charge. I won't have those xenos stepping all over you—"

I knew my face betrayed my thoughts because his lips grew thinner, and the gray in his hair started turning platinum. "My lord, with all due respect—"

Chloe's arrival drew my attention, stopping me mid-sentence.

"Thank you, Chloe."

"My pleasure, dear." She set the bowl at my right hand.

At once, I began eating the bits of food. "You remembered the ham? You are a wonder."

"Of course, agapi mou. There's a slice of eliopsomo at the bottom."

"Thank you, Chloe," I called as Chloe disappeared.

My body warmed slightly, not nearly enough, but I felt better. Less mushy. I dared to look up at Grandmother and Thaddeus. He growled, which always sounded like thunder.

"The Athenas need to take better care of their whelps," he said, eyeing Grandmother. "Being raised abroad has damaged—"

Grandmother gave him that raised eyebrow as her entire body addressed him. "Mark your words well, Thaddeus."

"This"—he waved his hand at me—"makes us appear weak to the world. I am seriously considering recalling the Athenas from abroad. Honestly. Working as a Stitcher. Of all things. Now taking douleútria."

The silk around my wrist quivered like a viper itching to strike. I straightened to my full (and unimpressive) height, eyes narrowed. Then I sneered at him. "Of all things. An honest day's work. Living alongside mortals and immortals like we're all equal." I clicked my tongue. "Yeah. Real weak."

"Pherenike," Grandmother hissed, eyes round.

Thaddeus stepped forward, his massive chest coming to my eye level just inches from my face. "Who are you to—"

My heart pounded in my chest. *Man, this guy's huge. Good. He'll fall harder.* I hated that I had to crane my neck to look up at him, but I did. "We are the diplomatic arm of the Twelve, Zeus Thaddeus. Without us in the world, your precious trade agreements, the things that keep your coffers full and your bed filled with...warmth...the Eleven would be left—well, Atlantis should be a nice picture of what happens to isolationists."

His hair had turned completely platinum. *Bring it, big guy.* His voice dropped so low that only I could hear him. "You are a child, trying to play at being an adult. Go back home to your dead husband and your mongrel. I'd hate for something to hap—"

Oh no, he did not. My body burned, and the world around me slowed. He was going to die. My swords were in my hands without realizing it, but Grandmother caught me and shoved herself between us. "Leave my home, Thaddeus."

"You will tame your tongue, Pherenike."

I growled. "You threaten my family again, old man, and I will bathe in your blood."

Grinning at me, he let lightning play along his fingertips. "An unwise Athena." He snorted and opened his mouth, but Grandmother took him by his corded forearm. The two disappeared.

I could hardly breathe, barely able to see Chloe staring at me with widened eyes.

"Pherenike," Chloe called, hands up like I was a wild animal.

"He threatened my son," I hissed, shaking. "He threatened my son."

"No," Grandmother said, appearing exactly where she had been standing moments before. "He was goading you, child."

I realized the silk on my arm was poised to strike if anyone came too close.

"And you fell for it." Grandmother granted Chloe a tender smile. "The usual."

I forced myself to see that Grandmother was fairly calm. My eyes closed. *Breathe, Huri. Calm down.*

"Have some tea, dear," Grandmother bade me once I opened my eyes. Apparently, Chloe had brought out a tea service.

"He threatened Eli," I said but sat. "He tried that nonsense with me when I got pregnant."

Sitting at the table, Grandmother gave me a long-suffering look. "He threatened Apollo Sophus's grandson the other day. Thaddeus likes to poke every bear he can find as often as he can. And you're an easy target."

I glared at the spot Thaddeus once inhabited. "He'll learn not to poke this mama bear."

Grandmother snickered into her tea. "By the stars, child, you're so much like your grandmother." Her eyebrow arched. "My mother," she said when my brow furrowed. "She was the fiercest person I've ever known. A temper." She whistled with a shake of her head. Her eyebrow peaked over her left eye. "But she learned how to harness it."

Fighting the impulse to roll my eyes, I stared at my tea before taking a sip. "Point taken, Grandmother."

She exhaled and nibbled a scone. "Now, what's this about work?"

I exhaled, wondering how to walk the line between confidentiality and concessions. She was the current delegate for the Greek pantheon in the Amaranthian Society, which meant she had an ear everywhere, including StS.

"Part of our investigation has led us here."

She beamed like a beauty queen who had just won the questioning portion. "Spoken like a fine politician."

I continued to stare at the spot Thaddeus vanished from, remembering how red his face had gotten when I told them I was pregnant. He was ranting about how no immortal before their first century should be having children. I knew he was about to order me to do something heinous based on what my distant cousins had whispered had happened with them when they had unplanned pregnancies.

He had pointed at my stomach. "If it's mortal, it will be terminated."

I had never been so angry in my life. "Mortal or immortal, this is my child. I don't care who you think you are, old man. But if you or anyone in or tied to this family comes for my child or my husband, I will dance on your ashes."

Thaddeus nearly slapped me for my insolence. Naturally, I didn't trust him after that. I never ate from his table while pregnant or brought Elias to Amaranthia to meet him. In fact, I did not see him again until the day after Luis died.

I was so blinded by grief that I stormed into his home and demanded to hear from his lips whether he'd had a hand in my husband's death. His guards promptly threw me out, but it took ten of them to do it. It was only a matter of days after that that I found, drained, and then starved the azeman who killed Luis. Grandmother sat with me afterward as I cried in silence.

"The love of mortals is deeper than anything we know, Pherenike. It is more euphoric than ambrosia and more deadly than your grandmother's venom," Grandmother had told me.

Grandmother laughed a little, jostling my mind back to the present. Toying with my hair, she said, "I'm glad Zephonia has seen to travel. I look forward to seeing you and perhaps Elias more at home."

Subtle. Super subtle. Of course she knew my partner's name and probably everything else. In the next moment, I realized that I would be able to come to Amaranthia more often. Oh no. What a gift Mama had given me in not teaching me how to teleport. A small hedge of protection. Now that was gone.

"I'm surprised Philomache didn't teach you."

I didn't have an answer for that implied question.

"I'm sure you must head out to your work. But I do insist you and your partner stay with us. I won't meddle or ask questions—"

Because you can find out from Janis exactly what's happening.

"But I'd like to get to know this new part of your life."

That was nice. I nodded. "I'll talk to her. But we may not be here that long. Depends on how things go."

She smiled, caressing my cheek. For some reason, having a grandmother who stopped aging at thirty always creeped me out. *I suppose, given our agelessness, that I'd probably freak out if she suddenly started aging.*

"I'm truly glad you've managed traveling. I've missed having you here since you finished your training."

Eyes down, I could only nod. While the girls had been in college, I had been splitting my time between Earth and Amaranthia. Grandmother saw to training me in more than combat. Being alive for centuries hadn't changed the violent tendencies mortals told stories about. During my time on Amaranthia, I had seen the beauty and the advancements of Amaranthian life. But I had also seen the darker parts. I had even been the darker parts.

I nodded again, recalling the long walks with Grandmother after training. It was the only redeeming thing about that period. I got to reclaim the grandmother of my childhood, the one who had once befriended my yiayia.

"Me too," I said because that was the polite thing to say. As much as I was a Greek, I was a Southerner too. And Southerners were always polite.

CHAPTER 28

I politely refused Grandmother's entreaties to take transportation to the surface. It'd only take more time and clog the already congested streets. Besides, I needed the walk. I eventually wound my way from my future home and the homes of the other rulers and arrived at the Tunnel Market.

In the Tunnel Market, a two-mile-long bazaar that bridged upper and lower Olympia, oiketes and freeman completed errands as salesmen hawked their wares. Children kicked a soccer ball between the legs of the adults. I couldn't help but snicker at the fact that even in Amaranthia, the mortals' sport had a strong presence. A giant shadow raced along the ground, drawing my eyes to the serene sky. An *ornisharma*, with its golden metallic wings stretched wide, glided overhead. Despite myself, I smiled at the machine, wishing that Elias could see it.

The thing that struck me most was how clean Olympia was. From each litter-less street to the pristine clothing, nothing was out of place. It always made me feel like I was in a romantically sanitized vision of history. Few mortals here knew any life beyond the confines of Olympia; fewer still were allowed to travel into the city-states of

Amaranthia. Somehow, it was still illegal to formally educate the oiketes beyond what their duties necessitated. Their healthcare was just enough to sustain them. I remembered the first time Mama snuck me into Olympia to show me that diseases the freemen could easily treat ravaged the oiketes. Many times, the mortal medicines Mama brought were too late to really help.

I glared at the temple that served less as the Aphrodites' home and more as their offices.

My nose twitched when the heady musk of rose and anemone wafted to me. I groaned inwardly when I spotted Adonis striding toward me from between the columns, along with a gliding Aphrodite Oenone. *Of course.* Adonis grinned his boyish grin at me.

"Pherenike," Adonis called with a wave.

I pretended not to hear as a girl of six dribbled a soccer ball between her feet and then danced around me. Seeing the girl made me pause. Already, her future was marked by the red-and-gold sash across her white dress. It meant that in a year, the girl would be taken from her family and into training to be one of my distant relation's servants. Based on her luxurious black curls and her dimpled cheeks, I knew someone was laying claim early. No doubt that was why she played outside the temple. For this girl, her duties would be far more than just cooking and cleaning. She would become a *hetaira* and would be sterilized shortly after her first period.

I closed my eyes at the memory that many considered being a hetaira to be an honor. At least, they felt that way until they grew too old and wrinkled to warm their lovers' beds. Then they watched their less desirable sisters have sons and daughters and grandchildren while they trained the next hetaira who would serve their former lovers. The girl passed the ball to a little boy with a similar sash and a similar future.

I hummed and pushed those thoughts aside. Both children were too close to Elias's age for comfort.

"What a small world," Adonis said with a clap to my back, jolting me from my thoughts.

"We're seeing too much of each other." I greeted Adonis with a punch to his arm and then turned to Oenone, who was adjusting the strings of pearls in her hair. "Oenone. A pleasure as always."

"Welcome home, Pherenike." She placed a delicate kiss on my cheek and fought to avoid my gaze. It must have been because her grandmother was still upset about Delphine's punishment. "What are you doing here, Pherenike?"

"Working, actually." I winced at Adonis, whose playfulness disappeared.

"Here? Can't you take some time off?"

"I'm actually on my way to the field office now."

"Then we'll walk with you," Adonis said at once, which gained a sigh from Oenone. "You're such a killjoy. How often do we get to see Pherenike here?"

"Not infrequently enough," Oenone muttered.

I failed at hiding my laughter. "Really. I'm just going to the office and then heading to Pakanahuili."

Oenone beamed at the girl playing soccer until the girl bumped into her. I didn't miss the flash of anger that swept over her face for a brief moment.

"I'm so sorry, my lady," the girl whispered, eyes downcast.

Oenone cut her eyes at me. *Yeah, I'm watching you.* "Fair child," Oenone said and caressed the girl's face to bring up her chin. "You've got to keep your feet light. Chest tall." She pulled up her volumes of skirts and dribbled the ball between her sandaled feet. She passed the ball to the girl.

"Thank you." The girl laughed and hurried away, doing just as Oenone instructed.

Oenone patted each pearl and pleat of her dress back into place and looked at me with an almost challenging eyebrow raised.

Priss. My lips twitched to keep from snickering as we started off toward Old Town, which pretty much began at the temple. "It's so nice to see you take such an interest in educating your *pornai.*"

Oenone sighed and rolled her eyes. "Your thoughts about my

subjects are made so primitive by your prudish American ways. If this is what living abroad gives us, I shall endeavor to put forth laws to keep us all home, as is proper."

"Well, thank the Lord that you're not actually in charge of anything but giving mediocre blow jobs."

Oenone huffed and stomped her foot. "My exploits are never mediocre." She grinned at Adonis. "Wouldn't you agree?"

Adonis let out a tight laugh and threw his arm around my shoulders, dragging me away. "You're both so witty." His lips moved to my ear. "Seriously, you need to not jump down everyone's throat when you see them."

I pushed him away; Oenone's perfume clung a little too well to him. "I give back what is given to me."

"Let's go, Adonis. Pherenike's prudishness dampens the air like a wet rag."

Jerk. My silk loosened into striking position at my wrist, but then I sensed silk nearby. Coming from Oenone's shoes. Was she actually wearing silk sandals? Without a thought, I snagged one of the stitches along the seam of one of the sandals. Oenone staggered a little when the sandal practically unraveled with each step. *Petty. I know. But don't judge.*

Adonis's eyebrows rose at me. "Seriously?"

"Go on, Adonis," I said. "Your lover's waiting."

His lips thinned. "You're being childish."

My mouth dropped open. Well, perhaps the shoe was childish, but the rest? "You're too good for her," I whispered and crossed my arms. "Even if you are a complete Neanderthal."

His dark-gray eyes, almost blue in the right light, creased at the corners as a tender smile curled one side of his lips. "Yes, well, the only other who is remotely worth my time is still in love with another man."

"And she doesn't date her cousins. Even if only distantly related."

"Adonis, let's go!"

He grinned and kissed my cheek, lingering. His proximity

reminded me that Luis had been the last man to be this close to me. "Makes it all the more naughty. Happy hunting. Cousin."

I had to punch his arm for that and hurry away as I wiped away his kiss. *So gross.*

Trying to forget Adonis's weirdness, I made my way into the outskirts of town. It was no less clean in this area, but the smell of disease wafted past my nose. The Olympia Field Office was in an abandoned house on a back street close to the northeastern wall of the city-state. It looked like a hole in the wall compared to Nashville's FO. When I walked inside, I saw it was manned by five stewards, all cramped into a single tiny room. I had forgotten how small it was—I had first seen it when I snuck in one night to speak with a steward about joining.

The steward had gone pale and instructed me to apply on Earth and not to mention them, which is why I had dutifully forgotten the field office. The five seemed to be waiting for me and immediately escorted me to the teleportation room.

"Just speak your destination, my lady," one bade me. None seemed to want to even look at me lest they get in trouble.

"Pakanahuili," I said as soon as the steward stepped away.

The stone room spun for a moment before I dropped into darkness and then landed as if the ground rushed to greet my feet. My knees buckled as my eyes adjusted to the brightness.

"That was quicker than I expected." Zephonia pushed herself away from the entrance to the teleportation room. "Let's go."

I looked down at my bracelet when it buzzed, hoping that news about Rose was awaiting me, but no. Mama had sent a picture of Elias playing in a tree. Twenty feet up and hanging upside down. I had to have a serious talk with my mother about safety.

"I'm sure he's fine, Huri."

"So, where do we start? Shouldn't we speak to the steward handling Frank?"

"No. Things aren't so simple here. I want to look around first."

I followed her out into the streets, fighting to ignore how invigorating the air was. I fixed my mind on Elias. Zephonia stopped at an ornisharma awaiting us in front of a library building that spanned several blocks.

I raised my eyebrows at Zephonia, who hopped right in.

"Well, come on. Surely this isn't the first time you've seen a glider."

"I may have been born in the sticks, but not that far in the sticks. How'd you swing this?" I hopped in, which sent the ornisharma into the air before I could really sit.

Zephonia lifted an eyebrow, fingers drumming against the controls. "I've my ways."

The force of the takeoff knocked me into my seat. *Show-off.* "So, where're we headed?"

"Krujë. There is a village on the outskirts of Pakanahuili that is full of dhampir and their mortal parents. I've placed several there. Never had a problem before."

That was one thing I liked about Pakanahuili and the other Amaranthian city-states sprinkled throughout the Americas. They were a melting pot of the cultures that fled the Old World, mirroring the bigger cities with their cultural districts. They weren't like the majority of Amaranthian city-states, which remained fairly homogenous, like Olympia or Sliasthorp, where the Norse had made their home.

I studied my partner discreetly, noticing how her furrowed brow was somehow firmer and the crow's feet were disappearing. That knot between her eyebrows, however, seemed incapable of leaving even as Amaranthia began to reclaim Zephonia's body. I realized that knot meant the inner workings of Zephonia's mind were running at a blazing speed. Zephonia's fingers were even worrying the only bit of jewelry she wore, a plain silver ring on her left middle finger. Something was missing.

"Where's your pipe?"

Zephonia was silent and staring out of the ornisharma as the lush forests surrounding Pakanahuili sped by. She blinked after another moment. "I left it at the office."

I winced. *Bless her heart.* "It's not your fault, Zeph."

She managed a slight wince, youth returning to her face with each passing second, but she said nothing in reply.

I sent a message to Elias through Mama and added a note about not letting him climb too high. Mama sent a picture of the network of webs he and Yiayia had woven to catch him. And another of the two swinging from a stand of Yiayia's silk. *No winning.*

As my eyes grew heavy, I noticed several white spots poking out of the lush green of a hillside. When Zephonia sat straighter, I realized this was our destination. The ornisharma touched down on the side closest to the hills. Zephonia waved for me to exit and clicked a remote, which made the ornisharma vanish.

"Here we are," Zephonia said as she pointed toward a cluster of houses a few hundred yards away. "His house is this way."

I followed in silence, preferring to keep quiet rather than hear myself talk. The walk was short. Frank's new home was a log cabin the size of an efficiency apartment, but it was well maintained. It looked like there were the beginnings of a garden in the backyard.

Leading to the door were mossy stone steps that looked carved from the hill the cabin rested on. Fresh bits of stone showed through like they had been cleaned. I knelt down and touched the pathway. *Seems Frank doesn't like the mossy rocks.*

Zephonia pressed her hand to the middle of the door. After a click, she entered, needles at the ready in her left hand. I followed, keeping an eye behind us. A gasp from inside brought my attention, especially when Zephonia's body left mine. Beyond Zephonia, a plump woman plopped into a chair. She looked like she was a living time capsule, dressed like a medieval peasant.

"I am cleaner. Do not harm," she said, hands up.

I approached, senses acting in concert to determine what the woman was. "*Sterblich*," I whispered to Zephonia. *Mortal.*

"Who are you?" Zephonia didn't sheathe her needles.

Her eyes were wide as she let her eyes sweep the two. "Stitchers? Yes. I am Yeta. I take care of Frank."

Zephonia sheathed her needles, so I closed the door behind us. "Where is Frank?"

Yeta cowered into the chair. "I do not know. I come each day to care and feed him, but this four days and he is not here."

Zephonia nodded at me, which I took to mean I needed to look around. "Has he been acting strange?"

"Not much. He is looking for window lots. To always know that I am near. Wants me in soon. Always the same with the...new ones you Stitchers bring. Scared yes but is safe here. He would learn."

I studied the house. It was as spotless as a century-old cabin could be. I began looking in drawers and cabinets, but nothing. Maybe he wrote something down, but the cabin was devoid of paper or even writing utensils. My eyebrows met.

"Do they not provide paper and pens here?"

Zephonia and Yeta immediately stopped mid-sentence and looked at me. I addressed Yeta and repeated.

"Yes. Yes. Always. Why?"

Zephonia straightened and rushed to the fireplace. She growled. "When was the last time you cleaned the hearth?"

"Not yesterday but day before. I think. First day, I tell you I think he is out exploring. Second day, I think he must find girl he likes, so I clean for him. I put ashes in bin like he asks. I show you."

She escorted us to the backyard where Frank had started what looked to be a compost pile. My shoulders dropped, knowing from Rose's around-the-clock gardening vigilance that compost piles had to be turned every three days or so. The ashes, though waterlogged, were still resting on top.

212

Zephonia glanced at me before studying the ashes more. "I need some tongs or tweezers from the kitchen."

Once I placed tongs in her hand, Zephonia was using them to pull fragments free. I winced. Nothing was legible, only gray paper. Even so, Zephonia pulled out a baggie from her pocket and sealed in the larger chunks of ashes with a few scoops from the decimated pile, even labeling the baggie.

"Keep this with you," she said as she straightened.

I slipped it into a deep pocket at my waist, breathing in the fresh air. It always amazed me how rejuvenating Amaranthia was.

Zephonia barely glanced at Yeta. "Thank you for your help, Yeta. You are free to go."

"He must be okay, yes?"

"We hope. I'll let you know when I find him."

I watched Yeta leave, eyebrows meeting. "What're your thoughts?"

"If we're not done by afternoon, take that back to Bridget. I'll need to know if anything was written on there. Good catch, Huri."

I normally would've swelled a little at the compliment, but Zephonia was staring into the woods behind Frank's cabin. I looked toward the house when Zephonia did. Every window was shuttered and curtained from the back.

"You feel that?"

"Feel what?" Zephonia said.

"I feel like we're being watched. Listen. The birds are quiet."

Zephonia circled the house, staring at the ground like it would reveal its secrets. She winced and started moving outward from the cabin.

I, however, studied the trees. I hated feeling like I was being hunted. I knew it all too well from when Grandmother had Artemis Mykale train me. Mykale's training was to give me a ten-minute head start on a game of cat and mouse.

"Want me to take a look?" I pointed to the sky.

"Yeah. Not too far though."

I leapt into the air as Zephonia slipped into the woods, her normally gray bun reddening with each passing moment. I spotted a break in the trees that turned out to be a pond shadowed by a small rock face. It looked like a stone giant had thrust a hand out from the earth and had been frozen there. Only insects rippled the pond, which couldn't have been more than a few dozen yards wide. The unease grew when I saw a telling bit of scorched earth. I circled, eyes zeroing in on the spot to confirm my suspicions. With a swallow, I wheeled down to Zephonia, who was now her classically youthful self. I did not want to be the one to tell her.

Zephonia's eyebrows rose as she stared up at me. I totally wasn't hiding in the tree. "You found something?"

I did not want to be this messenger. "I found a burn mark by a pond," I admitted after I shifted.

"Show me."

At those words, Zephonia set out at a run, following me. Within minutes, we arrived at the pond. Zephonia slid to a stop when she saw the scorched earth. I alighted beside her and returned to normal. With her straight needles, Zephonia nudged a pair of shackles. I knew what they were for. They bound a vampire in a kneeling position, wrists to ankles. Whoever did this had him facing the rising sun and an easterly wind must have been blowing because his ashes and the burn mark flew backward to the west.

As Zephonia straightened, I spotted tears racing down her cheeks. She touched the blackened grass and dirt, whispering in a language I did not know. Then she began to sing an ancient song, both terrible and mournful. Half-images filled my mind like a language made not of words but of sensations. As she sang, we gathered what evidence we could. Once we were done, Zephonia swiped her bracelet.

"Janis, it's...yeah, they got to him. I...I don't know. He wouldn't have said anything." Her chin trembled. "Yeah. Well, just send a team. You've got my location."

I watched Zephonia sit on a stone beside the water, shoulders and back bowed. "I'm sorry this happened, Zeph."

Zephonia stared at the burn mark, brow knotted. "This is bad, Huri."

"I know, but who could've said anything? Why?"

"That's only the small part." Zephonia's hands worried one another. "Means whoever's selling those Cherries has an extensive reach."

"I get that. I mean, they've got people here."

Zephonia snickered. "Ah, chickadee. You don't get it. The Earth vampires don't take too kindly to their Amaranthian kin. The Amaranthians are a bunch of pompous lords who only bring over their select favorites if...if they actually do deign to take themselves to Earth for a romp. Those turned on Earth stay there. And the Earthlings aren't too happy that their overlord daddies keep so well-fed that they become daywalkers. And don't share in the fun."

I blinked, eyes roaming the ground. "So you're saying an alliance isn't likely."

She saluted me with a blade of grass. "It's why I chose to get Frank topside. Most transfers can live here, no problem. In fact, I can count on a single hand the number of times a transfer has gone missing, let alone..." She indicated the crime scene with her hand.

My eyes were flitting along the ground, watching tiny crabs shuffle toward the water. "So then there must be an alliance."

"And that's the rub," she mused, fingers shaking from missing her pipe. "Imagine what it would take to get two...enemies, for lack of a better term at the moment...two enemies to join up."

"It explains why it's so hard to get through the shell companies to an origin."

"Your endless digging for the past couple weeks is showing me that this thing is deep, chickadee. And I've had my doubts that Earthling vampires have the kind of technology to pull off something like the Cherries."

Zephonia stood when women began to pour into the clearing through the trees, their wrinkles and limps silkening into youthfulness with each second. Nodding at my packages, Zephonia pointed at the air.

"I'll take care of this. You need to get those to Bridget."

"I can..."

Zephonia raised an eyebrow as she pointed toward the air, all trace of vulnerability gone. "Hop to it. I've got this. We need to make sure this is him."

Fine. I launched into the air, ignoring the stares from the other stewards, and blinked out of sight, hoping and praying I didn't end up in Olympia again.

CHAPTER 29

I didn't see my partner at all the rest of the day. The next morning, Zephonia still wasn't back, but she had messaged that she wouldn't return until the next day.

I rested my head against the desk, mind running amok with Klara and Alexis's website to find Rose and a mockup of the article Jerome's reporter friend was doing on the issue with immortals and the public school system. My bracelet vibrated, jolting me back to reality. "It's Huri," I said without looking down.

"Results are in," Bridget said.

"On my way." I hung up and rushed down to the lab, where Bridget was waiting.

I swiped my bracelet to enter. "I'm seeing a lot of you these days," I said.

Bridget's arms were crossed and lips drawn.

My shoulders drooped. "It's him, isn't it."

Bridget handed me a file. "I didn't have a lot to work with, but what I could use from the inside of the shackles...they were definitely on Frank." She frowned. "And based on the burning, it's not a stretch to believe it was him."

Skata. "I was hoping we were wrong. For Zephonia's sake."

"She was fond of him. She has a weakness for the turned. Something about having their lives ripped from them and their world turned upside down gets her every time."

"Any luck processing some of the footprints?"

"Working on it. You got one good print in the ashes. Looks to be male, but I might be able to match the treads to some databases. I'll let you know what else I come up with, but I'm going to need some more."

"She's got the crew working the scene now." Another dead end. If only I could get past these shell companies. I opened my mouth to speak before closing it again, which made Bridget's eyebrows rise.

"Go ahead."

"I've been trying to track down the shell companies, but financial stuff is not my thing."

She pointed at the door and started farther into the lab. "I've got a girl who can help you. These ancient families are a labyrinth. She and her team have been working on recording histories of the ancient families."

"Why do you think it's one of them?"

"Because Zephonia showed me how far back you've gotten. Julie might be able to help you find connections. She's also pretty good with financials."

I paused with Bridget at an office that looked like a library and a trading floor had a baby. She knocked on the glass. A woman with a severe bun the same color as her dark skin turned with reading glasses perched on the end of her nose. She motioned us in and turned back to her paperwork. There were no chairs, only a stool in the corner; the tables were all at the perfect height for the woman to stand and work. With a sniff, I realized Julie was a mortal, one of the few in the office.

"Julie, this is Huri, Zephonia's greenie."

"Hello," she replied without glancing up. "Don't cross my line. I don't need you all glitching my tech in the middle of a search."

Bridget indicated the crime scene tape. My eyebrows rose, but I didn't cross the tape. Instead, I approached the table.

"Bridget was telling me you've been studying financials for the ancient lamia families."

"Yes."

"I wondered if you could take a look at what I've found."

A bell dinged on the computer, causing Julie to rush over and investigate. "Leave it there. I'll look it over and call you."

I furrowed my brow at Bridget, who smiled and nodded.

"Thanks, Jules."

She saluted us without a look back. *I hope that means something good.*

CHAPTER 30

Days turned into weeks before Julie finally called me back. I stood over the virtual recreation of Frank's murder scene on one of Julie's amazing tables. I exhaled as I studied the location of footprints and paths once again. All the information gleaned from the sweep the stewards performed weeks ago. Who would have the means to pull this off? A file slapped down, canceling the program.

Julie was standing there, arms crossed and lips pinched. "You're giving me rabbit holes."

Finally, someone else can feel my pain. "It's what I've got," I answered. "That's why I needed help."

She sucked her teeth and looked away. "I have pored over every corporation here and in my files. None of them match."

"Well, they might be wrong or missing—"

"Are you saying I've screwed up?" The whites of Julie's eyes were even bigger now.

Diplomacy, Huri. "I'm saying that there's got to be something out there we're missing. There's a trail somewhere."

Julie growled and started typing on the screen at the end of the table. The documents that I had amassed floated before us. "I have looked through each of these corporations. Beyond the shared meaning of their names, I can't find anything. I've tried to find connections through every known house. Nothing."

My frown deepened. "What about the names of people who started them?"

"Same as you. All I found is a bunch of dead mortals with no ties to houses."

I shook my head.

"But I did find that they were dead before they signed those papers."

That made me look up.

"Which made me cross-reference their names with vampiric aliases. No dice."

"What's the deal?" I hit the table. *Dead ends again. So annoying.*

"But there is one good lead here. These two"—Julie pulled the virtual files forward—"Have immediate family who are still alive.

"Justine Frances has a daughter who lives outside of Mobile. Name: Bama Frances. Alfredo Martinez has a son who lives in Miami."

"Same as Lisa Fuentes. She's from Miami."

"Really." Julie started typing and pulled up a map. "Interesting. Their addresses are just a couple of miles apart."

I smirked and started typing. "Let's see their financials."

Julie grinned. "Thinking they got paid off?"

"Maybe."

"These guys are going through a lot of trouble to cover their tracks."

"I know." I exhaled. "Not the best sign."

"You kidding? I love a good puzzle," Julie said and started working on Martinez's financials.

"I got nothing on Bama."

"Try five thousand down to three." She grinned and pointed out the amounts to Ramon Martinez's account. "See. On the regular. Cash."

"Nothing for Bama Frances." I frowned at the hologram.

"She looks old-school." Julie smirked. "She might just be hiding things under a mattress."

I snickered and started on Lisa Fuentes. No children. No living relatives.

We both looked away. *These dead ends make me wanna cuss.*

"We'll need them all tracked down anyhow." Julie wiped her face. "I'll start looking for patterns between Fuentes and Martinez."

I nodded. "I'll keep digging into Justine and Bama Frances."

"Have you had any luck with the list of pharmaceutical companies Lamiens Alliance gave you?" Julie asked.

"Zephonia is talking with the few labs nearby. I don't think it's going well."

"Like they're dead ends?"

"Yeah. Most are mortal-run, so it wouldn't make sense to manufacture the Cherries."

"We need to go through the employee lists."

"I think she's getting the employees who would be in contact with the equipment Lamiens Alliance gave us." I paused and looked at Julie. "What about the equipment? If this is super hard to make, the equipment—"

"Great idea," Julie said with a snap of her fingers. "Maybe we can track the sales. Maybe get a name."

Julie started her research, cutting her eyes at me.

"What?" I asked at last.

"How'd you get into this?"

My eyebrows met. "Being a steward?"

"No. Research in general."

I blushed. "Oh. Well, my friends and I tried to write an exposé on Rose's dad. I was a journalist for my school."

"Seriously?"

I nodded. "They lost interest when we couldn't pin too much on him besides being a dad who was never around. Anyways. I caught the bug."

Julie snickered.

"How about you?"

"History major." She smiled a little, but that turned into a frown a moment later. "My brother got in with some unsavory folks." She licked her lips as she stared at her hands. "I...I felt so helpless. I mean, you guys are stronger than me and have these abilities and... all I've got are my books."

That's awful. But I get it. Here I am supposed to be protecting my loved ones. And all I've done is fail.

"No offense," she added.

"Believe me. None taken. I get it."

"But it hit me one day that these people have been operating like businesses and not always legally. Turns out that I wasn't able to make his murderers pay for his death, but I hit them in other ways." She laughed. "Who would've thought my books could be weapons?"

"One grandmother exiled my other grandmother," I said softly and shrugged. "I...I have seen too much not to want to do something. Not to mention, all my friends are mortal." *Hold it together, Huri.* "I spent my life hiding who I was from them, trying to keep them safe. But..." My eyes watered as I stared at the holographic screen.

"So, it's true your friend was attacked by a tick."

I nodded. "I'm hoping but...been a few weeks now." *Months really.*

"I'm sure you'll find her."

"I'm just hoping." I winced. "Look at us. Here immos thought giving mortals the Americas would solve inequality issues, but we segregated ourselves so much that mortals don't know the dangers certain immortals pose." *So dumb.*

"You couldn't have prevented this."

I wish I felt that way. "Looks like the Frances women bought a farm outside of Mobile. Not too long before Justine's death."

Julie rubbed my back but didn't force the subject. Maybe I

should've told the girls sooner, warned them. There were times I'd worried about Klara, but somehow, she'd managed to stay out of the predators' way. Maybe if I had been open with them...I looked down at my unanswered calls from this morning and hoped my dearest friends wouldn't pay for my silence.

Julie pointed at her screen. "Look at that. The vampire philanthropists are on the list for labs with the right equipment for manufacturing."

I nearly plowed over the crime scene tape to join her. "Who?"

"That Lamiens Alliance. Their logo is all over the initial lab work for the Cherries. They were the outside lab Captain got to run the forensics test on the drug. Remember?"

"Oh yeah." My frown deepened. Maybe I hadn't been paranoid about Enrica after all.

CHAPTER 31

Elias swung from branch to branch like the love child of a trapeze artist and a monkey. Showers of auburn and yellow leaves helicoptered to the ground in his wake.

I smiled. My boy was meant to be in the air. It was so nice to have a moment of normalcy after failing to infiltrate some of the local houses. Beatriz wasn't making any headway, either.

My stomach and throat switched places as he flipped, nearly missed a tree limb, and then caught himself on a lower branch with a deft swing. He landed, legs wobbly, eyes wide, mouth agape. It was so impressive that I actually grinned at him.

"That was insane!"

Poor thing had scared himself so much that his legs shook before he managed to dash into my arms.

I cradled him to my chest. His tiny heart thumped so hard that I could feel it beating through both our shirts. "You all right, sug?"

He swallowed hard and then exploded from my arms. "That was so cool. Did you see that? I can't believe I caught myself I thought I was going to fall but I caught myself and it was amazing I've got to do that again."

"No, you don't," I said. "I've had enough of a heart attack for the day."

"But that was so cool."

I pulled him into a headlock and ruffled his hair. "Insanely." My bracelet buzzed. It was a text, but I didn't recognize the number.

Something large fluttered by us. *Maybe I should open it.*

"Holy cow! Did you see that thing? It had to be the biggest butterfly I've ever seen."

My body turned cold. *Rose.*

"We should get those nets like at the circus so that I can...Mom?"

My hands started shaking when pictures started coming through of a hotel room with a very naked trio on the bed. I let out a squeak, turning the bracelet so that Elias wouldn't accidentally see.

Two males. Twenty to thirty years old. One blond. One brunet. The woman looked to be about the same, but it was the angle. She had black hair down to her breasts.

"Mama? Are you okay? I promise not to fall, but the net would catch me just in case the webs don't. Then you won't have a heart attack."

"Shh!" I shook even more as I rushed inside to the big mirror in my office. I scrambled to open the holographic keyboard and started begging Rose for details.

He stomped in after me, arms crossed.

"I'm sorry, baby, but it's Rosie." *Where are you?* Based on the camera angle, she must've been watching the three on a hotel room bed. The light fell onto the bed behind her. Eastern facing then. Corner?

"What?" He practically ripped his vocal cords to ask the question. *PB.*

I couldn't look away from the first picture I had seen of my sister in months. She was alive. She looked beautiful, even with the silver tainting her honey-colored eyes. Then I was crying when Rose finally gave me a name.

Nikolai Smirnov.

I screamed. That was the name of the guy she had that last dinner with. The guy from Firebrand Records. *But that name is fake.*

Before she could text more, Rose sent the chilling line: *They're back. They'll kill me if they find me with this.*

I knew better than to text Rose back. No matter how badly I wanted to.

I scried both Zephonia and Beatriz as I forwarded the texts to both, closing out any images Elias could see inadvertently.

"Is she okay? Where is she?" he begged, tugging on my shirt.

I ignored Elias when both answered nearly at once, their heads filling the large mirror.

"You just got this?" Beatriz gasped.

"Thank the Lord," Zephonia breathed. "She's semi-okay."

I could only nod, squeezing Elias to me. He was starting to cry from excitement. "Hush, baby. I gotta talk. Just wait." I managed to stare straight ahead and closed my eyes like that would drown out Elias's worried questions. "She's in Palm Beach. That's what PB is."

"I'm going to put a tracker on the number," Beatriz told us.

It felt like hours before Beatriz yelped. "Lab confirms. Cell is in Palm Beach. They're tracking. We'll have our girls pick the owner up."

"They'll be gone by then," I said.

"Our people will get there soon," Zephonia said, voice soothing.

"I'm already sending a travel freeze for her," Beatriz announced. "I'll have the lab work up facials for the ones in the video. You stay put, Huri. I've got this. Let me do my job."

"I hear ya," I said with a sigh. *Best chance we've had in months. Please, let her come home.*

It felt like hours before I got another call. I was sitting on the couch with Elias, eating cookies and ice cream. We were staring at Pater's mirror-TV hybrid without really seeing it. Elias had stopped asking if I thought Rose was okay. I wasn't sure which I hated more: the constant questions or the ensuing silence.

"They've brought in two sirens," Zephonia said. "Beatriz is questioning them now."

"I want to see."

"It's being fed to your mirror."

Sure enough. The mirror in the office dinged a moment later.

Elias sat straighter.

"Stay here, bud. I'll let you know what I find out."

He nodded and appeared to remain still. I knew, however, that he silently padded to the office door and listened. Which is why I put cuffs on each ear for privacy.

The mirror showed the blond siren sitting in an interrogation room. Beatriz entered as soon as she saw that I was watching. A second feed from a pendant from Beatriz's necklace appeared once she sat down across from the siren. He grinned at her like all men did.

"I've never seen such a beautiful Stitcher in my life."

"Yeah. I've never heard that one before." She lifted the file to show those watching from the pendant. "Christofer Messini."

I scribbled down his name.

His smile faltered as he leaned back, draping his arm along the back of the chair. "What can I do for you?"

"Tell me about her." She set Rose's photo in front of him.

"Never seen her."

"Perhaps you know this woman then." She pulled out another photo, this one of the dark-haired beauty.

He grinned at the second image. "Now that I remember." His smile faltered as Beatriz set down additional photos of the three together. "So? Having a ménage à trois isn't illegal."

"These pics didn't take themselves, Christofer. Tell me how I got these photos of you and your friend. And it better be truthful. I've got your friend in the other room waiting to corroborate your story."

"What's in it for me?"

I growled. "Not having my talons rip off your tail."

"This girl"—Beatriz tapped Rose's picture she'd sent from the

228

condo—"Was kidnapped over three months ago. She's the daughter of a senator, Chris. She's also dear friends with someone very close to reigning members of your pantheon." She chuckled. "Shall we say... her friend's blood is a little purer than yours."

"Good for him. What's this have to do with me?"

"Tell me about the encounter."

He grinned like a shark.

"Start with how you met her."

"She came up to me, actually. Asked me if I had any *ouzo*. We flirted, but her friend was the most fun. This chick claimed she only liked to watch."

"Did she seem happy to be there? Under duress?"

"Look. I don't have to force women."

"I didn't say that. I mean, did the woman act unusual? Say anything to you?"

He frowned and looked away. "No. Only thing weird was that she was worried about the guys with them."

"Guys. Who's that?"

"Two giant Norse-looking dudes. They let them go around and have fun, but they stood outside the room." He grinned. "Not that that bothered me any."

"Could you describe them? Did you hear any names?"

"Look. What's the deal here? This girl looked just fine. Not kidnapped or anything."

The camera shifted away a few inches. I could see Beatriz lean backward in the other feed as she extended a piece of paper.

"That your cell phone number?"

He got quiet as he read the text messages printed out there. The shade of white he turned was perfect. He closed his eyes as he pinched the bridge of his nose. "Look. I don't know about that. I didn't send that text."

"I know. She did. Deleted it, apparently."

He shrugged and leaned back. "I didn't do anything wrong. I was focused on her friend."

"Get a name on her friend?"

"No."

Beatriz snorted under her breath.

"Look. Names complicate things."

"Of course. Did they mention anything or anyone else?"

"No. Not that I remember."

"And these two Norse guys. Were they mortal?"

"At first, I thought they were ticks. I mean, the girls' eyes were silvered for sure, but the Norse dudes were day-siding it. No way they were ticks. They must have been bodyguards. That's what we both thought afterward. Ask him. Some rich girls looking for fun."

I growled but straightened the next moment.

"You catch that?" Zephonia asked over their scry.

"Yeah."

"Sounds like we have a bit of a connection." Zephonia exhaled smoke. Even with the distance, I could almost feel it.

I was scribbling notes. "Not too many daywalking vampires. They gotta be connected to the Cherries."

"It's thin." Zephonia hummed. "But it's something."

CHAPTER 32

I kept waking up from seeing Rose with those sirens and some random guys from the Norse pantheon. Those guys were just as egotistical as the rest. I pressed my palm into my eyes, trying to be rid of my nightmare's image of Rose's lifeless, silvered eyes as her corpse lay beside Luis's.

Bodies piling up in my life. I tried not to think about the fact that airport security took pictures of the backs of their heads, but nothing else. Not even the aircraft was registered. I struggled not to dwell on how little we had. I'd exhausted every avenue to that recording company with Nikolai Smirnov.

All I knew was that I had to get answers. Something. I had to bring Rose back. I couldn't lose her too.

Just like Dennise from Cool Kats had hinted: Rose had to be part of a house—and as Zephonia pointed out, one that was involved with Cherries. Fake Lisa Fuentes with Dave, working in the weight-loss clinic, came to mind. I needed to get her tracked. So far, the only daywalking vampire I knew was last seen at that clinic with his lips all over Lisa.

The next morning, I could barely drop Elias off quick enough at

Yiayia's house. I only felt slightly bad. Solving Rose's case would bring the gleam back to Elias's eyes.

For once, I beat Zephonia into the office. The cloud floated up to seat me as I pulled together all the information we had on Lisa Fuentes. It wasn't much. While we were receiving the creepy shadow box of fangs, Lisa left the apartment with a duffle bag and never returned. One of the neighbors emptied out everything onto the curb and put a rental sign in the window. She hadn't even been seen at the weight-loss clinic. Fake Lisa had ghosted us.

How was a mortal giving orders to a house? Then I remembered Dennise mentioning mortals who were nearly vampires. Maybe Fake Lisa was one of them. I rummaged through files on the houses in the area. Surely those files contained a list of possible donors.

Nope. We had nothing on donors. Probably because of how short-lived they were. My fingers drummed the keyboard, wondering how I would track people who were presumed dead. My eyes narrowed. I had only looked at recent missing persons in the Nashville area. Maybe I needed to broaden that to include other areas and also go back a few years.

I glanced at the files Julie and I had worked on together. Perhaps there was a geographic connection between these folks and Fake Lisa. I had to narrow the search a few times because the computer kept crashing, but by the end of the day, I was grinning at the screen.

"Hello, little mouse," I said as I stared at Tiffany Silva of Gulfport, who was reported missing after she ran away from a foster home. She popped up two years later in Miami and then went missing again. There was a Tiffany Silva living in Nashville on the outskirts of town toward Clarksville. And she looked exactly like Fake Lisa.

I printed the address and hurried out the door, barely saying two words to anyone.

CHAPTER 33

I leaned against the trunk of a tree, thirty feet up, and watched. Tiffany Silva paused outside the local Kroger to answer her phone (*definitely a morrie*), switching all her bags and the giant creamy leather purse into one hand to open the car door at the same time. *Perhaps I should take Tiffany in the parking lot.* It would be poetic. Not to mention convenient, given where she was parked: on the side of the building where there weren't any cameras. But I waited.

I followed Tiffany on her mundane errands until she headed for a warehouse not far from her house. An expensive black import parked nearly at the same time Tiffany did. My feathers stood on end when Enrica Fontana—*how had I not connected her last name?*—stepped out of the black sedan to greet Tiffany like they hadn't seen one another in ages. They slipped into the warehouse, hands clasped.

I totally missed this Fontana. A daywalker...those sirens said the Norse dudes could've been daywalkers. Plus, Lamiens Alliance has the equipment to make the Cherries. Gah! Such an idiot.

As a tiny owl, I shot through a broken window at the top and flew through the building until I reached the sound of the voices.

Then I shifted and hunkered down in the shadows in what was once the warehouse's office.

I found Enrica biting Tiffany so tenderly I nearly turned away from the moment. It felt at once deeply intimate and yet sexless. They seemed like lovers who had moved beyond sex as the only form of intimacy.

The office looked like it was used rather frequently. The chairs were secondhand but well maintained. There was a whiteboard with symbols that probably made sense to a chemist or mathematician. My heart started racing. *Enrica's behind the Cherries. Not Fake Lisa.* Now I just had to prove it.

Taking out my bracelet, I held it up to record.

Enrica drew Tiffany to sit in a chair. "How are you?" Enrica asked, unable to release Tiffany's hand.

"Just the usual stuff. I get tired of these idiots. You?"

"Nothing worth speaking of."

"They still don't suspect?"

"Not that I can tell. They're pretty closed. But Filomena would say something if they did. She'd feel like she'd have to come to me as a concerned friend."

They both shared a snicker. *Jerks.* No doubt Janis would relish sending this vulture to prison when she learned how they'd played her.

"How are the trials going?"

Tiffany reached into her purse and handed over a spiral notebook. "It'd be easier if I could use an Excel file."

Enrica started leafing through handwritten notes. "It's promising," she whispered after a few moments.

"I agree. How are talks?"

"Tedious but hopeful. I've gotten several strigoi houses to back us. I've almost got enough votes. I just hope we get it in time."

"You will, baby," Tiffany said with a kiss to Enrica's fingertips.

"I just need to get Aleksandr's father. He'll sway the council."

Hmm. Who's Aleksandr? The pronunciation pointed to a non-English variation.

Tiffany beamed at Enrica. "You will. I know it."

"All our holes are plugged? I don't need the Stitchers finding another provider."

"Yeah. After the last one, everyone's staying in line."

"Good." Enrica indicated the notebook before sliding it into her purse. "Thank you for this. I know it's a risk meeting me before things are done."

"We're almost there." Tiffany pressed her forehead to Enrica's. "Then we'll be free."

Fat chance now.

"I have to go. Another meeting." The two embraced and kissed tenderly. "Be safe, my sweet ambrosia."

"You too." Tiffany sniffled. "Just think. Next time we meet, this will all be over."

Next time, you'll be behind bars.

"You're coming out too, right?"

"I have to make sure shipments are ready to go. You go ahead."

My heart thudded in my tiny owl chest. I knew I needed to call Zephonia, but any sound would set them off. And I needed to find out what Tiffany knew about Rose. It was clear that Tiffany was Enrica's second-in-command, a special donor. Enrica, for all her talk of being a philanthropist, was obviously the head of a house. *How did I miss this? Enrica Fontana. Even her last name points at shell companies. No way Tiffany doesn't know about Rose.*

Unwilling to move from my perch, I waited while Tiffany bid Enrica goodbye. Tiffany returned and sat at the desk and made a few calls to the major dealers. Then she packed up to leave. I flew behind her and shifted. In the next moment, I stabbed her slightly with a sedative needle.

Tiffany flailed momentarily, but I caught her and hauled her upstairs into an open room. My internal warning system screamed at me. But I had to find Rose before it was too late. That was all.

But I needed this job. I needed to support my son. This had been my dream.

But how could I do that if Eli kept losing those closest to him? Not to mention that Rose was my oldest and dearest friend. My sister in all but blood. Rose would do anything to save me if the situations were reversed.

Be wise, Pherenike.

I bound Tiffany to a beam and set up the mirror to capture the interview. I inhaled and exhaled, nostrils flaring as I tried in vain to calm myself. *Keep it together.* Next, I pulled out the vial of Aletheia's Tears from my backpack. My hands shook a little when Tiffany groaned.

You've got this. Keep calm. I stood in front of the mirror. Fighting to think of the right words to cover myself and to find Rose without letting Zephonia down, I licked my lips and prayed for help. For something to come to mind. My heart thudded against my ribcage when Tiffany started mumbling incoherently.

I took a deep breath and pressed the mirror. It came to life. "Copy this recording to Steward Zephonia Weber."

Zephonia's portrait appeared in the top right corner of the mirror.

"I am Stew—Steward Huri Rojas of the Nashville Field Office. I have discovered a nexus of operations for the drug known colloquially as Cherries at 13246 45th Street on the north side of Nashville. I am now switching on my stitch marker to notify my partner of my location. Zephonia does not know where I am or where I was headed the last time she saw me. Behind me is Tiffany Silva, who is a donor for Enrica Fontana, the owner of Lamiens Alliance. I have been tracking her under the alias Lisa Fuentes in connection with the Cherries and have been led here. I was unaware of Lamiens Alliance's connection until moments ago. She and Ms. Fontana met in this building to discuss shipments and exchanged a notebook with some sort of trial findings. I am going to administer Aletheia's Tears to secure an unbiased interview with Ms. Silva concerning her involvement in the Cherries and in...in Rosaline Brandt's abduction."

"What...where am I?"

Here we go. "I've given her the standard sedative to ensure her cooperation." I looked back when Tiffany jerked against her restraints.

"Who the hell are you?" Tiffany flicked her hair aside to look at me. "You've no idea the hell that's about to come down on you for this."

You're trying to find Rose. Tiffany's a drug dealer. "Actually. I'm well aware," I said softly.

Zephonia's face immediately popped up on my bracelet, but I swiped it away.

"Hi, Tiffany. I'm Steward Rojas. No doubt you are unaware of many of the laws of the Amaranthian Society governing immortal and mortal crimes. The gist is that you're peddling an illegal drug that harms your fellow mortals—"

"I get a lawyer."

"Your lawbreaking sets you firmly under Amaranthian—not US —laws and jurisdiction. We have no lawyers because of Aletheia's Tears. The Tears allow you to speak with complete candor. Now. You're abetting immortals who are perpetrating crimes against mortals; therefore, your crimes fall under StS's jurisdiction. Not mortal police agencies." I held up the vial. "Again, I'll repeat that the Tears will allow you to speak with candor about any subject I ask. It's painful if you resist. I am administering it intravenously to prevent undue injury." I drew the appropriate amount in front of the mirror to show I knew the right dosage and then injected Tiffany quickly.

She screamed and thrashed, but the effects of the Tears had her spewing insults and profanities that would make most sailors blush.

I sat cross-legged in front of Tiffany while still allowing the mirror to have a full view of the scene. "I'll start with easy questions to get you used to the Tears' prompting."

It took several questions to establish the baseline for the Tears.

My hands shook. *Which question do I ask first?* I didn't have a lot of time before Zephonia would arrive.

"Let's start with this woman." I pulled out a picture of Rose and placed it on the ground.

"Who is she?"

My heart bottomed out. Nothing in her delivery revealed a lie. "Her name is Rosaline Brandt. She's the daughter of Senator Sturgeon Brandt. She was abducted about three months ago."

"OK."

"I know daywalkers took her. You're in with daywalkers. Where is she?"

"Gahd." Tiffany laughed. "Cops are idiots no matter if they're mortal or immortal. I don't know every daywalker. Just Enrica."

"And David Spangler. Who normally wouldn't be a daywalker." I raised an eyebrow.

"He won't be walking any more days now, will he?" She snickered at her own joke and then froze, realizing her mistake.

"Who killed him?"

Tiffany clamped her mouth shut. Her face turned red and then blue until she couldn't hold it. "I had him killed. Cristofer Polini and Randy Collins did it."

"Who sent the package to Steward Weber?"

"Randy. Had his friend slip it into the Stitcher's mail." Tiffany screamed and started cursing.

"And Franklin Howard?"

Again, she screamed and raged. "Some guys in Amaranthia. I don't know. Enrica saw to it. She has friends on the other side."

"What is her involvement?"

It took minutes of agony for Tiffany to finally speak, interspersing her testimony with so much cursing that I had a hard time understanding her. But I got the gist.

"So, she created the Cherries. Got it."

"I will kill you!"

"I'm sure. Now, back to Rose." I tapped the picture. "Who kidnaps donors long-term?"

"All the houses do. Gahd. Do your homework! Every house does. I do not know this girl. I don't run in their circles."

My stomach soured, and my skin ran cold. *No. She has to know something.* "Don't lie to me. Where is she?"

"Probably dead. No clue."

No. No. Tiffany knows the daywalkers. She knows who has Rose. She has to. "I'm losing my patience."

"I can't lie," Tiffany screamed.

My hand wrapped around Tiffany's throat. Before I knew it, I slammed her against the beam. Face pressed to Tiffany's cheek, I panted, fighting the vengeance roiling like a volcano just before eruption. The silk along my arms rose like a cobra ready to strike. "Try again!"

"Check the tick clubs. They're always hosting the bigger houses. Gahd. I don't know. Girls everywhere."

"Huri!"

Like plunging into icy water, I realized Tiffany really didn't know. I'd lost my only link to any kind of clue to bring Rose back. I slid away from Tiffany. I could only stare at my hands. *She doesn't know. Rose will never come back.*

"Huri, where the hell are you?" Zephonia called from below.

Tiffany cackled. "Mommy can't save you. You're screwed, bitch."

Water burst from my eyes. "She doesn't know."

"She's here!"

I felt someone jerk my shoulders. Zephonia's muddy-river eyes were waiting, but that was all I could see. "She doesn't know, Zeph."

Zephonia sighed and crushed me into her arms. "I know, honey."

"I'm never going to see her again," I wept.

"Wait until my lawyer hears about this. Your asses. Your jobs. All mine," Tiffany roared.

"I'm sorry," I whispered. "I'm so sorry."

239

"I have to put these on you until I figure out what's going on, Huri."

I held out my wrists and let myself be handcuffed to a column. "I'm never going to see her again."

"Zephonia," Beatriz called. "You've got to see this. Shipping dates. Everything. This is where they'll send it out."

I wept against the beam. *I've been such a freaking idiot. Worst steward in history. Worst detective. I couldn't even find my sister. I couldn't save my husband. I can't protect my son.*

Zephonia's footsteps retreated down the stairs. Tiffany laughed as if told the best joke ever.

"Great job, Stitcher. You've totally screwed your whole case."

I glared at her through my waterlogged eyes.

"Nothing you find here will be admissible."

My eyes darkened. "You're a glorified drug dealer. Your actions lead to death. Addiction. Rape."

"Sometimes you've gotta roll in the mud to get where you want to go. Just wait. You're going to see. We'll be on top."

"Yeah, on top of what? A pile of dead bodies?"

"On top of luxury and a pile of cash. Enrica and I will—"

I laughed loud and hard. "Enrica? She's a tick. You're a donor. Ha. You're dinner."

"She will lay waste to your little career."

"Dinner. That's probably why she made them in the first place. She wanted to pimp you out, just like she did with David."

Tiffany's eyes narrowed.

Hit her low and hard. Just like Grandmother taught you. "How many other vampires has she let feed off of you, her sweet ambrosia?"

"Shut up."

"I bet it's not the same when those guys sink their teeth into you. I saw how you were with her." I whipped my eyes clear. "Love. As much as an addict can love cocaine. But it's the closest thing you've got to it. And she's pimping you out to these low-level dealers to get the data she needs. And all for what? Some cash?"

"You're full of it. She does love me."

"You're food. You're dinner. Nothing more."

"She's my mate."

I let out a sharp hoot of a laugh. "Mates plump up like an actual tick. It's a physical change when vampires fall in love. How do you not know that? I don't see her rounding out and getting all fat and red for you."

Tiffany's eyes rounded, words silenced.

"Didn't know that. Do your homework, dinner-donor. But that's going to be over now. You're nothing but another David. Another Franklin. You're a leak that'll need plugging."

"Shut the hell up."

"Was it worth it? Your life? Traded for what? Prison time. If you survive detox. No one has. You'll still be nothing but a petty drug dealer who got taken by her partner."

"We're not dealers. We're manufacturers. We're going big. You'll see."

A crunch brought our eyes up. Zephonia and Beatriz stood there, arms crossed. Beatriz's otherworldly smile made beauty look as terrible as the eyewall of a hurricane.

"How big?" she asked quietly.

Zephonia popped her pipe into her mouth. "Yes, how big are we talking? Please, don't stop on our account."

Tiffany's eyes bulged. Her face turned red, then violet, and finally blue. I grinned when Tiffany's scream of rage and defiance ripped the words right out of her throat.

Beatriz skipped over to the mirror and pressed the stop button. "I believe that will do. For now."

CHAPTER 34

My ears rang from Captain Janis's yelling. I wanted to curl into a ball and hide in the corner. The entire NFO could hear Janis berating me. In the basement even. The labbies started filtering up to stand in the detectives' office to witness my tongue lashing.

"Suspended for four weeks," Janis roared as she paced back and forth. "The desk will be your freakin' best friend after that, child."

I couldn't look at Zephonia, who puffed like a dragon by the door. I had never seen so much smoke come from a pipe before. It threatened to overtake the entire office.

"You're lucky you had the brains to keep it as official as possible."

"And that you found anything worth using," Zephonia growled.

"That's beside the point. The only reason I'm not firing you..."

Is because of what I am. Curse that title.

"Is because you were only a halfwit and not a complete nitwit. And I hate it. You should be on the street. You want to go rogue? That idiocy is best served in Olympia. Not here. Remember that sign as you walked in on your first day? And every damn day after? 'No heroes. Only heroines,' it says. Did you not read the sign every single time you entered this building? You threatened the integrity of not only your partner but the whole field office and the entire organization. You nearly blew the case. All because you don't know how to keep yourself in line."

"You don't know how to trust your fellow stewards!" Zephonia barked with just enough power behind her voice that I felt every ounce of her fury condensed into a single sentence. "We are your people. Your sisters-in-arms."

Atlas must've slammed his burdens squarely on my back.

"Two of those weeks will be unpaid. You will sit at home and fester. Hopefully, the hit to your paycheck will remind you of that independence you claim to hold so dear. The other two will be spent in realignment therapy."

"What is that?" I dared to ask, unable to look at either.

"It's to help you get your head on straight," Zephonia growled. "Help you deal with whatever insanity took you down this path."

My insides roiled, bringing up my eyes. I caught my words before they gushed out of my mouth.

Zephonia grinned darkly. "Hit a nerve. Spill it."

"Spit it out," Janis shouted. "Get this junk out. Now."

"No." I panted to keep my temper contained in a box. My wrath rattled its cage.

"That's an order, Rojas." Janis got in my face. *Get away from me.* "Why in God's name would you threaten everything we've worked for?"

I leapt to my feet, nearly knocking over the captain. "I am my sister's keeper," I shouted. "Bia was too busy with other cases. I had to save her." Those words hit home. My chin trembled. "I have...have to save her."

Janis winced. The sight of compassion, despite the anger, triggered my waterworks. But I buried them deep. My captain's hands gently held my face. They were rough, as if from hard labor. "You can't save everyone."

I glared at her. "I know." I couldn't even think his name lest he suddenly appear.

"No, you don't," Janis whispered. She tapped the left side of my chest. "No, you don't. You are an Athena. You're not really meant to know." Janis winced. "But you will. We all do."

I looked away and licked my lips. "I won't give up on her," I said at last. My chin trembled again. "I...I can't."

"We're not either," Zephonia promised and put her hand on my shoulder. "But you're not alone."

Janis exhaled. "What you're feeling is what every family feels when we can't help them or it takes too long."

I didn't know what to say, so I nodded.

"You get a grip on this, and it can help you be a better steward," Janis said with a pat to my arm before heading back to her desk.

"Shoot," Zephonia said. "It can make you a better *person*."

Janis flicked a hand at me. "Badge and needles."

My skin froze. I never wanted to hear those words again. I pulled my badge off my belt and drew up my shirt to reveal the leather sheath that housed my needles and brass knuckles. After I unbuckled it, the sheath gave way with a tug. It had begun to feel like a second skin, no longer unusual. The air chilled the dampness where the needles once were.

For a long moment, I stared at my badge and needles. My hands shook as I handed them over.

Janis passed me a paper. "This is the name of the therapist. Set up the appointment. You can't come back until you've gotten at least three sessions each week. That's twelve sessions."

"I will."

"Good." Janis nodded toward the door. "You're dismissed."

I paused at the door and turned to look at Zephonia, whose face was a mask, her steely bun steelier than I remembered from my first day. "I am sorry, Zeph. Captain."

I couldn't look at either to see if they accepted my apology. I probably wouldn't have in their place. And definitely not in Rose's place.

CHAPTER 35

When I returned to my little home, I didn't know what was worse: the look on Yiayia's face or the pride on my son's.

"You need to let them do their jobs. How would you feel if someone did that to your case?" Yiayia quite nearly slammed the door in my face.

Elias burst through the closing door. "Serves them right. They should've found Aunt Rosie by now." Elias beamed. "Now you can visit that school."

"Eli..."

"Or just snuggle with me." He fluttered his long, black eyelashes at me.

I snickered. "The brightest side to any day." My arms wrapped around him and squeezed just enough.

And that's exactly what I did. I basked in being on call for my son. I spent most of my time fulfilling his every need, a first since I started working. The rest of the time, I was raining down my wrath on several punching bags in the backyard. That is, until it was time for Elias to come home from training with Mama. Then I'd stash them away.

Then, of course, Mama needed my help distributing flyers and medical supplies to Olympia and Pakanahuili since I'd learned to teleport. It was like I became a teenager who'd just learned how to drive and thus run errands. Again.

The thing I looked forward to the least was the therapist. But I dutifully made the appointment and showed up to the office.

It fit every therapy scene from a movie. So cliché. I imagined that the therapist, a woman, would wear reading glasses on one of those metal chains that clipped to the frames. The only unexpected thing was the sound machine in the corner. It reminded me of one Luis's crew bought us as a baby gift.

Dr. Ingrid Tremili entered and sat across from me in a cozy chair, adjusting her cat-eye glasses. They obviously weren't readers, but close enough. Plus, she smelled so much like a wet cat that I knew she had to be a feline shifter—definitely not part of the movie vibe.

"Hello, Huri." She reached across the coffee table and shook my hand. "It's lovely to meet you. I'm Ingrid."

I returned the greeting, fiddling with the hem of my shirt when I watched Ingrid fold her legs underneath her as she picked up a clipboard. *Why isn't she wearing shoes? So weird.*

"So, what brings you in today, Huri?"

Seriously? "Didn't Captain Janis give you details for my sessions?" I didn't want to think of the therapy part. My life was not open to discussion with strangers. This was just a way to pay my penance and get back to work.

"Yes, but why do you think she ordered therapy specifically?"

I was careful to keep my hands still, careful not to purse my lips or touch my face. All of those gave away clues to my underlying thoughts. And I couldn't do that. "I believe it's because I allowed my emotions take control."

Ingrid scribbled on her clipboard. "I can see why you would think that."

I chewed the inside of my cheek. "Why do you think she ordered therapy?"

A smile luxuriated across her face like a house cat stretching in a window seat. "Did she tell you that I am a therapist for many stewards across the US?"

"No." I looked away. "I was a little too worried about keeping my job to ask for your credentials."

"This will go easier and swifter if you simply answer questions rather than posing them in return, Detective."

I shrugged. "Forgive me. It's in my training."

Her smile softened a little. "I know. You've been conditioned to hide who you are and what you feel, Athena Pherenike."

My face flushed, and I couldn't control it. *Titles.*

"You wear many faces out in the world, Huri. In here, you get to shed them."

Sure, Doc. I stared at my fingernails, discreetly checking the clock in the reflection of my bracelet. Forty more minutes.

"Let's start with something other than work." Ingrid shifted to sit cross-legged. "I saw you have a son."

"I do." *Stoic, Huri.*

Ingrid actually laughed. "Tell me a little bit about him."

I exhaled. "I'm restricted with how much I can discuss my family given how tightly everything relates to my pantheon."

"OK." Ingrid laced her fingers before her. "What can you talk about?"

"Things related to my job as a steward," I said at once.

"So, why did you allow your emotions to get the better of you?" Ingrid smirked. "In your job."

That hotel picture with Rose's altered irises, silvered over like mercury replaced them, filled my memory. The fear there. The desperation. "My cases and Rose's disappearance...seemed to intersect. It was admittedly tenuous...the connection."

"You didn't trust your colleague to do her job."

I blinked and then stopped. Eye blocking. I had to stop doing that. But Yiayia had said the same thing as Ingrid. So had Zephonia and the captain. "It's not that simple."

"You withheld information on the case from the primary investigator, Huri. To what end?"

"To save Rose."

"Not to bring the kidnapper in yourself?" Ingrid's smile tightened. "Not to be the hero? Go it alone? Show you don't need anyone? That you're above the system?"

My jaw clenched. I prayed hard to keep my emotions in check, but they bubbled like lava just beneath the surface. "I only wanted to save Rose."

"Yes, but you had to believe that your colleague was failing at the job. That you would be better suited." Ingrid leaned back and crossed her legs. "You do see that, right?"

"You have a child." I indicated a pinch pot and a crude origami fox. "If someone kidnapped her, would you not be out there doing all you could to help the investigation?"

Ingrid's jaw tightened this time. I reveled in her loss of composure. "Indeed. But Rose is not your child."

"She's as dear as my sister, my blood." I exhaled. "My skills aren't like others'. I'm capable of more than just putting up missing person posters."

Ingrid laughed mirthlessly. "Yes, your...skills. They make you all the more dangerous when you lose control."

I jerked as if someone punched me. *Dangerous. Am I dangerous?*

Ingrid leaned forward. "Power...corrupts. In all its forms, whether that power rests with mortals or immortals. It turns into pride. Humility...dampens that power and stalls the corruption. Harnesses it into meekness. Strength and power under control." Ingrid paused. "Where do you lie on the spectrum, Athena Pherenike?"

My jaw tightened. Unbidden, the silk around my wrist sharpened to needle points. "My friends keep me humble."

"They keep you humble." Ingrid relaxed into her chair as she hummed and took notes. "And yet you wield your power—I mean, skills—to save them. Sounds as if they are, then, your weakness. Possibly something to exploit."

This sounded just like my pantheon. *Idiocy. That's what this is.* "My mortal friends are not a weakness," I shouted as I stood. "If you are like the others, then I have nothing else—"

Ingrid's eyes softened. "No, Athena, they are your strength. Which is why you fight so admirably to keep them."

I gasped at this woman's words, the truth of them seeping into my gut like cool spring waters. Would this woman stop playing devil's advocate? I'd had enough of that in my own mind.

"No doubt you fear what you will become without them once they die."

I threw myself back into the chair. I hated therapy. Officially. But I couldn't muster the energy to counter Ingrid's words.

"We're done for now. I'll see you on Wednesday."

I trudged out of the office and slammed the door.

CHAPTER 36

Ingrid's words didn't plague me at all after that first session or the ones that followed. I wasn't dangerous. And dangerous to who? My friends and family? How was trying to find Rose a bad thing? How was securing their well-being a danger?

Luis's face filled my mind alongside his murderer's just before the monster turned to ash.

I growled as I paced in the kitchen. No. That creature had it coming. Deserved his death. I completely ignored the fact that I'd interrupted Beatriz's investigation then as well. Or at least I tried to ignore it until Beatriz sent her usual countdown message for how long it would be until I was back at work.

Only ten more days.

Beatriz hadn't taken my screwup as hard as Zephonia had. My partner, however, had barely spoken to me. Even Elias had noticed.

"You've got to check on her," Elias told me as I tucked him in bed.

"Who?"

"Ms. Zephie," Elias said as if it were obvious. "I want to have playdates."

I rolled my eyes. "Is that all you think about?"

"I wouldn't have to if you'd let me go to school. And that's what you said I'm supposed to do if one of my friends has an owie."

I sighed and kissed his forehead. "You're relentless."

He beamed up at me like an entirely too-innocent angel. "Good night."

The next morning, I stood outside Zephonia's door with a cup of her favorite coffee in hand. No one had answered. I didn't want to snoop to see if anyone was in the backyard, so I waited on the front steps.

After another few minutes, the door opened, making me jump to my feet. "Are you ever going to go away?" a breathless voice asked.

Skata. You've got to be kidding me. My shoulders dropped. "You."

Hans gave me a tight-lipped smile, sweat dripping down his brow. "Me. What do you want?"

"I came to speak with Zephonia."

"Well, that's obvious. But one, she doesn't want to talk to you. And two, she's not here. She's having a grandma weekend. Took all the grands to breakfast."

"Then what are you doing here?"

Hans crossed his arms. More defined muscles than I remembered (or wanted to notice) rippled beneath that t-shirt. *Stop it, Huri. You're married. Well sorta.* "HOA found out about the twins...and me." He frowned. "No-immo policy."

Wow. That beyond sucks. "Sorry, man. You gonna fight it?"

He scoffed and rolled his eyes. "And subject my kids to effigies burning in the yard?"

"Fair." I shook my head. "I'm sorry that it happened."

Hans relaxed his arms. "Thanks."

Silence drifted between us. I tried to look anywhere but at Hans filling up Zephonia's doorway, looking like he'd just been exercising. He wasn't a small man. *But I could still take him.*

252

"Bring a peace offering?"

I nodded and shrugged. "Claudette's place was closed. Otherwise, I would've brought cupcakes."

That actually brought a smile to his lips. It was small, but it was also nice. "Coffee's the next best thing. You...uh, want to bring it inside?"

"Yeah. Sure."

Hans extended a hand for me to enter first as he tousled his hair out of his eyes. They weren't muddy-river brown like Zephonia's. They were more hazel. I did my best to ignore how arresting they were as I passed. At least, they were arresting when he wasn't being a jerk.

"Remember where the kitchen is?" he asked as he closed the door.

"Yeah. Zeph has had me and Eli over to play with the kids a few times."

He nodded as he fell in step beside me. "The twins always rave about him afterwards."

I smiled. "They're great kids." I set the cup down on the counter, watching Hans grab his mug and pour his own.

"Thanks. But it's not my doing. Mom knows what she's doing."

I winced. "She told me about their mother. Seems like you're doing right by them."

He frowned and hid behind a sip. "Sirens never really stick around. Off serving the pantheons."

"You did."

He smirked, making one dimple appear. "I'm also a man. Not nearly as valuable. Just thought she'd be different."

I leaned my hip against the counter. "What are you going to do? About the house thing."

He blew out a long breath and stared right at me as he considered his words. I did my best not to squirm. Most men didn't look me in the eye so intently. "Don't know. Just happened day before yesterday. I just started looking for real estate agents. I'd love to just rent it out to spite them, but I need the money from it to get into another one."

"I get that. Rent is awful."

Hans snickered, eyebrows meeting. "You pay rent?"

Don't you dare blush, Huri. "Yeah."

"You mean, your family doesn't own the whole block?"

I scoffed. "No. I don't take their money."

He leaned up against the counter as he studied me.

"What?"

"Why don't you?"

"Because...I just can't." I shivered in disgust. "Complicated."

"Uncomplicate it."

I exhaled wearily. "Come on. You know why. Or you can imagine why based on your own experiences."

His eyebrows met again. "Because of my ex-wife?"

"What she does. Nabs mortals to serve immortals. My pantheon...family...whatever...does the same thing. Exiled my grand-mother for standing up to that nonsense." I growled into my coffee.

Hans laughed and shook his head.

"It's not funny."

"Gawd, you're so much like her." Hans groaned as he smiled. "You want some cookies?" He fished out a box hidden in the top cabinets. I frowned at the stomach muscles peeking out of his lifted shirt. *Lord have mercy, does this man have a V cut? He's supposed to have a dad-bod.*

"Like who?"

"Mom. Total idealists." He extended the plastic sleeve to me.

My shoulders relaxed as I took a chocolate-covered graham cracker. "That's not a bad thing."

"It's not. Just explains a lot." He shrugged as he pulled the wrapper away from the sleeve of cookies. He set the sleeve of cookies on the counter. "She really thinks a lot of you."

I actually blushed. Again. "So, have you looked into other neigh-borhoods?"

He groaned and shook his head. "I don't know where to begin. I looked where Laura is, but nothing for sale there."

"I bet an agent will know."

"Yeah, look at this." He motioned for me to join him by a laptop on the counter. When he pointed at the screen and I didn't come, he frowned at me. "I don't have cooties."

"Such a man. I have cooties for mortal tech, Hans."

His cheeks reddened. "Oh. Yeah. Well, this here. It's a filter for no-immos policies."

I scoffed. "Like to filter out places without them?"

"No. To show all the places that are immo-free."

That made me roll my eyes as I took a cookie. "Just like with schools. They're another immo-free zone."

"That's what I'm worried about. Laura's kids don't have that problem. Their blood's too diluted. Mine? They're like baby rattlesnakes."

I winced and slid him another cookie. It hit his hand. "My kid turns into a spider. Remember?"

Hans stared at the cookie for a while and then took it. He held my gaze. He obviously had something to say. What snide comment would he make? He closed the distance between us. "What are you doing about the school thing? Mom told me what happened. I can't imagine."

"Avoiding the subject." I knew if I stepped back that it would look awkward. So I stayed put. Even if this was the first time in years I'd been this close to a man I hadn't needed to put into a headlock. Adonis totally didn't count. And Hans smelled like he had just been for a short run. I loved how Luis smelled after working out. Such a weird thing I missed.

His laugh burst out, making a riot of color dance in my mind. "Avoidance. My favorite way to handle things."

I dared to smile. "Elias's old teacher told me about an immo-friendly school. The pamphlet looks promising, but I'm still freaked out."

"And Elias wants to go."

I rolled my eyes. "Understatement."

"Let's look it up. I need to find a place for my rattlesnakes. You need to see if it's potentially safe for him."

Interesting. "You actually think he's got a good idea."

"Don't know yet." He looked back at me from the computer. "But if this means so much to him, he deserves your due diligence."

I was the one staring and studying now. He typed something on the keyboard and then looked back when I didn't say anything. "What?"

"You're not a total jerk."

That actually made him wince. "Fair. I was a jerk to you." His wince curved up into a smirk. "And you're not a totally pampered princess."

I rolled my eyes and crossed my arms, not trusting myself not to hit him. The girls and Luis used to tease me that that was how I flirted. And I was so not flirting with Zephonia's son. "That's what you thought of me?"

"Actually, yeah." He smiled like a boy with a new toy. "So, what's the name of the school, princess?"

CHAPTER 37

My mirror in the entryway flashed just before someone knocked on the door. I'd been sitting on the couch, knitting a hat for Elias and staring off into space. With a sigh, I swiped the mirror and found Zephonia's face there.

Without hesitation, I practically threw the door open.

Zephonia held up a bag from the Sanguine Bakery. "You got coffee?"

I grinned and then stifled it to a diplomatic nod. "Warm this time." It had been two days since I'd been to Zephonia's house. Almost a month since I'd seen her.

Zephonia followed me to the kitchen and waited in silence as I poured the coffee. It didn't escape my notice that she had bags under her eyes.

"What's wrong, Zeph?"

She actually gave me a tender smile at the nickname. But the smile was short-lived. "I'm not supposed to talk to you about this. But I need to get this out."

My heart sank. It was about Rose. Or I probably did something super wrong and didn't know it. Safest to keep silent.

"There's a leak at the office." Zephonia took a deep pull of the coffee like she would her pipe, wincing at the temperature.

A leak? Like the roof? That's not right. Oh no, she's not talking about the watery kind. "Oh, man."

Zephonia nodded and pulled out cupcakes. She laid into one like a kid looking for the prize in a Cracker Jack box. "Hasn't happened in decades," she mumbled around the mass of cupcake in her mouth. "Literally before you were born."

I passed a barstool from the island to Zephonia and then plopped onto mine. "How do you know?"

Zephonia held up a finger as she finished chewing. After a moment, she cleared her mouth with another sip of coffee. *Hurry up already.* "So, too many things are going wrong."

Zephonia took another maddening sip.

"You...we've been raiding the bigger houses."

My blood surged. They were actually following my hunches for Rose.

"They're emptied moments before we get there."

I couldn't help my fist clenching.

Zephonia's eyes glanced down at my hand, making me hide it below the counter.

"What does Janis say?"

Zephonia exhaled. "She...doesn't know. Or it's possible she's choosing to ignore it."

"You haven't told her your suspicions?"

"Not yet. No proof."

I leaned forward. "Who do you suspect? I bet it's Violet. She's always in on gossip."

"You just don't like her." Zephonia exhaled and covered her face. "It could be anyone. No one. Just seems that every time we get traction, something goes wrong. Maybe I'm looking for something that isn't there."

I nodded. "That package with the fangs and tongue did end up getting delivered without going through the post office."

Zephonia straightened like a soldier snapping to attention. "I forgot about that."

"Remember that time I was missing files?"

Zephonia's face reddened. "Yeah, then they came back. Like they were never missing."

I winced, mind glazing with the memory of reaming myself out for misplacing those files.

"And then there's Frank's murder."

"Yeah, there's no way someone outside the office could've pulled that off."

"The only thing that didn't get tipped off was your...arrest of Tiffany Silva. But that's because you didn't tell anybody beforehand."

My heart pounded. "Zeph, I would never—"

Zephonia smiled weakly. "Huri, you didn't even know about the raids. You've been out."

I put a hand on my chest like that would somehow let me breathe again.

Zephonia winced as she leaned across the counter and squeezed my hand. "I wouldn't have come to you if I suspected you, chickadee."

The nickname nearly undid me. It was hard to swallow those blasted emotions as I squeezed back.

"I need to talk this out before I bring it to Filomena. She trusts the stewards."

"Well, anyone has access to our desks."

Zephonia nodded. "But not everyone has access to our mail."

"Didn't Janis have us review the footage?"

"It was totally clean." Zephonia wiped her mouth with a napkin. "I watched it myself. Whoever it was knew our blind spots."

"So, who has access to the mail?"

Zephonia winced. "The front desk stewards."

"They'd be able to snag files since they drop off mail daily."

Zephonia groaned into her coffee. "I hate this."

"How are you going to bait them?"

"Only way is to plant a false trail."

Silence drifted between us. I wasn't sure what to say. I wanted to say something profound.

"I've missed this," Zephonia said at last.

My heart warmed as my stomach soured. "I'm sorry, Zeph. I really screwed up."

Her smile still looked a bit injured. "Just trust me next time, chickadee."

I nodded. "I've gotten so used to doing everything alone."

Zephonia saluted me with her cup. "Been there too."

I raised my mug. "To no more Lone Ranger nonsense."

Zephonia's smile didn't look so forced this time. "Hear hear."

"So how are things going with getting Enrica?"

Zephonia scoffed. "That's something else that tipped me off. She's always one step ahead of us. She's claiming that Tiffany went off the rails and tried to peddle it on the streets." Zephonia let out a slow exhale. "Even claims she has the authorization to develop the drug. It's a mountain of legalese. She's now being so cooperative that we're snowed under from going through the evidence. So far all that evidence is just a bunch of unrelated paperwork."

My eyes widened. "What does Tiffany say about that?"

Zephonia winced. "She's not in her right mind at the moment."

I should've guessed. "Withdrawals."

"Yeah. And we're not allowed to give her the very drug that we're fighting against."

Skata. "Maybe you could use Tiffany to pin down Enrica. Say that you're going to transfer her or something."

Zephonia nodded. "She'll either try to rescue her or—"

"Kill her." I shook my head at the memory of the last time Dave and Tiffany were together and how quickly his life ended after that encounter. There was no doubt Tiffany would meet a similar end.

"Well, I need to head back home. Watching the twins while Hans meets with a real estate agent." She half smiled like she knew a secret. "But you already knew that."

I fought to keep impassive. "Mama knew a good agent. I just passed the info along."

Zephonia squeezed my shoulder as she passed. "I'm glad you two are getting along."

"As long as he's not a jerk, we're good."

Zephonia snickered. "He's all right when he stops trying to control everything."

I did not open my mouth on the subject. It still felt weird that Hans had been sending me messages since I visited Zephonia's. It was such weird texts, too. Usually, questions like, "What about this house?" or "When did Eli stop having accidents?"

"Let me know how it goes." *Maybe that leak was helping whoever had Rose.*

"I'm sure you'll hear it from Hans."

I laughed and shook my head. "The leak, Zeph."

"Oh." Zephonia's laughter slowly died. "I hope I'm wrong, though."

Me too. It was one thing to have stewards turn into mavericks. It was a whole other thing to have a spy for the bad guys in our midst.

CHAPTER 38

I hid my face behind my hands as Alexis and Klara read the pros and cons lists Elias and I had made. Hans and I had found out that the school seemed to be as welcoming to immortal as mortal children. It was in their mission statement. I promptly forced the image of Hans's glowing face when he looked back from the computer and thanked me for sharing a place that might be good for his kids. He had looked so relieved that it made me feel guilty for not touring the school yet.

So, I headed home and made Elias make an "I Want To Go To School Because..." List.

"Wow, Huri," Klara said as she plopped into the seat beside me.

"Yeah, I mean, I knew he was smart, but this is next level." Alexis shook her head as she continued to read.

"What do you think?" I wiped my face. "I mean, if I do this and he gets hurt again...I don't know that I can take it on top of...of Rose." My eyes cut to the refrigerator where Luis leaned, munching on an apple.

Their eyebrows rose almost as one as they exchanged looks. Apparently, Klara was ordered to speak first. "I'm not a mom," Klara began. "But I remember being a kid. I'd be pretty upset if my mom didn't take me seriously after something like this." She waved at the paper.

I pulled the list back over. It wasn't a list of pros and cons so much as bullet points of why Elias wanted to go to school.

The first one: "I'm not frade to go to scool. I'm scared not to go." Granted, his spelling was off in several places, but it didn't lessen the impact.

"We'll go with you," Alexis said. "I can contact some parents on social media."

I worried my bottom lip. *Am I really going to do this?* "Parents first. If there are some immortal parents..."

Alexis smiled and squeezed my hand. "We've got you."

Within days, I'd spoken with enough parents to know that I had to see the school. When the fifth immo parent raved about how wonderful the school was, I knew I couldn't avoid a tour. Even so, I scheduled an Elias-free tour first. Just in case.

I chewed my bottom lip—it was getting to be a bad habit—and sent a message to Hans. *Talked to some parents. Going to go look at the school.*

He immediately typed back: *You need me to go with you?*

My eyebrows rose. That was unexpectedly sweet. *Thanks. But I've got it. I'll let you know how it goes.*

It was so different from the public school, from how non-prison-like the building was to the smiles on the kids' and teachers' faces. It was warm and cozy and full of art. Some classes even played background music to help kids focus. Most importantly, I watched a werewolf cub transform during recess. No one said anything. He romped and played with his mortal friends like this was a regular game.

For the final tour, I brought Klara and Alexis with me and Elias.

The sight of Alexis with a clipboard like she was some sort of Inspector of Schools made me snicker to myself. As soon as Elias saw the kindergarten room, he hurried right on in and joined a group reading in comfy beanbag chairs.

Klara smiled and joined him silently, helping him pick out a book.

"He is so bright," the principal said with a smile.

"Yes," Alexis said with a grin and looked down at her paper. "He is quite advanced. What do you have in the way of curriculum that can challenge Elias? He can already read chapter books."

The principal looked to me, eyes wide. "Seriously?"

I nodded. "He just started, but yes. He can read and understand just about anything."

"And he's adding and subtracting two-digit numbers," Alexis said.

"Perhaps we could test him and see where he really falls. If he's doing so well, he may be more advanced than I expected."

Alexis nodded so imperiously that I nearly snickered. "That's a wonderful idea. Let's get the testing scheduled." She hurried the principal along to the office.

Klara joined me in watching Elias read to some of the students. "He fits in pretty good here."

I nodded. *He's amazing.* "He's far more affable than I am."

Klara bit her bottom lip and turned her back so that the kids couldn't see her. "Is the little girl in pigtails..." She raised her eyebrows.

"Yeah, she's a werewolf pup," I whispered.

Klara's cheeks flushed. "She was so sweet to Eli."

A small smile twitched at the corners of my lips.

"I'm just surprised she was turned so young."

The little girl giggled and approached. Klara yelped and jumped at her sudden appearance. "My mommy borned me like this." Then she headed over to the bathroom on the other side of the room.

Klara's face turned completely red. *Bless her heart.* I knew that Klara hadn't been around many immortals...or at least ones that weren't shady.

The teacher approached with a smile. "Would it be okay if Elias joined us for recess? If you have the time."

"Absolutely. I'm sure he'd love that."

My smile deepened as she called them all to line up, asking Elias in particular. It was so good to see Elias swinging and laughing between another little boy and girl. They were racing to see how high they could swing. After a few minutes of contented swinging, his gaze focused on me then the kids and the teachers, and then back to me. His jaw clenched. And I knew right then that he was going to do something.

"Elias," I called and shook my head. "Don't." *Whatever it is. Just don't.*

At the apex of his swing, he leapt out, and as he landed, he shifted. It felt like the wind got blasted out of me by a centaur's kick. His top half, as ever, was still Elias, but from the waist down, he sported slender legs, an iridescent blue. Klara grabbed my forearm. At first, I thought Klara was trying to hold me back, but the wide-eyed gape on Klara's face made me realize she'd never seen Elias transform.

"My grandmother's Arachne, Klara. Remember?" I whispered and pried off her grip.

The kids all stopped and stared. The teacher and I locked eyes. Then the teacher put on her sternest face. "Now, Elias, we're not allowed to jump off the swings like that. You could get very hurt."

Bless her. She didn't freak out.

He stared at the children who could be his friends. They were shocked to silence. Another class came running out to the playground. I rushed to Elias's side as they all skidded to a halt. They had to have a few more years on Elias.

"Change back," I hissed through my tight smile.

Elias still stood there, chewing his bottom lip. Red was coming to his nose. *Oh no. He's going to cry.*

One boy pushed forward. He, too, smelled like a werewolf. "Wow. An orb weaver spider. They have some of the strongest webs on the planet." He ran up to Elias, staring up at him like he was a movie star. "Can you spin webs? I'm Jason. I just got done doing a report on orb weavers. Can you spin webs? Are they sticky? Wow! You're so tall."

Elias blinked several times as if it took him a minute to process what the boy said. *Me too, kiddo.* "I'm Elias."

"I've never heard of a werespider. I'm a werewolf. My sister goes here too." He pointed at the girl with pigtails. "You wanna play?"

In a blink, Elias was back to having only two legs. "You're...you're not scared of me?"

Jason laughed. "Dude, I love spiders." He pointed at his Spiderman t-shirt. "I wish I could turn into one. Does your whole family turn into spiders? Oh! Let's go do the jungle gym. Who's your favorite superhero? Mine's totally Spiderman."

My eyes burned when Elias looked back with a trembling grin. I forced myself to nod and waved him away. He and Jason both scampered off, talking about all the bad guys Spiderman would definitely beat.

Alexis wrapped her arm around my shoulders. "Scheduled his test for tomorrow."

A gasp escaped me, and I turned away to hide. Klara came to my other side and bumped me.

"That's one brave kid you've got," Klara whispered.

My throat was so tight that I could barely speak. "He is."

CHAPTER 39

After my final therapy session, Janis sent the clearance to return to work on the following Monday as planned.

I nearly cried from relief. *I'm a total wreck.*

It wasn't long after that when I received a message from Zephonia with information on a new case. "We got a fresh body while you were on vacation," Zephonia wrote. "I want you up to speed for Monday. And keep an eye out for an announcement from the captain."

A few hours after that, Janis sent a message that was too long to read on my bracelet. I entered my home office and accessed it on my larger mirror.

It was a recording. Zephonia's voice came through as she held an envelope addressed to the captain. She was walking to the front desk where Violet was sorting papers and mail.

"Can you make sure you get this to Filomena, Violet? Her office is locked for the day. She wanted to make sure it got locked back up."

"Yeah, she's gone. I'll get it to her." Violeta then waited for Zephonia to leave before opening the envelope, reading the contents, and then scrying someone from her bracelet. She spilled everything about the fake report.

I scowled but felt vindicated. Violet had been too much of a pain. I turned off the video and exhaled. It was too much watching another steward get arrested by her own colleagues.

I sent a message to Zephonia. "Called it."

With a weary exhale, I refilled my cup with decaf and returned to my home office, ignoring my story collage, and flipped through the files on my large mirror.

The victim was mortal, nineteen, female. I winced at seeing that she was brutally drained. A prayer escaped me in hopes Christina Jones felt as little pain as possible in her final moments. Poor thing even had a stab wound that the labbies said looked to be from something the size of a butter knife. But that was an older wound that had been slowly healing. Her parents had reported her missing over a year ago.

I propped my head against my hand as I flicked through each documented trauma. It was obvious Christina had been a donor for a house. She had gained weight since her last-known photo, and her body sported healed bite marks too numerous to count.

"I'm so sorry this happened to you," I whispered, fighting against the thought that Rose was probably in a similar situation.

Christina had been dumped in a field like someone wanted her to be found. Two huge moths dotted her arms and legs. Something about the moth's pattern tickled my brain. I grabbed the lukewarm files and started thumbing through them until I found Sierra Lenora Reynolds.

I stood when I spotted the butterfly wing in one photo. With a flick, I held up the photograph next to the mirror with Christina's photo. The wing decoration was too similar to discount.

"Scry Zephonia Weber."

I clamped on my ear cuff and waited for her. Zephonia answered from the mirror in her kitchen. She looked like she was about to pour a stiff drink.

"Zeph, sorry to bother you, but I found something," I said quickly in case she was about to hang up on me.

"Yeah?" Zephonia threw back the drink like a shot.

My eyebrows met. "What's up? You okay?"

"Watch the news, chickadee."

What? I shook my head. "News? I just saw Violet's arrest. But I found something with the new case. And Sierra Lenora Reynolds. It's a link."

Zephonia straightened when I held up Sierra's picture. "Oh. It's a butterfly. They pool on dead bodies all the time."

"It's a moth. Same kind as is in Christina's picture. It's huge."

Zephonia's eyes widened as she set down her glass. "We...wait. A moth."

"Yeah, it's weird. It's the size of a man's hand. It's huge. I've never seen one do this."

"Pooling. They do that with dead bodies. Even butterflies do it."

"Yeah, but two of the same kind in different places? Are there any immortals tied to moths? I've never heard of any."

Zephonia cursed and covered her face. She shook her head and started fiddling with her mirror. "Look at this."

My bracelet and mirror vibrated. I opened the message to see a press conference with Enrica as well as council members of the Amaranthian Society and the CDC. Grandmother was standing beside Enrica.

"Enrica Fontana, the founder of Lamiens Alliance, has just been granted the green light to manufacture and test synthetic lamia venom on mortal subjects," the voiceover said as Enrica stared right at the camera and grinned like the cat who caught the mouse.

The picture fell from my hand. "No," I rasped. *No, this can't be happening.*

"We were just about to execute the warrant for her arrest."

"Zeph..." I sank into my chair. *Grandmother. How could she?*

"It wasn't you necessarily." Zephonia poured another drink. "Not you and Tiffany. We tried to get her, but she has her teeth in the council." She exhaled.

"Dang." My forehead clunked onto the desk. "I didn't know. I've been keeping my nose clean." I groaned. "Trying to."

"Happened just an hour ago." Zephonia shook her head. "But look at the guy beside your grandmother."

I knew Zephonia didn't mean it as a jab, but it felt like it. Keeping my words tucked safely in my mouth, I adjusted the image so that I could see him. He was huge. Like Conan but so blond he looked like he had white hair. He dressed like he was a modernized lord of old with his three-piece suit and some fluffy sort of tie.

"See that broach pinning his ascot?" Zephonia took a long drag and exhale of her pipe.

"It's a moth."

"He's a *wurdulac*. They're only supposed to be in Usal Mountains."

"Russia. But what's this wurdulac thingy? What are they?"

"They're vampires, Huri. Old ones. They shift into these moths instead of bats."

My eyes widened. "Huge Nordic bodyguards. Isn't that what the siren said?"

"What?"

"Do they all look like him?"

"Yeah, they get mistaken for the Norse pantheon all the time. I'd really ream you for this if they weren't so freakin' rare."

I jumped to my feet. "Aleksandr. She...she mentioned an Aleksandr. Weird pronunciation. Do you..."

Zephonia was already typing on her holographic keyboard. "Wife Vivienne of House Vessiks. Son Aleksandr..." Zephonia lapsed into some colorful German that I hadn't learned. "Aleksandr Nikolai Vessiks."

My cry of rage quite nearly shook the whole house.

"The son is in Nashville. They have a presence here, Huri. A house."

I nearly upended the table, cursing in Japanese (much more satisfying), but it just thudded the wall.

"Huri! You'll wake Elias!"

I gripped my hair, water springing to my eyes. "All this time. All this time, Zeph."

Zephonia pulled over Beatriz's file on Rose. "Beatriz has been visiting the local houses since seeing your notes from home." Her lips creased. "She hadn't gotten to Vessiks yet."

"Then we go tonight."

"That's not how it works, Huri. You know it. We don't even know if they're keeping her there."

My mind filled with the glorious image of smiting the entire house.

"Don't go rogue, Huri. We need the stewards to move against a house of this much power. Vengeance Laws won't protect you. His father is right beside your grandmother. You'll start a war."

Good. Let their blood flood the ground. No, Huri. I growled and clamped my eyes shut. "I know," I raged and threw myself into the chair.

"We will stake him to the wall, Huri. Let's make it legal. So he will pay for his crimes."

I shook. The taste of vengeance on my lips would burst through my mouth like the finest pinot noir, subtle and fruity and dry all at once. And unflinchingly intoxicating.

"Mama?"

My body straightened when Elias entered, blurry-eyed and clutching his Spiderman plush toy. "You okay, agapi mou?"

"I heard yelling."

"I'm so sorry, baby. Mami was just reading something. I got a little excited. Go back to bed."

"Can you sit with me?"

I looked to Zephonia, who gave me a dark grin. "I'll call you once we're ready to move. Just tend to Elias."

I stared at my son for a brief moment before nodding. "Will do. Come on, buddy. Let's snuggle up in my bed."

CHAPTER 40

Mama passed me my sword, which my silk armor enveloped at my thigh. "I've got Eli."

Alexis and Klara rushed through the door. Both their mouths fell open when they saw me in my dark-gray silk armor. I tapped my forehead for my helmet to reveal my face.

They hurried forward, Klara with the strongest coffee in town and Alexis with a jar of olives and a package of ham.

"I can't bake," Alexis said with a shrug as she looked down. "But we've been keeping them in stock."

"As a backup," Klara added and passed me the coffee.

Mama grinned. "No better ambrosia than a sister's thoughtfulness. Eat up, love. We're still waiting on Zephonia."

Klara nodded at my armor. "Badass. Just needs some leather."

Alexis's eyes misted. "You're sure this is the guy."

"He's the head of the house here. It fits." I stuffed the olives into my mouth first and chased them down with the coffee. It was a strangely invigorating combination. "I don't know if he's got Rose, but this is the closest we've been."

Klara's fingers drummed her chin as she continued to assess my attire. "You're totally missing something. But what's taking so long? I mean, it's been at least an hour or more."

"I don't know. They probably have to wake everyone up," I said.

Alexis tore open the package of ham and started pulling out chunks and practically force-feeding me. *Forget that.* I plucked them from her hand and popped them in my mouth. Alexis said, "Just stay safe. Taking on a whole pack of vampires."

Mama and I smirked at each other. As my body began to hum with the gifts from the friends I claimed as sisters, I realized what Zephonia meant.

It had been dumb not to trust my sisters. All of them.

My bracelet vibrated off the edge of the counter. The three crowded close but out of eyesight.

"Huri," Beatriz greeted me.

And I knew then, just by the sound of her voice. "It's Rose."

"We...we found her. It's what took so long."

My eyes welled as I looked at my family. "Is...Where is she?"

"Gruhn's parking lot."

I rushed to the door. "I'm on my way."

"Call us when you can," Mama shouted from the door as I sped away in Big Blue.

Gruhn's was barely ten minutes away. Somehow, I knew that Rose had been trying to get to me. I called Zephonia as I raced through the streets.

"Chickadee?"

"Zeph." My voice cracked.

I heard something that sounded like metal being sharpened. "What's wrong, Huri?"

"It's...they found her. Bia just called."

Zephonia swore, and something hit a wall. "Good Lord, we can't catch a freakin' break. Where?"

"Gruhn's."

"Consider me there."

Just as I pulled up, I hung up. Blue and red lights lit the night. I managed to get the car in park before leaping out.

"Beatriz!" I shouted over the chattering of radios and police. Then I saw the sheet covering a body. "Rose? Rose!" My body trembled as I ran past the police. One caught me, but Beatriz called him down.

"She's a steward. Let her through."

I managed to remember myself and what I was, but it was a chore. Beatriz's face was drawn and her nose red.

"Is..." I could barely form words. Beatriz hugged me hard and tight. "She's not...she can't be."

"Hey." She cupped my face in her hands. "Let me read you the scene. Work. We gotta nail this guy."

I nodded. "Let...me...let me just see her first. Give me a minute."

Six months. Six months and I thought I would never see my sister. Six months and I never thought I would hold her hand, touch her hair. Six months and Rose had never given up. All the hours and...

"Of course, Huri." Beatriz walked me forward and pulled back the sheet.

I gasped. She looked like she had taken a beating. More than.

"Multiple bite marks." Beatriz shook her head. "When we got here, there was a whole mess of moths all over her. Strangest thing I've ever seen."

I felt a growl rise up at that. It was him. I'd found him. Only too late.

I took in the stilettos on the ground beside Rose, covered in blood and gore. They were beside markers where stewards were photographing them. My body vibrated like a volcano, remembering how I took Rose and Klara and Alexis into my backyard regularly and made sure they knew how to defend themselves.

"She put up one hell of a fight, Huri," Beatriz whispered, voice breaking.

"Get the hell out of my way, son," Zephonia growled and held up a badge. "I'm a steward."

I managed to put on the gloves Beatriz handed me as Zephonia knelt beside me. With a tender kiss to my forehead, Zephonia helped expose Rose's hands and arms to let me hold her hand. I brought Rose's hand to my lips, but Zephonia stopped me.

"Wait," Zephonia whispered. "Look at her lips."

I obeyed. "She fought hard, Zeph."

"Beatriz," Zephonia began. "We need to get the body moved for scene mop up."

I swatted a huge moth away, forgetting for a moment what that meant. Then I leapt to my feet. "You're under arrest, you bastard. Capture the moths!"

Another steward taking pictures shook her head. "It's called pooling. Butterflies do it too. They drink any liquid."

My silk shot out and stabbed the nearest giant moth as my sword leapt into my hand. The wurdulac shifted just before I sliced him in half. Zephonia charged next, sinking her sedative-laced needles into his abdomen.

"Don't let'm get away," Zephonia ordered.

But the other wurdulacs had already vanished into the shadows.

"Screw Vengeance Laws," I roared as I made my way to the car. "I'll have his head."

Zephonia grabbed me by the arm and swung me around. "You're your grandmother's daughter." She jerked my arm. "Act like it."

I nearly unleashed my fury on Zephonia, but then a gurney came rolling up. Watching them put my sister's body in a bag melted me. What would I tell Elias? The girls?

"Get in, chickadee." Zephonia pushed me into the back of the van with Rose and shut us inside, bracelet to her lips.

"Jerome," Zephonia began. "I'm so sorry for the call. We've found her."

I stared at Zephonia. How could I forget to call Jerome?

"I...I hate to...just a precaution in case..." She nodded at whatever he said. "I know. That's why we're taking her to the steward's clinic."

"Steward's clinic?" I whispered.

"Right away. If...well, you know we don't have a big window."

"What's going on?"

Zephonia nodded, looking away from me. "Thanks, Jer."

As soon as she hung up, I turned Zephonia back around. "What's going on, Zeph?"

Zephonia swallowed. "I don't want to give you..." She picked up Rose's fingers. "It's blood. On her lips too. There's a chance it's her attacker's blood."

My eyes rounded and nearly doubled in size. My body began to shake.

"If that's the case...we've got to...Jerome's people...they have a way to curb the effects of vampirism. They've been hunted nearly to extinction."

I stared at Rose. "How...I didn't think anyone could be...I mean... it's impossible and..."

"I may be wrong, but we can't take that chance." Zephonia winced, staring down at Rose. "That whole 'rising from the grave' thing is a story for a reason."

Skata. "How do we know?"

"We'll know when it happens. I have never seen anyone turn. But based on the stories, we'll know."

As long as she's alive...after a fashion. I held fast to Rose's hand during the entire ride. I wouldn't let her go even as they unloaded her. The stewards at the clinic had Rose out and were rushing her into a room.

A steward dressed as a nurse approached once Rose was strapped to the bed. "We've a donor on standby."

"Thank you," Zephonia said. "We'll alert you at the first sign."

I planted myself directly beside Rose, allowing Zephonia and another steward to collect samples from Rose's body. I wept when they had to do a sexual assault examination. Both gasped at what they saw.

Witnessing the process of collecting samples and cataloging her injuries, taking pictures with tape measures, made me fantasize about all the tortures I would inflict on this Aleksandr and his house. *Let them all burn to ash in the sun. Starve achingly slow.*

Enrica was somehow connected. I didn't know how, but I was sure of it. I'd kill whoever it was. No. I'd beat them within half an inch of their life-in-death and let Rose have her revenge. If Rose survived this. *No, she will. She will survive.*

"You all right?" Zephonia asked once it was all done.

I couldn't speak, only shake. *I'm not okay. Not yet, at least.*

Zephonia bit her unlit pipe, lips thin and brow furrow in a knot. "You'll avenge her, Huri. And I'll be there with you. We'll not let this stand."

I stared into Zephonia's eyes. The browns of her irises reminded me of the fury of a river that overtakes its banks. I'd never seen her anywhere near wrathful, but Zephonia was there. It calmed me just a little, the impending realization of revenge.

I rested my head against Zephonia's shoulder. For minutes, we sat there, waiting for some sign from Rose. The door opened, and nurses came in, followed by Jerome, who had a messenger bag thrown across his torso. His body stiffened when he saw her, pale as death and just as cold and still.

I looked to Zephonia when the nurse began moving Rose's hospital gown around her abdomen. "What's going on?"

"I...I don't know how to say this...but she's pregnant. There's a baby in there."

Sure enough. As soon as the monitors were attached, the fluttering of a heartbeat spiked on the monitors. *Skata. She's pregnant? Impossible.*

"What?" Jerome stumbled against the wall.

That's when Rose started thrashing.

"Jerome. Do it," Zephonia ordered.

He swallowed hard and nodded. "I've got it."

"Poppi!" Rose shouted, thrashing.

278

The nurse rushed to the bed and hit the button to raise Rose's upper body. I had never seen Rose look more sinister than when she opened her eyes and set them on her human nurse. The ferocity of a starved predator twisted Rose's features into something out of mortal nightmares.

I pushed the nurse back when she exposed her wrist to her. "No!"

"She'll burst the restraints if I don't."

"There are other ways," Zephonia said and waved at Jerome.

The nurse wrestled admirably but futilely with me. "I won't allow her to be experimented on."

"Let me get her consent," I said.

The nurse huffed and blew her hair out of her face. "Fat chance. They're not tame 'til they feed."

The air behind me moved. I looked back in time for the tip of Rose's fingernail to draw a crimson line the size of a paper cut along my neck. I growled and leapt on top of Rose, pinning her arms.

"Rosie. Listen to me!"

"I will taste her blood." Rose snapped her teeth.

Before I could stop the nurse, the woman pressed her wrist to Rose's lips.

Rose latched on like a leech. Water burned my eyes. She was feeding on a mortal, sucking like someone dying of thirst. The moment the nurse and Rose locked eyes, I felt Rose grow still. Like a sleepwalker coming to, Rose looked around. My heart ached for the nurse whose silver-lined eyes never strayed from Rose.

"Look at her, Rose. You're doing to her what *he* did to you. She's you."

Rose closed her eyes, two quick tears racing out past her lashes.

"There's another way," I said, holding Rose's rock-hard hand to the bed. "Let go of her. There's another way."

Her body shook beneath mine.

"Look at me. Please, Rosie."

After I begged several more times, Rose looked at me. Her bloodshot eyes were no longer lined with silver. They were their old hue. But I couldn't see Rose, the sister I loved, staring back just yet.

"You're safe, Rosie. Let her go. Let me help you."

No one moved for several moments. Then Rose blinked a few more times, looking at the nurse and then at me. More tears fell until she released the nurse's wrist like a dog dropping a bone.

"There's another way?"

"Yes," I whispered. "Jerome says it will work."

Rose stared at the nurse once again as another nurse came in, and wrapped the first nurse's wrist with gauze, and half-carried her out. "OK."

"Out," Jerome ordered everyone.

Zephonia nodded to another nurse-steward, who glared but obeyed. "You better know what you're doing, Zephonia."

I left reluctantly and stationed myself at the window. Jerome shut the curtains with a snap.

The growling and snarling inside the room had me pacing before the door. Rose screamed the word *poppi* over and over. Zephonia chewed her pipe and spoke to someone over the bracelet. I assumed she must be updating Beatriz.

Somewhere in the back of my mind, I knew Mama and the girls and Rose's parents would want to know, but I couldn't bear to speak with anyone until I knew her condition. Screaming was good. But at what cost? Turning into the thing that stole her life?

The screaming stopped. I trembled from the effort of keeping myself from barging into the room. The sink turned on inside. I threw open the door and found Jerome wiping her face clean of something red and sticky.

"Huri," he scolded.

The husk of some sort of fruit lay on the bed. It looked like a giant fig. Those had been at Rose's house before she disappeared. The baby's heartbeat pulsed on the screen beside the bed. "Is...is she okay?"

He stared at me and then at Zephonia, who entered without

letting anyone else in. "It would have been better to get it in her before she woke. We'll see."

My hands shook as I sank back into my chair. Jerome took up his post on Rose's right side. Zephonia started to sit beside me, but her bracelet rang.

"I've got to take this. I'll be right outside."

Once Zephonia left, I looked across Rose's body to Jerome. I hated that I hadn't kept up with him like I should've. We'd spoken almost weekly immediately after her abduction. The time between check-ins slowly lengthened when weeks turned into months. "Will it help her...now that..." I couldn't say it.

He nodded. "It should. My father saw it work on a friend. It won't change what she is now, but it'll...it dulls the cravings. Over time, I've heard they become like dhampir."

We stared at her in silence.

"Thank you for coming, Jerome."

"I'm just glad that she's...she's home." He nodded, bending over to hold her hand and kiss her fingertips. "That's all that matters."

Rose's head tossed and turned, lips moving in silent speech.

"Man, she put up a fight." Jerome stared down at her beaten hands. Already, the bruising and cuts were reknitting.

"She was just minutes away from me, Jerome."

He looked over at me. "You stake these bastards to the wall, Huri."

I nodded. "You know I will."

He nodded once as if that was enough and the discussion was closed. "Listen, she'll need to eat one of these every time she wants to feed. She'll fight back for a bit, but after a few feedings, she'll want the figs more than...you know."

"You can't leave, Jerome."

"She may not want me around. Vampires have an aversion to us." He smiled sadly. "I just want you to know in case. But I'm sticking around until we see how she reacts."

I eased back into the chair. "I'm going to wait to call her parents until we find out what's going on with her."

"I agree," he said. "We need to make sure they're not in danger."

I'd forgotten that part.

"Thanks for staying, Jerome."

He cast Rose a lovesick look.

We waited through several nurse checks. Jerome and I stared. We'd each experienced this with our own children: a sonogram of a fluttering little baby.

"Is it...okay?" I dared to ask the sonogram tech while she checked on the baby.

"Amazingly. But dhampir are a resilient lot. They're hard to kill even this small. Hard as diamonds." The tech shook her head at the screen. "Poor thing. I've never heard of a do—I mean, a victim—getting pregnant before."

Jerome swallowed hard. "It happens with mated couples."

That's right. Like Paul and Claudette and their dhampir daughter. What had happened to Rose? Did I really want to know?

"How...how far along is she?"

"Hard to tell. Dhampir grow faster than most of us. We'll know more when she wakes." The tech winced, patting my shoulder as she started toward the door.

The scent of the mortal tech had Rose's nose twitching and her body jerking against the constraints. Her eyes flared open, revealing that beautiful honey-brown of her pre-bitten days. But they had a feral, unseeing light to them.

At once, we shoved the tech out. Jerome force-fed her the fig. I nearly tore him away from her when he practically suffocated her with the fruit, but then Rose was eating with relish, even licking the juice from his fingers when they got in the way. He actually laughed then.

"That tickles, Rose."

She grinned tellingly, eyes closed. "Those fingers are precious, Rome."

Our eyes widened.

"Play that one song." She paused as if listening to him speak. "No, the one you played when we were kids."

Then she was back asleep.

I couldn't hold in my giggle and raised an eyebrow at him. The smile on his face shamed the sun.

"Rose?" he dared to call. "Wake up, baby."

It took her a minute, but her lips curled into a snarl. "Go away. I'm sleeping."

"Rose," I called this time. "Rose, it's Huri. Can you hear me?"

Rose tried to shake her head, but the strap across her forehead kept her too still. She thrashed until I dared to press my hands to her face.

"Rose, it's Huri. You're safe."

"Let me go. Let me go."

Then her eyes surged open. My heart warmed at the sight. Rose was there. My Rosie was shining back out of her gaze. She was alive. Rose was alive. *Thank you. Thank you. Thank you.*

Rose's eyes leaked tears as she fought to look toward my voice.

"Huri? Is...I...am I dreaming? I can't move my head."

I managed to get into Rose's line of sight. It made Rose cry out, weeping openly.

"Oh, thank God. Poppi. Is Poppi okay?"

"What's a poppi?"

"The baby. I'm...I'm pregnant and..."

I exhaled a wet sigh. "Yes, honey. Baby's fine."

"Don't let them take her from me. She helped me remember *me*. I forgot me and all...and keep her safe, Huri. Don't let them..."

"Poppi?" I barely kept myself from blubbering. *She's already given the baby a name?* "Poppi's fine, Rosie. She's strong like her mama. Listen."

Jerome turned up the baby's heartbeat.

Rose's eyes widened, and her mouth dropped open. She let out a wail as a grin split her face. "She's...I...that's her little heartbeat. Holy cow." She laughed as she cried, relaxing into the bed. "Poppi, I can hear you. You made it. We made it. I told you I'd get you out of there."

I laughed with her, trying to hide my concern. *A baby from a monster and she wants to keep it?*

"Where...who else is here? Why can't I move?" She swallowed hard. "I thought we were dead."

"You...you've been turned, Rose." I felt my own body go cold. "You're restrained so you don't hurt the medical staff."

She swallowed hard. "I...I'm...I'm..." She closed her eyes, pushing out tears. "I'm one of them now?"

I gave Jerome a long hard look. He closed his eyes and came closer, taking her hand.

"Sort of," Jerome said.

Rose let out a cry of shock. "Jerome." She breathed his name as if it had a meaning of its own.

He dared to caress her cheek with the back of his fingers. "Welcome back, Rosaline."

Her breath caught, eyes closed as she reveled in his fingertips tracing her battered cheek. "I'm so sorry."

He scoffed. "No, there's no apologies here, beautiful. You are back, and I don't care about anything else."

Her chin trembled.

The nurses had filled the window and door. *Great. Not even two seconds of privacy.*

"Rose. The nurses need to come in and check you." I squeezed her hand. "Jerome, explain things."

He did at once. Rose listened through the tears. At the end, she nodded.

"I'm okay. I'll do whatever it takes. Just...do you think it'll hurt Poppi? The turning? The fruit?"

"No one knows," I admitted. "I don't know anyone who has turned while pregnant."

Rose shook, eyes closed. "What happens if I don't take blood? Do...what...what is Poppi?"

"A dhampir. Half mortal, half vampire. And all the ones I know can go with or without. They just like rare steaks."

That made Rose giggle.

I beamed at the return of my sweet friend. *She's back.* "You ready?"

"So...Jerome, one last thing." She winced. "I don't mean to sound mean or anything but...why do you stink?"

He laughed hard. "Y'all don't like fruit bats. Tend to lose your appetite around us."

She snickered. "Seriously?"

"I'll start smelling like heaven after a couple more figs. No worries."

"And a shower," I said with a punch to his arm.

"I don't want to hear it. You look like Catwoman."

Our laughter brought in the nurses.

CHAPTER 41

The sight of the nurses made Rose sit straighter, like a girl giving her best side to an approaching date. My insides turned when saliva started dripping from the corners of Rose's lips.

Her body stiffened and pressed against the constraints. I had a feeling that she was testing whether her body was now strong enough to break free. Rose's biceps and forearms flexed and rippled beneath her pale skin. I was beyond grateful that the straps holding her in place were as unyielding as she was now strong.

Rose growled and jerked against the constraints.

"We should get her a donor soon," one nurse said and rolled up her sleeve.

I swear, something needs to be done about this whole conflict of interest between donor nurses and the newly turned.

"No," Jerome said at once.

"Yes. Who's first?" Rose entreated with a flirtatious bite to her bottom lip. Then she shook her head as if something had ahold of her.

"She's going to go mad. It's impossible to fight it."

I patted Rose's forearm with a gentle smile. "Just until the end of day," I assured them, eyebrow raised at Jerome, who nodded discreetly. "Then a cup. No donors."

"Are you okay with this course of treatment, Rosaline?"

Eyes closed, she growled but nodded. "It's best."

The nurse clicked her tongue at the three of us. "Very well. If I feel you can't handle things, I'll see to it that you're fed immediately. I can't have you going mad."

"She won't," I promised. *I hope.*

"Now, Rosaline—"

"Rose." She hummed a tune like she was trying to block the nurses out and squeezed Jerome's hand. "Please."

"Rose," she allowed. The nurse glanced at Jerome. "If we could have some privacy, please."

"No." Rose's eyes flared open. "No. He can't leave."

"I need to discuss your medical conditions, Rose. He might be uncomfortable…"

He squeezed Rose's hand back, but his hand shivered. I chewed my bottom lip, uncertain how to proceed.

"Oh. You must mean…yeah…ok." Rose looked anywhere but at Jerome. "But not far. Right? You won't leave, will you?"

My insides turned to mush when he laughed softly and kissed Rose's cheek. "I'll just get some coffee. I'll be right outside."

She tried to nod but couldn't. Tears leaked out of her eyes when his skin left hers. "Thank you," she whispered.

When the door closed, the nurse moved her bed to sit her up a bit straighter. Somehow the constraints never slipped. Her throat caught, and a seductive light filled her eyes. I had never seen Rose act anything like this. It was unnerving.

"Rose."

She clamped her eyes shut.

The nurse checked her monitors like she needed something to fiddle with. "I…I don't know if you're aware, but anytime we have assault victims come in…we have to do a rape kit on them."

That stole the seductive light from Rose's eyes.

"It does appear that you were sexually assaulted."

She swallowed hard. "I'm...I'm not surprised. I don't remember much."

"Also...you are pregnant, Rose."

Her eyes cut at me. "I've known for a while. It's why I tried to escape."

The nurse's shoulders drooped a little. "We can have a termination procedure done as soon as you're ready."

Rose's eyes flared open, and her canines snapped into place. I moved between Rose and the nurse. "Don't hurt Poppi. She's all that helped me remember who I am. Tell them, Huri."

The nurse's eyes widened as they settled on me like I had answers I didn't.

"Nothing's going to happen to the baby, Rosie. It's protocol to offer." I gave the nurse a look that told her to go along. *Come on, lady. Say something helpful.*

"My apologies. I...I just assumed."

"Popcorn in my belly," she told the nurse. Her hand jerked. I knew it was to move hair from her face. She always did that to soothe herself. "I only remembered me when I felt the popcorn in my belly. I escaped because of Poppi. Don't you dare..." She began crying, bringing water to my eyes. The horror she had been through. "I can't do that again. I tried it already. She...I can't do that to her again."

Oh, Rosie. Why'd you have to go through this? Rose fixed me with a look of utter desperation. It ripped my heart into pieces.

"No one's going to hurt her," I promised, bending over to kiss Rose's forehead. "Everything's okay, Rosie. I'm sure we can have an obstetrician come check on my niece or nephew," I told the nurse as much as Rose.

"Absolutely. We'll schedule a consult."

Rose relaxed when I nodded and squeezed her hand. "OK," she said. "But just know. Nobody hurts her." She now looked to the nurse with that same desperate-to-be-understood look. "She saved me.

288

Poppi saved me." Her eyes fixed on me. "You need to take care of her. If something happens to me, Huri."

Water filled my eyes at such a statement. "You're going to be just fine."

"Father will fight me. You're my power of attorney. Our guardian. Mine and Poppi's." Her jaw clenched like she was preparing to do something insane. "Now, I want the paperwork drawn now. Before anyone else..."

"We can set up that paperwork," the nurse said, casting me an uncertain look.

"Yes. Right now." Rose growled and thrust her chin at the door.

The nurse gave her a tender smile that told me the woman was humoring a madwoman. Within moments, a midwife brought in the paperwork for me to make decisions about Rose's care. A pen never felt heavier in my hand.

This's crazy. "You're sure?" I asked, pen poised above the line.

"As a heart attack," Rose said so calmly I consented. "Just until I get out of the hospital."

Once the midwife departed, I bade Rose to rest after a leisurely meal of figs. It didn't take long for sleep to take over. I practically collapsed into a chair from relief. *I'm not qualified for this.*

Jerome entered a moment later. "You okay?"

"She gave me power of attorney over her medical decisions."

He whistled. "Not her parents?"

I leaned back. My bracelet buzzed. When I looked, there was a message from Hans.

Hey, princess. Mom and Jerome filled me in. Praying for you and Rose.

Despite myself, I smiled at his words.

Jerome cleared his throat, which got my attention. "You might want to change how you get notifications." A smirk curled up one corner of his lips.

"Don't be peepin'." I rolled my eyes. "Jade okay? You've been here a while."

"With my mom. But I do need to get back."

"I've got Rose. Take care of Jade." Shouts filtered through the door from a distance. "You might want to slip out before her parents get here."

"Too true," he said, eyeing the door. "I'll be back with lunch."

The shouting drew closer. "Hurry. That sounds like them." I shoved him toward the door and then in the opposite direction of Phyllis's tower of debutante hair and Sturgeon's booming voice.

"Good luck," Jerome whispered and practically sprinted away.

I plastered on a smile as I closed the door behind me. "Right here, Phyllis. Sturgeon."

"Move out of my way, Huri." Sturgeon tried to barrel through the door.

I gripped his arm and held him in place. "We need to speak first."

Phyllis blustered when the nurses stood guard beside me.

"What is the meaning of this?" Sturgeon jerked his arm away.

"Rose is sleeping at the moment. Please lower your voice."

"I will see my daughter now," Phyllis said and crossed her arms.

Lord have mercy, these people are annoying. "You will stay right here. It's not safe."

"Not safe?" Phyllis said and looked to Sturgeon.

I leveled my best Athena gaze at him. "Will you two shut it? She's been turned."

"It's not safe for you," one of the nurses piped up. *Finally. Maybe they'll listen to medical professionals.*

"You're not her mother," Phyllis ordered and forced herself into the room.

I swore under my breath and got between her and Rose. In one glance, I could see her eyelids wiggling as if she were feigning sleep.

"Lord have mercy," Phyllis rasped, covering her mouth.

Phyllis nearly touched Rose's arm, but I grabbed her hand. "I'm trying to protect you both," I whispered. "As you can see, she's completely transformed."

"She won't hurt us. She's our daughter."

Idiots. You'd think they'd understand not to touch vampires.

"What happened to her?" Sturgeon asked like Rose was on her deathbed.

I could see Rose's throat working. No doubt she was having a horrible time controlling herself.

"Based on what we've gleaned...she escaped from the vampires who abducted her. I'm not sure how yet. She needs rest from the transformation and...I wouldn't touch her yet, Phyllis. She needs time to become accustomed to...to mortals."

Phyllis swept away to the windows. "Why are these open? She'll burn." Phyllis closed them with a snap.

I slipped my fingertips into Rose's cold palm. "She's perfectly okay to be in the sun. The ones who turned her aren't affected by the sun."

Phyllis's fingers fiddled with the hem of her shirt as she and Sturgeon kept two feet away from the edge of the bed. "She put up a fight. Bless her heart." She covered her face with her hand and wept. "My baby girl. What'd they do to her?"

I gripped Rose's hand hard like an alarm as the door opened. *The obstetrician. Not now.*

"Hi. I'm Dr. Harris."

Rose squeezed back hard, confirming my suspicions.

"Senator Sturgeon Brandt. My wife Phyllis. We're Rosaline's parents."

"Nice to meet you both. I'm here to check on my newest patient. Rose, can you hear me? I'm here—"

Sturgeon stood up so quickly that the chair ground noisily across the floor. "You're an obstetrician," her father said, pointing at the monogrammed word on the doctor's lab coat. I couldn't argue that the man wasn't observant. "Why does my daughter need an obstetrician?"

I cringed at the tone, knowing exactly what that meant. When Rose dared to open her eyes, Dr. Harris's pale brown face was waiting. Dr. Harris read my gaze and Rose's before she nodded once. Her shoulders squared to Sturgeon as she moved between Rose and her father.

Instantly, I liked this woman.

"Why are you here, Dr. Harris? Rosaline! What is going on?"

"I'm going to need you to leave, sir. I need to examine my patient."

"Rosaline," Phyllis called. "Honey, what's going on?"

"The hell I am. You will tell me what's going on with my daughter."

"I'm pregnant, Father," Rose said, clearing her throat.

I put up a hand when Sturgeon stepped closer to Rose. "You wanna be dinner?"

"How is this possible?" Phyllis asked like she hadn't graduated top of her class. I never understood why Phyllis always played dumb.

"I think it's apparent *how*, Phyllis. The question is why the...why it wasn't terminated immediately."

Rose jerked as if hit, but I squeezed her hand. "I'm keeping the child."

"No," Phyllis hissed. "Absolutely not."

Rose's entire body seemed to coil like a snake readying to strike.

Sturgeon sucked his teeth. A sure sign he was furious. "You've just been through hell and the gods know what else. You're...Doctor, she's in no condition to make this decision."

Rose's jaw clenched so hard the veins were beginning to show in her face. I pointed to the door. "Out, Sturgeon."

"Rose and I have medical matters to discuss. Steward, please, show Mr. and Mrs. Brandt to the waiting room. We just set a pot of coffee to brew."

Sturgeon bristled when I extended a hand to the door. "I've every right to be here. She's my daughter."

"You keep this up, Sturgeon, and she'll burst her restraints," I told him in a low growl. "You want her to live with the guilt of attacking you, her father, on top of everything else? I don't."

As she walked to the door, Phyllis gifted Rose with a tender smile that was so full of love-light that I was reminded of my own mother. "Huri's right. She's barely holding herself together, Stu. Let's give her a moment." She paused at the door when Sturgeon exited. "Let us know when you're ready to talk, sugar. If your father's not calm enough, we'll leave him out."

"The hell you will," he shouted from down the hall.

Phyllis simpered like a young girl and then closed the door.

Dr. Harris exhaled, watching Rose, and then laid a hand on her forearm. "You okay?"

Rose couldn't stop shaking, rage usurping the places the venom once lived. She gritted her teeth. "Fig. Huri."

After a look about the room, Dr. Harris found what she needed, but I had already beat her to it. "This is the treatment they spoke of?"

I lifted it to Rose's mouth to eat.

Rose devoured the huge fig, juices cooling her rage until she sank back into the bed. Her hand rested against her belly as tears dripped out of her eyes.

"I'm sorry," she whispered, barely able to look at the doctor.

Just like Rose. Worrying about decorum in the worst of circumstances.

"For what? You've been through hell and back." Dr. Harris held her hand. "Believe me. I know."

The sincerity in the doctor's voice drew my eyes.

"You were turned," Rose said.

She nodded with a wince. "Fifteen years ago."

"Does it get easier?"

Dr. Harris was silent for a long moment. "In many ways, yes. This hunger will subside. But in many ways, you are totally new."

Rose exhaled a wet sigh and then wiped away tears. "Have you seen anyone like me?"

"My specialty is dhampir," Dr. Harris said. "Mostly free, mated couples. I travel the world to tend them. Huri and a Jerome asked for the best."

Rose let out another wet gasp and held a hand out for me to take. I didn't hesitate. "They're the best."

"You make us all better," I said, feeling far too sentimental at the moment.

Dr. Harris smiled and nodded. "I'll admit I haven't seen any in your situation, turned during pregnancy, but I've tended many lamia pregnancies and even a few mortal pregnancies. I'm quite certain everything will be okay."

Sweat pooled between my hand and Rose's as she chewed her lip. I could only imagine what she was reliving at that moment.

"Can you tell me when you started noticing symptoms? Anything about the pregnancy?"

"A few weeks ago. No more than a month. I thought the weight gain was because of the food and all."

Dr. Harris pulled out a cone-like stethoscope. "May I listen as you speak?"

"Ye...yeah..." Rose shivered from the cold metal on her skin.

"Nausea, vomiting?"

"Yeah. My breasts ache."

The doctor hummed, brow furrowed as she moved the cone around.

"Is Poppi okay?"

The doctor pulled out a tape measure and measured her baby bump. "Poppi? Oh, you've named the baby?" Dr. Harris beamed. "Good sign. Dhampir have a remarkable bond with their mothers."

Rose's tears burst from her eyes. "But she's okay?"

Dr. Harris stared deep into her eyes. "Is there anything I should know, Rose?"

Her chest heaved. And Dr. Harris simply waited. Silent. Nonjudgmental. Rose breathed so heavily and her pulse raced so fast on the monitors that I feared her heart would burst. "Several of the vampires hit me in the stomach. I think I had some broken ribs. And...and..."

"You tried to perform an abortion on yourself."

That made my heart rip apart for Rose. She'd once miscarried in college. It nearly undid her. I could only guess what she felt now.

Rose cried out and wept. Her hands moved toward her face, but the restraints jerked them back. She yanked on them for a moment and then dissolved into more tears. "How'd you know that?"

"It happens a lot with female donors. Never works."

I couldn't contain the waterworks either now. "Oh, Rosie." I had to be ugly-snot crying all over my poor friend, but I couldn't help it. Rose just clung to me and sobbed. I whispered silent prayers over her. It took several minutes for her to finally steady her breathing.

After a few moments, Dr. Harris took the corner of Rose's sheet and cleaned her face. I swore I now loved this woman.

"The baby's heart is strong. Poppi sounds fine."

"But what if I hurt her?"

"Honey, it's impossible to kill a dhampir in the womb without killing the mother. It's like trying to kill an adult vampire. They're incredibly resilient. Even then, it takes skills, like Huri here has, to do it."

"But they said that if a vampire mated...they'd kill the...fetus." Rose wiped her nose.

Dr. Harris winced and shook her head. "They have to kill the mother to get to the child. Lamia offspring are practically indestructible."

Rose's rage rekindled in her eyes. "You mean they killed all those women and children to hide their indiscretions? Like we're something dirty to take out?"

"Unfortunately, that is exactly how they see it."

I took a box of tissues and cleaned my own face, remembering how Thaddeus had practically ordered me to do the same to Elias.

"Here. Put this in your ears." Dr. Harris fitted the earpieces of the stethoscope into Rose's ears as she pressed the huge cone to a specific spot on Rose's bump.

Rose beamed as fresh spring-like tears filled her eyes. "That's her heartbeat? Huri, listen."

I obeyed and was rewarded with the fluttering cadence of a healthy baby. "Such a strong heartbeat."

"It's incredibly fast." Dr. Harris grinned back at Rose. "Like hummingbird wings."

"It's not too fast?"

"Not at all. Now, I know you're dealing with a lot, so I won't overload you with more than what you have at the moment." Dr. Harris pulled out two cards. "This one has my contact info. I have a support group for mortals with immortal pregnancies. We'd love for you to come. Also, this is a therapist I work closely with. She works with a lot of mortals and immortals. Particularly with trauma. Please, talk to her. Her name is Anne Billingsworth."

"I'll look into it." Her head nodded as if on automatic.

Dr. Harris patted her hand and walked to the door.

"Thank you, Dr. Harris."

"It's my pleasure, Rose. I'll have my staff scry you for an appointment." She graced Rose with a smile. "Just rest as much as you can. One moment at a time."

CHAPTER 42

Hours later, I was failing to hold the suspect binder steady. Rose's bruising was slowly lifting, but between her change, the pregnancy, and all the injuries, her body was overloaded with what to heal first. We hadn't had much chance to speak since Dr. Harris's visit and the subsequent talk with her parents. Rose seemed more settled since Dr. Harris. Even after her parents left and Zephonia and Beatriz had entered.

Time for answers.

After checking the medical documentation myself, I handed Rose the bottle of Aletheia's Tears. "Poppi will be just fine. Truth won't hurt the innocent."

As Rose drank down the Tears, I was a bundle of live wires when I set a book of pictures on the table in front of Rose. With a scrying mirror hung on the wall directly across from Rose, Zephonia and Beatriz surrounded Rose's hospital bed, knitting needles ready.

"Take your time," Zephonia told her as she chewed her pipe stem. "We're recording this to make it legal. You have to publicly accuse your attackers as an immortal. But given the laws surrounding the newly turned, it would be safest for you to do it as a recording."

Rose nodded and looked to me. Since no mortals were allowed into the room at the moment, she was free of her head restraint, and the ones on her arms were slackened. "Don't fight the Tears, Rosie. It's painful. Just let whatever needs to come out be said. Hold nothing back."

Rose flipped through the photographs of vampires and mortals. She said nothing at first. Beatriz was noting which pictures she paused at, the yarn moving through her fingers and needles at blazing speed.

We all straightened when Rose flipped the picture over to a vampire whose features in-life would've been albino. He looked paler still. His smile in his identification picture was charmingly cocky. Rose's hands shook. She looked at me.

"This is Nikolai?"

Rose nodded. "Everyone called him that." Her fingernail tapped the name below. "I never heard him go by this name. Aleksandr Vessiks."

How was her voice so steady? Maybe it was just the Tears. Or maybe she had shed too many. I cut my eyes to Zephonia, who studied Rose with her unlit pipe in her mouth.

"It's not uncommon for them to take different names over the years. This was his name at birth."

Rose's eyes met Zephonia's. "What?"

Beatriz cleared her throat. "Aleksandr was born to two wurdulacs, Vyacheslav and Vivienne. Just like mortals are born." Beatriz pushed a lock of her golden hair from her shoulder. "It's mainly how vampires are made. Most are not turned."

"Yeah, we mostly see folks turned on accident. Getting chosen... that's like once in a mortal lifetime," Zephonia added.

"You're sure that's him?" *Never forget that face, Huri.* I shoved my hands in my pockets to keep from ripping the vile picture into tiny shreds.

"Yeah, that's him." Rose stared at the picture, brow furrowed. "I... I can show you the others I saw."

I let myself be the one Rose spoke to while Zephonia recorded the process and Beatriz took notes. Rose had never spoken more freely than at that moment under the Tears' influence. I fought to hide the horror of hearing which men and women raped her and fed from her and beat her. She even discussed men and women who weren't present in the book whom she had seen at the parties.

"Oh. And Mayor Renford was at one of the parties."

My mouth fell open at these words. "He never said a word." We'd spoken to anyone Rose might contact or know.

"I thought he would for a while. Hoped he would, at least." She frowned. "How many times had we all hung out together for birthday parties? But he looked right at me and immediately turned away." She shrugged. "I haven't told Father that yet."

"Don't say anything until we get Nikolai arrested," I warned her. "Sturgeon'll probably do something stupid."

Rose snickered. "True."

The interview lasted as long as the Tears stayed in her system. She even drew maps of the building they'd kept her in.

"I wish I could remember more." Rose fiddled with imaginary dirt underneath her fingernails.

"Don't you worry, Rose," Zephonia told her, touching her leg. "This is a mountain of information. We can definitely build out this case and others with what you've given us."

"Others?"

I nodded. "Some of our cold cases in the area have the moths in common. We think this house of wurdulacs may be responsible for their deaths."

Rose blinked several times, eyes round. "I had no idea."

"You are definitely helping a whole lot of families get answers they never thought they would get."

Rose merely nodded, eyes going to me. "What will you do to him?"

I glanced to Zephonia and Beatriz, who came and sat beside Rose. "We arrest him," Beatriz told her. "Much like the mortal law enforcement would. Our laws are different after that. He will be given a trial. The consequences of his actions are for the judge to decide."

I relaxed when Beatriz withheld just how involved Rose might be.

"Good." Rose nodded. "Do you have enough to arrest him?"

Zephonia scoffed. "More than."

Rose turned her gaze on me. There was real emotion and true fight in her eyes. "Don't get hurt."

I grinned at Rose, glad she understood that I was going, that I needed to be the one to bring him in. "You got it."

"We'll send in Huri's mother while we process everything," Zephonia told her.

"Thank you." Rose teared up. "For everything."

CHAPTER 43

I sat curled up on the couch at home with Elias. Mama had gone in to relieve me at Rose's request after Sturgeon tried to get a psych evaluation done to gain power of attorney. After that, he was expressly forbidden access to Rose at her insistence, and Rose added Mama as the immortal equivalent of a medical guardian. My body ached at the thought of all Rose had gone through, all she had to fight through to be free. My eyes rested on the folder hiding the picture of my sister's abductor.

"You're sure she's okay, Mami?"

I paused to consider my words. "In many ways, she's our Rosie. But she's different too. It's a big adjustment."

Elias ate popcorn without seeing. I could feel him lift a piece to his mouth. "When can I see her?"

"A few more days, I imagine. She's got to get her thirst under control."

"But she'd never hurt me."

Resting my cheek against his head, I hummed a laugh. "That's something neither of us are willing to risk. She told me to tell you that she misses her Eli."

I felt him smile against my t-shirt. "I can't wait," he said.

"We'll have to think of a way to celebrate. Do you think you could make her a drawing or something? I know she'd love that."

"We should go to that bakery. The one with the yummy cookies."

I grinned. "Sounds good, cookie monster."

He snuggled deeper, and I soaked in his affection to purge and recharge. It wasn't long before I had to tuck him into bed. He fell asleep without an issue. *Thank goodness.*

I sat back on the couch, file spread across the coffee table as I sipped water. My eyes were misting when I studied Rose's pictures at the crime scene before I got there. Her entire body was covered in giant moths, like some photograph from an up-and-coming artist.

I tapped on the mirror that served as our TV. A video of the Council signing the approval of the new wonder drug came over the screen. I frowned at the immortals approving the new drug. Even Grandmother had put her name down. But no mortal in sight. My lips thinned at her betrayal. My hackles rose when Enrica took her turn. She seemed to be sneering directly at me from the camera lens. Next came the wurdulac.

Rose had told me about this sadistic man. He'd be another addition to the Smiting List.

My bracelet warmed. Without bothering to look, I answered, figuring it was Mama or Zephonia.

"Pherenike."

"Grandmother." I tried not to inflect so much bite into my tone, but I failed, naturally.

"You've heard already."

"You've made your decision."

A scuffling sound came through my ear cuffs before Grandmother appeared right in my living room.

"Grandmother, privacy!"

She winced. "Pherenike, please, listen."

Flipping my file shut, I glared at her. "Do you know how many people will die because of this?"

"I was thinking of Rose. I know how much she means to you, and when you find her, she'll need something to help her overcome the addiction."

I stopped where I was, mouth dropped open in mid-rant. *That's right. She doesn't know.*

"This drug can help her when she's free. We just have to find her. Any leads?"

My chin trembled. "You...you did this for Rose?"

"Of course, asteri mou." Grandmother's normally steady chin trembled. "The numbers are promising for victims and—"

"She...she escaped just yesterday," I whispered, voice cracking. "She was turned on accident."

The color changed so quickly in her face that I could hardly keep up.

"I would've told you, but they don't know she's al...not..." I didn't know what Rose was now. "We didn't want them to try and claim her."

Grandmother took my hand and kissed it. "That's not—are you okay?"

My chin trembled, but I managed a nod. "She's...what she went through, Grandmother." Tears leaked out. "She's been..." She nodded her understanding. "And she's pregnant. Wants to keep the baby. And her father is going nuts. She named me and Mama her proxies instead of her parents. To protect the..."

Grandmother pressed me into her arms and chest.

"She's...she's a vampire. They put her in a cage. Did horrible things to her."

"Ssh, Huri. Breathe, my love."

I wept into her hair as she rubbed my back. "I don't know what to do, Grandmother."

She held me so tight that I felt like she held me together. It was the same way she'd held me when I was a child. She let me slowly return to breathing normally. I exhaled and wiped my eyes.

"Keep a strong head, Pherenike. You are either all reason or all heart."

I could only nod, remembering all those times she told me that a true warrior was the child of both reason and passion. Grandmother took her sleeve and wiped my cheeks. "I am happy that she has returned as whole as we could've hoped."

I nodded again. "I keep telling myself that."

"When she is ready, I need to speak to her."

That made my eyes go round. *The douleútria. I'd nearly forgotten.*

"Have you told her about...your mother's side?"

"Just before she disappeared. She didn't have much time to process it."

"I ask because...she's in a unique position to help those who are like her. It might prove therapeutic."

Oh, so not about the douleútria? "I haven't heard of any who live after the addiction."

"They are few, but with this drug, they might increase." Grandmother shrugged. "Perhaps with an advocate, we can get some real change happening." She gave me one of her looks that said she was making a point.

"I'll find the right time. But I don't know how receptive she is. She abhors politics."

Her eyebrows rose over the same gray eyes all we Athenas shared. "She may not have a choice now, between her father's position and being turned. I can help...alleviate some of it, help her navigate. Once they find that she's turned, they'll be after her to join the house. By force, if necessary. Especially with a dhampir in her belly. They'll terminate it after birth."

I swallowed hard. "I can't lose her again."

"Then do your part. Make her your douleútria to give her a house. Go after the bastard. Bring him to justice at Rose's hands." Grandmother nodded grimly. "It's her right now that she's no longer mortal."

I hadn't considered that part. The retribution part. Vengeance Laws were now in Rose's favor. I exhaled, making a mental list:

- Find this Nikolai idiot.
- Kick his ass.
- Arrest him.
- Let Rose kick his ass.
- Test out if Rose can be around Elias.

Grandmother left me in better spirits than when she'd come. My mind throbbed, and my heart ached, but I still managed to let sleep drag me under.

CHAPTER 44

From the cover of trees at the edge of House Vessiks's property, I soaked in the details of the mansion before me. It was on the west side of Nashville, closer to the river, and looked every bit the expansive plantation-style mansion of the Antebellum South, with three-story white columns and a porch and balcony that stretched like a welcoming hug to invite all inside.

It would've been beautiful if I didn't know the welcome was more of a choke hold than a hug.

I cut my eyes over at Zephonia, who was pinning her long silvery locks into a bun, pipe hanging out of her mouth. She was also in full armor.

She was hard to miss.

She looked like someone had vomited a rainbow of yarn from the era of disco and love all over her. In truth, it was a hand-woven garment that deflected most blows. My spider-silk armor, stronger than even the usual StS armor, was blackish gray, like the feathers of the owls I often shifted into, and it was made to my body's exact specifications. Before I left, Klara had tried to accessorize it with a leather utility belt. I already looked like Catwoman. No need to add

Batman to the mix. Besides it just wasn't necessary when my silk could hold anything I needed.

"OK. Just so I'm clear about the absolute dumbest, most asinine law in existence. We're supposed to just walk up there and arrest him. Just the two of us."

"Yep."

"In his own house."

"Yep. That's the law."

"Two against an entire freakin' house. Tell me again why this wasn't better my way."

Zephonia snickered. "You're so cute sometimes. Your way is solo. But you're a heroine now. Not a hero."

Whatever. "Who made that idiotic law?"

"Immortal politicians." She shrugged and pulled on a matching granny-square cardigan.

"That's madness, you know."

"You know the plan."

"I know." I rolled my eyes. *Stupid plans make me grumpy.* "Get captured. Send up the signal. Rain hell down on the bastard."

Zephonia grinned around her pipe. "We've had him under surveillance since yesterday. He's relatively unguarded. Apparently, he's in a rage lately."

My eyebrows rose, and a dark smirk curved my lips. Rose was no doubt the reason for the rage. *Good.*

"Keep your head, chickadee. Force is used as a last resort."

Yeah. Yeah. I'll last-resort the idiot into ashes. "I hear you, Zeph."

Zephonia walked out of the woods and across the lawn to the cobblestone driveway. "You read up on the wurdulacs?" she mumbled out of the side of her mouth.

"Yes." *Who would want to shift into a bug? Creepy.*

Zephonia stared straight ahead at the door. We could see curtains moving in the windows. "Most of the people in here will be mortal servants."

"I don't intend to hurt the mortals," I whispered.

"They might try you. The donors always try to protect their feeders."

"I know, Zeph."

Zephonia exhaled and brought her hand to the door. "Here we go." She knocked twice.

No one answered.

Zephonia rolled her eyes and knocked again. "This is Steward Zephonia Weber and my partner, Steward Huri Rojas. We are here to speak with Aleksandr Vessiks."

Silence deepened, like a viper coiling before a strike.

"We're authorized to use forceful entry if needed, Aleksandr. We'd prefer not to."

An intercom scratched. "It would be foolish for you to try," a man answered. "What do you want, Stewards?"

"I'm doing you the honor of coming to you rather than taking your indiscretions to your father," Zephonia told him. "If you don't open, I'll just speak with him instead."

There was a long pause.

"I have no idea what you're talking about."

"Very well. To Daddy we go, sugar." Zephonia tapped my shoulder as she walked away.

My back turned to the door, and a moment later, it opened.

"He will see you now."

Zephonia cocked an eyebrow at me. *Good call.*

A crimson-clad servant escorted us through the opulent foyer to quadruple doors below the double staircase. Another five similarly dressed servants stationed themselves along the staircase and even more along the upstairs landing. Beyond the doors lay a dining hall. It looked like the Renaissance took over the room. *So pretentious.*

At the head of the table, amid a pile of paperwork, sat a version of the man in the photo that Rose had pointed out. He wore a patch over one eye, giving him the effect of a ghostly pirate. I couldn't contain a grin at his obviously scorched eye. Blackened veins spread out from beneath the patch. *Good job, Rosie.*

He was red-faced and plump like a ripening strawberry. A wine glass sat before the papers. The liquid looked a little too thick to be wine.

Seeing him made me want to rush across the room and beat him until his body drained of his donor's blood. Zephonia brushed up against me pointedly.

"So, what is so pressing that you interrupt my business, Stewards?"

My nostrils flared, sensing more vampires concealed along the wall tapestries. *This place smells repugnant.*

"We have a series of mortal homicides, and the evidence suggests that your house might be involved."

Nikolai huffed and resumed perusing his paperwork. "I'm sure that the strigoi are responsible. We take pride in caring for our donors."

Zephonia placed a photo book on top of his paperwork and opened a file with Sierra and then Christina. "Curiously, in each of these photographs, I find a moth of unusual size. Definitely not native. Very much like the markings of your people." She flipped each picture until it came to Rose. He flinched at seeing her. "This one is a curious case. Verily encased in moths. The only one given such treatment."

His face flushed. I relished seeing his wounds were even more grievous than I had hoped. *Nicely done, Rose.* Battled a vampire and did it as a mortal.

"We naturally traced things back to your house, Aleksandr. Or do you prefer Nikolai? We've found a few aliases."

"I don't know this woman. Or any of these individuals." His throat caught as he flicked the book shut. "But I will do a full investigation and provide you with the results. Rest assured that House Vessiks is in full compliance with the law."

My hand twitched, which caught his eye. Zephonia gave him a gentle smile, the kind a teacher gives to an ignorant student.

"Rosaline Brandt had a great deal of evidence on her body. The fluids on her person trace directly back to you and…" Zephonia's lips thinned. "Every male wurdulac under your rule, it would seem."

"Aleksandr Vessiks," I began, pulling out cuffs. I ignored the vampires who came out of hiding now. There were only five. "It is my deepest pleasure to place you under arrest for the kidnapping and murder of Rosaline Brandt."

He sneered, fangs lengthening, as he leered at me. "Ah, so you're the sister steward, minus blood resemblance."

Adrenaline permeated my blood as the anticipation of sinking my needles into his chest snaked a grin across my face. "You should come peacefully." *But please, don't.*

"I never took a liking to immortal blood. But for you…I'll make an exception."

Zephonia sighed. "So, I take it you're not coming peacefully."

I tapped my forehead, making my helmet appear. "Don't worry, Zeph. He'll be begging for prison soon enough."

He launched himself at me, fangs bared.

I unsheathed my wooden needles and rolled with his charge. My fists pumped into his gut, making him howl, just before someone barreled into me. Several hands seized me as Zephonia let out a battle cry. Between the limbs, I saw my partner being dragged away under a sea of bodies. Darkness swarmed my eyes.

CHAPTER 45

"Are you awake?"

I groaned at hearing Zephonia's voice so early in the morning.

"Chickadee, you need to wake up. Like now."

The sound of male voices jerked me back into reality. "Where are we?" I winced at the coming headache.

Zephonia exhaled and relaxed against the pole at her back. She was shackled, but they'd apparently given her a stool to sit on. *Such kind ticks.* "Dungeon. It's absolutely medieval down here."

Zephonia's description was pretty accurate. From the stone walls and iron tools that looked a little too much on the torturous side to the torches hanging on the walls and the stench of decaying bodies, this creepy dungeon was all sorts of medieval. I pulled on my arms, but they were shackled above my head. The jangle of chains brought in two Norse-god-like men. They looked like twins. Maybe they were.

"Oh look," I said. "It's Tweedledee and Tweedledum."

"You Stitchers are such lightweights." Tweedledum punched me in the gut.

I had expected it, but that didn't change the fact that he hit like an anvil. "You hit like a boy. Unshackle me. I'll show you how to hit like a woman."

"Look what we have here," Tweedledee said as he rifled through Zephonia's knitting bag.

Tweedledum gripped and tore at my silken armor, hands roaming places they shouldn't. *So original.* "Come out of that suit, and I'll show you what a woman's good for."

"Be careful, you goons! If you make me drop a stitch, I'll make you wish you died for real the first time."

"Watch your mouth, old woman." Tweedledum pushed her shoulder.

"Hey! Have a little respect," Tweedledee hissed as he backhanded his twin's arm.

"Aw, honey. I'm used to it. These young'uns aren't raised right anymore. Not like you, darling. Looks like your mama did right by you."

He actually winced. "Our nana. Mama died when we were little. House war."

"My word," she breathed. "I'm so sorry to hear that."

I cocked an eyebrow at Zephonia. *Are you seriously being nice to these idiots?*

"Nana made up for it."

Tweedledum groaned and rolled his eyes. As much as I hated him, I kind of agreed with his sentiment.

"I'm glad for it...what's your name, son?"

"Robert. Most folks call me Rob."

"Big guy like you? Robert's such a strong name. You mind if I call you Robert?"

His brown eyes got big. "Don't mind at all, ma'am."

"Aw, you two gonna start courtin'? Shut your stitchy—"

"Language," Robert scolded as he and Zephonia exchanged a roll of the eyes. I snickered to myself. *Where's my popcorn?*

"Hey! Stop that! She's the enemy."

"Love your enemy as yourself, man."

The evil twin's mouth slackened as he shook his head. "You some kind of hippie now?"

"Means he was raised right." Zephonia raised her eyebrows at Tweedledum and shrugged her shoulders. "What happened to you? Separated at birth?"

"Yeah, well, I raised myself on the streets. Where it don't matter if you got manners or not. You still gonna get shot. So sit down and shut up."

Robert gave his brother what Zephonia liked to call "the hairy eyeball."

"She'll stake you just like the rest." The twin spat. "Can't trust a cop."

Zephonia exhaled. We needed to send the signal and soon. "You criminals are all the same."

"Not wrong," I said.

"You don't know me. Get Catwoman here ready. Boss wants her."

Zephonia rolled her eyes. "I know your type. Low-level with a sordid past. Blames the whole world for all his troubles." She paused. "Can't man up and own his mistakes."

I grinned when he turned back to glare at Zephonia. *Button pushed.*

"So, Mama died...Daddy didn't want you...Nana, well, it's obvious that Robert was the favorite. He's a gem." She winked at Robert before glaring back at his brother. "That's why you like this... existence. Gives you a power trip over those weaker than you. It's why you threaten little old ladies with their knitting."

His smirk turned sinister. "You mean this stuff?"

Just for effect, she glared at him. "Don't even think about it."

Get him, Zeph.

"Come on, man. Do you know how long that takes?" I said.

"I'm doing more than just thinking." He ripped her needles and yarn apart. Finally. He frogged it. I smiled at the sight and relaxed back against the pole.

"Oh no." Zephonia leaned back and crossed her legs, glancing at me. "Not that."

"Ribbit. Ribbit." I gave Zephonia the smallest of nods. *Come on, calvary.*

"Gawd, you're such a jerk." Robert backhanded him and put her things back in the bag. "Can't you be civil?"

"Do your job, Rob." Tweedledum took a medieval catchpole and grabbed hold of me around the neck. "Get her chain."

The rusted spikes on the inside of the catchpole pressed against my throat. "Oh. You've got me now," I said as Robert unhooked the chain from the wall and tossed it to his brother. "Whatever will I do."

"Shut up. Let's go." Tweedledum jerked me forward.

"Where are you taking my partner?" Zephonia studied her fingernails.

"She's going to get a very special welcome to House Vessiks." Tweedledum grinned with a wiggle of his tongue.

CHAPTER 46

Tweedledum attached me to a pole in the center of the cage. Based on the few details Rose gave, I knew this was the place that had broken her. It was much bigger than I originally imagined. There was the railing where I imagined the sadistic watched the spectacles below like an even more sinister Colosseum. A metallic floor dotted with holes let the blood and fluids drip down. And there was the darkness at the edges where nightmares hid before pouncing on their victims.

Then there was Nikolai. Maybe twenty feet away. He sat in a chair, feeding on some woman as she had sex with him. His eyes stayed on me, mouth still on the woman's neck.

"This used to be her favorite way to—"

The ringing in my ears drowned out his idiocy. Somehow, I controlled the rage. In my mind, I stroked it like a pet lioness. Zephonia had warned me that being captured would happen. I had to trust her. But I wasn't leaving without my revenge.

"Nothing to say?"

I stared at a point above his head and kept silent. He couldn't see my eyes, but he growled when I ignored him. Just as the woman was peaking, he slit her throat, bathing himself even more in her blood.

Bastard. You're going to die.

When he pushed the woman's body off his lap, I glared at him before deciding to change tactics. My gaze drifted downward, and I let out an uncontrollable laugh behind my helmet.

"Dang, Tiny Tim. No wonder she tried to escape. You should really start exercising more. And stop taking those supplements your buddies are on."

He threw the blade at me. It bounced off my armor, but it still left a bruise. With abandon, he hurled himself at me next, beating me and slashing at me. *Thank you, Pater and Yiayia, for the gift.* Even though my armor held true, his blows were still devastatingly strong. Some ribs were weakening under the bombardment.

He paused in his rage and screamed at me. If he had been a dragon, he would've bathed me in flames. Then I realized, as he stood there panting and soaked in blood, that he looked much like another vampire. The flush to his face and body wasn't just from his victim's blood.

"You're in love with her," I breathed, eyebrows meeting. *Did I just say that out loud?* Maybe they were mated. But wouldn't both have to feel the same?

Nikolai straightened and glared at me. "You don't know what you're talking about."

"I know a mated vampire when I see one." For a brief moment, I felt a twinge of sympathy for him, knowing from my research that in most houses, any vampire who found a mortal mate would be doomed to exile. He would be considered as unhinged as a mortal falling in love with a cow. Only by killing their mate would they be allowed to remain in power.

It also explained how Rose got pregnant. Dhampirs were only conceived between mated couples. A vampire in love was quite literally a different species, one compatible with mortals.

But that brief moment of sympathy was obliterated as I gazed at the dead woman on the floor and my lungs fought for oxygen. These vampires twisted love into their own dark image.

"It's curious that you're still swollen like a tick ready to pop." I licked my lips as if tasting the sweetness of my words instead of my own blood. "Is this why you don't want to see your father?"

He backhanded me. "Shut up."

"You love her even after she took your eye along with your dignity."

He screamed his rage and pain and began raining blows on me again. The bout was shorter. I took the time to check for any other immortals in the giant room. I could smell another two, but those scents were muddled because of the distance and his overwhelming scent. I'd have to bank on there being more than two.

"I would've given her everything," he rasped.

"You are a sadistic idiot," I growled. "I know what horrors you put her through. No true vampire or man, for that matter, could do that to his mate. You know nothing of love." I grinned behind the mask. "I would avenge her blood by bathing in yours if I could."

His fangs elongated as he snapped at my face. "Too bad she's mortal."

Laughter crackled out of me. "Too bad I'm a steward," I corrected. "I'm bound to haul you in, you pathetic tick."

He flicked a hand at me, splattering me with the dead woman's blood. "You're the one in my chains. Getting a beat down. But let's say you succeed. Unlikely. But I'll humor you. I'm protected by Laws of Survival."

I whistled and shook my head. "Wow. It's obvious your position wasn't earned based on your intelligence."

He rushed forward and licked the side of my masked face. "What would a Stitcher know of positions?"

Feeling his body pressed up against mine again, knowing this body violated my sister, undid my control. A tiny amount of silk from my suit slipped into the shackles on my hands and feet.

"You're nothing but a scared little girl in a suit," he said, hands roaming places they shouldn't. "It's why you wear it—so I can't show you just what position you should be in."

No originality. I head-butted him and slipped from my shackles. As he staggered back, I rubbed my wrists. The near-silent creak of vampires' tentative steps pricked at my hearing. Crimson-clad mortals stepped into the light along the rails above me. I couldn't spot any weapons, but that didn't mean they weren't armed.

"How did you do that?" Nikolai asked, cracking his nose back into place.

My hands brushed my hips. Two short swords surfaced. I loved the knitting needles, but these beauties had been with me since I came of age. The edges glinted in the torchlight. I smirked when he straightened and his colleagues stopped.

"Will you not come peacefully, Nikolai?" I laughed. "I'd hate to have to take your other eye."

He vanished into a giant moth as five vampires streaked in.

"Coward."

I marked the path of the moth. *Double doors at the back.* Without pause, I charged after him, spinning around the leading wurdulac, who turned out to be a woman. I sliced her arm, dropping her to her knees. I technically couldn't turn them to ash without a wooden stake, but I could definitely dice them into compliance.

As soon as my blade slid off her arm, I had to bat aside the talon-like fingers of another wurdulac. The sight of their friends howling limbless on the ground made the others pause. I didn't wait for more to come; instead, I ran through the doors.

I was just in time to see Nikolai standing in an elevator as the doors closed. I rushed down the hall, stabbing the controls with my sword. The elevator screeched to a halt. I could hear him prying at the doors.

"There's a set of stairs to the right," a female voice said.

I turned toward the voice, sword tip leading, and stopped when I realized the woman was a mortal. *Holy cow.* This was the woman from the hotel pictures Rose sent.

"He's probably headed to their old room. It's where he's been staying the most these days."

"You're helping me?"

A smirk luxuriated across her face. "Good luck, Stitcher." With that, she walked away, munching on an apple.

I bounded up the stairs the woman indicated, shifting to catch up. No one minded the silent owl flying overhead. I spotted him turning a corner. I followed his scent and bloody footprints. My lungs burned when I shifted back and paused before a door that had closed just a moment before.

Take a second, Huri. I waited as he banged around in the room, trying to prepare myself for seeing the room he'd kept Rose in. Hardening myself, I kicked the door open. He stood with a gun raised at me. I ducked behind the wall just as the bullet whizzed by. He laughed like some maniac from a movie.

"Your aim's off," I called. "Happens when someone stabs your eye out with a stiletto."

"You don't know when to give up."

His voice was closer. I shifted and perched on a sconce on the wall. It creaked under my weight. As he exited, he fired his gun at my assumed position. *Fool. No one ever looks up.* The idiot charged out a beat later. He grunted when he didn't find me there. I alighted behind him, shifted, and sliced his back. He howled, swinging wildly behind him. I ducked easily under his arm as he tried to shoot at me.

The noise of the gunshots shattered my hearing, sending me off-balance long enough for him to reverse his grip to pistol-whip me. Stars erupted in my vision. *Skata. That hurt.* I growled through the pain and focused my attention on the silk in my suit. The silk formed tiny spikes all over my body. He kicked my swords out of my reach and shot at me. The suit held true, but the pain that exploded in my leg felt like it didn't. He aimed for my chest.

"Say hi to Lina for me." The name Rose said he called her made my skin cold.

I sent the silk from one arm to his gun, knocking it wide as a shot grazed my arm. Again. I threw out another bit of spider silk to grab my dropped sword as I kicked his knee.

The moment my sword was back, I pressed the tip to his ribcage. And pressed seductively and slowly. His painful howl caressed my senses and raised the hair on my arms and back like the loveliest chills. Just as he was about to drop to the ground, I took out my petrified yew needles and stabbed his right hand to the wall.

His howls of agony were a symphony. "That's for stealing my sister from her family. Putting us all through hell!"

"Huri!"

My armor formed needle-like points, and my fists pummeled his ribcage. "This is for every bite that marred her beautiful skin."

His blood saturated his white shirt like a masterpiece.

"This is for every moment you stole her body from her."

"Huri, don't!"

I stabbed his left hand to the wall. I grinned at seeing him barely conscious from the pain. "I should stake you through the heart right now." I pressed my second pair of needles to the skin over his heart. His eye flared with life. *Good boy. Wake up for this.*

"You don't have the guts," he growled, blood dripping from the corner of his mouth.

Zephonia skidded to a halt beside Beatriz.

I could've done it. I could've taken his life as surely as he stole Rose's. I pressed the tips of the needles into his chest a bit more. The smell of burning flesh tickled my nose. The lioness in my chest roared its pleasure.

But I knew if I did, I'd rob Rose of her own chance to punish this imbecile. I also knew that I'd lose the only job I'd ever wanted. Most importantly, I'd lose the respect of my son.

My silk helmet parted. In the reflection of my sword, I could see my face. Bloodlust twisted my features from classical Greek beauty to hedonistic predator. I reveled in how dangerous I was. Powerful even. Nikolai's eyes widened as he tried to move deeper into the wall to get away from me. I leaned in and inhaled, eyes closed. The scent of his fear intoxicated me, nearly made my needles sink deeper into his chest.

"You're wrong," I purred in a whisper. "I would love nothing more than to spill your guts onto your feet and then show them to you. Let you heal, and then do it over. And over. And over. But that's not the job." My body shook in protest as I stepped back, withdrawing my needles from his skin. "You're going to pay for what you did. In front of the world." A predatory grin filled my face. "I can't wait to watch."

I picked up my other sword and slammed the hilt into his head. His head lolled to the side.

"Twitch the wrong way and I'm staking your heart this time. Screw the paperwork," I growled at him, sliding to the ground as the pain from the gunshots assaulted me through the lifting haze of adrenaline.

A throat clearing brought my eyes as my silken suit moved to needle-like points. It was just Zephonia and Beatriz. "Ladies."

Zephonia raised an eyebrow at Nikolai, slumped with only his staked hands holding him upright.

"I didn't kill him," I defended, regretting that fact a little more now. "He's under arrest."

Beatriz snickered, eyebrow raised at Zephonia.

"I guess that's the most I can hope for, chickadee. We could've helped you if you remembered your stinkin' ear cuff."

I blushed and pulled out the golden cuff, putting it on my ear. "This one?"

Zephonia sighed and rolled her eyes. "Come on. Let's get you tended. You look like death warmed over." She took me by the elbow.

"Ow! Not that one. Bastard shot me."

"You forgot the mouth guard too," Zephonia said as Beatriz fitted a muzzle over his face.

I half expected him to wake and snap at Beatriz, but he didn't. Maybe I hit him harder than I figured.

"I did good not to kill him."

"I'm surprised you didn't." Zephonia threw my good arm around her shoulders when she saw I could barely put weight on my left leg.

"Yeah, well." I cut my eyes back at Beatriz as she floated a stone slab with Nikolai on it behind us like a strange gurney. "I like my job."

Zephonia laughed a musical laugh that made even Nikolai smile in his sleep. "Bless your heart, honey."

Just as we entered the foyer, Nikolai woke with a start. Zephonia leaned me against a wall and began singing, which made him stand. She paused her song long enough to whisper, "I'd kill you for what you've done. But that's illegal these days." She hissed a song into his ear that made him scream and even weep. When she was done, he walked out of the compound without another word.

CHAPTER 47

I paused before Rose's room at the clinic. I looked through the window, my eyes sweeping the room. It wasn't the first time that I'd come and noted Jerome's absence. He was in the habit of dropping off the figs at my house rather than visiting Rose at the stewards' clinic. Each reason for his absence seemed as plausible as the next. But I figured Rose's keeping the baby was a heavy factor.

So proud of her. She was doing well enough to remain chained to the chair instead of the bed but not well enough to go out in public. Rose enjoyed the figs from the chair beside the window. Mama was in the room along with Phyllis.

The three were laughing together like they never had before. It warmed my aching heart to see the unity among them. Phyllis had always resented Mama's relationship with Rose, and Mama had always criticized Phyllis for how she treated her daughter. But as they caressed Rose's burgeoning belly, the three were one.

I hated to interrupt their moment, but I'd promised to see her once the arrest was done. *Just get in there.*

The three looked up at once. Rose and Mama were on their feet. Phyllis could only gasp at the sight of me.

"Tell me he's worse," Mama breathed. Thunder rumbled overhead as her eyes darkened.

A crooked grin filled my face, and, not for the first time, I wondered who Mama's father was. "He's a little more holey than usual."

Rose stared into my eyes. "Does he know?"

"Oh, no. I want to see his face when he sees that you're alive."

"What happened?" Mama asked, voice hard as a storm.

"Law says only two can go in." I shrugged and swallowed. "Zeph and I had to take a beating before the stewards could lawfully be called in. House Vessiks has fallen. Thankfully, Zephonia fared better than I did."

Rose's body trembled, and her once golden skin paled even more. "Did...did he hurt you?"

I knew what she meant. "No. Pater and Yiayia's armor doesn't let anything pierce it. But that doesn't mean that I'm immune to things."

"What does that mean?" Phyllis asked softly.

Mama raised my shirt. Rose growled at the sight as Phyllis gasped.

"I'm fine."

"The hell she is," Zephonia growled as she entered and closed the door. "Bastard shot her twice."

"I'll rip his throat out," Rose snarled and leaped for the door until her restraints jerked her back down into the chair.

I caught her arm with my left hand. "You need to know what's going to happen."

Rose paused long enough for me to limp to a chair and looked at Zephonia.

"You're going to need to come out." Zephonia exhaled. "Problem is that House Vessiks will try to lay claim to you and your child."

Rose glared at Zephonia. "I am not going back to them."

"I know," Zephonia said. "But it's the law that any turned vampire must be cared for by the turning house. It prevents...issues."

324

"How do I get around that?"

I exhaled. "If another house were to take you, it's possible, but that would start a war." I pointed at Rose's belly. "Dhampir aren't well-liked. To put it gently."

Rose swallowed hard, shaking as she turned away.

"There is a house you could join," Mama said.

"Whose?" Rose scoffed. "They're all awful."

"Mine," I said.

Zephonia smiled at Phyllis and cleared her throat. "Phyllis, could you help me with a statement? I wanted to make sure to get yours before it slipped my mind."

Phyllis looked from me to Rose. She rose from her seat so slowly that it was obvious she didn't want to go. "Of course. You okay without me, honey?"

"Yes, Mother. I'll be just fine."

The three of us waited until the door shut before I continued. "You could become my douleútria. You were abducted before I could mention this." I bit my bottom lip as I held Rose's gaze. "You'd be my lady-in-waiting. Like an adviser. Klara and Alexis have already agreed. It would allow me to legally protect you."

Rose stared into my eyes so deeply that I knew she was putting the unsaid bits together. Her gaze moved from Mama to me. "This will...protect you as well? Keep us all together."

"Yes."

Rose nodded. "What do I have to do?"

My pulse regulated a bit more. "You have to take the Tears and give witness before my grandmother."

Her eyebrows met. "Yiayia?"

"No, my mother," Mama said quietly.

"Oh." Rose whistled a little. "Well, let's do it. The sooner, the better. Right?"

"Mother," Mama called into her bracelet. "She's ready for you."

After a moment, Grandmother appeared beside Mama. Her eyes fixed on Rose. I could see her jaw twitch in displeasure. But there was something else there. Like she was looking at a hated memory.

"Hello, Rose. I'm so happy to meet you at last."

Rose stared at the three of us, each in turn. "Wow. How did I not put together the resemblance before?"

I snickered, as did my family. "She's agreed."

"Excellent." Grandmother took out a vial from her pocket and handed it to Rose as a scroll appeared in midair. "Let's get this done."

Rose downed the contents and nodded to us.

"Do you swear that you will serve Athena Pherenike faithfully and without coercion as both friend and adviser to the best of your abilities?"

"I do."

"Do you swear that you will not and have not divulged her identity as Athena to any mortal not within the employ of any pantheon or the Amaranthian Society?"

My heart clenched. I should've remembered this part. No doubt, she'd told Nikolai.

Rose considered her words. "The only people I've told are Klara and Alexis. And I...I didn't say she was an...Athena. Just immortal."

Grandmother stepped closer. I couldn't believe this either. Grandmother even checked to make sure the vial was empty. "You're certain. None of your captors knew?"

"No. Not from me. Nikolai's father knew. Tried to throw it in my face. That he knew you, Athena." Rose's nose turned red as she looked me in the eye. "I...I couldn't do that again. I'm so sorry, Huri."

I exhaled a breath I'd been holding since the day Rose outed me. "Forgiven and forgotten, Rosie. Without question." I kissed Rose's hair.

"I won't ever do that again," Rose whispered to hide the tears springing to her eyes.

Grandmother smiled tenderly at us as she finished with the terms of the contract. "Once the baby is born, I expect you all to attend sessions together in Olympia."

"Of course," I said at once.

"Please bring Elias and the new little one along. I love babies."

After a round of hugs, Grandmother vanished just as Zephonia peeked into the room. I gave her a thumbs-up, which prompted her to escort Phyllis into the room.

Phyllis beamed and put a gentle hand on her daughter's shoulder in greeting. "I was just telling Zephonia that we need to change the narrative a bit."

"How?" Rose breathed. I could see from her wide eyes that she was getting overwhelmed again. I couldn't blame her.

"You confront the law. Fight to change it." Phyllis kissed Rose's forehead.

Rose's eyes widened. "No. You know I hate politics."

"It might work," Zephonia said. "Too few mortals come back alive from living in a house."

I exhaled, remembering Paul and Claudette. "I bet most are too scared to challenge their house." I cut my eyes at Mama. "This must be what she meant."

"Who?" Rose asked.

My eyes widened. "Grandmother. She came to visit me after the ruling on the Cherries. She told me she did it for Rose. That when Rose was ready, to talk to her. That Rose could help others like her."

Rose shook. "This is all I'll be known for. All people will see me as. I'll be nothing but the victim who asked for it."

"I know, sweetie." Zephonia put her pipe in her mouth. "But your fight for freedom is not over."

Rose stopped at those words. I watched her lips go thin. "What do you think?" Rose whispered.

"I don't know what I would do in your position, Rosie." I limped the few steps to her and took her hand. "We know the backlash you'll face. This has to be your decision. I will do everything I can to protect and support you."

"You say that like you know which decision I'll make."

I smiled. "I think you know how far you're willing to go. I mean, you turned that idiot into a vampire pirate."

Rose smiled darkly as she sighed. "I don't know what to do first."

Phyllis patted her back. "We need to have a press conference. We're prepped for it already."

"Am I that predictable?"

"It was going to happen even if you didn't say anything. But I think you need to be the one who speaks. I'll get your father over to hash out details."

Rose swallowed hard. "I haven't even told the girls."

"I'll start writing," Phyllis said at once. "Call your father. We need to show a united front."

Rose nodded and shakily retrieved her phone. Sparks flew from the device. With a roll of the eyes, she looked at me and Mama. "How do you stand it?"

CHAPTER 48

I fidgeted with the cerulean silk yarn in my fingers. In all the bustle of finding Rose alive and arresting the prick who kidnapped her, I had forgotten to tell the two most important people. Well, I had told them Rose had been found, but not everything. I closed my eyes, hating all the secrets that I'd been keeping.

My eyes lifted when I heard Alexis and Klara's car doors close. They burst through the door just as I stood. Both women's tears trailed down their cheeks. Alexis nearly dove into my arms, halted by all the bruising and cuts.

"What the hell," Klara breathed, touching my battered cheek.

I smirked and winced. "He looks worse."

"Who did this to you?" Alexis demanded, looking around like the perpetrator was in the house.

"I arrested Rose's attacker." I rolled my eyes. "Dumb immortal laws." I indicated my face as evidence. "But sit."

"So, you found her?" Alexis took my hand. "You look awful. Are you okay?"

A smile took my face. "I'm fine. And yes. She escaped. She's safe now."

Klara let out a gasp and clutched her chest, pacing. "Where is she?"

The smile faltered. "She's...she's in a clinic." My bottom lip trembled. "She's...lord have mercy, there's no easy way to say this. She's been turned."

Alexis and Klara froze.

"She fought hard to get free. They were killing her. Somehow, she had their blood on her hands. She...she drank it." *Stop shaking, Huri.* "She's one of them now. It's why you can't see her yet."

"The hell I can't," Klara said, voice deep as a growl. "She's our sister. She won't hurt us."

"She will. Even she's afraid. She's asked me to hold off on bringing you to visit. She's scared that she'll hurt you."

Alexis fanned her face. "But she's okay besides this? She's alive and...after a fashion...I mean, she's our Rosie?" More tears rained down her cheeks.

I needed a drink to quench my thirst and give my hands something to do. "She's still our Rosie. Just not safe for you right now. But soon." I grabbed a glass of water and took a deep sip. "See, Jerome, well, he has a way to reverse it a bit. We're testing it out to see if it'll work. She's still struggling with being around Phyllis, even. We have to keep her under supervision." I wiped my face. "But that's not all."

Alexis exhaled and nodded that she was ready. Klara crossed her arms.

"She's pregnant. She wants to keep it." I swallowed hard. "Like raise it, even."

Klara's legs gave out. My silk snapped out and jerked a chair under her before she hit the ground. Alexis's mouth fell open and then closed.

"Can that happen?" Alexis asked. "I mean, it's part of whoever took her?"

"Yes. It's rare and hard to explain, but the short answer is: yes."

Alexis's tears stormed down her cheeks. "She wants to keep that monster's baby?"

I winced. "The baby made her remember her life before. Gave her something to fight for." My eyes widened as I remembered seeing Rose whisper to Poppi as she listened to the baby's heartbeat through the stethoscope. "She escaped to save the baby. She says that Poppi—that's what she calls the baby—saved her."

Klara's reddening face started to drain back to normal coloring. She and Alexis stared at one another for a long minute. Some unspoken communication happened between them.

"Well, we'll have to get a fabulous baby shower planned," Klara huffed. "She's going to need a ton of help. Single mom and all."

"We're sure we shouldn't talk her out of it?" Alexis whispered as if she didn't want to.

"She's made me and my mom in charge of her medical affairs if something happens to her," I said. "She even kicked out Sturgeon and said he's not in her life if he doesn't accept Poppi. She's not budging."

"Poppi?" Klara snickered.

"Cause her belly feels like popcorn when the baby moves," I admitted with a smirk.

Alexis nodded. "OK. We're doing this then." She grinned. "Who's ready to be an auntie all over again?"

"Now, let me assume this whole meeting was to get us over the shock?" Klara said.

"Yeah, she wanted me to tell you all after we arrested Nikolai."

"And he's in immortal jail or whatever?"

I nodded.

"Good." Klara's fist hit the table. "Did you stake him to the wall? Even a little?"

"Yeah. A little bit."

"Forget him," Alexis said. "Let's call Rose. I want to hear her voice and see her face."

I retrieved a hand mirror and whispered the words for Mama's. Mama grinned when she saw the three of us.

"There're my girls." She set the mirror in Rose's hands. "It's for you, sweetie."

Alexis and Klara gasped at seeing a beaten Rose, but I had to admit that they kept their countenance better than I could've imagined. After gushing over how happy they were to see her and that she was back, Klara tossed her blue hair over her shoulder.

"OK. So, we need to get down to business. While you're laid up in bed, you have homework. We need to know which room you want for the baby's room. Start getting decor ideas together. We need to plan a gender reveal party and baby shower eventually."

Rose's round eyes filled with more tears. She nodded. "I think I can do that."

"Good. I'm going to talk to some friends who know dhampirs. Poppi might have needs we should be prepared for," Klara said, eyes distant as she tapped her chin.

"We need to start stocking up on diapers," Alexis put in. "That's what Eli needed more than anything."

Rose laughed and burst into tears, the mirror falling onto the bed so that we could only see the ceiling for a moment. "Man, I love y'all," she said once her face came back into view.

"And one more thing," Klara said. "You listen to me, Rosaline Marie Brandt. I don't care what's going on now. We know you won't hurt us. But I imagine this's scary and stuff. And I'm...I'm..." Tears choked her throat.

"She's trying to say that we're ready to see you when you're ready, Rosie," Alexis said with a pat to Klara's back.

Rose looked to Mama, who whispered something we couldn't hear. Rose nodded and swallowed hard. "Once I'm...yeah, let's do it now before I'm out. They can hold me down here."

CHAPTER 49

Four days later, I stood in the kitchen, putting the finishing touches on the potato salad that Rose always raved about as I stared into the backyard. Elias and Pater swung from branch to branch above Rose, whose face was bright with laughter despite the bruising that remained.

My chest warmed when my attention rested on Klara and Alexis talking to Claudette and Millie. Zephonia and Mama stood off to the side, sharing a drink along with Yiayia.

Luis's throat cleared as he appeared beside the sliding glass door, leaning on the doorframe. "You're doing it."

"I'm doing no such thing," I whispered, looking down.

"I'm proud of you, cariña. You're making a new family for yourself."

"You're still my family, papi," I said.

I turned to find Grandmother. I gasped and clutched my chest. "What is with you? Doors!"

Her eyes caressed my face. Not even acknowledging her issue with boundaries. "I'm going to have to do something about that preposterous law. Two stewards for an arrest."

I twisted my lips into a wry smile. "We're taking on enough unfair laws at the moment."

Grandmother's smile radiated. "Just as I like it." She shifted from foot to foot, staring out at Yiayia, who was calling up taunts to Pater and Elias. "I have a rather large favor to ask you."

My hackles rose. It was the first time that Grandmother had said anything like this to me. I wondered if she was going to try and use me in some political game at some point. "I'm not sure I like the sound of that."

She gave me a file with a picture of a man with a debonair smirk. It was an old photograph, perhaps from the turn of the twentieth century. "This is Ixion." She blinked, unable to take her eyes off of Yiayia.

My eyebrows met. "The guy who was all into Hera Gaia like centuries ago? I thought they got rid of him."

Grandmother's hand shook before she hid it in the folds of her dress. "Arachne says he's the one who framed her."

The folder dropped. "Excuse me?"

"Arachne was part of the rebellion. Ixion was, too, but he only wanted to break up Gaia and her husband. According to Arachne, Gaia refused him, and he flew into a jealous rage. Said he'd get his revenge. Again, according to Arachne, Ixion used her as a patsy."

My lips thinned. "And no one believed her?"

"The evidence was damning. She was found with the weapon in her possession. It was before Aletheia perfected her tears. No one suspected Ixion. Right afterward, he even accused her publicly. Providing evidence of his innocence. Ixion died not long after that. I saw his body myself."

I wagged his photo. "But this is him."

"Near as I remember him looking." She swallowed hard. "Gaia's said she's had dreams about him."

"And?"

"And it's a hunch, Huri," she snapped, wincing a moment later. "Forgive my tone. It's just...I gave Arachne the Tears years ago."

My heart softened a little when a tear traced down her cheek.

"After your mother told me about you." Grandmother flicked away two more tears. "It's how I got Gaia to remove the curse."

I stared at the file in silence. It was terribly thin. There had been sightings here and there, but always blurred photographs that might have been him. The last one was two weeks ago.

"I realize it's a long shot." She exhaled. "She can't know."

I nodded, knowing what kind of harm that would do to Yiayia. "I'll find him."

Grandmother's chin trembled as she finally met my gaze. "I love your grandmother, Huri. She was my dearest friend. I never wanted..." More tears tumbled down her cheeks. "I've tried to..."

I saw it then. How Grandmother must have begged Gaia for mercy on her friend, who cursed her rather than killing her. Gaia never really liked the Athenas, so Grandmother probably came up with the idea for her to banish and curse Yiayia as punishment. "I know."

Grandmother caressed my face as she exhaled a millennium of worries. "Thank you, Pherenike."

I drew Grandmother into a long hug. Words failed me, mind reeling from all she had sprung on me. I only knew one thing: I could exonerate my grandmother. If I found a ghost.

"I should go," Grandmother said as she slid from my embrace.

"Stay. Celebrate with us."

"Oh no. I have a mountain of work to do. Politics never sleeps."

"Yeah, well, you need a vacation."

Grandmother dried her eyes with a laugh. "When you take one, I will."

"Done. I'm holding you to that."

With one last laugh, she kissed my cheek and vanished.

I stared down at the file for a long moment, considering how wrong I had been about Grandmother. With a nod, I entered my office and pinned the picture of Ixion on a free wall.

"Huri, where in the world are you? We're starving," Zephonia called.

"I had to hunt something down," I answered, memorizing Ixion's features.

Zephonia paused at the door. "May I?"

"Absolutely."

We stared at Ixion's photo in silence.

"Everything okay? I thought I heard thunder." Her eyebrows rose as she looked about the room.

Chewing my lip, I blinked a few times to ready myself. "I'm going to need your help, Zeph."

"This guy?"

"Yeah, he framed my grandmother."

Zephonia straightened and stared at me until I finally met her gaze. "Then let's find the bastard."

Pink filled my cheeks when pride drew Zephonia's lips into a rare smile.

With a quick nod, I pointed out the door. "Wanna help me carry things out? I imagine Pater and Elias have worked up an appetite."

"I hope you made that steak rare. Rose looks like she's ready to come out of her skin."

My face fell as I looked out the window for Rose.

"I'm messing." She smirked. "Sorta."

I bumped her in retribution as my silk snaked out and opened the sliding glass door. As we placed the food on the tables, everyone hurried to their seats.

Finally, my immortal family could be themselves around my mortal family. My insides beamed at seeing Elias yammering on to Rose about school and his friends there. My new friends were chatting with the old. My heart warmed at seeing my father lean over and kiss my mother as tenderly as a first kiss.

I toyed with Luis's Maltese cross, failing at not missing him as deeply as a desert misses the rain. With grateful prayers that my family was as whole as could be again, I resisted the urge to imagine him beside me. Instead, I basked in the laughter and the smiles and stood to raise my glass. Everyone turned their attention to me and lifted their drinks.

"To family, born and made."

"To family," they toasted as one.

Klara smirked at Rose, me, and then Alexis. "And may God have mercy on anyone who tries to come between us."

Laughter danced through the air, but we held one another's gaze in silent affirmation. "Amen to that," I said and raised my glass to my friends and to Yiayia, who promptly kissed my cheek.

CHARACTER LIST

Huri Pherenike Rojas Arachne: Future Athena, daughter of Philomache and Timon
    Elias Dareios Rojas Arachne: Son of Huri and Luis Rojas
    Luis Rojas: Husband of Huri Rojas, murdered by an azeman
    Athena Philomache Arachne: Wife of Timon Arachne, daughter of reigning Athena Alcis
    Timon Arachne: Husband of Athena Philomache, son of Arachne
    Arachne: Mother of Timon, convicted of treason
    Athena Alcis: Reigning Athena, mother of Philomache

Rose (Rosaline Brandt): Huri's oldest friend, daughter of Phyllis and Sturgeon Brandt
    Phyllis Brandt: Wife of Sturgeon, mother of Rose
    Sturgeon Brandt: Husband of Phyllis, father of Rose, US Senator for Tennessee
    Jerome: Rose's love interest, father of Jade

Klara Marie Barnet: makeup artist, Huri's friend
    Alexis: marathon runner, Huri's friend

Zephonia Weber: Huri's partner, mother of Laura and Hans

Hans Weber: Son of Zephonia, father of Lucas and Yasamin Weber

Captain Filomena Janis: Captain of StS Nashville Field Office

Bridget: Head of Forensics at StS Nashville FO

Violet: Steward, receptionist at StS Nashville FO

Kari: Steward, receptionist at StS Nashville FO

Julie: Steward, historian at StS Nashville FO

Beatriz Ortiz (Bia): Steward, detective at StS Nashville FO

Paul Browne: Husband of Claudette, father of Millie, co-owner of Sanguine Bakery

Claudette Browne: Wife of Paul, mother of Millie, co-owner of Sanguine Bakery

Millie (Mildred) Browne: Daughter of Claudette and Paul Browne

Zeus Thaddeus: Reigning Zeus

Zeus Adonis: Heir of Huri's generation

Aphrodite Oenone: Heir of Huri's generation

TERMS

Stewards of the Shield (StS): An organization of immortals and mortals under the jurisdiction of the Amaranthian Society. They investigate and prosecute criminal acts perpetrated by immortals against mortals.

    Steward: a woman in the employ of StS

Morries (slang): mortals
    Immos (slang): immortals
    Demi (slang): half-mortal and half-immortal
    Stitchers (slang): Stewards, at times derogatory
    Donor (slang): a mortal who is addicted to lamia venom
    Tick (slang): derogatory term for vampire (lamia)

Nixie: river siren, subspecies of human
    Pemba: bat shifter, subspecies of human
    Lamia: vampire, subspecies of human
    Strigoi: lamia, nightwalker
    Azeman: lamia, daywalker
    Wurdulac: lamia, moth shifter, daywalker

Asteri mou (Greek): my star

Agapi mou (Greek): my love

Eliopsomo (Greek): Greek olive bread

Ouzo (Greek): Greek liquor

Yiayia (Greek): grandma

Pater (Greek): Father

Oiketes (Greek): slave or servant

Hetaira (Greek): courtesan

Pornai (Greek): prostitute

Ornisharma (Greek): Amaranthian airplane that resembles a metal bird

Pan de jamón (Spanish): Venezuelan bread with ham, olives, and raisins (Huri's ambrosia)

Mi cariño (Spanish): my heart

Mi amor (Spanish): my love

ACKNOWLEDGMENTS

In true Adams fashion, I have to start way back at the beginning. You're forewarned.

At fourteen, I had no idea where I was going with my life. (What teenager does?) But God knew. He gave me an English teacher who gave me a book list. It had *The Hobbit* on it. Before then, He gifted me with an insistent father who nagged me for years to read that blasted thing. I had no idea that a book could change a person's life. But it did. So, thank you to both Dad and my Father for knowing what I needed even when I didn't.

When I was about eighteen, my then-boyfriend put a book in my hand, *The Crystal Shard*. I read it, and with all the haughtiness of a young person, I thought, "Hey, I can do that. I can write a book." And that's what I've endeavored to do ever since. Thank you for the book —and to R.A. Salvatore, thanks for showing me that fight scenes aren't just in the movies.

When I first started writing, Mom and Granny Pat both suffered bravely through the fumblings of my first handwritten books and short stories. Both gave (and continue to give) unfailing encouragement and suggestions. While I always wanted to have my book published before Granny Pat passed, to place it in her hands and to see her place it on her shelf, I know she would be proud now. Thank you for never failing to see the best in me.

Fast-forward to the present: Mom and Holly, you constantly listen to my insane ideas and are usually the first and last eyes on my stories. Your unflinching support, encouragement, feedback, and love are the inspiration for many of the scenes in this book. Thank you.

Eugenio, we are opposites in so many ways, but God has known what we've both needed. Your accountability has helped smash down my complacency and fears to bring this book to completion. Your encouragement to turn this dream into a goal and then to birth it into existence has pushed me to new heights. Thank you for helping me transform my vision into reality.

Titus and Theo, being your mom has been the most rewarding, gray-hair-inducing, and inspirational experience I have had. God knew that I needed you. Thank you for your love, support, and inspiration. You're both all over my heart.

Teca, you're my oldest and dearest friend. We might be miles apart, but writing about sisterhood in this story made me feel a little closer to you. May we grow into crotchety old women together!

A huge thank you to my beta readers: Taylor, Rebecca, Ubriel, and Lillian. Your insights have helped refine *Stitchers* into its final form. Thank you, Amanda Sumner, for your incredible editing suggestions and patience. You're an amazing editor!

There are moments when my thoughts have failed to flow down through my fingertips and onto a virtual page. Writing this section is definitely one of those times. Not because I don't have anything to say, but because I'm overwhelmed with the memories of all the wonderful people who've encouraged me on my *Stitchers* journey. Even if I haven't mentioned you by name, know that your fingerprints are all over the pages of this book. Thank you.

AUTHOR'S NOTE

Every book I write deals with issues that are dear to my heart. Addiction and human trafficking are prominent in this one.

Addiction touches so many lives and families, including my own. With every purchase of this book, I am donating a portion of my profits to a local addiction recovery group.

If you're struggling with addiction, stake it to the wall. I'm rooting for you from afar.

———

Human trafficking. Let's call it what it is: slavery. Many don't realize that slavery exists today, but it is the most profitable and contemptible business on the planet. And it's still going strong. When you purchase one of my books, I will be donating a portion to a charity that helps free modern slaves.

The fight for freedom isn't over. But it's my hope that one day soon, we'll see that happen.

WHAT'S NEXT?

The greatest gift you can give any author (besides buying their book) is writing a review. Whether you loved it or hated it or are somewhere in between, your insights help readers find the right books for them.

So, please take just a few minutes and drop a review on your favorite bookstore's website or on Goodreads. Word of mouth works great, too!

The...third? greatest gift (I hope I counted right) you can give an author is to sign up for their newsletter. If you want to get all the latest updates on my new releases, news from my world, and newsletter-exclusive freebies, follow this link: https://www.ashleaadams.com/book-newsletter-sign-up.

About the Author

Ashlea Adams is a speculative fiction writer in the Florida Panhandle. She was born in Hopkinsville, KY, and spent her childhood persuading others that there was (and is) in fact a dragon on the moon (not a man). This love for the fantastic has led to her passion for speculative fiction today. When she's not staying up too late writing in her own little worlds, she is usually knitting socks or chasing down her two sons in the humid Florida heat.

facebook.com/ashleanadams

instagram.com/ashleanadams

goodreads.com/ashleaadams